When Canad[...]vels in high school, s[...] for such an awesome job. [...] two decades without publishing, but r[...]ed inspired by the romance message that if you hang in there, you'll find a happy ending. In May 2012, Mills & Boon bought her manuscript in a two-book deal. She's since published more than forty books with Mills & Boon and is definitely living happily ever after.

Kate Hardy has been a bookworm since she was a toddler. When she isn't writing, Kate enjoys reading, theatre, live music, ballet and the gym. She lives with her husband, student children and their spaniel in Norwich, England. You can contact her via her website: katehardy.com

USA Today bestselling author **Sasha Summers** writes stories that celebrate the ups and downs, loves and losses, ordinary and extraordinary life occurrences. Sasha pens fiction in multiple genres and hopes each and every book will draw readers in and set them on an emotional and rewarding journey. With a puppy on her lap and her favourite Thor mug full of coffee, Sasha is currently working on her next release. She adores hearing from fans and invites you to visit her online.

The Christmas We Almost Lost

DANI COLLINS

KATE HARDY

SASHA SUMMERS

MILLS & BOON

All rights reserved including the right of reproduction in whole or in part in any form. This edition is published by arrangement with Harlequin Enterprises ULC.

This is a work of fiction. Names, characters, places, locations and incidents are purely fictional and bear no relationship to any real life individuals, living or dead, or to any actual places, business establishments, locations, events or incidents. Any resemblance is entirely coincidental.

Without limiting the author's and publisher's exclusive rights, any unauthorised use of this publication to train generative artificial intelligence (AI) technologies is expressly prohibited. HarperCollins also exercise their rights under Article 4(3) of the Digital Single Market Directive 2019/790 and expressly reserve this publication from the text and data mining exception.

® and ™ are trademarks owned and used by the trademark owner and/or its licensee. Trademarks marked with ® are registered with the United Kingdom Patent Office and/or the Office for Harmonisation in the Internal Market and in other countries.

First Published in Great Britain 2025
by Mills & Boon, an imprint of HarperCollins*Publishers* Ltd
1 London Bridge Street, London, SE1 9GF

www.harpercollins.co.uk

HarperCollins*Publishers*
Macken House, 39/40 Mayor Street Upper,
Dublin 1, D01 C9W8, Ireland

The Christmas We Almost Lost© 2025 Harlequin Enterprises ULC.

Claiming His Christmas Wife © 2018 Dani Collins
Their Christmas Dream Come True © 2006 Kate Hardy
Christmas in His Bed © 2016 Sasha Best

ISBN: 978-0-263-41919-1

This book contains FSC™ certified paper and other controlled sources to ensure responsible forest management.

For more information visit: www.harpercollins.co.uk/green

Printed and Bound in the UK using 100% Renewable Electricity
at CPI Group (UK) Ltd, Croydon, CR0 4YY

CLAIMING HIS CHRISTMAS WIFE

DANI COLLINS

To the wonderful team at Mills & Boon Modern.

I've had the privilege of working with several editors in London and they've all been fabulous and supportive.

Thank you for turning my imaginings into these iconic books with the red banner and circled embrace.

It's a dream come true! Xo

CHAPTER ONE

"Mr. *Travis* Sanders?"

"Yes," he confirmed shortly, willing the woman to hurry to the point. His PA had interrupted a high-level meeting with this "extremely important" call. "What is this about?"

"Imogen Gantry. She's your wife?"

Memory washed through him in a rush of heat and hunger. He tensed against it and glanced around, lowering his voice. That broken teacup had been swept firmly under the rug four years ago.

"We're divorced. Are you a reporter?"

"I'm trying to locate her next of kin. I'm at…" She mentioned the name of one of New York's most beleaguered public hospitals.

Whatever old anger had sent him soaring at the mention of his ex-wife exploded in a percussive flash. He was blind. Falling. Wind whistling in his ears. Air moving too fast for him to catch a gulp.

"What happened?" he managed to grit out. He was dimly aware his eyes were closed, but she was right there in front of him, laughing. Her green eyes glimmered with mischief. Her hair was a halo of flames licking at her snowy complexion. She swerved her lashes to cut him a glance. So enchantingly beautiful. Gaze clouding with arousal. Sparking with anger. Looking so wounded and vulnerable that last time he'd seen her, his heart still dipped thinking of it.

He'd quickly learned it was a lie, but that didn't make any of this easier to accept.

Gone? He couldn't make it fit in his head. He had told her he never wanted to see her again, but discovered he had secretly believed he would.

From far away, he heard the woman say, "She collapsed on the street. She's feverish and unconscious. Do you know of any medication we should be aware of? She's awaiting treatment, but—"

"She's not dead?"

He heard how that sounded, as if that was the outcome he would have preferred, but leave it to Imogen to set him up to believe one thing, contort his emotions to unbearable degrees, then send him flying in another direction. That betraying, manipulative— If he could get his hands on her, he'd kill her himself.

"And she was taken to *that* hospital? *Why?*"

"I believe we were closest. She doesn't seem to have a phone and yours is the only name I've been able to find in her bag. We need guidance on treatment and insurance. Are you able to provide that?"

"Contact her father." He walked back toward the door to his office, saying to his PA behind her desk, "Look up Imogen Gantry's father. He's in publishing. Maybe starts with a *W.* William?" He hadn't met the man, only heard her mention him once or twice. Hell, they'd only been married fifteen minutes. He knew next to nothing about her.

"Wallace Gantry?" His PA turned her screen. "He

appears to have died a few months ago." She pointed to the obit notice that said he was predeceased by his wife and eldest daughter, survived by his youngest daughter, Imogen.

Perfect.

He knew better than to let himself get sucked back into her orbit, but what else could he say except, "I'll be there as soon as I can."

Imogen remembered sitting down on the curb. It hadn't been a nice, rain-washed boulevard of freshly mown grass beneath century-old elms with a stripe of sidewalk, then an empty canvas of manicured lawn to her mother's rose garden, ending at the wide stairs to the double-door entrance of her childhood home.

No, it had been a freezing, filthy inner-city curb where the piles of snow had turned to a layer of lumpy muck atop a century's worth of chewing gum and other disgusting things. The damp chill on the air hadn't squelched any of the terrible smells coming off the grate at her feet. She shouldn't have touched the post she had braced herself against and she had thought a car would likely run over her legs as she sank down. At the very least, one would drown her with a tsunami of melt from the puddles.

She hadn't cared. The side of her head had felt like it was twice as big as the rest. Her ear, plugged and aching, had begun screaming so loud the sound had been trying to come out her mouth.

She had tried to pretend she didn't have an ear infection because those were for children. Her sister had got them, not her. She hadn't gone swimming recently. She hadn't known how it could have happened, but there she'd been like a damned toddler, nearly fainting with the agony of it, dizzy and hot and sick.

She'd had to sit down before she fell down. A fever was nature's way of killing a virus, so why hadn't this run its course? And who passed out from such a silly thing, anyway?

Her vision had dimmed at the edges, though. She had felt so awful she hadn't cared that the wet snow had been soaking through her clothes. Her only thought had been, *This is how I die.* She'd been okay with it. Her father would have loved this for her, dying like a dog in the gutter a week before Christmas. Even Travis would probably conclude that she had got what she deserved. If he ever found out, which he wouldn't.

It had been a relief to succumb. Fighting was hard, especially when it was a losing battle. Giving up was so much easier. Why had she never tried it before?

So, she had died.

Now she was in—well, this probably wasn't heaven, not that she expected to get in *there*. It might be hell. She felt pretty lousy. Her body ached and her sore ear felt full of water. The other one was hypersensitive to the rustle of clothing and a distant conversation that bounced painfully inside her skull. Her mouth was so dry she couldn't swallow. She tried to form words and all she could manage was a whimper of misery.

Something lifted off her arm, a warm weight she hadn't recognized was there until it was gone, leaving her with a profound sense of loss. She heard footsteps, then a male voice.

"She's waking up."

She knew that voice. Her eyes prickled and the air she'd been breathing so easily became dense and hard to pull in. Her chest grew compressed with dread and guilt. She couldn't move, but inwardly she shrank.

She had definitely gone to hell.

A lighter, quicker footstep came toward her. She opened her eyes, winced at the brightness, then squinted at a tastefully sterile room in placid colors that could have been the one her father had occupied the last months of his life. A private hospital room. For an ear infection? Seriously? Just give her the pink stuff and send her on her way.

"I—" *I can't afford this*, she tried to say.

"Don't try to talk yet," the kindly nurse said. Her smile was stark white and reassuring against her dark brown skin. She took up Imogen's wrist to check her pulse, the nurse's hand soft and warm. Motherly. She checked her temperature and said, "Much better."

All the while, Imogen could almost but not quite see him in her periphery. She was afraid to turn her head on the pillow and look right at him. It was going to hurt and she just didn't have it in her yet.

"How am I here?" she managed to whisper.

"Water?" The nurse used a bendy straw, the kind Imogen had never been allowed to use because they were too common. A gimmick.

She got two gulps down her parched throat before the nurse said, "Easy now. Let me tell the doctor you're awake, then we'll give you more and maybe something to eat."

"How long…?"

"You came in yesterday."

A day and a half in a place like this? When her bank balance was already a zombie apocalypse running rivers of red?

The nurse walked out, sending a smile toward the specter on the other side of the bed.

Imogen closed her eyes again. So childish. She was that and many more things that were bad. Maybe her father was right and she was, simply and irrevocably, *bad*.

A shoe scuffed beside the bed. She felt him looming over her. Heard him sigh as though he knew she was avoiding him the only way she could.

"Why are you here?" she asked, voice still husky. She wanted to squirm. In her most secretive dreams, this meeting happened on neutral turf. Maybe a coffee shop or somewhere with a pretty view. She would have had a cashier's check in hand to pay him back every cent she'd been awarded in their divorce settlement—money she knew he felt she'd conned out of him. Somehow, in her fantasy, she found the words to explain why she'd taken it and he had, if not forgiven her, at least not despised her any longer.

Maybe his feelings toward her weren't that bad. He was here, wasn't he? Maybe he cared a little. Had he been worried for her?

She heard a zipper, which made her open her eyes out of curiosity—

Oh, *no*.

"You went through my things?" She clamped her eyes shut against the small red change purse that had belonged to her mother. It held Imogen's valuables—her driver's license, her debit card, her room key, the only photo she had of her with her sister and mother, and the marriage certificate stating Travis Sanders was her husband.

"The nurse was looking for your next of kin." Oh,

this man had a way with disdain. It dripped from a voice which was otherwise deep and warm with an intriguing hint of Southern charm.

She was a connoisseur of disparaging tones, having experienced a lot of them in her lifetime. Neighbors. Teachers. Daddy dearest. Inured as she ought to be, this man cut into her with scalpel-like precision with his few indifferent words.

He didn't care if he was the only person left in this world whom she had any connection to. He found his brief association with her abhorrent when he thought about her at all.

"It's my only other piece of identification."

"Birth certificate?" he suggested.

Burned after an argument with her father ages ago. *So* childish.

She wanted to throw her arm over her eyes and continue hiding, but her limbs were deadweights and the small twitch of trying to lift her arm made her aware of the tube sticking out of it.

She looked at the IV, the ceiling, *him*.

Oh, it hurt so badly. He had somehow improved on perfection, handsome features having grown sharper and more arrogantly powerful. He was clean-shaven, not ruggedly stubbled and human-looking the way she remembered him when she dared revisit their shared past—hair rumpled by her fingers, chest naked and hot as he pressed her into the sheets.

Whatever warmth she had ever seen in him had been iced over and hardened. He wore a tailored three-piece suit in charcoal with a tie in frosted gray. His mouth, capable of a sideways grin, was held in a short, stern firmness. Flat gray eyes took in what must appear like soggy laundry dumped out of the washer before it had even been through the rinse cycle. That's about how appealing she felt. While he was...

Travis.

Just thinking his name made her throat flex in an agony of yearning. Remorse.

Why was she always in the wrong? Why was she always falling down and getting messy and driving people away when all she wanted was for someone, anyone, to love her just a little? Especially the people who were supposed to.

Oh, she really was a mess if she was going to get all maudlin like that.

Pull it together, Immy.

"Is there someone I should call?" Flat silver dollars, his eyes were. When she had met him, she had thought his gray eyes remarkable for being so warm and sharp. The way he had focused his gaze on her had been more than flattering. It had filled up a void of neglect inside her.

Today they were as emotionless and cold as her father's ice-blue eyes. She was nothing to Travis. Absolutely nothing.

"You've done enough," she said, certain he was the reason she was in this five-star accommodation. She flicked her gaze to the window. Snow was falling, but the view was likely a blanket of pristine white over a garden of serenity.

"You're welcome," he pronounced derisively.

Oh, was she supposed to thank him for saving her life by further impoverishing what was left of it?

"I didn't ask you to get involved." She ignored the fact that she kind of had, carting around their marriage certificate instead of their divorce papers. *Where had those ended up*, she wondered.

"Oh, this is on me," he said with unfettered scorn. "I came here thinking—well, it doesn't matter, does it? I made a mistake. *You*, Imogen, are the only mistake I have ever made. Do you know that?"

CHAPTER TWO

Travis heard her breath catch and watched her eyes widen in surprise at how ruthlessly he'd thrown that direct hit.

He didn't feel particularly bad about knocking her when she was down. He was speaking the truth, and she was showing an annoying lack of appreciation for his helping her when he could have hung up at the sound of her name.

He should have. Imogen Gantry was the epitome of a clichéd, spoiled New York princess. Self-involved, devious and intent on a free ride.

She didn't look like much right now, of course. What the hell had she been up to that she had wound up in an overcrowded, understaffed emergency room, unable to speak for herself?

"Be happy I had you transferred. Do you know where they took you, when they scraped your frozen body off the sidewalk? What were you doing in that part of the city anyway?"

"If I told you, you wouldn't believe me." Her green eyes met his briefly, glimmering with indecision as she wavered toward telling him something, then decided against it. The light in her gaze dimmed and she looked away.

Drugs, he had surmised darkly when he'd heard where she'd been picked up and seen how gaunt she was. It seemed the only explanation. Blood tests hadn't found anything, however. No track marks or withdrawal symptoms, either.

She'd been raging with fever, though. Had a terrible ear infection that had thankfully responded to the intravenous antibiotics. It was something that should have been dealt with sooner, the doctor had said. She could have lost her hearing or wound up with meningitis. He'd looked at Travis as though it was his fault she was so ill.

That had been when she'd been transferred here to this enormously better-equipped private hospital. Travis had been trying to remember her birthday and searching for her details online only to discover she didn't seem to exist anywhere but in the flesh. He'd found a handful of very old posts, selfies with other socialites at whichever clubs had been the it spot around the time they'd married, but aside from her father's obituary, which was short and stated no service would be held, there was nothing recent about her online.

Her father's house had been sold, he quickly discovered, and Travis hadn't been able to find her current address. He'd had to write down his own. He had acted like her husband and approved her treatment, underwriting the cost. What else was he supposed to do?

Whatever they'd given her for the pain had knocked her out for almost twenty-four hours. Given how bedraggled she'd looked, he'd deduced she needed the sleep.

She still had dark circles around her eyes and an olive tinge in her normally ivory face. The hollows in her cheeks he put down to some women's desire for a skeletal frame in the name of fashion, but she was overdue for a manicure and her hair was limp and dull.

Looking at her, all he felt was pity at her condition. Tired anger. He had known he was making a mistake even as he married her, so why had he gone through with it?

The doctor came in at that moment, along with the nurse who elevated her bed. The doctor wanted her to finish her course of antibiotics orally and said she was anemic. Needed iron.

"You're run-down. Burnt out. I'm prescribing a few weeks off work, along with high-potency multivitamins and proper eating. Get your strength back."

"Off" from what? Travis wondered acridly. She hadn't held down a real job in her life.

"Thanks," Imogen said with a tight smile, folding the prescription in half once, then held out her hand to Travis.

He gave her the worn silk bag that was all she'd had on her when she collapsed, like she was some kind of runaway. It might have been good quality twenty or thirty years ago, but it was frayed and faded now. Ugly.

"So, I can go?" She indicated the needle still feeding medication and fluids into her arm.

"Oh, goodness no," the doctor said. "You'll have another dose of antibiotics and an iron infusion. We'll talk tomorrow about discharge, but I would think later in the week—"

"I can't afford this," she cut in. "Please." She lifted her arm. "I'd rather you remove this even if I have to pay for it. I'm squeamish."

"Mrs. Sanders—"

"Gantry," she said at the same time Travis said, "We're divorced."

The doctor sent a perplexed look between them.

"My ex-husband isn't paying for my treatment. I am."

Travis had to raise his brows at that, but was far less surprised by her next words.

"And I can't. So." She crossed her arm over her body toward the nurse. "Please get me out of here as quickly and cheaply as possible."

"You're not well," the doctor said firmly. "She's not," he insisted to Travis, causing an annoying niggle of concern to tug on his conscience.

Why did she get to him like this?

Her stupid arm was too heavy to hold up and even her head needed to flop back against the pillow. "Is this pro bono, then?"

She knew it wasn't. She knew suggesting it put Travis in a tight spot. He'd brought her here. He would be liable if she refused to pay.

"I'll pay for her treatment," Travis ground out, tone so thick with contempt she cringed. His next words, resounding with sarcasm, sawed right through her breastbone to scratch themselves into her heart. "You can pay me back."

"I'll pay for my own treatment," she said, capable of her own pointed disdain. If she knew nothing else, she knew that she would not go deeper into his debt. "But my bills stop now. Bring me whatever forms I need to fill out and get this needle out of my arm. Where are my clothes?"

"I threw them away," Travis said.

"Are you serious? Who— Well, that's just great, isn't it? Thanks." She looked at the nurse. "I'll need some pajamas. Heck, throw in a hot meal, since I'm spending like a drunken sailor anyway."

"Like an Imogen Gantry," Travis corrected under his breath, just loud enough for her to hear it.

She glared at him. "Don't let me keep you."

He had the nerve to look at the doctor and jerk his head, ordering the man to confer with him outside the room.

"Don't you talk about me," she said to their backs. "Did you see what just happened?" she asked the nurse.

"Let's finish this dose of medication before we talk about removing your needle. I'll bring you some soup."

Imogen fell asleep in the time it took the nurse to come back, but felt a little better after a bowl of soup and a glass of vegetable juice. Half her weakness in the street had been hunger, she realized. Apparently, the human body needed to eat every day, and sneaking a few maraschino cherries from the bar while she scrubbed the floor behind it didn't count. #ThingsTheyDon'tTeachYouInSchool.

The nurse removed her needle after giving her some pills to swallow, then helped her shower and dress in a pair of drawstring pajamas and a T-shirt with yellow birds on it.

After all that activity, even finger-combing her hair was too much. Imogen used a rubber band she begged off the nurse to gather her wet hair into a messy lump, then sat in the chair, trembling with exertion, pretending she was fully on the mend, fishing for the thin slippers that would no doubt cost her a hundred dollars apiece.

She signed forms that promised the hospital both her useless arms and legs and tried to be thankful Travis hadn't thrown out her boots with her jacket. She snuck a blanket off a linen cart on her way to the door, but it was still going to be a long, hellish walk home, looking like one of New York's finest. It would be dark soon and was still snowing, growing dusky at three in the afternoon. Her debit card would combust if she so much as tried to put a subway fare on it. She had no choice.

"Bye now," she said as she passed the nurses' station with a wave. "Add this to the bill," she added with a point at the blanket. "Thank you."

"Ms. Gantry," the motherly nurse said in protest. "You really should rest."

"I will," she lied. "Soon as I'm home." She would swing by to see one of her employers on the way, though. See if she still had a job with the biker bar's janitorial staff after blowing her shift last night with this unplanned excursion to the right side of town.

She walked out of the blasting heat in the space between the two sets of automatic doors, and winter slapped her in the face. It immediately sapped 90 percent of her energy, making her sob under her breath as she began putting one foot in front of the other. The cold penetrated before she took ten steps, but she pushed on, doggedly following the looped driveway toward the gilded gates that suggested this place was heaven after all.

It began to look like a really long way just to get to the road. She had to stop and brush snow off a bench dedicated to a hospital benefactor, rest there a moment. She felt so pathetic her eyes began to well. At least her ear didn't hurt like it had. It was just a dull ache.

There was always a bright side if she looked for it.

Nevertheless, panic edged in around the meditative breaths she was blowing like smoke in front of her face. She was shivering, teeth chattering. How was she going to carry on?

One day at a time, she reminded herself, closing her eyes. One footstep at a time.

Before she could rise, a black car stopped at the curb in front of her. The chauffeur came around and opened the back door. She already knew who would get out and tried to pretend she was bored, not so very close to beaten.

Even her father hadn't crushed her as quickly and thoroughly as one irritated look from this man did. He wore a fedora and a gorgeous wool overcoat tailored to his physique. His pants creased sharply down his shins to land neatly on what had to be Italian leather shoes.

"You look like a gangster. I don't have your money. You'll have to break my knees."

"Can those knees get you into this car or do I have to do that for you, too?"

The air was so cold, breathing it to talk made her lungs hurt. "Why do you even care?"

"I don't," he assured her brutally.

She looked back toward the hospital doors. As usual, she'd come too far and had to live with where she had ended up.

"I told the doctor I would get you home if you insisted on leaving and make sure a neighbor checks on you."

The drug dealer across the hall? She would *love* for him to come and go.

She clutched her purse against her chest, inside the blanket she clenched closed with her two hands. She stared at the flakes appearing and melting on her knees so he wouldn't see how close to tears she was.

"I'll find my own way home," she insisted.

Travis, being a man of action, didn't say a word. He swooped so fast she barely had time to realize he had picked her up before he shoved her into the back of his car and followed her in. Abject loss struck before she'd even had time to process the safe feeling of being cradled against his chest.

Dear *God* it was deliciously warm in here. She bit back a moan of relief.

"Now," he said as he slammed his door and sat back, shooting his cuffs. "Where is home, exactly?"

"Didn't the hospital tell you? They seemed so keen to share everything else about me. What is my blood type, anyway? I've never bothered to find out."

He only nodded toward his driver, indicating the man was waiting with more patience than Travis possessed.

They were really doing this? *Fine.* A perverse urge to let him gloat over his pound of flesh gripped her. Maybe if he saw she was being thoroughly punished, he might quit acting so supercilious and resentful.

She stated her address.

The driver's frown was reflected through the rearview mirror, matching Travis's scowl.

"Would you be serious?" Travis muttered.

She shrugged. "You wanted to know what I was doing in that neighborhood. I live there."

"What are you doing, Imogen?" he asked tiredly. "What's the game? Because I'm not letting you screw me over again."

"No lift home, then?" She put her hand on the door latch.

He sighed. "If I drive you all the way over there, what happens? You get into the bed of some sketchy thug your father didn't approve of?" His lip curled with disgust. His eye twitched, almost as if the idea of it bothered him. "Does he spank you the way you've always needed?"

"Hardly necessary when you're doing such a fine job of that." She glared at him, but holding his gaze was hard. It felt too intimate. They had never played erotic games, but suddenly they were both thinking about it.

While she grew hot, she watched him shut down, locking her out, jaw hardening and a muscle ticking in his cheek.

She swallowed. "I plan to crawl into my own bed and hope I never wake up."

"Tell me where you really live," he said through his teeth.

"I just did." She didn't bother getting emotional about it. It was the doleful truth that her life was so firmly in the toilet, she was barely surviving it.

She let her head rest back and must have dozed, because suddenly he was saying, "We're here," snapping her back to awareness of being in his car.

"Okay. Thanks," she said dumbly, looking behind her to see if it was safe to open her door against traffic.

"You're going through with this, then." Travis swore

beside her and went out his side, then motioned her to come out his side. He had to lean down and help her climb to her feet.

She clung to his hand, shaking, longing to lean into the woolen wall of his chest. Longing to beg, "Don't leave me here." She was scared *all the time*, not that she had the dim sense to show it. It might be a different neighborhood, but the apprehension was the same as she'd always felt in her childhood. Weakness would be pounced upon. She never showed it if she could help it.

She had never been *this* weak, though. It took a superhuman effort to release him from that tenuous connection of grasping his hand—not just physically, but because she felt so lonely. So adrift.

Why was it so freaking cold out?

Shivering, she fumbled her key from her purse and moved to the door of her building. It wasn't locked. Never was. The entryway smelled like sauerkraut soup, which was better than some of the other days.

Travis swore as he came in behind her and set a hand on her upper arm, steadying her as she climbed the stairs. His looming presence, intimidating as it was, also felt protective, which made her heart pang.

"Hey," one of her neighbors said as she passed them on the stairs. She was off to work the streets in her thigh-high boots, miniskirt and fringed bra beneath a faux fur jacket. "No tricks in the rooms."

"He's just bringing me home."

"Don't get caught," the woman advised with a shake of her head. "You'll get kicked out."

Imogen didn't look at Travis, but his thunderous silence pulsed over her as she pushed her key into the lock and entered her "home."

It was the room where she slept when she wasn't working but so depressing she would rather work. It was as clean as she could make it, given the communal broom was more of a health hazard than a gritty floor. She didn't have much for personal effects, having sold any clothes and accessories that would bring in a few dollars.

There was a small soup pot on the only chair. It usually held a bag of rice and a box of pasta, but she had dumbly left it in the shared kitchen overnight a few days ago. She was lucky to have recovered the dirty pot. Payday wasn't until tomorrow, which was why she hadn't eaten when she collapsed.

Sinking onto the creaky springs and thin mattress of her low, single bed, she exchanged the damp blanket she'd been clutching around her for the folded one, giving the dry one a weak shake. "Can you leave so they don't think I'm entertaining? I really can't handle being kicked out right now."

"This is where you live." His gaze hit her few other effects: a battered straw basket holding her shampoo, toothbrush and comb, for her trips to the shared bathroom; a towel on the hook behind the door; a windup alarm clock; and a drugstore freebie calendar where she wrote her hours. "The street would be an improvement."

"I tried sleeping on the street. Turns out they call your ex-husband and he shows up to make you feel bad about yourself."

His "Not funny" glare was interrupted by a sharp knock and an even sharper, "No drugs, no tricks! Out!"

"Would you go?" she pleaded.

Travis snapped open the door to scowl at her landlord.

"He's not staying—" she tried to argue, but of course she was on the bed, which looked so very bad.

"We're leaving," Travis said, and snapped his fingers at her.

She flopped onto her side with her back to both of them.

"Imogen."

Oh, she hated her name when it was pronounced like that, as if she was something to be cursed into the next dimension.

"Just *go*," she begged.

"I'm taking this," he said, forcing her to roll over and see he held her red purse.

"Don't." She weakly shook her head. "I can't fight you right now. You know I can't." She was done in. Genuinely ready to break down and cry her eyes out.

"Then you should have stayed in hospital. I'll take you back there now."

She rolled her back to him again. "Take it, then. I don't even care anymore." She really didn't. All she wanted was to close her eyes and forget she existed.

With a string of curses, he dragged the scratchy gray blanket from her and threw it off the foot of the bed. Then he gathered her up, arms so tense beneath the thick wool that her skin felt bruised where it came in contact with his flexed muscles. He was surprisingly gentle in his fury, though, despite cussing out the landlord so he could get by and carry her down the stairs.

"Travis, stop. I'll lose all my things."

"What things? What the hell is going on, Imogen?"

CHAPTER THREE

IN THE FIVE minutes they'd been upstairs, a handful of jackals had begun circling to case the car. His chauffeur stood ready to open the back door and Travis shoved her into it, wondering why he'd got out at all.

To see how far she would carry her charade, of course, never dreaming she would take him into a dingy firetrap of a room that was where she *actually* *slept*.

He couldn't even comprehend it.

Snapping a glare at her, he saw there was no fight left in her. Her mouth was pouted, her eyes glassy with exhaustion, her hands limp in her lap.

If she weighed a hundred pounds right now, he'd be stunned. It wasn't healthy, even for a woman barely hitting five and a half feet tall.

"I can't afford the hospital. Can you please just tell my landlord I'm sick, not stoned, and let me sleep?"

"No." He slammed his door and jerked his head at his driver to pull into traffic, wanting away from here. As far and fast as possible. "Do you have gambling debts? What?"

"Oh, I backed the wrong horse. That's for sure." She rolled her head on the back of her seat to quirk her mouth in an approximation of a smile. "What's that old song about not being able to buy love? Turns out it's true."

"Which means?"

She only sighed and closed her eyes, almost as if she was trying to press back tears. "Doesn't matter," she murmured.

"Explain this to me. You had a lover who stole all your money? Tell me, how does that feel?" He ignored the gas-lit inferno that burst into life inside him as he thought of her with other men, feigning great interest in her reply instead.

Her brow pleated and she turned her nose to the front, eyes staying closed. Her lashes might have been damp.

"You seem obsessed with my many lovers. Accuse me of anything, Travis, but not promiscuity. You, of all people, know I don't give it up easily."

That took him aback a little. He didn't understand why. They were divorced. It shouldn't matter to him how many lovers she'd had, so why was he needling her about it? He *presumed* she'd taken some. With her libido?

Sexual memory scared through his blood, lifting the hairs on his body and sending a spike of desire into his loins.

He ignored how thinking of other men enjoying her passionate response put a sick knot in his gut. He had long ago decided he was remembering it wrong, anyway. He'd been high on personal achievements when they'd met, which had lent optimism and ecstasy to their physical encounters. Whatever had been roused in him hadn't been real or wholly connected to her. It certainly hadn't been worth all she'd cost him.

As for what she'd felt?

"Right," he recalled scathingly. "You want a ring and a generous prenup before you sleep with a man. You haven't found another taker for that? Of course, you only have one virginity to barter, and sex without that sweetener?" He hitched a shoulder, dismissing what had felt at the time like an ever-increasing climb of pleasure as she grew more confident with him between the sheets.

His ego needed her to believe his interest had already been waning, though. He still felt embarrassed for going blind with impulsive urgency in the first place, unable to let her get away. He had married her in a rush, on the sly, because he'd known deep down that they wouldn't last. A fire that burned that high, that fast, guttered just as quickly, which was exactly what had happened. A blur of obsessive sex had quickly dissolved into her walking away with her prenuptial settlement and a demand for a divorce.

"Wow," she said, voice husky. "That's hitting below the belt, isn't it? You're welcome, then, for releasing you to enjoy much better sex than I was able to provide."

He wasn't sure how her remark caused his own to bounce back and sting him so deeply. Maybe it was the fact that, try as he might to claim disinterest, he'd never found another woman who'd inspired such a breadth of sexual hunger in him.

That was a good thing, he regularly told himself. Maybe he hadn't erased her from his memory, but he didn't want or need the sort of insanity she had provoked, either.

No, he had spent the last years very comfortably dating women who didn't inspire much feeling at all, only returning to the land of turmoil when his PA had interrupted his meeting yesterday morning.

Had it only been thirty-six hours? Such was Imogen. She was a hydrogen bomb that cratered a life in seconds, completely reshaping everything around her without a moment's regard.

He remembered her prescription and drew the paper from her purse, handing it to his driver, instructing him to drop them in the front of his building before filling it.

When they arrived at his Chelsea building, however, the doorman was busy corralling paparazzi away from the entrance. It was a common sight when one of his celebrity neighbors had just arrived home. The sidewalks were teeming with Christmas shoppers, too. Even some carolers dressed in olden days' garb.

"Take us to the underground," Travis instructed, beginning to feel weary himself. He had only been home for a few hours of sleep last night, arriving late and leaving early, wanting to get back to the hospital. The urgency to do so had been...disturbing. Now he was compelled to get Imogen into his apartment so he could finally relax, which was an equally unsettling impulse.

"You don't want to be photographed with an escapee from the psych ward? Weird," she murmured. "You realize I don't just *look* like a homeless person? I am one. My landlord will have my stuff on the stoop and my room let to someone else by now. Thanks for that, by the way."

"Still have some spit and vinegar, though."

"Literally, all I have left. Why did you bring me here? Because I'm quite sure you're not inviting me to live with you and I'm quite sure I won't take you up on it if you do."

He didn't know what he was doing, but he hadn't been able to leave her in that roach-infested garbage pail of a building. He imagined she would only discharge herself if he took her back to the hospital. Bringing her to his penthouse was his only choice.

"You're going to have that nap you're so determined to take. I'll use the silence to figure out what to do with you when you wake up."

Imogen wanted to sneer at him, but it took everything in her to open her door when the car stopped and it wasn't even her own steam that did it. The driver got out and opened it for her. He helped her out and Travis came around to slide his arm across her back, helping her into the elevator where he used his fingerprint to override a security panel and take them to the top floor.

He kept his arm around her and she couldn't help but lean into him. It felt really, really nice. For a split second, she experienced a spark of hope. Maybe he didn't hate her. Maybe this was a chance to make amends. She couldn't change the past, but the future was a blank whiteboard.

Then she caught sight of their reflection and her glimmer of optimism died. At one time, she had *almost* been his equal, when her family had had money and she had been a product—not a shining example, but at least a product—of an upper-crust upbringing.

Since then, however, he had skyrocketed from

wealthy architect who dabbled in real estate to international corporate mogul, taking on prestigious projects around the globe. An honest-to-God tycoon who lived in the city's best building on its top floor. He was way out of reach for the black-sheep daughter of a paper publisher and far, far beyond taking up with a match girl—which she could aspire to be as soon as she stole some matches.

She had thought dying in the street was rock bottom. Then Travis seeing how broke she was and the way she had been living had felt like rock bottom. But this was rock bottom. Riding an elevator up to what might have been her life if she'd played her cards differently, while she faced how completely and irrevocably she had fallen down in his estimation, was beyond demoralizing. It was shattering.

Until this moment, her life had been a mess, but her heart had held some resilience. She had possessed some spirit. Some hope that one day she would be able to face him and make amends. That belief had got her out of bed and off to her many awful, minimum-wage jobs. But that was gone now.

The doors of the elevator opened to a foyer of marble and mahogany. Floating stairs rose on the right with a bench tucked beneath. A side table stood on the other side. An impressionist painting the size of Central Park hung above it.

From inside the lounge, out of sight but not out of earshot, Imogen heard an excited voice cry, "Papa!"

As tiny footsteps hurried toward them, Imogen began to disintegrate, each particle of her breaking away and sizzling agonizingly into utter despair.

She was such a fool. *This* was rock bottom.

***

Travis bit back a curse as Imogen pulled away from him, swinging a look on him so betrayed and shattered, it cut like a scalpel directly into his heart.

He had to look away to his niece, Antonietta, as she appeared from the lounge. She came up short at the sight of them, recovered in the next second and continued her pell-mell run at him, arms up and wearing a wide smile.

"Zio!"

He picked up the three-year-old sprite.

She threw her arms around his neck and made a production of kissing his cheek with a loud, "Mmmwah!"

Gwyn, his stepsister, appeared with a sleeping Enrico drooped on her shoulder. She faltered as she took in that Travis had a woman with him, one who didn't exactly look like his usual type. She wasn't the judgmental sort, though. She quickly recovered with a welcoming smile. "Hi."

"I completely forgot what day it was," Travis told her.

"No problem. I'm Gwyn." She came forward with her free hand extended.

Imogen's gaze sharpened with recognition, but if she said one wrong word to Gwyn...

"You're Travis's sister." Imogen unfolded one arm to shake hands. "Nice to meet you. I'm Imogen."

"Good timing. I've just made coffee," Gwyn said toward Travis. "Let me put Enrico down. I'll be right back."

Imogen's brain was reengaging from its tailspin, where she had briefly been convinced Travis was married with children. She occasionally stalked him online, as one did with an ex. He dated a lot but hadn't seemed serious about anyone, so, for a moment, she had been struck nearly dead with shock. By a loss so acute, she hadn't been able to withstand it.

Shut up, misguided girlish fantasies.

She and Travis were *so* over.

As for his sister, when Gwyn had had a spot of trouble a few years ago with an international bank scandal and a global leak of nude photos, Imogen had followed it for different reasons than the rest of the world's lurid curiosity. While she and Travis had been married, he hadn't even *mentioned* he had a stepsister. It had been a shock to see his name associated with the headlines not long after their split. Imogen had combed every story she could find then, trying to figure out why he'd been so secretive about his family.

At the same time, she had drawn a line in the sand for herself. She hadn't told her father that she had an in with that particular story. She and Travis had been firmly on the outs by then, her father's business failing miserably, but she refused to exploit him. Between her divorce settlement and her mother's trust fund, Imogen had been sure they were only a few short months from having her father's company back on its feet.

The core of her reluctance to use Travis, however, had stemmed from the deep agony of rejection Travis's letting her go had rent through her. She hadn't even told her father she'd been married, fearful of his reaction.

He would have approved of Travis, of course, but there was no way she'd wanted Travis to meet her father. Then, when her marriage fell apart…well, who needed that sort of scathing disappointment added to her pain? Her father's derision would have expanded exponentially under the news she had failed to hold on to him. It was bad enough she had deluded herself into believing Travis had had real feelings for her.

The entire thing became so humiliating she had preferred to be as secretive about their marriage as Travis had been.

He led the way into the lounge. It was tastefully decorated for the season with festive garlands around the windows, fairy lights winking in the potted shrubs from the terrace and a tree that looked and smelled real. The presents beneath were professionally wrapped but with cartoonish paper that would appeal to children.

"Mama said I have to ask you if those are for me," the little girl said, one arm still firmly around Travis's neck as she fixed her gaze on the gifts.

"And Enrico, yes."

"Can I open them? *Per favore*, Zio?" she asked very sweetly.

"Not yet."

She gave a little pout of disappointment.

Italian? Imogen sank down on the sofa so she wouldn't fall down.

"You never mentioned your sister," she commented. All he'd told her was that he was close with his father, who lived in Charleston, and didn't see much of his mother, but she also lived in that city.

"Gwyn's mother married my father while I was at university, but passed away soon after. Gwyn and I didn't grow up together."

They seemed close now, if he was giving the woman access to his apartment when he wasn't even here. He'd been cautious about letting his *wife* into his personal space, constantly picking up behind her and uptight that the few things she'd brought with her hadn't fit with his existing decor. At the time, she had put it down to the shift from bachelorhood to living with someone, but she knew now it had been more than a territorial thing. He hadn't wanted her there at all. It still made her throat raw to think of it.

"This is Antonietta." He was still holding her. "We call her Toni."

The little girl cupped her hand near his ear and whispered something.

The corner of his mouth twitched. "Toni Baloney."

Toni giggled and hunched her shoulders up to her ears. "What's your name?"

"Imogen. My sister used to call me Imogen the Imagination Magician."

Toni widened her eyes in excited wonder. "I love that name."

He didn't just have family, but a fun and loving one. Huh. Why would he have felt a need to hide that from her?

"Come eat your apples and cheese, *topolina*," Gwyn said as she returned, waving Toni toward the snack at the elegant glass-topped pedestal dining table.

Travis set the girl on her feet and she skipped across to climb up and kneel on a velvet-upholstered chair.

Imogen hadn't been allowed at the grown-up table until she was twelve.

"The doorman let us up because you left notice that we would arrive today." Gwyn came over with coffee, cream and sugar, then seated herself where she could watch Toni. "I thought that meant you remembered we were coming. I was going to text, but I got busy with the kids. If we're imposing, I'll ask Vito to move us to a hotel."

"It's one night. I forgot, that's all." Travis seemed to blame Imogen for his absentmindedness with the cool glance he flicked her way as he sat.

Imogen lifted her brows, wondering how he was going to explain her presence now that his worlds had collided.

He didn't bother, only sat back with his black coffee. "Vito had meetings?"

After a beat of surprise, Gwyn nodded. She smiled at Imogen. "We just got in from Italy. My husband often has business in New York, so we make a stop here, adjust to the jet lag, let the kids leave fingerprints all over Zio's furniture, then head to Charleston."

"To see Travis's father?"

"Henry, yes. And the bank has offices there. Vito checks in and works on and off while we visit Nonno. For the last few years, Henry has been coming to us for the holidays, but this year is his seventieth birthday. It's right before Christmas and he's having a party, so we came to him."

"Sounds fun." Imogen deliberately offered nothing about herself.

"It should be."

Silence reigned as they all blew across coffee that was too hot to drink.

The corners of Gwyn's mouth wore the tiniest curl. She was clearly dying to pry, but was far too polite to ask. Or knew Travis would talk when he was ready and not before. Imogen had come up against that perversely closed-off side of him herself. In fact, the things

Gwyn had just told her were probably the most she'd ever learned about his personal life.

"Toni, do you see an elephant in this room?" Imogen turned her head to ask.

Gwyn snorted and almost spilled her coffee.

Toni sat up on her knees and swung her head this way and that. "No."

"Mmm… My mistake. I thought there was one."

Travis sent her a warning look.

"We've taken up both guest rooms, but the kids can come into our room if need be," Gwyn said mildly.

"Is there an aquarium?" Imogen asked Toni. "Because I feel like someone is fishing."

Gwyn had to scratch her nose to hide the laugh she suppressed.

Toni cocked her head, sensing opportunity. "We can pretend to fish in the pool."

"It's too cold, *topolina*," Gwyn said. "When Papa gets back and Enrico is awake, we could maybe go to the indoor one downstairs. You and I are going to have a little sleep first, though. Soon as you finish your snack."

"And Imogen?"

Imogen plucked at the pajamas she was wearing, certain that was what had prompted Toni's question. "I'm going to nap, too, but by myself."

Travis looked at Gwyn. "Would you have something that Imogen could wear when she wakes?"

"Of course. I'll find something right now."

Gwyn took Toni upstairs and Travis finished his coffee, watching Imogen while wishing for something stronger in his cup. He knew he should check his phone.

He'd been ignoring it since walking out of that meeting yesterday. Finding Gwyn here reminded him he had a life beyond Imogen. A trip to Charleston in a few days for his father's birthday and the family Christmas celebrations.

He couldn't think of anything, however, except the woman who had had a way of consuming his thoughts from the moment he'd met her. She had walked into his brand-new offices here in New York four years ago, as he'd been expanding beyond Charleston, starting some of his most prestigious architectural projects to date.

She'd introduced herself as a writer for one of the cornerstone publications in New York and proceeded to interview him. Her auburn hair had rippled in satin waves as she'd canted her head at him, listening in a way that had made him feel ten feet tall.

"Let's talk more over dinner," he had suggested after an hour of growing ever more fascinated by her engaging curiosity and earnest little frowns. Her legs were lithe stems beneath a black miniskirt, propping up a notebook where her handwriting looped in big swirls and *t*'s that she crossed with a sweep of her slender wrist. Her breasts had looked to be the exact fit for his palms. Everything about her had looked like a perfect fit. She had been, not that he had had confirmation that first night. Dinner had turned into an invitation back to his old apartment, which was when she had confessed to being a virgin.

"At twenty?" he'd chided with skepticism. "How is that possible?"

"Probably because I don't know what I'm missing," she had shot back, laughing at herself yet surprising him into laughing, as well.

That quick wit, that unvarnished honesty, had convinced him she was exactly what she appeared—a journalism student from a good family with a bright mind and a cheeky wit that would keep him on his toes. There was absolutely nothing to dislike in that package.

The packaging had been the lie, of course. Mislabeled. Ingredients not as advertised. Definitely looking shopworn these days.

Finishing her coffee, she set down her cup, bringing him back to the present.

"You don't want me here. I'll go." She looked around, frowning. She was probably looking for her purse, which was in the pocket of his overcoat. He'd hung it in the closet at the door. It could stay there for now.

"Where to?" he prompted. Goaded. He was fed up with her thinking she had options when clearly neither of them did.

She swallowed. "I'll talk to my landlord—"

"No," he cut in.

She turned a look on him that sparked with temper. "What do you want from me, Travis?"

"Let's start with an explanation. Where did all my money go?" He waved at the fact her worldly possessions consisted of pajamas she hadn't been able to pay for out of her own pocket. "Where did *yours* go?" She hadn't been rich, but she hadn't been destitute.

She blew out a breath and sagged into the sofa, pulling a tasseled cushion into her middle.

He braced, waiting to see if she would tell the truth or lie yet again. Wondering if he would be able to tell the difference.

"I was trying to save Dad's business."

"Publishing," he recalled.

"Newspapers and magazines." She gave him a pained smile. "Print media."

He recalled what she'd said in the car. "'The wrong horse.'"

"Such a dead one, yet I beat it like you can't even imagine. Your money, my trust fund. Dad sold the house and liquidated anything that wasn't already in the business. We threw every penny we had at it. Then he went into care, which was another bunch of bills. My name wound up on everything. I couldn't declare bankruptcy while he was alive. It was too humiliating for him. We were pretending it was all systems go while I sold furniture and clothes and Mom's jewelry to make ends meet. His cremation was the final straw. I was behind on rent and got evicted. I wasn't really keeping up on friendships by then and owed money to the few friends I had left. I wanted to start over on my own terms, so I found something I could afford and that's what I'm doing."

"That roach-infested brothel is your idea of a fresh start? Why didn't you come to me?"

"Oh, that's funny," she said with an askance look. "What would you have said?"

Everything he was saying now, but he wouldn't have let her get to where she was passing out on the street from neglecting her health.

"You married me to get your hands on your trust fund. Didn't you?" She had never admitted it, but he was convinced of it.

She hesitated very briefly before nodding, eyes downcast. Guilt? Or hiding something?

"I wanted access to it so I could help Dad." She had

the humility to shake her head and quirk her mouth in self-contempt. "Not exactly an economist over here. I knew better. Digital publishing was all I learned at school, which he thought was useless." She shrugged. "I tried to convince him to start doing things online, but old dogs..." She smiled without humor. "It would have been too little, too late, even if he'd bought in."

"So, you're broke."

"I'm in a hole so deep all I see is stars."

"You're telling me the truth? Because if it's addiction or something, tell me. I'll get you help."

"I wish it was. There would be pain relief, at least. Escape." Her smile was a humorless flat line.

He drummed his fingers on the arm of his chair, frustrated by what sounded like brutal honesty. Nevertheless, he muttered, "God, I wish I could trust you."

"What does it matter if you do or don't? I mean, thanks for the hospital, I guess. I'll try to pay you back someday, when I can afford a lottery ticket and happen to win the jackpot, but—" she flicked a helpless hand in the air "—our lives won't intersect after today, so..."

Her heart lurched as she said those words, trying to be laissez-faire about it.

He narrowed his eyes. "That would be nice if it were true, but I've just taken responsibility for your hospital bills. For *you*. What am I going to do? Turn you out on the street? In the middle of winter? I happen to possess a conscience."

"Meaning I don't?"

"It was pretty damned calculating, what you did."

"You're the one who set the terms of the prenup,"

she reminded him. "That was all you. All I did was sign it."

"And took the money after three weeks of marriage."

"Oh, I should have given you my virginity for the bragging rights of saying I was once Travis Sanders's lay of the day?" She blinked her lashes at him, pretending her shields were firmly in place when she was silently begging him to contradict her. To say she had meant more to him than that.

She *had* been willing to give it up without a ring in the heat of passion, if he would only remember. He was the one who had proposed and led her to believe he cared.

A muscle pulsed in his jaw. "I'm surprised you haven't sold our story, if you needed money so badly."

She pressed her lips together, but he was quick enough to read her expression.

"Considered it, did you? I cannot believe I thought we had a shot," he muttered.

"Oh, did you?" She leaped on that. "Did you really? How about you step off your high horse a minute and be honest about your own motives. Why did *you* marry *me*?"

"You know why. You refused to sleep with me until I put a ring on it."

"And you wanted in my pants so bad, you wanted bragging rights to my virginity so bad, you made our quickie marriage happen." They'd known each other a *week*. "Then what? Did you take me home to meet this wonderful family of yours, all flushed with pride in your darling bride? You didn't even tell me you had a sister." She thumbed toward the stairs. "She hasn't got a clue who I am. Does your dad?"

His stony expression told her that was a hard no.

"At no point did you think we had a shot." The words were coming out thick and scathing, but they tore up her insides, sharp as barbed wire, seeming to affect her far more than him. "You were mortified that you'd succumbed to marriage. Every time I said, 'Let's go out,' you said, 'Let's stay in.' The one time we ran into someone you knew, you didn't even introduce me. You didn't just skip the part that I was your wife. You didn't acknowledge me to them *at all*."

His cheek ticked and he looked away, not offering an explanation, which scored another fresh line down her heart.

"You wouldn't let me change my status online and said it was because you wanted me to yourself. Then you went to work every day, leaving me alone in that big apartment where I wasn't allowed to touch anything."

"You claimed to be writing for your father, if I recall. Why did I never see any of those articles?" So scathing.

Her face stung, but she wasn't about to get into her father's lack of love for her. One spurn was all she could relive at a time, thanks.

"You were planning our divorce before you said, 'I do.' That's why you drew up the prenup. All you cared about was keeping the damage to your reputation at a minimum. You invested *nothing* in our relationship except what I took when I left, certainly not your heart. Our marriage was as much a transaction on your side as mine. I bruised your *ego* by walking out before you told me to leave, not your feelings. Tell me I'm wrong."

Please. She silently begged him to give her a rosier view of their flash-in-the-pan romance. Her whole body tingled, ions reaching out for a positive against this negative charge consuming her.

"Fine," he bit out. "You're right. I knew it was a mistake even as I was saying the words."

His words skewered into her. She swallowed, wishing she had died in the gutter, rather than survive to face this.

"You're welcome for remaining your dirty little secret, then," she snapped. "For what it's worth, you're one of thousands of mistakes I've made. Not unique or special at all."

"You don't know when to quit, do you?" he said in a dangerous voice. "Aside from the day you walked out, of course."

"Oh, you started that. You know you did."

"A husband is allowed to ask his wife why he needs to top up her credit card before it's a month old," he said through his teeth.

"Your exact words were, 'I don't care where it went.' You didn't want to know about my life any more than you wanted to share details about yours. I quit kidding myself at that point. It wasn't a marriage if you were suffering buyer's remorse. I did you a favor by walking out."

"That's one way to frame it."

"Yeah, well, I keep trying to do you the favor of walking away again, but you keep forcing me to sit my butt back down. Why is that?"

"Because you owe me, Imogen." He leaned forward,

hand gripping the arm of his chair as though trying to keep himself in it.

"I owe a lot of people. Get in line."

The sound of the elevator had them both holding their stare but clamming up while the animosity cracked and bounced between them.

A superbly handsome man appeared in a bespoke suit. Little sparkles came off him where snowflakes had melted across his shoulders and in his dark hair. He was clean-shaven, calm and confident, not taken aback in the least by the sight of an orphan in hospital pajamas huddling on Travis's designer sofa.

"You must be Imogen," he said with a heart-melting Italian accent, coming forward to take her hand in a gentlemanly shake. "No, don't get up. Vittorio Donatelli. Vito, *per favore*."

"Gwyn texted you?" Travis surmised.

"And the photographers downstairs inform me that Imogen is your wife. *Congratulazioni*," he said to Travis with a blithe smile. "They asked for a comment. I told them I'm very happy for you, of course."

"Are you kidding?" Travis closed his eyes and Imogen was pretty sure steam came out his ears.

"I didn't say a word," she swore.

"You didn't have to, did you?"

"My passport lapsed! My student card was long gone. Sometimes you need more than one piece of ID. Why would anyone give a care who I was married to? I'm nobody and you're just one more businessman in a city of—" She cut herself off as she saw a look pass between the men.

Gwyn, she remembered. Travis's sister was notorious clickbait.

"It's not her fault," Travis said to Vito.

"I will assure her of that, but you know what she's like." Vito's smile was pained as he rubbed the back of his neck and excused himself to go upstairs.

"For what it's worth, that's one of the reasons I never told a soul you and I were married," Imogen said. "Once I saw what the online trolls were doing to her, I not only didn't want to be part of it, but I had enough people willing to pile on me. It would have only made things worse for her to be associated in this direction."

He stared at her. "You really want me to believe you were thinking of her?"

And him, but what was the use in trying to convince him? "You either believe me or you don't, Travis. I can't make you do anything."

It hurt to acknowledge his mistrust. All of this was even more excruciating than being one more anonymous hard-luck story in a building full of society's rejects.

"It's actually your fault that our marriage has been exposed, you know," she pointed out. "Some orderly probably saw you acting like a big shot, transferring your wife to Celebrity Central. You in your tailored suit, flashing your gold-plated phone. You should have left me at the first hospital and none of this would be happening."

He picked up his phone and said, "It's last year's model. Off the shelf."

"Whatever. You made me look important. I wasn't trying to be."

"Let's skip the blame shifting and get to mitigating the damage. You really owe me now." He tapped and rolled the phone along its edge on the arm of his chair, thoughts hidden behind an expression gone granite hard. "This is going to be all over the gossip sites. Maybe the financial pages and television news outlets. I imagine they'll dig up the date of our marriage and the divorce settlement."

As much as she had rationalized taking that settlement, she had always felt ashamed of herself for demanding it.

He had been contemptuous in fulfilling it, making clear that whatever physical infatuation he'd felt toward her had firmly run its course. She repulsed him on every level.

She had dreamed ever since of paying him back, just to soften his harsh opinion of her, but she knew from her childhood what a lost cause that sort of aspiration was.

"It won't be long before my father is calling me, asking whether this report of my marriage is true."

"What do you want me to do?" She held up her powerless hands.

"I'll tell you what I want you to do. *Don't humiliate me again.*"

Was that what she had done? Because when she had been standing there, wanting to make explanations about her father's business and how painful her relationship was with him, she'd felt pretty damned humiliated to realize Travis didn't care one iota that she had reasons and responsibilities and that she suffered. He had decided she was a faithless spendthrift well before she'd returned from her father's office that day.

"This is what you're going to do," he said in a voice so hard it couldn't be scratched. "You're going to say our marriage was youthful impulse and we parted ways when we realized our mistake. After your father passed, you began doing charity work, which is how you happened to be on skid row when you needed medical attention. I'll make suitable donations to back that up. Then we're going to show the world that we might have parted over artistic differences, but I had the taste and sense to marry very well. You're going to stay with me, pretend we're reconciling and act like the kind of wife you should have been."

Bad girl. I didn't say you could come out of your room. Get back up there.

She swallowed back the bitter pill in the back of her throat. "Is that what I'm going to do?"

"Unless you're ready to start making a living the way your neighbor appeared to earn hers, you are going to do exactly what I tell you to do."

"You don't see the irony of introducing me to your friends and family now, when I'm not actually married to you, when you were ashamed to call me your wife before?"

"It galls me," he assured her, leaning back and catching at his pant leg as he crossed one over the other, flinty expression belying his relaxed pose. "But the cat is out of the bag. We're going to groom it and put a pretty collar on it and keep it from scratching up the furniture."

"And somehow this pays off my debt to you."

"It keeps it from getting worse."

Oh, she doubted that.

The walls were closing in another inch. They'd been compressing on her for months. Years, even. No options. It was a trapped, helpless feeling and she could only sit there with her hands knotted into fists and breathe.

"You don't have anywhere to go," he pointed out, as if she wasn't sickeningly aware. "How do I look if I put you on the street? No, we're rediscovering each other. At *Christmas*. It's very romantic," he said with thick sarcasm. "The press will be very positive."

He said the last in a way that was more of a threat. *Mind yourself, Imogen, or you'll stay in your room.*

"How long will this last?"

"Until I feel the attention has died down enough we can part without it being noteworthy."

"But I'll still owe you for the hospital bills." She flicked nonexistent lint from her pajama pants. "Too bad you won't have sex with me. Otherwise, I could pay that down *exactly* the way my neighbor does."

"I didn't say I wouldn't sleep with you. I said you need to work harder to make it interesting."

For a moment, all she heard was a rush in her ears. Her face grew hot. She wanted to believe it was anger, but it was embarrassment. Acute insecurity. No matter what she did or how hard she tried, she was never enough. It was a hot coal of humiliation that burned a hole in her belly every single day.

"Well." She clung fiercely to what shredded dignity she had left, but she was dying inside. "I've only had one lover and he taught me all I know, so blame yourself. But after that remark, I'd rather give it away to strangers on the street than sleep with you again." She stood.

He shot to his feet, arm jerking as though he would stop her in her tracks.

She wasn't walking out, though. As he had pointed out so ruthlessly, she had nowhere to go.

She tucked her elbows into her sides, avoiding his touch. "Powder room?"

He gave a brief nod toward the far end of the kitchen.

She locked herself inside, then splashed cold water onto her burning eyes.

CHAPTER FOUR

Travis took zero satisfaction in having pierced her shell. There had been such hurt in her for a moment, the kind of betrayed shock that came after a sucker punch, he had thought she was walking out on him and his heart had lurched. He'd been ready to physically stop her.

Even though letting her go would be the healthier choice for both of them. He *was* hitting below the belt, but there'd been something in her flippant remark about paying him off with sex that had struck a raw spot. Her accusation of his treating their marriage like a transaction and having buyer's remorse was stuck in his craw, too.

Was that how he had viewed it?

He certainly hadn't looked on marriage as a sacred vow. His parents had divorced. It was something people did. That had allowed him to see a viable exit strategy even as he was proposing. She wasn't wrong about that.

I bruised your ego by walking out before you told me to leave.

He hadn't been ready, that was true. He had still wanted her—still did, if the way his blood had leaped at her talk of trading sex was anything to go by. Cop-ping to that would give her the upper hand, though, and she already had too much of his attention.

One lover? Really? *Impossible.*

She had said earlier she wasn't promiscuous. Okay, he was willing to believe she was fastidious, but to want him to believe she'd only been with *him*? Lying about that was worse than all the rest, almost as if she knew it was his Achilles' heel.

He couldn't let himself believe anything she said, but in all their sparring today, nothing had landed so hard on him as the way she kept insisting she hadn't been with other men. If it was actually true—

It couldn't be. It would leave him reeling. And she had overturned his life enough.

His phone rang, vibrating through his hard grip when he'd forgotten he was even holding it. It was his father. The rumors had reached him via a friend who'd seen something online. Travis promised to explain once they were in Charleston. No escape from this charade now.

The reality of pretending to be enamored with his ex-wife began to hit him. Better to manage the PR with her under his nose, however, than let her loose to ruin herself, maybe even him, all over again.

One lover.

Why did he want to believe that so badly?

The elevator pinged as his driver delivered her medication. Gwyn came down the stairs as he accepted it and followed him back to the kitchen.

"I shouldn't have had the coffee," Gwyn said with a yawn. "Vito is fast asleep, but I'm wide awake so thought I'd start dinner. I left a dress for Imogen in your room. Is she still here?"

"In the powder room." He glanced down the hall, heard the water running. He moved to check her prescription and shook out a couple of pills to give her when she came out.

"Is she staying for dinner?"

"Yes."

"Did you talk to Henry?" Gwyn pulled vegetables from the fridge.

"Yes."

She paused to send him an exasperated look. "You were so angry with me for not speaking up when everything was happening with the bank. You know I want to help if you need something, right?"

"Cooking dinner is always appreciated."

She rolled her eyes, moving around his kitchen with familiarity.

This was one of the reasons he invited them to sleep here instead of a hotel. She provided some of the only home-cooked meals he ever ate.

Imogen had been a good cook, he recalled. That had been why he preferred to stay in. That and who wanted to get dressed again after sex? Today was probably the first time since they'd married that he had walked into an apartment with her and not stripped them naked in a matter of seconds.

Gwyn started garlic sizzling along with basil and oregano, saying, "We could stay an extra day. I could take her shopping if you like."

He had been suspicious of Gwyn and her mother when his father had moved them into his home. He'd since learned that beneath Gwyn's stunning exterior was a heart of pure gold. Her longing for family ran so deep, and her determination to stitch one together was so dogged, she had somehow pressed him into forming ties with her husband and children. He had enormous affection for her.

Which was why he didn't want her to get hurt.

"Don't get attached," he said in gentle warning. "This is damage control. It's not going to last."

Her optimistic expression fell into concerned lines. "But I want this for you."

He shrugged off her picture-perfect life. "I was never cut out for marriage and kids."

She dismissed that with a snort. "Vito would have said the same thing four years ago. *We* started as damage control."

"Vito didn't know what he was dealing with. Imogen doesn't possess your lovable nature."

Gwyn flushed and grinned at the compliment, but her smile fell away into embarrassed regret as she looked past him.

He turned to see Imogen had emerged from the hallway, expression stiff after hearing what he'd just said.

I can't do this, Imogen thought as she put on the sweater dress Gwyn had left for her. It hung off her like a sack.

It wasn't just how frumpy she looked. It was symbolic of how she didn't fit into Travis's world *at all*.

She had spent virtually her whole life trying to belong where she didn't. An interloper in her own family, the wrong crowd of friends, her father's choice of degree and a husband ashamed of their marriage. She couldn't go downstairs to eat with his family and pretend she was a *good wife*. One with a *heart*.

She was so very *dis*heartened by all of this that she pushed the dress off her shoulders so it fell to the floor, then crawled into the bed. Travis's bed. She honestly didn't care what he would think of her being so proprietary. What was he going to do? See it as a boring, extremely unimaginative attempt at seduction and revile her for it?

No need to sing another chorus of that, husband darling.

Curling into a ball, she brought the blankets up to her chin and fought tears as she tried to think. She had to figure out how to get back on her feet. Pull up her socks. Put things back to rights so she could get out of here, but it was all so horribly uphill.

She honestly didn't think she was that bad a person, just someone who had made some really dumb mistakes out of blind optimism. That wasn't the sort of character flaw that should leave her in such a ditch. It seemed really unfair.

It shouldn't be this hard to...

...sneak into Juliana's room.

She was so *hungry*. Her belly growled like a monster, but Daddy had locked her door, swearing really loud and angry, telling her to stay there this time. But she wanted out. She wanted to ask Juliana to bring her some bread. Or braid her hair. That always made her feel better. She was so sad. So lonely. All she had done was run up the stairs. She knew she wasn't supposed to run in the house, but he had told her to hurry and she had forgotten her hair band. He hated when her hair fell onto her face. Said it made her look like a stray.

Mama was saying things downstairs, making him shout even more. Mama's voice was soft, like she was crying, but Daddy's voice came through the floor like thunder, shaking Imogen's bed: "I told you!" and "Never should have had her."

He didn't want her and she didn't know why. The tears she'd been holding back began to seep through her closed eyes to wet her lashes. She couldn't help it. She pushed her face into the pillow so he wouldn't hear her sob. If he came to the door and heard her crying, she had to stay in longer. She could only come out if she was *good*.

Please come, Juliana. Please.

Like a miracle, the mattress shifted next to her. A soft "Shh" sounded near her ear as warm arms engulfed her. But these arms weren't her sister's soft, skinny arms. They were hot, muscled arms that enveloped her in a way that felt even safer.

"Travis," she whispered.

For a moment, she thought she was waking from a different bad dream. One where she and Travis had had an awful fight and she'd gone back to her father. They were still married after all. His skin branded her torso and thighs as she slithered close and melted against him, deeply relieved and instantly growing sensual, wanting to feel his body with all of hers. He smelled amazing and made her feel so cherished. His hand caressed down her spine, stirring her blood.

He was aroused, all of him stiffening as she slid her hand down his abdomen.

His muscles tensed and his hands shifted to press her away. "Don't."

Reality crashed onto her like an anvil dropping onto a hapless cartoon character.

With an anguished, mortified gasp, she rolled away and fought out of the tangled blankets. Her eyes released a fresh sheen of tears, frustrated, angry ones that choked up her chest and made her whole body shudder in confused reaction. She was half aroused, half traumatized by the betrayal of waking up *into* a nightmare.

Throwing her legs off the edge of the bed, she sat up, head pounding with a sudden rush of blood. She cradled her skull in two hands, elbows digging into her thighs, and consciously dragged her breaths into a slower cadence, grappling to face harsh reality all over again.

She was grown up and not even the married Imogen. She was the divorced, abandoned, impoverished one.

"You still have those?" He touched her back. "You're shaking."

She shrugged him off and used the edge of the sheet to wipe her cheeks. Then she used her forearm to hide her breasts in the dark while she stood and searched through the shadows for her hospital clothes.

"Where are you going?"

"I'm hungry." It was true, but she needed away from him so she could regroup. The dream had only happened a couple of times while they'd been married, but he had held her and stroked her then, soothing her and making love to her, encouraging her to bond with him in ways she couldn't risk again.

Not that he was offering, practically pushing her away like she was toxic.

This arrangement was going to be excruciating.

She hurriedly dressed and he followed her downstairs wearing jeans and nothing else. She averted her eyes from the smooth planes of his chest, the dark stubble coming in on his jaw.

The light over the stove was on, casting the kitchen in a soft glow. As she took yogurt from the fridge, he brought a box of muesli out of the pantry.

She sprinkled some over the yogurt in the bowl and took it to the table.

He brought over a glass of water and a capsule from her prescription. She'd had one before going upstairs to change, but had fallen asleep and missed the one she should have taken after dinner.

"Do you want toast? I can warm the leftovers."

"This is fine."

He touched the backs of his fingers to her cheek.

She pulled away, emotions so raw, even a gentle caress against her skin was liable to bruise all the way to her soul.

"I'm checking for fever."

"I'm fine." She lifted her hair off her neck where it was still damp with sweat from her dream.

He stayed beside her, fingertips going into his front pockets. "I suppose you still won't tell me what those are about?"

"They're just something I fake to earn your sympathy. Don't fall for it."

He swore under his breath, walking away then, standing to look out on the covered pool, blanketed with snow. His silhouette was heartbreakingly strong and beautiful against the glow.

His voice was marginally less confrontational as he asked, "Have you ever talked to anyone about them?"

"Why?"

"So they might stop."

"I'll sleep down here so I don't wake you."

"That's not the point." He swung around. "You

sound like you're in pain. You wake up with your heart pounding. You can't enjoy that."

She only took another bite and chewed, making herself swallow.

"Maybe if you talked about it, your mind wouldn't create monsters while you sleep."

"It's a memory."

A beat of surprise, then he asked very carefully, "Of a monster?"

"I wasn't molested. Don't freak out." She tipped the bowl and scraped yogurt toward the bottom side. "It's a replay of a no-good, rotten day when I was a kid." One of many, actually. "But sometimes, if I don't wake up right away, Juliana comes to visit me. So it's worth it to me to let it happen."

"Juliana is your sister?" He sounded almost gentle. "The one who passed away?"

"Yes."

"Why didn't you tell me that before?"

"Because I didn't want to." She chased the last bite and ate it. "I liked when you felt sorry for me and snuggled me. It felt nice. And I was afraid you might go to my father about it if I told you."

"Why?"

She threw her pill into her mouth and drank all the water, discovering she was super thirsty. She took her dirty dishes to the sink and poured herself more water, turning to lean against the sink and gaze across the miles of space between them.

Dare she pry open the darkest closet in her heart and show him the ugliest skeleton? Her dignity was long gone and that was all she had ever wanted to protect. Her father wasn't here to make it worse.

"Keep in mind I was twenty when you and I married. I've grown up a lot since then. I've had four years to realize Dad was the wrong horse to give a rat's behind about, but back then, I was still holding out hope I had a chance with him. I wasn't ready to cut the pulsating, infected cord that bound me to him."

"What kind of chance?" She couldn't see his frown, but she heard it in his voice.

"That he would love me." She took a sip to clear the constriction that began to squeeze her throat as she said it aloud for the first time. She had always known it, but now it was real. Acknowledged. *Fact*.

"Imogen—" his tone said, "Silly girl" "—lots of teenagers fall out with their parents."

"He hated me, Travis. *Hated* me."

"Why?" He still had that overly patient cast to his voice, like she was being dramatic or something.

"Ask him," she suggested with a scrape of humorless laughter in her throat. "I asked him once if my mother had had an affair. I thought maybe I was some other man's kid and that's why he couldn't accept me. He said, no, he just didn't want me."

"He said that? Those words? To your face?"

"He did. My parents' marriage was a business merger and he only agreed to Mom having Juliana because he needed an heir, but he didn't want another one. Mom wanted Juliana to have a sibling and wanted another baby for herself. She even tried the argument about an heir and a spare. He said no, but she stopped her pills and got pregnant anyway. He had taken to my sister. Mom thought he would warm up to me once I arrived. He didn't. I think hating me so openly was his way of punishing her for going against his wishes."

"This is the father you spent all my money bailing out?"

"You're entitled to your outrage." She tried pouring more water on the fire in her throat, but it stayed scorched and agonized. "I'm sure Mom is rotating like a rotisserie chicken in her grave over it."

"Why would you—?"

"Try to make my father love me? Because I was his child. He should have loved me. Isn't that the way it's supposed to work? But he didn't. Why, I don't know. Why didn't *you* love me? Because I'm bad? *Unlovable?*"

"Imogen." He said it like an imprecation and his hand came up.

"Don't feel bad about saying that." She waved off any nudge of conscience he might be experiencing over what she'd heard him say to Gwyn. "Maybe I'm not lovable. If so, it's his DNA that did that to me. He didn't know how to be anything better than he was and neither do I. I *tried* to be like Juliana. She was so good and sweet. He loved her. Everyone did. I did. You would have."

She looked for more to eat in the refrigerator. Some of Toni's leftover apple and cheese sat on a plate with plastic wrap. She took that out and looked for the bread.

"Was he an alcoholic or something?"

"No, just a bitter, cruel bastard. He used to lock me in my room without dinner to get me out of his sight. If I talked too loud or had raindrops on my clothes or got a better mark in spelling than Juliana, he would point at the stairs."

She carefully arranged the cheese and apples on one slice of bread, eating the chunk that didn't fit.

"I was smarter than her. A lot smarter. She struggled to read and sometimes I did her homework for her. I think that was part of his animosity. He liked being superior to everyone around him. I was always coming back with a joke or asking for more information. If he didn't know the answer or I got a laugh, he thought I was trying to make him look stupid."

"You should have told me."

"Why? What would you have done? Told him to love me? I knew when Mom and Juliana died that it was a lost cause. I just wasn't ready to admit it."

She pushed the heel of her hand down on the sandwich so it was thin as paper and about as appetizing. Her heart felt equally mashed to nothing. A nauseating ache had sat in her chest her whole life as she'd tried to figure out why she was such a disappointment.

"Want to know what he said that day, after the police came to the house?"

"Probably not," he said, grim and low.

She concentrated on cutting the crusts from her sandwich so she wouldn't have to lift her gaze. She was so ashamed of the memory, still so utterly devastated, that she didn't know where she got the courage to recollect it, but it was part of this ghost that needed exorcism.

"He was already angry. He had had to pick me up from my dance lesson because Mom didn't show up. She had slid off the road, into the river with Juliana. The police found them hours later. I was supposed to be in my room, of course, but when I heard someone at the door, I snuck out to see if it was them. I was at the top of the stairs as they explained what happened. Dad thanked them and closed the door. When he saw me, he said, 'The runt is the one who is supposed to drown.'"

"Is that *true*?" Travis's fists were so tight she could see the bulge of veins in his forearms all the way from over here.

"That was his reaction," she said, voice scraped raw by the past. "I couldn't even process that I had lost my mother and sister, but all he said was 'Go to your room.' Then he locked himself in his study until the funeral."

She had needed Juliana so badly then, but all she'd had was one hug from a housekeeper who had helped her find something to wear.

"I was eleven, just young enough to believe if I tried hard enough, he would change and learn to care about me, since I was all he had left. I worked really hard at school, hung around with all the spoiled preppy kids who came from families he admired. I didn't find one person I had a single thing in common with, but I *tried*. I took a degree in journalism, even though I was more of a fiction person. All the profs said my work was too purple. I wrote for Dad's dying rags, even though he only assigned me fluff pieces and only published my work if he absolutely had to. You thought I interviewed you as bait, trying to con you into our marriage, but I saw what an up-and-comer you were. My article was actually really good, but he cut it at the last minute. I tried to sell it to his competitor for you, because it was good press. We had a huge fight about it. We fought a lot and I always stormed out, saying awful things, but I always crawled back. They say the definition of *crazy* is to keep doing the same thing expecting a different result. I'm certifiable."

She ate her crusts out of habit. She cut them off

because she didn't like them, but knew better than to waste food, so she always got rid of them first.

"I was feeling pretty full of myself when we married. I almost quit and walked out of his house for good. I didn't need him if I had you, right? Then I realized you didn't actually care for me, that you only married me for my virginity. Seemed better to go back to the devil I knew, then. At least I had something he wanted. Maybe I could save his company and finally earn his respect."

She didn't know if he was even breathing. He stood so still, he could have been carved from marble. It made it easier to talk around the drill bit hollowing out her chest, leaving curled shards of her soul on the floor. She was confessing her sins to a statue, not a real person. It was a relief to finally get it all out.

"In the end, he hated me even more than you do, because I saw him at his weakest. I spent a solid year looking after him until I just couldn't do it anymore. Physically. He was too heavy for me to get into the bath. I had to put him into care. He hated me for that, too. I shouldn't have been born, I wasn't his favorite, I didn't save his business and I abandoned him to strangers—even though I spent hours every day with him at the home, fetching anything his nonexistent heart desired. I don't know why he was such a twisted, awful person. I'm sorry I was born to him, too. And embarrassed. That's why I never told you. I mean, who wants to admit her own father didn't love her?"

She picked up the sandwich, knowing she needed to eat it but feeling quite sick now, not sure she could swallow a single bite.

"Whenever I go to bed hungry and feeling sorry for

myself, I dream I'm locked in my bedroom again. If she can, Juliana sneaks in to make me feel better. You're the only person it's ever bothered because you're the only person I've ever slept next to. But I don't expect you to believe any of this. I'm a bad apple who never should have been born."

She bit into her sandwich and forced her jaw to chew.

The crying in her sleep was real. That much he knew. She sounded like a child when she was in the throes of her dream and came awake so shaken and confused, there was no way she was faking it.

He remembered the first time her tears had woken him, just a few days after he'd moved her into his old apartment. They'd had a fight earlier that evening about whether to tell anyone they were married. Rather than take her out for dinner, they'd had makeup sex until they fell asleep, utterly exhausted. He had thought she was crying about their fight when he woke to hear her sobbing. It had been eerie to realize she was asleep. He'd felt guilty, then worse, when touching her had scared the hell out of her.

"It was just a bad dream," she had dismissed after his soothing turned to lovemaking and her soft weight lay pliant against him. Embarrassed, she had risen to make bacon and eggs in the middle of the night.

"You should have told me after the first time," he said now, trying to fit this new information into his vision of her as a lying schemer. His father had tortured Travis in his own way, but it had been by pushing him into a state of passive helplessness. His father had never, ever, deliberately hurt him. Neither of them were the type to be effusive, but he didn't question his father's love or pride in him.

"Why?" she asked between bites. "What would telling you have changed?"

He didn't know. Would he have tried to keep her away from the man? He had known things weren't all roses there. The other time she'd had the dream had been a couple of weeks later, mere days before she'd walked out for good. She'd seen her father and had arrived home late, clearly upset.

He had assumed she didn't want to talk. He hadn't asked why she was so withdrawn.

You didn't want to know about my life any more than you wanted to share details about yours.

He hadn't wanted to open up, so he hadn't asked her to. He had preferred to kiss her out of her mood, keeping their sharing to the physical pleasure they offered each other. The times when he had sensed she was looking for more from him, some sort of emotional intimacy, he had withdrawn.

Why? Because his mother had cheated on his father and left. Their divorce had been brutal, the fallout nasty, but he would deny carrying a lifetime of scars. Perhaps he was wary of becoming as besotted with a woman as his dad had been, having seen the damage it could do. Mostly he didn't like to talk about it because it was water under the bridge. And none of what he'd experienced was so bad he had nightmares about it.

He had forgotten all about her nightmares. If he had known that hunger brought them on, he would have woken her to come down for dinner earlier. When he'd seen her asleep in his bed, however, something in him had eased. He'd told himself it was the relief from conflict. He wouldn't have to manage her interactions with his family. Who knew what she would say next? What damage she would cause?

I'm a bad apple who never should have been born.

He had made himself catch up on work after his houseguests went to bed, but he hadn't been tired enough to fall asleep once he'd crawled into bed beside her. He had been lying there, fighting memories of the other times they'd shared a bed, when he'd heard her breathing change.

Moments later, she had rolled onto her stomach and sobbed into her pillow as though she couldn't take whatever was being done to her. It was horrible. Of *course* he'd woken her to bring her out of it.

She'd known it was him right away, snuggling into place against him as if no time had lapsed at all, arousing him to the breaking point between one heartbeat and the next, with only the graze of her soft skin against his own. Her hand had moved with delicious familiarity and he'd nearly slipped into the erotic world where only the two of them existed.

He couldn't let her manipulate him like that, though. He had put a stop to her seeking touch and she'd reacted with such a jolt, it had only hit him as she pulled away that she'd still been half-asleep.

The fact her reaction hadn't been a deliberate act of manipulation, but her subconscious still reacting to him, was strangely gratifying. There was a part of him that had wondered if all her responses back then had been manufactured to wring a dollar value out of him, but the sensuality that had so ensnared him had, at least, been real.

"See?" she murmured, brushing her fingers over her plate. "Telling you has just made both of us uncomfortable and it changes nothing." Her cheeks looked hollow, her pleated brow fraught with embarrassment and despair. She rinsed the plate and put it into the dishwasher. "It shouldn't happen again, but I'll sleep down here, just in case."

"Go back to bed."

She gripped her elbows. Her narrow shoulders hunched up. "I don't want to sleep with you."

No? He would dearly love to test that, but only said, "I'll stay down here."

"I don't want to put you out."

He snorted.

The flash of injury in her expression was a bolt of lightning, jagged and searing, lasting only milliseconds but smacking him in the chest, leaving him breathless and seeing nothing while she walked away without even wishing him a good night.

It wasn't.

After tossing and turning, Imogen had slept late, waking to hear Travis in the shower. She went downstairs to find his sister and her family gone.

"Toni took her gifts?" she guessed when he came downstairs.

"Saved me packing them, so I said yes to her taking them."

That was when she learned they were going south to his father's birthday and having Christmas with the bunch of them.

"You can't ask me to participate in that. I can't afford gifts." She hadn't celebrated since her mother and sister had been alive.

"It's very low-key," he said dismissively. "Until the kids came along, we didn't do gifts at all. We still don't exchange between adults. Gwyn bakes cookies and makes a nice dinner."

It would still be awkward and painful, making her feel like an outsider yet again.

She had silently prayed the doctor would caution her against flying, getting her out of it, but an hour later the jerk had peered in her ear and pronounced, "Settling down nicely." He had approved her for travel provided she kept up with her antibiotics.

Since then, Travis had been expediently making decisions on her behalf, seeming to grow more impatient with her by the minute. "Stop asking how much everything costs," he muttered as he herded her along Fifth Avenue. "You need clothes."

"Normal clothes. Not..."

Not designer jeans at two grand a pair and cocktail dresses straight from the cover of *Vogue*. Imogen was currently changing out of a new dress to replace Gwyn's. This one was also a cable-knit, but it clung to her flyweight frame. It was so cute it had her reliving her three-year sentence on the fashion desk.

The cheeky lace-up sides on this forest green sheath add panache to a seasonal standard. Pair with a knee-high dress boot and an open-front trench for a day of shopping, then loosen the skirt laces for cocktails and clubbing.

The snug knit and low neckline flatters the most modest curves. Ramp up the fun factor with a bright red scarf and a bold lip, or drop in some drama with patterned black tights and a boho bracelet.

Now he was badgering her into ever-more-elegant eveningwear. And badgering the boutique's owner while he was at it.

"I don't care if frosted colors are made of titanium and on sale for ninety-nine cents. They're too ashen for her. Bring something vibrant. Jewel tones." He had an artist's eye in a businessman's head. The foundation of his fortune was real estate, built on his father's success in that arena, but Travis's vocation was architecture. He had shot into the stratosphere based on his ability to bring contemporary form and function to classic building design. "Yes, more like that."

An assistant was allowed past his gatekeeper surliness and came into Imogen's spacious changeroom with a sapphire-blue gown draped over her arms.

"Sorry," Imogen murmured on his behalf.

The woman brushed it off with a warm smile. "A day of spoiling is always a treat, isn't it?" She helped Imogen into the dress.

Spoiling? Was that what this was? Imogen was already in French lace underwear the last attendant had forced on her at his command. This didn't feel like indulgence. It felt like an assertion of his wealth and power over her, while putting further obligations upon her.

"Shoes," the young woman decided after zipping her. She hurried away.

"Can't you tell your father I have the plague and leave me here while you go to Charleston?" Imogen asked, poking her head out to where he lounged on a sofa, sipping champagne and scrolling through his phone. "You don't want me to meet him," she reminded him.

"He wants to meet you."

"But I don't know what you're expecting of me. What are the rules?" What was the punishment if she broke them?

"Rule one is to quit fighting me on every little thing." He lifted his gaze. "Let me see."

"It's too long. She's bringing me shoes."

"Get out here."

In all her years of trailing behind her father to galas and award ceremonies, she had never once worn a gown, only cocktail length. Deep down, she was loving this. She felt like a princess with silk whispering against her legs and tickling the tops of her feet. The cut lifted her modest bust and the shade turned her eyes to the color of the Caribbean Sea.

But she wasn't wearing makeup. Her hair was in a ponytail and she was so, so sensitive to his criticism. He had made a face at Gwyn's too-big dress, insisting they find something else immediately, as if he couldn't stand to be seen with her looking less than 110 percent. He had then nodded curtly to accept the green knit, barely looked at the jeans and showed zero interest in her shiny new boots. He wasn't enjoying this. It was something he had to do because she had ruined his life. *Again.*

She devolved into that most primitive of female desires for approval by hoping she looked pretty enough to please him. She picked up the skirt and hesitantly walked out to present herself.

He didn't move except to scan his critical eye up and down her with slow, thorough study. Finally, he took a sip of his champagne and said, "That will do." His gaze went back to his phone.

Her heart sank through the floor. She shifted her weight, standing on that stupid, pulsing organ that wanted and wanted and wanted.

The attendant hurried over with a pair of strappy black heels dangling from her fingers.

"Don't bother." Imogen picked up her skirt and turned to go back into the changeroom, blinking the sting from her eyes.

"Imogen." *Bad girl.* "Try on the shoes."

"Why?" she tossed over her shoulder. "You've made your decision."

The distracted attention he'd been giving her focused in so tightly, she felt the heat of his gaze like a laser that burned patterns into her skin. Like an electric lasso that looped out and held her in place while jolting her with a thousand volts.

"And now I've decided I want to see it with shoes."

The attendant heard the silky danger in his tone and crouched before Imogen. "We'll see if it needs hemming." She eased each of Imogen's feet into the shoes.

Imogen held Travis's gaze the whole time, staring him down even though she had no power here. Even though she was scared spitless of his anger.

Show no fear.

The young woman stood back and said, "Oh, yes, that's lovely. Don't you think, sir?"

Imogen waited, holding his gaze, waiting and waiting, while he said *nothing*.

"Would it kill you to be nice for five minutes?" she blurted.

His scathing gaze went down the gown to the French label shoes, coming back with a pithy disdain. He was being more than nice, his askance brow said, spending this kind of money on her.

She tightened her hands into fists. "Just buy me a leash and parade me around naked, then, since all you really want is the ability to yank me to heel."

His expression didn't change except for a bolt of something in his eyes at her temerity. He set aside his glass and stood, dropping his phone onto the cushion as he walked toward her, still holding her gaze. He jerked his head to signal the attendant to make herself scarce.

Imogen's heart pounded, but she held her ground.

"Now you've gone and made it look like we're fighting." He traced his fingertip up the throbbing artery in her throat, ending under her chin to tilt her gaze up to his.

His expression was mild, his eyes glittering with fury.

"And how things look is all you care about, isn't it?" She kept her voice low. "Was I not pretty enough to be your wife? Is that why you were so ashamed of me? Is that why I have to wear all these fancy labels and be seen, not heard?"

His touch shifted to hold her jaw in a gentle but implacable hand. "If I want to stop you talking, I know how to do it."

"Yes, you know all the best ways to hurt me and you can't resist standing on each of those bruises, can you?"

"*Does* it hurt, Imogen?" He lowered his head so his

mouth hovered near her own. "Last night when you reached for me, were you thinking about how good I made you feel? Four years seems a long time to go without sex. I don't believe you have."

The bastard. She ought to shove him away, but when she lifted her hands, it was only to splay them on his sides. She did think about the way he'd made her feel. Had every single day for the four years since she'd last touched him. Of the very few dates she'd been on, none had roused so much as a desire to kiss another man.

"You've been throwing it around like hard candy at a parade, I suppose?"

"Want some?" He slanted his head to take one microscopic nibble of her bottom lip.

The tiny contact strummed through her in a tremor of acute need.

This did hurt, but she was losing track of whether this was the pain of his derision or the pain of not having what she craved more than anything.

Her hands shifted, splaying wider to feel more of him while sliding to his waist and pressing. Encouraging him to come closer. Trying to pull herself into him.

"I do," she said in a thready voice, knowing it was a mistake to offer herself. She half expected him to shove her away, triumphant.

Instead, an atavistic light filled his gaze. His hand shifted to catch behind her neck and he crushed her mouth with his own, hot and possessive.

His other arm went around her and her chest collided with his. Time folded. The past crunched into the present and exploded into golden light and shattered defenses. Panic should have been her reaction, but all she felt was relief. Oh, he was rain after a long drought. Her whole being filled up with rejuvenation, swelling and reaching and opening for him. This man was the only one who did this to her, mind spinning away so all that mattered was that she wear his spicy scent on every inch of her skin. That he gather her into his powerful physique and ravage her with a hunger only exceeded by her own.

She twined her arms around his neck and pulled him down, encouraging the pressure of his mouth to the point of pain, trying to erase the ache of longing that had held her in its grip these four long years.

He met her anguished yearning with a ravenous type of control, body so hot around hers, she stood in a conflagration while he blatantly dove his tongue into her mouth. She was his. His action seemed to drive it home to her.

She couldn't deny it. She kissed him back without inhibition, greeting his tongue with her own, rubbing against him in open invitation. *Take me. All of me.*

It was exactly the way she had given herself over to him every time in the past. Even as she was cringing inside at her wantonness while celebrating the joy of being back in his arms, he was dragging his hands to her shoulders and pressing her away.

Her knees were too soft. She had to cling to his wrists to stay on her feet. It was mortifying.

His expression was avid and flushed. Aroused? Maybe. But sharp and accusatory, too. Angry but smug. He'd been teaching her a lesson.

Well, all she'd learned was that she couldn't trust either of them.

"I actually hate you right now," she told him in whatever was left of her voice. Then she carefully turned and closed herself into the changeroom so he wouldn't see that her lashes were growing as damp as the rest of her.

CHAPTER FIVE

"We're done for today," Travis said over his shoulder to the women standing across the room and pretending not to goggle at his spectacle with Imogen. "Package everything up."

He took out his credit card, drained his champagne, and went back to reading work emails so he wouldn't follow Imogen into the changeroom and finish what they'd started.

I actually hate you right now.

Given that he was lurking in the back of the boutique, waiting for a raging erection to subside, he was feeling quite a bit of animosity toward her, too.

He'd barely slept, trying to assimilate all that she'd told him last night with the way he'd viewed her all these years. Would things have been different if she'd told him? He was annoyed that he didn't know and hadn't been given a chance to find out.

Then she'd balked at going to Charleston and was pushing back on him with every purchase he was making, further shortening his temper.

Meanwhile, he'd been going out of his mind, watching her try on tight jeans that cupped her pert behind. He'd tried not to notice her bare knee between the hem of her skirt and the top of her boot when she sat beside him in the car or the way the neckline of her new dress framed the upper swells of her breasts. It reminded him too much of the way her soft body had felt slithering close to his oh-so-briefly last night.

When she had walked out in a gown that turned her skin to rich cream, one that made her hair catch lights and shadows and transformed her eyes into mysterious pools while it lovingly showcased the delicacy of her figure, he'd been almost beside himself with latent arousal.

And she wanted him to be *nice* to her? Nothing about this was *nice*. It was base and frustrating and colored with dark emotions he couldn't seem to identify.

"I'm ready." She appeared in the green dress, her waist so impossibly narrow, the gold belt sat like a small Hula-Hoop atop her hips. He kept forgetting how sick she'd been, but her face was pale enough to remind him.

He looked for the fire of defiance beneath her mask of obedience, the one that kept lighting his own temper, keeping him fighting. He waited for a sneer of sarcasm, but all he saw was tension and a hint of redness lingering on her lips from their rapacious kiss. She didn't meet his eyes, only offered a wan smile to the shop owner. "Thank you for all your help. I'll wait in the car."

Travis walked her out, leaving his driver to deal with the packages.

"What game are we playing now?" he asked as she turned her face away from him the moment he slid in beside her and closed the door. "Silent treatment?"

"Of course not. What would you like to talk about?"

She folded her hands in her lap and brought her face to the front, but this woman had never been so polite.

"You're angry that I kissed you," he surmised.

"Of course not," she said in that same ultrareasonable tone that was ultraprovoking in a passive-aggressive way. "You've demonstrated that you are allowed to do whatever you please with me."

Behind them, the driver closed the trunk. It shook the car, but the real impact was that precise little shot she'd taken with her loaded words.

When the driver opened his door, Travis barked, "Give us a minute."

"Of course, sir." He closed the door and moved to the curb in front of the car, shooing away the handful of photographers who'd been tracking them today.

"You didn't enjoy that kiss? It was something I *took*? Is that what you're saying?" The clench in his belly tightened.

"Whether I enjoyed it doesn't matter, does it? That was the point you were making. Whatever you do to me is a reaction—punishment—for what I did and continue to do to you." Her voice shook and her knuckles were white until she very deliberately relaxed her hands, drawing a breath that she let out in a slow measured exhalation. Like she was enduring something intensely painful.

"It wasn't a punishment, Imogen." Unless—*I actually hate you right now.* "*Did* you enjoy it?" His heart lurched, wondering if he had actually gone insane because he'd been sure they were both reacting with exactly as much passion as the other.

"Yes." Her voice belied that clipped answer. "You could have had me right there in the middle of the floor in a shop. Is that what you need to hear? Does that make you happy? How much is enough, Travis? How completely do you have to humiliate me before I'm sorry enough for ever having entered your life?"

She finally looked at him, but her eyes shone with angry tears. Shame raked at his conscience with sharp claws.

"I wasn't trying to humiliate you."

"Right," she said scathingly, hand turning into a fist again. "Just tell me the rules and I'll stop breaking them. The penance isn't worth it."

"It wasn't..." Agitation had him turning in his seat toward her.

She tensed. Braced herself. Winded him with the very idea that—

"I'm not going to hit you!"

"I didn't think you were," she claimed, but she held herself in wary stiffness, her sharp gaze on his.

He ran his hand down his face, trying to get a grip while his brain went ballistic.

He still wasn't sure what to make of the things she had said about her father last night. She hadn't said anything about violence, and he didn't believe she would have tried so hard to win over a man who had raised his fists against her. It had sounded more like her father was withdrawn and bitter, perhaps from grief, capable of lashing out, but Imogen was a dramatic person. He had wondered if she had exaggerated, trying to earn sympathy and forgiveness. She had flat out warned him against believing her.

But this reaction of hers was pure instinct and dread inducing in the extreme. He didn't even want to ask, let alone hear the answer, but he made himself do it.

"Did he hit you? Your father?" He would dig him up and kill him again.

"No."

"Imogen."

"Stop saying my name like that."

"It's your name."

"And you say it like I'm stupid and wrong and you can't stand me. You don't have to use your fists to hurt people, Travis." Her elbows were tight to her ribs, her body so tense she looked like she would snap.

The runt is the one who is supposed to drown.

He didn't want to believe her father had been that cruel because he would have to face that he had let her go back to Wallace. Had driven her there. His nostrils stung and a bonfire of culpability burned under his heart.

"Just tell me the rules and I'll follow them," she said again, voice strained. "Don't contradict you in public. Wear what you buy me. What else?"

"Imo—"

She flinched.

He closed his eyes. Gentled his tone, even though she was so infuriating he could barely control himself. "This isn't a test. It's not tennis. I wasn't trying to score a point with that kiss." Not entirely a lie. He had just wanted to *know* whether her reaction in the past had been real or manufactured.

"You're going to find fault in me no matter what I do. At least give me a fighting chance because I can't live with being smacked down all the time. You want me to act like we're in love when we're in public? Is that what I'm supposed to do?"

He scratched his brow. Sighed.

She flinched and looked away.

Really? She was so sensitive that a noise of frustration was a lash of a whip?

"Imogen." He managed to say it softly. His hand twitched to reach out, but he was afraid to touch her now, uncertain how she would take it, how she would feel it, wound as tightly as she was. He had never in all this time imagined he had the power to hurt her. Not that deeply.

"Do you expect me to have sex with you?" Her unsteady voice held a throb that sent a spear of aching tension through him.

"I don't expect it, no." Want? Yes. How the hell had things disintegrated into this?

"Because I don't know how to make it 'interesting'?" Her face was turned away, but her hand came up to swipe her cheek. "I was busy trying to help Dad. Taking care of him was a full-time job around my real one. That's why I didn't sleep with anyone else. I mean, I went out a few times, but just the odd dinner. So, yes, it has been a long time and that's why I reacted today, okay?"

She said it with enough vehemence he knew she was just trying to save face with him, but it still landed and stung. He had damned near devoured her and he hadn't been going without.

"I'm not built for casual sex. I don't know why. It's always bothered me."

Every single word this woman said baffled the hell out of him. "Why would you aspire to be good at casual sex?"

"Because it would be nice to connect with someone without getting hurt."

"If you're saying I was too rough, I'm—"

"Shut *up*, Travis. You don't expect to have sex with me. Fine. Do you expect me to pay you back for these clothes? That's why I kept asking how much—"

"No," he cut in, pinching the bridge of his nose. "You need clothes. Stop asking what I expect. I expect you to let me help you back onto your feet and not get yourself into another situation like this again. I expect you to take care of yourself and eat when you're hungry and get enough sleep and take your medication. If I sound overbearing and frustrated it's because I cannot believe you let things get to this level and that you're fighting me on fixing them."

Her mouth was pouted, her brow cringing at his harsh tone while her jaw worked, searching for a defense. "I don't want you to resent me more than you do."

"Well, you're going to love my next demand, because I expect you to tell me how much you owe so I can take care of it."

"No." Her knuckles stood out sharp and white on her tight fists.

"Your debt collectors are calling my office. I have to address it."

"You're not responsible for what I owe! Definitely not for what my father racked up."

"They don't care who pays, as long as they get their money." Keeping his father's business going when it had teetered on the brink had taught him exactly how financial vultures worked, compounding late fees faster than you could write a check. "We can do this the easy way or the hard way, Imogen. The easy way is for you to give me a list and we zero it off, quick and neat. The interest is the killer, so the longer you put it off, the worse it gets."

She scowled and hung her head. "I don't—" she began.

"It's like the debt clock," he cut in dryly. "While you waffle, it keeps rolling higher."

"Okay, fine! I'll need to go online when we get back to your apartment, but can we go somewhere first? I want to give you something. At least I can get that much off my conscience."

"What?"

"Your rings."

By the time they had driven to the converted brownstone in Brooklyn, where a handful of windows were framed with strings of colored lights, he had stopped speaking to her at all.

"I didn't feel desperate enough to sell them" had been the words that had flipped his switch into incensed silence. She had heard what he was thinking, though. Had known he was picturing that horrible little room in the sauerkraut-smelling building. If that wasn't desperation, what was?

Imogen bit her lip as they climbed from the car in front of Joli's building. If Joli wasn't home, Travis was really going to lose his bananas, but he'd been so busy taking her to task for "starving on the street," she hadn't wanted to get into the fact that, without her old cell phone and its helpful contact list, she didn't have Joli's number.

She buzzed the apartment with Joli's name on the plate and thankfully Joli answered.

"It's Imogen."

"I wondered if you would turn up. Come in."

"Who is she?" Travis asked as they climbed the stairs of the modest but well-kept building. This one smelled like nutmeg and cinnamon, thanks to neighbors preparing for the holidays.

"One of Dad's editors. She was a freelance journalist for years and went back to it after our flagship folded. She sent condolences when Dad died, but we haven't been in touch much since she went out on her own again."

As they arrived on the third floor, a door opened. Joli was heavyset and wore her gray hair in a no-nonsense, flat, boyish cut combed straight down on her forehead. Glasses that needed cleaning and a cigarette hanging out of her mouth were pretty much her signature look.

"How are you, kid?" She nodded at Imogen. Not the affectionate type, far too analytical and objective as a lifelong newsperson, but a trusted ally for years.

"The architect," Joli said when Imogen introduced Travis. "When I saw your names in the headlines this morning, I dug up your article on him and reread it."

"What? Why?" Maybe the bigger question was *how?*

Joli's studio apartment bordered on something from those shows about hoarders. Filing cabinets were covered in stacks of thick folders and surrounded by bulging cardboard boxes. Her kitchen table was a layered workspace of cuttings and notepads. Papers with brown mug rings sat on the coffee table while her desk in the corner was a computer poking above a mountain of spiral notebooks, colored index cards and full ashtrays. The whole place reeked of stale cigarette smoke.

"Bit flowery," Joli said with a wink, retrieving a

few pages from next to her computer. "But solid. He should have printed it." She offered them to Imogen.

"Oh, no—"

"Thank you." Travis took the papers and folded them in half.

"Travis," Imogen protested, trying to take the pages.

He ignored her, folded them again and tucked them inside his suit jacket.

She tightened her mouth and turned back to Joli. "I came for my rings. Do you mind?"

"In the fire safe." Joli crossed to the safe beneath her desk. She bent to dial it open. "Who are you working for these days?"

"I'm not writing. I had to sell my computer."

Travis sent her a frown.

Imogen shrugged. "It would have been stolen otherwise. At least the cash fit in my bra."

His next question should have been "What bra?" but the cash was long gone, too.

He asked instead, "Is that why the rings are here? You were afraid they'd be stolen?"

"I used to leave them with Joli when I went into the office, so Dad wouldn't see them. He would have told me to sell them."

Joli picked through old tapes and USBs, then came across a sealed envelope that had Property of Imogen Gantry written in bold print across it.

Imogen tore the envelope open and waited for Travis to offer his hand, which he did very slowly, radiating skepticism. She poured the rings into his palm, where the two bands sat like a platinum figure eight. An infinity sign weighted on one side with baguette diamonds, a pillow-cut stone with matched baguettes on the other.

She loved those rings. *Loved* them.

Which was why she hadn't been able to bring herself to sell them, no matter how dire her circumstances. It was heartbreaking enough to return them to the man who'd given them to her. She had to do it without touching them, without even looking at them for very long, or she might cry.

It wasn't even because they were so beautiful. They were stunning, but it was what they had meant when he gave them to her. What she had believed they meant. As fairy tales went, they had symbolized a happily-ever-after commitment that was pure and bright and magical. Sometimes she'd wondered if her biggest mistake had been in taking them off every day, hiding them from everyone and only wearing them in the privacy of Travis's apartment. Maybe if she had worn them around the clock, the spell would have stuck.

And maybe she had a rich imagination.

She handed the torn envelope to Joli. "I'd love some freelance work if you have any leads. Ad copy, anything."

"Email me," Joli said in her gravelly voice.

"Thanks."

Travis waited until they were in the car to say, "You said you didn't have any friends to lean on."

"Did it look like she has disposable income or a sofa I could use?" She made a face. "She's very independent and wouldn't dream of asking anyone for anything, except maybe what I just asked for—tips and leads. I knew if I went to her for money, she'd tell me to sell the rings and I didn't want to."

He had tucked them into his pocket and sat with his elbow on the armrest, finger resting across his lips. "Explain that to me again." The exaggerated patience in his tone grated; it was so supercilious.

She shrugged. "As long as I had them, I felt like I had *something*. I wasn't at zero. Also, selling them wouldn't have made a dent in the debt, so what was the point in giving them up and still being broke?"

He was searching her expression, picking apart her words. She could feel it and held her breath, realizing she had been hanging on to this link to him, needing it.

She decided to change the subject, even though it meant asking for another favor.

"It would be helpful..." she began, twisting her hands in her lap. "I mean, if you're serious about helping me get on my feet, it would be helpful if I could borrow a computer. I've kept a toe in with freelancing. It was just hard to hustle work when I had to get to the library around my other jobs. Half the time they kick you off after an hour and I wasn't picking up my emails fast enough. I'd get back to people only to hear they'd already offered it to someone else."

A beat of surprise, then he nodded. "I'll buy you a laptop."

"Just a loan. Please."

He only reached into his jacket. She thought he was getting his phone, but he pulled out the pages Joli had given him.

"Don't read that!"

He hesitated. "Why not?"

"Because I don't want to know how you react."

"How do you expect me to react? She said it was good, didn't she?"

She jerked a protective shoulder. "I wrote it when things were very different between us. I don't—don't want to see your reaction. Put it away."

"When we first met, I thought you were unlike anyone I'd ever met before." He folded the pages and tucked them back into his pocket. "I still don't understand you."

"I'm defensive. I wouldn't think I'd need to spell that out. I'm afraid you'll think that article is too full of awe. You'll see again what a green, starstruck little fool I was and laugh at me for it. If that's how you get off, go ahead." She waved with annoyance at his lapel. "Get it over with, then."

He lifted his brows. "Can I suggest something to you? Your father is dead. You don't have to denigrate yourself in his absence."

Nice advice, but it was going to be humiliating no matter what. He would realize how much he had meant to her and might even guess how gutted she was now. That would make today's kiss and his rejection that much more intolerable. Maybe he deserved to know how full of regret she was, but it was too mortifying to still be half in love with a man who had never cared for her at all.

"Is that why your father refused to publish it? Did he think it was biased?"

"I doubt he even read it." The cityscape grew as they crossed the bridge.

She felt his stare and turned her head to see something smoldering in his dark expression, something that made her abdomen tense.

"You should have told me how bad it was, Imogen."

"It doesn't matter," she muttered, looking away, hurt

for some reason. Maybe because his reaction was too little, too late. Maybe because she was angry with herself for not confiding in him. "There's no changing it. I'm over it."

He raised his brows in disbelief.

"That's why I was starting over the way I was," she defended. "Yes, it was the hard way, but I didn't want anything from my past to come with me. Nothing connected to him. That's why I carried my marriage certificate. At least I could pretend I had your name instead of his."

Hours later, Travis was spending way too much time lifting his gaze from his screen to the view out the door of his office. Not to look at the tree, either.

They'd come home to a lounge put back in order, toys stowed in the closet again, wet wipes back under the sink in the powder room.

Travis had bought a new laptop on the way home, which Imogen had taken to the sofa after changing into tights and a long sweater. She kept shifting, bending and straightening her legs so the hem of her sweater fell to reveal the slenderness of her thighs. She absently pushed it back toward her knee and rubbed one socked foot over the other. They were fuzzy white socks that made him want to squeeze her arches and toes like one of Toni's plush stuffies. She played with her hair, tickling the fanned end against her thoughtfully pursed lips. She arched and plumped the pillow behind her back, pushing her breasts against the knit of her blue sweater, then relaxed with a soft sigh that vibrated through him all the way over here.

Fantasies of walking out there, taking that laptop

from her startled hands, settling over her and making love to her on the sofa consumed him.

Their kiss earlier was still clouding his brain and now he had a pair of rings and her article to confound him along with the rest of what she'd revealed. It all spun him back to the heated moments in the back of his car the night before they married. They'd been parked outside her building, his driver having a cigarette somewhere. He'd had his hand up her skirt and she'd been trembling from the most exquisite orgasm he'd ever witnessed.

He would have done anything, *anything* in that moment. It was all he could do to restrain himself from claiming her completely right there in the street. Instead he commanded grittily, "Invite me up."

Their clothes had been askew, her body still quivering and damp, her lips parted as she tried to catch her breath. When her eyes blinked open in the light through the fogged windows, they'd been hazed with lust.

Something like agony had pleated her brow and she had bitten her bottom lip before she swallowed and lowered her lashes in a kind of defeat. "If that's what you want."

They had been nose to nose, the air charged with intimacy. Every nuance and breath had imprinted on him—not that he had let himself revisit that memory in the time that had since passed. It was far more comfortable to resent her as a world-class manipulator.

If he had been manipulated, however, it had been his own hormones and conscience.

"Isn't that what you want?" he had asked.

She'd been honey and heat, pliant with surrender

against him, lips clinging to his as he'd succumbed to the need to taste her mouth once more, keeping the fire burning hot between them. Caressing her so she'd gasped and arched in offering.

"It is." Her voice had throbbed with longing. "But I was saving it for my husband. For a man who—" She had buried the rest into his neck, her damp mouth making his scalp tighten.

A man who what? Loved her? His hand on her mound had firmed with possessiveness as he felt pulled apart. In those moments, he had only half believed she was a virgin. Her shocked gasp under his initial bold touch, however, and the way she had shattered with shy joy, inclined him to think she'd never let anyone touch her this intimately before.

As he'd continued fondling and necking with her, he hadn't seen her virginity as the prize so much as feeling irrationally jealous at the idea of her being with other men. He had wanted to make her his in a way that went beyond the physical.

As she'd rested her head on his arm and gazed up at him with surrender, he'd read the melancholy in her trembling smile.

He could have pressed her to let him have her that night. He could have taken her virginity without the rings, but she would have regretted it. On some level, she would have felt cheapened by giving in without a commitment between them.

Travis Sanders's lay of the day.

His stomach tightened as he recalled how that hadn't been enough for him, either. Not in those moments. So, he had said the words. *Marry me. Tomorrow.* He'd spent the night drawing up the prenuptial agreement, thinking he was being sensible in the midst of pure recklessness.

"That's it." Her voice snapped him back to his office while a ping at his elbow notified him of yet another email arriving.

She was talking about the folders and links and contacts she'd been sending him over the last hour. Now she stood in the doorway and glanced around the office he rarely used. His real office was only blocks away and he traveled to site so often that when he was in his actual home, he preferred to unplug and unwind.

Imogen's gaze narrowed on the folded papers he'd left on the corner of his desk. She hugged herself defensively. "Did you read it?"

"No," he lied, not ready to confront his feelings on how she'd portrayed him and revealed herself. Straightening, he pulled himself back to the immediate matter at hand. "I've been messaging with my accountant. He said at first blush there are several items that should be settled as part of your father's estate and not carried over to you."

She made a face of mild disgust. "I knew I should have hired an accountant, but won't their fees wash out whatever he saves me?"

"We'll see. He's preparing a release for you to sign, to let his office take over the probate of your father's will. He said the service provided by the home where your father passed is fine for seniors with modest assets, but they're not the right approach for something this complex."

"All right." She curled her socked toes. "Do you want me to see if there are steaks or something in the freezer for dinner?"

That wasn't the appetite gnawing so consistently at him.

It would be nice to connect with someone without getting hurt.

Wouldn't it?

"We'll go out." His voice sounded more gravelly and curt than he intended, making her stiffen and scowl warily.

"Why?"

She was entitled to her shock, and he had ulterior motives, but it bothered him that she was so suspicious. That he couldn't ask her to dinner without it being a thing that stirred up their past. This constant unraveling of threads he'd long thought tied off was exhausting. Especially since each thread was a viper that ended with a bite and a sting of poison. He sincerely wished they could move forward into something that wasn't so fraught.

"We're promoting a vision of reconciliation," he reminded her. "At least, the press release implies we're having a fresh try."

Her brows went up in a silent and disparaging, "Good luck with that."

He pushed aside his phone and rested his forearms on the desk.

"How things look *is* important to me. Partly it's who I am. Look around. I run a tidy ship. One of the reasons we went out first thing this morning was to give the housekeeper a chance to wipe down all the furniture. The kids make a mess and it's all I can do to wait until they're gone to clean up after them."

"You're a neat freak?" She looked at him in sudden

interest, mouth curving into a teasing smile. "Here I thought you were perfect."

"Worse. I'm a perfection*ist*."

Her smile didn't stick. Her humor dimmed and her lashes swept to hide her eyes. Because she wasn't perfect? Neither was he, much to his chagrin.

"It's my biggest flaw, but I come by it honestly. My mother spent my entire childhood wiping my face and hands, smoothing my hair and straightening my tie."

Imogen bit back a smile. "I may require photo evidence of that. Please tell me it was a bow tie."

"I was every bit as fastidious as she was. When I started high school, my father said he would give me a dollar per mark, provided I kept my grades above seventy percent. Who wants a pile of bills adding up to ninety-eight when you can have a crisp Ben Franklin?"

"There are easier ways to a skinny wallet, you know. Kind of an expert over here." She gave a little wave. "Ask me anything."

And here was the woman who had led him off his straight and narrow path into a wilderness of unpredictability. He forced himself to stay focused on what he wanted to convey.

"I was the school's top track athlete, I headed the debate team, played saxophone and organized a repair of a seniors' center after a storm damaged it."

"And dated the head cheerleader?" It was an accurate guess, but he wasn't stupid enough to confirm it.

"I also worked weekends at my father's office and assisted with conveyancing contracts. You can't miss dotting an *i* on those. I was voted best all-around student two years in a row. My life was as flawless as I could make it, my future paved in gold."

He ran his tongue over his teeth, getting to the difficult bit.

"Then my mother had a blazing affair. She shattered my father's heart and handed me a cloud of filthy rumors to wear as I finished out my high school years. Dad nearly lost his business and I had to drop my extracurricular activities to look after him."

Her smile faded and her gaze softened with concern. "Sick?"

"Alcohol."

"I'm so sorry."

He didn't want her pity. This was an explanation, not a therapy session.

"My marks suffered, which was untenable, and I got kicked out of school twice for fighting. I *hate* gossip and bad press, Imogen. I hate even more when I lower myself into reacting to it. I prefer to keep a tight control over myself and everything around me so it never comes to that."

Her mouth twitched. "I've noticed that. You play your cards close to your chest so you're always one square ahead of everyone else."

He narrowed his eyes at her. "You mixed that metaphor on purpose, didn't you? Knowing it would bother me. This is why you make me crazy."

"There could be a board game that uses cards and spaces. I don't know." She pretended innocence with a lift of her gaze to the ceiling.

That was the part that got to him. The mischief. The invitation to laugh at himself. He shouldn't be drawn to such capriciousness and maybe that's why he'd held back from truly committing to their marriage. He couldn't spend a lifetime with this much uncertainty. With a woman who wasn't 1,000 percent steady. In a moment of madness, he had wanted to lock her down, contain her, but he had quickly realized such a thing was impossible.

"I didn't expect our marriage to last," he admitted. "You're right about that."

Her lighthearted half smile died. She had one hand on the doorjamb and quarter-turned into it, looking as if she would rather walk away than hear this. Her profile paled, despite the warmth of the gas fireplace having left color in her cheeks a moment ago. She drew her bottom lip between her teeth.

"After witnessing the way my parents' marriage imploded, I knew I didn't want anything to leave a stain on me when ours fell apart." Maybe he'd even pulled what few supports they had had, encouraging it to collapse so he wouldn't have to wait for the inevitable. "We're very different, Imogen."

"I'm not perfect."

"You're creative. That's not a bad thing."

"You're creative," she pointed out.

"In a disciplined way."

"The right way."

Why her saying that wrung out his internal organs, he wasn't sure.

"Then why—?" Her voice cracked and she looked upward again.

The artist in him admired the beautiful line from her profile, down her throat and along her feminine torso to the curve of her waist. Artwork. She was absolute beauty without even trying. He took a mental picture, wanting to replicate that line somehow, somewhere. His muse.

Something deep within him kept wanting to preserve these moments of striking beauty she produced, the sound of her laugh, the scent in a room she had recently occupied. He wanted to press each memory into a book. Secure them in a safe.

But he couldn't. He had known that the first time and knew it even more indelibly now. A woman like her wasn't meant to be confined. It was beyond wrong.

He heard the vestiges of pain in her voice as she tried again and this time succeeded with voicing her question, if faintly.

"Why do you want to parade this messy *ex*-wife of yours in public? Shouldn't I be kept behind closed doors?"

Locked in her room, missing dinner.

The twisting, wringing sensation in him wrenched to an excruciating tightness. His chest grew compressed. "Gwyn's debacle arrived as I was expanding and taking on debt for a massive project in South America."

"The cathedral."

"For the Catholic church, yes. You can imagine how thrilled they were that my sister was being publicly shamed for nude photos and a raging affair with a banker. Please don't ever tell her how bad it was. She was going through far worse, but it demonstrated to me exactly how important my image is to my clients. I'm closing on something in Hawaii as soon as the holidays are over. I can't risk their confidence flagging because they fear I'm having personal problems."

"So, put on my Sunday best, mind my manners and clean up the mess I've made."

"I own some of this mess, Imogen. I know that."

"Because you never should have married me." She

was looking at her hand now, where she played her thumb against the plate of the catch. In a sudden move, she pulled her hand away and pressed her thumb to her mouth.

"Did you just cut yourself?" How? She really was a disaster waiting to happen.

"No," she lied around her thumb, scowling at him. "What time do I need to be ready?"

"Let me see." He rose.

"I'm a big girl. I can solve my own problems." She held her ground, tucking her thumb inside her fist and dropping her hand, not hearing the ridiculousness of her statement when his email was ringing like a stock trading bell with notes and questions from his accountant about her catastrophe of a financial situation.

Maybe she did hear it, though. She lowered her gaze and her shoulders heaved in a defeated sigh.

He gave her this one and stayed where he was.

"We have reservations for seven. Check the powder room for bandages."

She walked away and down the hall.

You look lovely.

Imogen was trying not to smooth her dress down her hips or fiddle with the neckline as they entered the restaurant. Her mind kept playing a loop of his quiet compliment as they'd left the penthouse. Was he pandering to her fragile self-worth after her hissy fit at the boutique? Making a comment on the fact she didn't look like death warmed over now that she was on the mend? Or had he meant it?

Maybe he was just being polite. Maybe she did look nice. She had always scrubbed up pretty well. Along with all the clothes, some makeup had been delivered. With her hair washed and styled, she looked as good as she could. This dress didn't hurt one bit, either. It was a figure-hugging crepe in panels of purple and ivory with a saucy zipper all the way down the front. Her shoes were a stunning confection of crystals forming a floral embellishment on an otherwise nude mesh with a sparkly heel. Chic and classy, but cheeky.

She desperately wanted to click them together to see if she could fix her life in a blink. On the other hand, this Technicolor world of his, where her mother's change purse had been replaced with a half dozen handbags with designer labels, was a nice place to visit. Even on her best day, she had never carried as much cash in her bank balance as the value of this quilted satin clutch, with its seed pearls in paisley patterns and enameled clasp.

Had he spoken with a hint of emotion in his tone when he'd delivered that succinct compliment? Or had it just sounded that way because she'd been so terribly desperate that he *not* find fault? Had he been forcing the words out? Was it a pity compliment?

Was she that far gone she was okay with that?

"The other half of your party is here. Let me show you to your table," the maître d' said, weaving them through the crush at the front of the restaurant to what seemed an exclusive section at the back, where tables overlooked Central Park. She had glanced longingly at the merrily lit-up carriages trotting down the paths there as they'd entered.

Watching them would be almost as good, but she balked and caught at Travis's arm. "Other half?"

"I invited a friend and his wife, someone willing to help with our PR problem."

Our? He wasn't doing *her* reputation any harm. She was the one dragging *him* into the dirt.

As Imogen recognized the couple waiting for them, and they stood for introductions, she must have dug in her heels because Travis's hand in her lower back firmed, pressing her forward exactly as her mother used to when she had wanted Imogen to greet her father after a business trip with a hug and a kiss.

"Nic. Rowan." Travis greeted his guests, then introduced her simply as, "Imogen."

"Gantry," she supplied. Nic Marcussen owned one of the largest news organizations *in the world*. His wife had been a child performer and was the daughter of a well-known starlet from British stage and films. "My father was Wallace Gantry. Travis may have neglected to mention that."

"He didn't have to," Nic said. "I know who you are. I don't have any hard feelings. My sympathies for your loss."

"I suppose professional rivalry is only an issue for the person in second place," she murmured dryly, making him release a surprised chuckle, then give her a look of reassessment.

Maybe he was amused because she had exaggerated her father's position. He'd been running dead last in their particular race, writing more than one inflammatory piece about rivals like Marcussen Media ruining publishing by encouraging the online platform. Meanwhile Nic had evolved with the times and had risen to the top. He could have gloated about that, but he allowed the conversation to move to other topics.

Imogen remained on guard, though, barely touching her wine and filtering every word that left her tongue. It wasn't the other couple that made her so tense. They were witty and relaxed and clearly in love, talking up their children and what sounded like such a perfect life that Imogen's heart contracted with envy.

While she felt like she was being tested with Travis looking at her each time she spoke, making her feel picked apart. She had lived her entire life like this, conscious of how she reflected on her father. Maybe she would have felt this same sense of being on display when she and Travis were married if they'd ever left his apartment, but one of the things that had drawn her to him most inexorably had been a sense that, when she was alone with him, she could be herself, accepted for exactly who she was.

No longer. As forthright as she'd been in the last two days, as much as she had owned up to her mistakes and tried to make amends, she continued to feel as though she fell short. It was agonizing, not that she let on, chuckling on cue and pretending the brush of Travis's thigh against her knee didn't turn her insides to butter.

They were starting dessert when Nic said, "Strong piece on the builder." He was speaking to her, but nodded to indicate he was referring to Travis.

"What?" The heat of a thousand suns swiveled onto her, drying her throat into an arid wasteland. She shot an accusatory look at the man beside her.

"You didn't tell her you sent it to me?" Nic asked.

Travis's flat smile at Nic said, "Thanks a lot."

"You said—" *Behave, Imogen.* She willed the pressure behind her eyes to stay there and looked to her crème brûlée. "He didn't," she replied with a forced smile. "Thank you."

She quickly changed the subject, asking after their home in Greece, and managed to get through the rest of the meal without snapping, but the short trip back to Travis's penthouse was a silence thick with the fulminating anger she was suppressing. She was trembling by the time they were in the elevator.

"I sent it across to him because I thought it was very—"

"I don't care what you thought," she cut in. "You *lied*."

"About reading it? Or about our reason for going to dinner?"

"Both."

"Look, I sent the press release on our reconciliation directly to him, as an exclusive. In return, he made a point of being seen with me, which telegraphs that any smear campaigns against me will have consequences."

The doors opened and she charged straight up the stairs to the guest room she had commandeered.

He followed and stuck out a foot to stop the bedroom door she tried to slam in his face.

She glared at him as she threw down her overpriced, mostly empty clutch—biggest lipstick holder in the history of accessories—and kicked off her insanely expensive shoes without care for their quality.

"Since he and I were on the topic of *you*," Travis continued relentlessly, "I sent across your article, requesting he forward it to one of his editors if he saw a place where you might fit. You seemed interested in freelance work."

"That's not how it works, Travis. Writers are a dime

a dozen and you have to earn your stripes. Do *your* friends send sketches from their wives for you to consider for your next big project, so they don't have to go through the pesky process of apprenticing at the drafting table? No. You expect them to climb through the ranks like everyone else."

"You've paid your dues. Why are you angry? He *liked* it."

"Great! Now what happens if he throws some work my way? Who do I owe for *that*?" She gave a useless pound of her fists into the air at her hips, making her elbows hurt. "You? *Again?*"

"You owe yourself because it was a good piece." He looked confused, like he genuinely didn't understand why he had to explain this to her. "It was thorough, insightful and entertaining."

"I don't care what you thought," she insisted, talking over him.

"Why the hell not?"

"Because you didn't care *then* how I felt about you. I don't need to hear *now* that you find those feelings quaint and pathetic."

He rocked back on his heels, expression shuttering. "That's not what I thought *at all*. For God's sake, Imogen, I thought it sounded as if—"

"It doesn't matter what you think it sounds like! I am being brutally honest with you at every turn," she cried shakily, throwing out her arms in agitation. "I have no ego left. No defenses, no self-worth. I've lost everything and I depend solely on you." She pointed at him in emphasis. "And you lied to me. I asked you if you'd read it and you *lied*."

He pushed his hands into his pockets and looked

away. The ceiling light was on, along with the one in the hallway. There was nowhere for either of them to hide.

"Do I not even deserve honesty from you?" Her whole body throbbed with agony at how little respect that showed.

A muscle pulsed in his jaw before he finally admitted quietly, through his clenched teeth, "I felt naked when I read it."

"*You* did," she choked, dipping her head to rub her brow. "Those were my gauche feelings on display, not *yours*."

"You—" He looked away. "Reading it made me remember the excitement and enthusiasm you showed when we met. I remember how encouraging you were. It was infectious and, yes, flattering." His fists were round bulges in his pockets. "You also captured how *I* was feeling. My passion and ambition for the future. All the aspirations I had for the company. It was uncomfortable to look back on that, mostly because I've lost some of that glossy outlook. I've become cynical and business focused. Reading it was like reading a letter from myself, reminding me why I pushed to expand, what I had hoped to accomplish. It was disturbing to see how far I've strayed from where I intended to be right now."

She searched his expression, which was closed off and resistant to telling her any of this. She wanted to ask where he thought he should be, but only said, "You lied because you didn't want to tell me that?"

"I don't process things as quickly as you do. I have to deconstruct before I can reconstruct. But if you want honesty, Imogen, my first thought was that I needed to thank you for documenting that time in my life. Reading that article renewed my sense of inspiration."

She blinked, feeling for the first time since she'd seen him again that maybe she did have something to offer him.

"At the same time, it was a gentle rebuke." He frowned. "Suddenly, I'm realizing why I haven't been entirely happy with my work lately. I forgot the passion that drove me to architecture in the first place. So, yes, I lied to you while I filtered through all of that."

For some reason, her stomach was full of butterflies, all flitting in different directions, tickling her heart and making her breaths feel unsteady. She didn't know how to process this, either. She was touched. Truly moved by having had some effect on him at all.

She tried to gloss over it by being flippant. "Does that mean I should say 'I'm sorry' or 'you're welcome'?"

"You can say 'you're welcome,'" he said with a sincerity that turned the floor beneath her to sand. "But maybe 'thank you,' as well, since I loathe revealing my missteps, but I sent the article to Nic anyway. I knew it was a stellar example of your ability. I couldn't refuse to let you use it to get work if writing is where your interest lies. But there was some self-interest there, too," he allowed with a tilt of his head. "I figured he could help you get started without putting my story on every desk in town."

"Oh." She was still holding on to her elbows, but much of her tension had drained away into a glow she was afraid to name. Pride? "That was kind. Thank you." She licked her lips. "But please don't lie to me again. It's upsetting."

"Is it? I hadn't noticed," he said dryly.

She quirked a half smile at his facetious lie and dropped her gaze, realizing that she stood beside the bed. He was inside her room, hand on the latch of the door.

"I do appreciate all you're doing for me," she said sincerely. "It's hard to accept it, though. If I lash out, that's why. I don't like being something that has to be tolerated. Not again."

"You're not."

"You're not doing this out of friendship or affection, Travis." She wasn't being emotional about it. It was a fact. "It's obligation because we were once very briefly married. That's all."

He didn't contradict her and that was, perhaps, the most painful response he could have offered.

"I wouldn't help you if I didn't think you were worth the effort, Imogen."

As she stared at him, absorbing those words, her heartbeats slowed and grew so heavy they became a hammer, chipping away at her breastbone. "Do you mean that?"

"I do."

She nodded, unable to thank him because she was too moved. Her composure was crumbling.

"Do you mind?" she said in a strained voice. "I'm going to take my pills and get some sleep. The boss of my life says I have to."

He stood there a long moment before nodding once. He closed the door as he left.

She sat on the bed a long time, eyes closed, tears rolling down her cheeks.

CHAPTER SIX

A FEW DAYS LATER, Travis booked them into the presidential suite in a Charleston mansion that had been converted to an exclusive boutique hotel. Their room had two floor-to-ceiling marble fireplaces, panels of Tiffany glass above the door frames, Italian chandeliers, a whirlpool tub in the bathroom and a twelve-foot Christmas tree in the lounge.

She was dying to say, "What, no piano?"

"I usually stay with my father, but his brothers and their wives are there, in town for the party."

"I'll try to make do," she murmured, noting there was a king bed and a daybed, along with a sofa here in the lounge that probably pulled out.

"You have an appointment at the spa. I'm seeing my barber and picking up my tuxedo."

"Okay." What else was she supposed to say? This was a play they were enacting. She had to report to hair and makeup, then say her lines without flubbing. "Is your father's party being held here?"

His mouth quirked. "A cruise of the harbor. I asked Gwyn to make all the arrangements and send the bills to me. She was going to book a paddle wheeler, but Vito's bank decided to buy a yacht to use for corporate events. He swears it was coincidence, but he likes to upstage me."

"Rivalries only matter when you're in second place. Someone said that to me recently." She circled a rivet in the upholstery of the chair she stood behind.

"You said it," he said dryly. "And when it comes to pleasing Gwyn, I'm forced to cede to Vito, so any sense of rivalry is pointless."

She smiled benignly, keeping her gaze on the chair. Lucky Gwyn.

"Are you all right? You've been quiet."

"Nervous," she admitted.

Suffering a hideous case of performance anxiety. After his kind words the other night, she had reminded herself not to let that affect her too deeply. To counteract any silly yearnings, she had counted up all the ways she could never rise to his level, which made for a depressing mood. She had decided to salvage some self-respect by repairing the damage she'd done, though. She would be the best fake wife he'd ever had.

Despite not having been a very good real one.

He left and she went down to the spa to let the proverbial birds and mice work their magic, massaging away her tension, painting her nails and pampering her skin, rolling her hair into fat twists of red-gold and lengthening her lashes to glamorous degrees.

When she returned to their room, she found a gown on the bed, this one in a rich amethyst. It didn't look as dramatic as the blue she'd brought with her, appearing quite plain and modest, but once she had it on, she saw its sensual elegance.

The draped back was so low, however, she couldn't wear a bra. That left her breasts thrusting against the sweep of velvet across her front. The cut of the skirt was narrow with a slit that rose nearly to her hip. Once she had her shoes on, she showed a lot of leg with each step.

She was swaying in front of her reflection, wondering who that red-carpet siren in the mirror was, when Travis returned.

He looked breathtaking in his tailored tuxedo. He was freshly shaved and his hair was trimmed into scrupulously perfect lines. And for once, in this single snapshot of time, with his compliment from the other night still floating like a love song in her ears, she was able to smile naturally as she looked on him, almost believing herself good enough for that ruthlessly handsome man.

Travis had walked into an electric fence as a kid—three wires he hadn't seen at summer camp because he'd been talking over his shoulder to a friend. The jolt had knocked him back so hard, he'd stumbled and landed on his butt.

That's how he felt as she smiled at him. Like he'd been chopped in the heart and the gut and the groin by a charge of something so strong, he came up short and had to catch himself on his back foot.

Dear God, she was a vision. He had known the color of that gown would accent the auburn and gold in her hair. He hadn't expected it to turn her eyes to emeralds and make her skin look delectable as whipped cream. The blue one from New York had been sexy on her, but he had taken one look at this dress on the mannequin and had known its simplicity would do her far more justice. It let Imogen shine through, from delicate shoulders to long limbs to the undeniable feminine mystique she possessed.

"You look beautiful." He felt something slipping from his grip and remembered why he'd run out. He offered the box. "I thought you might need jewelry."

"The rings?" Her smile fell away and her eyes widened enough to suggest panic. "No."

Her quick rejection was a fresh jolt, disturbing him. Why was she so adamant? Why did it sting that she didn't want to wear his rings?

"It's a necklace and earrings."

"Oh. On loan?" She was still wary.

"Yes."

"Okay, then." She came forward to take the box and opened it. "Thank you. They're lovely."

He watched her affix the earrings, thinking of her saying the night they went for dinner that he was only helping her out of obligation. Should he tell her that he'd spent a solid half hour choosing these for her, not because he was worried about how she looked, but because he wanted her to like them?

"Can you?" She lifted her hair so he could close the necklace.

He clasped the delicate chain and touched her shoulder, encouraging her to turn and face him again.

She smelled divine. He found his hand lingering on her shoulder, thumb lightly caressing the incredible softness of her skin. He barely resisted the desire to dip his head and taste her.

She shrugged and rubbed the spot where his hand had been, wiping away the goose bumps that had risen from her elbow up her arm. He wanted to rub them away himself, except he wanted to use a touch light enough to raise more. He wanted to draw her into his shirtfront and lick all the way up her throat until he was plundering the heat of her mouth.

"You're so beautiful. So sensual." His voice originated deep in his chest. "There couldn't have been only me." He hated the idea of her with another man. *Hated* it. But he couldn't blame her for it. Couldn't expect her to have been faithful to the vows he had made half-heartedly.

Her lashes flashed up, impossibly long and thick, making her look so innocent and vulnerable his insides ached. Shadows of hurt moved behind her gaze.

"You don't want me. What makes you think anyone else would?"

Until this moment, he hadn't believed she had been celibate. Now, as he saw how the breakdown of their marriage had only added to the rejections she had suffered from her father, battering her confidence into nothing, the truth impaled him.

She had denied herself sensual pleasure, not out of fidelity, but because she had been too hurt by him to risk another rebuff.

Remorse penetrated in a line from his throat to the middle of his chest, paralyzing him even as it stabbed excruciatingly deep.

"That's not true, Imogen." He took her arm again, feeling her stiffen at his touch, body already trying to pivot away from his. "I've said things to hurt you. Out of anger."

"I know." She closed her eyes, mouth not quite steady. "And it worked." She carefully removed her arm from his hand. Her eyes were glossed with tears as she looked at the door. "Can we not start a fight right now? I'm already worried how this will go."

"It will be fine."

She sent him a resigned look, as if she knew disaster was inevitable.

He didn't know how to convince her, though. How to repair the damage he'd done. With a nod, he moved to hold the door.

Imogen was doing well, *so well*. They had been among the last to board, tipping off Gwyn ahead of time to say they were running late so they could avoid the scrutiny of standing in the receiving line.

When Travis introduced her to his father on arrival, Henry was easily won over. It was painfully obvious he was dying for his son to marry and settle down.

Dark had fully fallen when the yacht left its mooring. The harbor was as still as a tub and the air crisp and clear under a fat moon and a blanket of stars.

Imogen felt as though she was an extra in a movie; everything was so perfect around her. The yacht was an elegant, ultramodern monstrosity with four decks, uncounted staterooms and an interior lounge of long sofas with a bar at one end. The whole thing was coated in holly and lights and wreaths and bows. On the outer deck off the stern, a small band from New Orleans played blues and jazz, Henry's favorite, apparently. They threw a few Christmas carols into the mix while the buffet dinner was served. Now people were starting to dance.

Most of the guests were in Henry's age bracket. They were curious enough about Travis's secret marriage and divorce to strike up conversations with them, but they confined their questions to an interest in where Imogen grew up and other nonthreatening topics.

Other guests were Travis's contemporaries, people he and Gwyn knew socially who also knew Henry. Some had worked for Henry during his years dominating the real estate markets in the Carolinas. They cast a few speculative looks toward Travis, but the South was known for its manners. Everyone was very civilized and the evening painless.

Until Imogen gaffed.

Of *course* she did. Of course it was *her*.

Gwyn was keeping Imogen firmly under her wing, giving her a rundown on who was who, frowning with distraction at a beautiful middle-aged woman who kept looking in their direction.

"She must be a plus-one. I don't recognize her. Do you remember her from the receiving line, Vito?" When her husband shook his head, she drew Travis from whatever thoughts had him drowning his gaze in his drink. "Who is that woman in the black-and-white dress, the one with the adorable pillbox hat?"

Travis glanced over, instantly arrested. "That would be my mother. You didn't invite her?"

"No." Gwyn's eyes widened in shock. "I've only seen one photo your father has of her when you were a baby. I'm sorry, but I can't even recall her name."

Now that Travis had noticed her, she approached. She was so much the beautiful feminine version of her son, it was uncanny. And she was younger than Imogen had expected. Her dark hair might have been colored to hide some gray, but it looked natural in its flawless chignon. Her skin was stunning, her makeup clever enough to take years off her already youthful appearance. Any woman of any age would be happy to have that figure.

"Travis, darling."

He stiffly allowed her to touch her cheek to his, then introduced them. Without being rude, Vito quickly excused himself and Gwyn to the dance floor, leaving Eliza Carmichael holding Imogen's hand with her ultrasoft, impeccably manicured and beautifully bejeweled fingers.

"How are you here?" Travis asked her.

"I came with Archie. Your father knew. He said he didn't mind."

"How long has that been going on?"

"Archie? It's a friendly date, not a romantic one. I wanted to see you. Meet Imogen." It was her clinging grip that got to Imogen. Eliza was cool and coiffed and smooth as silk, but there was something desperate in her hold on Imogen's hand. A plea.

"My son never tells me anything," she said, as if it was the oversight of a teenage boy neglecting to mention he'd asked a girl to prom. "I can't wait to get to know you properly."

"We have to mingle, Mother," Travis said flatly, running his hand along Imogen's arm until he had disengaged her from his mother's touch and could weave his fingers through hers himself.

Eliza barely flinched and her smile stayed pinned firmly in place. "Come for dinner tomorrow. Or any night while you're in town."

"We're at Dad's tomorrow and Christmas morning, flying back to New York right after. We're due in Hawaii by New Year's. It can't be changed."

Imogen hadn't known that "they" were going to

Hawaii, but that wasn't the issue right now. The issue was his mother was trying to reconcile with him and he was holding a grudge well past its expiration date.

"Why don't you come by our hotel for breakfast tomorrow?" Imogen suggested.

Travis's grip tightened, stretching the flesh between her fingers in warning.

"That would be lovely." Eliza held on to her Southern persona, warm without gushing, charming without being needy. "I'll look forward to that."

She moved away, but Travis was already tugging Imogen from the main cabin and down a hallway. What did they call them on boats? The passageway? It felt like a gangplank. He refrained from grabbing her by the ear or poking her spine with a sword point, but he was *mad*.

He ducked them into the first stateroom he found with an unlocked door, then snapped it closed and latched it behind them.

"Not your place, Imogen."

Oh, that got her back up. "Are you saying it is my place to put her in hers? I don't think so. And don't try to put me in mine. My instructions for this evening were to mind my manners. *You* were the one being rude when she only wants to spend a little time with you. That doesn't seem like an unreasonable request." What was wrong with him?

"It's called setting boundaries."

"Really? Because it looks like a refusal to forgive. You said she cheated on your father, not *you*. Your father was big enough to let her come to his party. Why are you angry about it? What's really going on?"

"Here's another boundary—don't try to get inside this. You know nothing about it."

"Does *she*? I've been on her side of that kind of hatred, Travis. It's not fair."

"Don't be so dramatic. I don't hate her. I see her on my terms, not hers and not *yours*."

"Why? What are you afraid of? That you might have to admit humans aren't perfect? You said you and she were alike. Was it so traumatic to see her mess up? Did it make you realize *you* could?"

"Take a step back, Imogen, because you are standing on my last nerve."

She was practically standing on his toes, chin hovering near the knot in his bow tie, genuinely angry on his mother's behalf. Being cut out like that was incredibly unfair. She knew exactly how that felt. From him, even.

"Fine. Don't spare her any of your precious minutes. I'll have coffee with her myself."

"You will not."

"What's the worst that can happen? You've never told me anything about yourself so I can't spill any of your secrets. All I can talk about is me and I don't reflect well in any of this, so your stellar reputation remains perfectly untarnished."

"I am warning you. *Do not* get involved."

"Oh, is your overactive need to control riled?" She poked him in the chest. She was that infuriated she just jabbed him right in the lapel, like pushing a button.

His hand shot up and grabbed her wrist. "My control is slipping by the second and you do *not* want to know what will happen when it's gone."

"What are you going to do? Kiss me into submission again? Prove that you can control me after all?

Go ahead, Travis. Go right the hell ahead." She knew it was a dare. Not to see if he would do it, but to hear him refuse to.

I've said things to hurt you.

Yes, he had. He'd said such hurtful things that she held her ground and dared him to say them again. To tell her he didn't want her. To *prove it.*

He swore in one explosive epithet. Then he dropped his mouth onto hers and she met him with her own pent-up anger. She thrust her hands into his hair and dragged him down and scraped her teeth across his bottom lip.

His arms banded around her and he crushed her tight to the pleats in his tuxedo shirt, fingers digging into her buttocks as he took control of the kiss and pivoted toward the bed.

The kiss changed on a dime, from anger to white-hot passion. His tongue dove into her mouth and she groaned as she greeted him, shuddering at the onslaught of sensations that accosted her—his familiar scent, his taste, his strength and the iron hardness behind his fly.

Then he was tilting them onto the bed, one hand stealing into the slit on her dress as they went. While he dragged his tongue down her throat, his palm claimed the heat between her thighs. He rocked his hand there until she was lifting into the motion, breathing, "Travis, please."

He rose enough to strip her panties down and throw them away, following the flow of the motion to drop off the edge of the mattress himself, onto his knees between her legs. He caught her thighs over his arms and grasped her hips, bringing her to the edge and his waiting mouth. Her skirt rode up and a silent scream gathered in her throat at the sudden, unavoidable, intimate contact. Ferocious, tingling heat flooded into her loins, pulled and gathered there into a coil of tension by his unabashed attentions.

Why this? Why make her feel so exalted? So worshipped and instantly swept away?

She arched herself to his pleasuring, hands clawing at the blanket beneath her, head thrown back and vision glazed by the rolling waves of arousal gathering strength as they radiated from her abdomen to her limbs, drawing her toward a screaming pitch.

She wanted to beg, but couldn't even lick her lips. Tension caught her up so quickly she could only pant and gasp for air and finally drown in the swirling joy of sudden, sweet release.

It wasn't enough, though. Even as her body pulsed in a flood of ecstasy, she ached for more. For all of him. Every inch of him covering her with his heat and weight.

While he pulled away, making her whimper in loss.

For about one second, as he rose to his feet, she thought he might have forced her into subjugation this way. He looked down on her, limp and wanton, and she knew he saw that she was utterly at his mercy. Her heart stuttered and stalled, going into free fall.

Then he tore off his jacket, dropping it behind him as he jerked open his pants, revealing his turgid shape, hard and ready. His knees hit the edge of the mattress, pushing hers further apart. He hooked his hands under her arms, moved her up the bed, and then his weight settled on her while the crest of his shape pressed for entry.

She was slick and aching, taking him in one easy thrust that brought a sting of homecoming to her eyes. She managed to hook one bare thigh over his, but their clothing was tight and in the way, providing an erotic mix of textures and constriction when he began to thrust. His pants were a friction against her inner thighs, the hidden button of his shirt poked her breast, the silk of his bow tie grazed her jaw before he dipped his head and kissed her deeply, thrusting and thrusting, smooth and deep. Familiar and rough-sweet.

She was dimly aware this was earthy and wild, but it was also what she needed. Unabashed and fierce. Her body responded to his steady, determined possessiveness by twisting under waves of acute pleasure. When he tightened his hold on her so she felt the full measure and depth of his thrusts, she moaned with gratification, nearly coming apart with the rising tension. She gloried in how he made her feel, never wanting him to stop, but no human body could stand this level of hedonistic intensity.

She scraped her nails across the crisp back of his shirt, catching at the waist of his pants to pull him in tighter. Faster. More. *Now.*

White light seemed to flash behind her eyes, then she was falling. Gathered in with implosive energy, then expanding into all the dimensions ever created. Each piece of her took part of him with her so they reverberated together, shock wave after shock wave, disintegrating into all corners of the universe, together forever.

CHAPTER SEVEN

HE COULD FEEL her twitching beneath him, still quaking with the final spasms of climax, breath still unsteady, but he was afraid to open his eyes and meet her gaze. That had been…

His mouth opened against her shoulder, a caress that made her moan and squeeze him with her intimate muscles, still reacting in latent pleasure to their collision.

Even so, his conscience was heavy. He'd been too rough. Too unrestrained. Not only that…

"I didn't use a condom," he said as he forced himself to extricate, rolling onto the bed next to her. The loss of her heat, her softness and elemental scent, nearly undid him. A growl of refusal to be denied locked in the base of his throat.

"Should I be worried?"

His heart lurched. "About disease? No." He had been a virgin of sorts for her tonight, having always worn condoms, even during their marriage. He had regular physicals, too, but… "Are you on the pill?"

"I'll take one of the morning-after kind."

A protest rose to his lips for no reason at all. He knew the precaution was for the best.

She sat up before he could decide what to say. Not even the sleeves of her dress were askew. When she stood to fetch her underpants and took her clutch into the bathroom, the only signs of their tussle were her ruffled hair and smudged lipstick.

He rose and straightened himself, locked in a kind of shock at how savagely they'd come together.

She emerged, makeup fixed, but pale and not meeting his gaze.

"Imogen." He put out a hand and she halted beyond his reach, something in her stiffness keeping him from moving close enough to touch her. "Are you all right?"

"Of course." She lifted her lashes, but her expression was the cautious one of supreme cooperation, like he'd seen after he had kissed her at the boutique. The one where she fell into line out of sheer defensiveness. His heart lurched.

"We don't want anyone to know. We should go back out." She veered around his outstretched hand and unlocked the door, glancing back before leaving without him.

He lingered, reached to straighten the blanket and hated himself a little more for erasing that small bit of evidence, when he would rather hang on to their moment of passion with both hands.

You don't want me. What makes you think anyone else would?

He had been astonished when she had said it. He could remember being astounded that she really had been a virgin on their wedding night. She had been so sensual and responsive, reacting to his lightest touch. She had said something at the time about dating in the wrong pool, not the sort of men she found truly attractive. He remembered being curious but not asking questions, because he was smart enough to know that sexual pasts were never good topics with current lovers.

His own past seemed tawdry against her standards, especially when he'd left her thinking he didn't want her.

I've said things to hurt you.
And it worked.

He'd been fearful he'd killed whatever she'd once felt for him when she had said that. He'd spent the evening sick with himself for kicking over what had actually been quite precious, long before he realized its value.

At the same time, he'd been fighting jealousy. He had no right to such a thing, but even Vito's eyes had lit with surprised appreciation at the sight of Imogen tonight and he was 10,000 percent devoted to Gwyn. Everyone was looking at Imogen, not because she was Travis's surprise ex-wife, but because she was that entrancing.

He was proud to stand beside her, but threatened. He wanted her, but so did everyone else. And there was nothing that gave him a claim on her except maybe obligation on her part for the help he was offering her.

All of that had been whirling in him as his mother showed up to act as any mother would on meeting the woman who might have been her daughter-in-law.

His mother's presence had reminded him that any sort of monogamy was an exercise in futility. It didn't matter how much he wanted Imogen. He couldn't have her. Not forever. Not in a way he could believe in.

The pressure had reached a boiling point in him.

Imogen getting cozy with his mother had been his snapping point.

He wasn't still punishing his mother. He wasn't that small. But the accusations Imogen had been throwing at him about being human had been all too accurate when primal forces had been taking him over. Then she had dared him to kiss her.

He hadn't been trying to control her. He'd barely been able to control any of that—which was a terrifying admission to make to himself. But the second he had touched her, he hadn't been thinking of anything at all. Nothing except pleasure. Ensuring hers, then enjoying his.

We don't want anyone to know.

He supposed that was for his benefit. She had pulled herself together and was out there putting on a brave face to protect his reputation, and all he wanted to do was go out and manacle her wrist with a firm grip, telling the entire guest list, "She's mine."

He wanted to drag her back in here and prove it again. And again and again.

The instinct, so base on the heels of acting like such a caveman, left him shaken. He splashed cold water on his face and pulled himself together.

When he finally returned to the party, he didn't spot her right away. The delay was just long enough for a knee of panic to kick into his abdomen. Then he found her outside, at the rail with his father.

He noted the wrinkles pressed into the velvet of her dress. Anyone else would imagine they had been caused by her sitting down for a few minutes, but he knew his own weight had imprinted those lines into her gown. He burned with primitive satisfaction as he approached. Burned in the sinful fires of wanting to do it again.

As he came up behind them, he heard his father offering a history lesson, pointing to heritage properties barely visible in the dark.

Unable and unwilling to go another second without touching her, he found her waist with his splayed hand. "Dance?"

She turned, revealing a brief flash of pain that nearly knocked Travis over the rail and into the water before she swept her lashes low, leaving an impression of having been chastised.

"If you'd like. Excuse me, Henry."

"You two have fun," his father said with an indulgent smile.

His father's pleasure against her wariness set Travis's heart on its edge. He took her into his embrace, but she felt stiff and awkward.

"He was only telling me about some buildings. It wasn't anything about you or us." The pang in her voice rang like a bell deep in his ears, sending painful echoes into his chest.

"I wasn't trying to cut that short." Maybe he was. What point was there in letting his father get to know her? He'd dropped by the house today with a half-assed explanation, which his father had only absorbed with a pained nod.

Forgive me for hoping your reasons for divorce weren't as insurmountable as mine with your mother. Of course, if I was still married to your mother, I wouldn't have Gwyn and her children, would I? I guess these things work out as they're meant to.

Was that his father's idea of something "working

out"? His first wife had cheated and his second had been diagnosed months after their wedding day, gone within a couple of pain-filled years.

Imogen's hand in his felt tense. All of her did. He was shoving a mannequin around the dance floor.

She had her chin tucked, hiding her expression. When he looked around to see if anyone had noticed, he caught Gwyn frowning at them with concern.

He drew Imogen toward the rail, where a shadow was cast by the bulkhead. "Imogen, I'm—"

"Don't say you're sorry. You'll make it worse." She kept her face turned toward the water, so the guests couldn't see she had a sheen of misery on her eyes.

"I hurt you." A cloud of remorse choked him. He sidestepped to shield her with his body and tried to enfold her, somehow thinking if he held her gently now, it would erase his fervent embrace from before.

"I hurt myself. I thought I was proving something, but now there's just one more thing to worry about. And for what? Nothing changes." She pushed away and pressed herself to the rail, looking up to hold back tears. He watched her visibly gather her composure, taking breaths to steady her shoulders and calm her profile.

"Are you two all right? Did your mother say something?" Gwyn appeared beside them, looking to him with concern.

Travis bit back a curse while Imogen quickly found a bright smile.

"I'm a little seasick. Please don't say anything." She squeezed Gwyn's arm. "You know what sort of rumor that will start. But maybe fetch me a ginger ale?" she asked Travis.

So quick with the lies it was terrifying, making the other thing she'd said a harsh truth: nothing had been changed by their lovemaking.

He went to order her drink, thinking he would never again attend a party on a boat. There was no escape when the seas grew rough.

Imogen's cheeks ached from the strain of holding a fake smile. Her shoulders were carved marble, her molars practically shaved down to nothing after grinding them to endure this interminable night.

It was after midnight, yet somehow the hotel concierge had come through for her and made a purchase from an all-night pharmacy, leaving her package next to the bathroom sink as she had asked in her brief call from the ladies' room aboard the yacht.

"Oh, for heaven's sake!" she cried as she read the directions. "Is nothing in this life simple?" Marching out of the bathroom, she found Travis unraveling his tie and pulling it from his collar. His jacket already hung off the back of a chair.

He stalled with surprise. "What's wrong?"

"Can you look up if these interact? There's no point taking both if one cancels out the other." She shoved the contraceptive and the antibiotics at him, then went straight back to the bathroom to remove her makeup, so overwhelmed and frustrated she was shaking.

She was still reacting to their impetuous lovemaking, not quite believing it had happened. After his claim that he'd only said things in the past to hurt her, implying they hadn't all been true, she had had a perverse need to test his desire. As they fought, she had goaded him. Part of her was thrilled to discover they were as explosive as they'd been during their marriage. But as physically exciting and satisfying as their lovemaking had been, all she'd learned was that he was capable of having sex with someone he disliked.

How devastating.

He came in to set both items beside her on the vanity. "They're fine."

She finished brushing her teeth, poured herself a glass of water and took her medication. Then she dropped the contraceptive into her palm and threw it into her mouth, right there where he could watch her take it and there wouldn't be any accusations later if things went awry.

He inhaled sharply, as though her action was a bludgeon that landed someplace very mortal and damaging to him.

"No discussion, then," he said in a strained voice.

"What's to discuss?" she asked after washing it down. "You don't want a baby with me. You're already sorry you even touched me. Do you mind?" She lifted her hair and turned her back so he could remove the necklace.

He slid the pendant free and set it on the vanity with a muted shower of gold links against marble. Then he surprised her by taking hold of her hips. The weight of his head came to rest against the crook of her neck and shoulder. The heat of his forehead almost thawed the rigidity gathered there.

"My only regret is that I didn't treat you more gently. You destroy me, Imogen." His voice was grim, but his breath feathered against the top of her spine. "When I'm with you like that, nothing matters. You're like a drug."

Damaging and ugly. Her heart skittered and swirled down a drain. "And you hate it. Hate me. *I know.*"

"I don't hate you." His hands tightened. "I don't hate how we are together. That is the problem!"

She shakily took off the earrings, but he didn't release her. His body heat and the press of his mouth on her hair remained while she set aside the earrings. She stared at their hooked shape against the marble, unwilling to lift her gaze to the mirror and see herself in his odd embrace. She stood in his hold as though his body was a compress, something that eased the ache while the injury remained.

His breath wafted against her skin again. His hands massaged gently on her hips.

"You're so fierce and dangerous to me, I forget that you're slight and tender and bruise easily."

"I'm fine. We had quickies before. If I wasn't into it, I would have told you."

He drew a deeper breath as he lifted his head, but when he released his grip on her hips, he folded his arms across her front, gathering her into him.

She felt so safe in that moment, with her one arm resting over his at her waist, her other hand catching at his strong wrist where his arm banded her collarbone, she let herself lean into him and close her eyes. His cheek rested against her head, lips near her ear. She felt the light kiss he placed there and nearly wept at the sweetness of it.

"I'm tired of the hurt and the blame and the guilt," she confessed in a whisper. "I'm tired of being a disappointment."

"You're not."

She drew away and turned to face him. "You don't want this. You don't want *me*."

His lips tightened into a grim line and he looked away, not at his reflection but in the other direction, as if he couldn't look at himself right then, either.

"I don't want to be at the mercy of the way you make me feel. You have always been too much for me. Never not enough. I don't know how to deal with the force that is Imogen. You're so beautiful and passionate. I make rash promises I can't keep, just for the privilege of touching you. I want you more than I can bear."

"I don't want to be your self-destructive impulse, Travis. I want…"

She wanted him to love her. To want her forever. Those had been her thoughts the first time, when she had been young and idealistic and had succumbed within a week to blind passion. She had saved herself for her husband because she had believed if a man married her, it would mean he loved her.

She was older and wiser now, but… "I want you to like me," she said shakily. "At least a little. I know I can't look to any man to complete me, but we ought to offer each other something besides orgasms. A lifetime commitment was an unrealistic expectation for both of us. I know that. We should have had an affair four years ago, but an affair now is madness. You resent me. I'm a charity case. It's too unequal."

"It's not charity. I'm helping you because I want to, Imogen. Because I *care*. I wouldn't forgive myself if I didn't." He set his hand against the side of her neck and looked her in the eyes.

I care. Silly, foolish hope began to thrum like a trapped bird in her chest.

"But trust is an issue for me." His thumb stroked against her throat. "That's not all on you. I didn't trust you when we married and I didn't yet have a reason *not* to."

"Then I lived up to your lowest expectations," she muttered.

"How much did you trust me?" he challenged quietly.

"You didn't *ask*."

"Fair enough." He acknowledged that with a tilt of his head. "But this *is* an opportunity for the affair we should have had. One without added pressures like marriage or ulterior motives."

"One without expectations of any kind? Not even a future?" She said the words so they both understood the rules, even though it was a heel on her heart.

"Yes."

That wasn't such a terrible thing. He did care for her in his way and the surrender of defenses and weapons between them would bring an approximation of the peace she desperately longed for. It was something.

Covering his hand, she turned her head so she could kiss the inside of his wrist.

His breath shuddered as he drew her in. She lifted her mouth for the press of his and it was pure magic. All the charged emotions flipped and became a magnetism, strong and electric, sealing them into rightness. His kiss was urgent but tender. Passionate but sweet. So, so sweet.

They stood there a long time, hands whispering across clothing as they kissed. She ran her fingers through his hair again and again, loving the short, spiky strands, so dearly familiar. He cupped her butt and took soft bites down the side of her throat, laughing with satisfaction when he made her shiver and moan.

"Still my fatal weakness," she said sheepishly, shrugging and drawing back to rub the lingering tingles.

"I'm going after the small of your back before we're done," he promised in a voice that hit like a velvet punch in her midsection. His fingertips tickled into those delicate hollows that took out her knees.

As she let him take her weight, she looked into the expression that convinced her she was someone worth the trouble, the one that was fierce and possessive, lit with approval and hunger and abject desire, all his attention on her. It was intoxicating to be looked at like that. This was why she had fallen for him the first time.

Closing her eyes so she wouldn't start to believe in the impossible, she ran her hands up behind his neck, reveling in the luxury to do so, and drew him down for another kiss.

He dipped and caught her behind the knees, carrying her to the bedroom where he set her on her feet by the bed. When he started to kiss her, she drew back a half step.

"I want to look at you," she told him shyly and started to search for the buttons in the pleats on his shirt. "Feel you."

He yanked at his shirt, pulling it from his waistband and rending the buttons to get it open before stripping it with a powerful twist of his tanned shoulders. When one cuff hung up at his wrist, he swore like he meant it, making her laugh.

"We have all night," she pointed out.

"You don't understand how badly I want to be naked

with you," he growled, making her laugh again as the shirt got trampled so he could jerk his arm free. Then he shed his pants and underwear in one swift move.

He straightened and all of her melted at the sight of this man. The handful of years had added muscle to his chest and seemed to broaden his shoulders. The taper to his flat abdomen and narrow hips was accentuated and sexier than ever. He was starkly aroused, flesh thrusting with desire atop the tense columns of his thighs.

As intimidating as he was, however, so broad and aggressive-looking, his hands were surprisingly gentle as he drew the dress down her shoulders. It fell to her elbows and the bodice drooped, exposing her breasts.

Her nipples, already hard points, pinched even tighter as he looked at her like he'd uncovered a treasure, seemingly having forgotten himself as his breath became audible and unsteady.

He lightly guided her hands down to her sides, so the dress continued its fall. It puddled around her feet, leaving her standing in only her midnight blue thong and a pair of high heels in black velvet with a velvet ribbon tied in a bow at each ankle.

The hiss of his breath deepened as his gaze took her in, crossing from shoulder to shoulder, singeing her quivering breasts and making her stomach suck in. Heat flooded into her loins, dampening the thong he lightly traced with the tip of his finger. Her thighs trembled in reaction to his touch, making her feel unsteady in her shoes.

Very slowly, excruciatingly slowly, he eased her thong down, exposing her inch by inch, making her clench in anticipation and bite her lip at the tease of it.

"Don't close your legs. Let them fall."

"Travis," she breathed, tortured.

"I know. I want you, too. But let me look." The lace finally fell down her legs, but that only left her helpless to the torment of his light caress. He traced and teased and had her moaning under the tickling touch that only incited, didn't assuage.

She reached to take him in hand, squeezing a message of what she needed from him. He grunted out a harsh curse and thrust into her grip, then caught her against him so the impact of hot skin against her own made her cry out.

They kissed then, madly and deeply. Without restraint. Wet and hot and with such lust she thought she would combust. She rubbed herself against him, needing the scrape of chest hair against her nipples, and lifted her knee against his hip, longing for the shape that stroked her sensitive flesh to invade and satisfy her.

Suddenly she was on her back, his big body over her, his hand cradling her jaw as he looked into her eyes.

"I'm supposed to be doing this properly." He found a condom and applied it.

"I can't wait." She hurried him, guiding him to where she wanted him.

He rolled, pulling her atop him. "Take what you want," he said grittily. "Then I'll do it my way."

She rose on her knees to impale herself, riding him to a swift peak, breasts teased by his wicked hands the whole way. But she was hungry, hungry, hungry and kept moving even as she was shuddering and lost in the ecstasy of climax. She wanted to gorge herself on him and kept going until she was clenched in the vise of orgasm a second time, this one even stronger and more satisfying than the first.

Only then did she melt onto him, all his hard muscle a hot ceramic containing explosive chemicals.

"Thank you," she murmured as she splayed herself on him.

"Oh, no, my beauty. That was for me and it was amazing. Now, though, now I'll give you something to be thankful for." He rolled so she was beneath him again, then slid away to kiss and nibble and lick, all the way down her front. He sucked at her nipples in turn, taking his time, and sighed his hot breath across her navel before threatening a bite of each hip and blew softly across her mound.

She writhed on the covers and her heel caught. He made a noise of sympathy, as if she was injured, and rose to his knees. He took off her shoes with great care, pressing his mouth to her ankles and biting gently against her calf. His fingertips teased behind her knees and he scraped his stubble against her inner thigh.

As the heat of anticipation built in her core, he sent her a wicked smile and rolled her over. His teeth nipped her buttock and his mouth opened in her lower back, the nerve bundles there so sensitized to his caress that she cried out, while goose bumps raced across her whole body and heat flooded into her buttocks and loins.

With a firm touch, he parted her thighs, making her gasp at the audacity of it. Then he was toying with her moist folds while pressing kisses to her back. Her scalp tingled and she couldn't speak, she was held in such a paroxysm of pleasure.

"I could do this forever," he said hotly against her nape. "Touch you, taste you." He settled over her, hot shaft branding the crease of her buttocks.

For long minutes, he braced himself over her like that, shifting and letting her feel his weight, his hot skin, imprinting his scent on her like an animal. Maybe it was a move of dominance, but it felt like something else. None of that strength and power was meant to hurt her, he seemed to be saying. He was reminding her she could trust him.

Her hips lifted of their own accord.

When he rose enough to let her roll onto her back and kissed her tenderly, she opened like a blossom, taking him between her legs, accepting the length of him with one smooth sink of his hips against hers.

She was lost in the miasma of sexual bliss, then. Caressing him, moaning with joy at each thrust, licking into his mouth, holding nothing back. Offering herself without reserve.

"Look at me." He stopped moving to smooth her hair from her perspiration-soaked temple.

She could hardly open her eyes. When she did, the intimacy was almost too much to bear. He held her on a precipice so fine and sharp she was ready to scream, body pulsing and aching for release.

His eyes glowed with fierce possessiveness. He knew he held her in the very palm of his hand, all of her given over to him without conditions. His voice was drugged and smoky, hypnotic.

"It's time. Come with me now."

He began to move in heavy, purposeful thrusts. A fresh wave of pleasure, mightier and more all-encompassing, engulfed her. As it broke and curled over her, he shouted his culmination.

They tumbled to the bottom, clinging to the other as the world shattered around them.

The phone jangled her from a deep sleep, making her gasp awake to the realization she was not alone in bed.

Travis was spooned so tightly to her, her skin pulled painfully as he shifted to reach past her and pick up the receiver before it could ring again.

"Sanders." His voice was gritty and sensual enough to curl her toes.

They'd done their best to rewrite the Kama Sutra last night, then fell asleep wrapped around each other. It had been greedy and gratifying, conversation limited to what they liked and wanted. She felt like she was his again, the way she had when they'd been married. His lover, his wife, his woman.

Careful, Imogen.

Whoever was on the line was female. Imogen didn't try to make out what she was saying. She was caught between a desire to fall back asleep and put off facing reality, and a flood of sensual memory that made her want to squiggle her butt into Travis's growing arousal.

She was tired and achy, but still bathed in sexual satisfaction, wanting only to snuggle back into his arms and stay there.

"We'll see you then." He hung up and let his hand land on her hip in a light smack that was cushioned by the covers. "Mother will be downstairs in thirty minutes."

"Okay, you were right. Breakfast was a dumb idea,"

she conceded, pulling the sheet over her head. "Enjoy your I-told-you-so."

He didn't say anything and didn't move. His hand was still resting on her hip and his chest grazed her back. He didn't even nudge himself against her butt, just let his swelling sex rest against the softness of her cheeks.

"Are you mad?" she asked.

"I'd rather stay in bed, so, yeah. I'm put out."

She lowered the sheet and made herself look at him.

Here was the man she had fallen so hard for, undeniably masculine with his stubble and short, spiky lashes and that air of smug animal pride as his gaze hung up on her mouth.

"Or are you asking if I'm mad that you put out? Hell, no. Last night was fantastic."

"Nice." She jabbed her elbow into his chest.

He captured her beneath him and gave one warning scrape of his stubbled chin against her smooth one, then planted a firm kiss on her lips.

"Shower," he declared, shoving himself off her and dragging most of the covers with him so they fell off the side and onto the floor. "Separately, or we won't leave this room for a week." He walked naked into the bathroom.

Travis wasn't carrying a grudge against his mother, despite what Imogen had accused last night. He had been angry when her infidelity was exposed. Of course he was. One minute, his family life had been stable and his parents' marriage—to his eyes—had been loving. Then overnight his mother's cheating had come to light and everything had blown up.

She'd moved out and all the little ways she had run their lives, things that Travis had taken for granted, were over. He'd not only had to take responsibility for himself, but his father had been a wreck, turning to the bottle in a way so distressing, Travis had worried about leaving him alone while he was at school.

As a result, he had resisted leaving his father to visit his mother, only going when he absolutely had to. She'd been living with her new lover anyway, so it had been beyond uncomfortable to join her. He'd been old enough to decide where he went and for how long and, yes, he had probably been punishing her by avoiding her.

The distance in their relationship had stuck through his last years of high school. When he left for university, he had developed a full enough life; he simply didn't have time for anything but his own ambitions. He'd checked in with his father quite often, but only because Henry had taken up with his office janitor, Gwyn's mom. It had been a strange enough romance he'd wanted to keep an eye on it, but mending fences with his own mother hadn't been a priority. Once his career had started in earnest and he moved to New York, he'd made do with calling her a few times a year.

Had her actions in his impressionable teen years left him thinking all women were inconstant? Perhaps. It was certainly another reason he'd been convinced his marriage to Imogen was unlikely to last.

Did he hate and blame his mother for that? Want to punish her for it? No. They simply didn't have a lot to talk about.

But as he sat down with her, he noticed for the first time in more than a decade that she was aging. There were lines cut into her natural beauty. He wondered uncomfortably if Imogen was right. Maybe he'd been unfair to Eliza, avoiding her this long.

He let Imogen carry the conversation, even though there was a certain danger in letting her speak for them as a couple. He was especially conflicted because he'd spent the last several hours trying to meld their bodies into one. They *were* a couple, but a temporary one.

That word *temporary* caused a tightness in him he didn't want to examine.

The women wound down from their agreeable comments on what a nice party it had been, how the weather had cooperated and what a versatile and accommodating band had been found for the occasion.

His mother cut him a wary glance before broaching the real purpose of their meeting. "I didn't even know Travis had been married."

"No one did," Imogen assured her with a sheepish wrinkle of her nose. "We were young. I was *very* young. Just turned twenty. No one should embark on a lifetime commitment before they're twenty-five, if you want my older and wiser opinion."

"How old are you now?"

"Twenty-four," Imogen said cheekily.

His mother's mouth trembled between a rueful smile and something more delicately pointed. When she spoke, he thought it might be more for his benefit than Imogen's. "Perhaps that's why my marriage didn't work. That, and the age difference between us."

Travis narrowed his eyes, tempted to dismiss it as his mother taking advantage of the situation to make excuses for her behavior, but even though he knew full well she was eighteen years younger than his father, he had never stood back and examined that gap in the context of how it might have affected their marriage.

"Was Henry as ambitious as Travis?" Imogen asked. "I found that part hard. I was trying to do my own thing, having zero success, while he was knocking it out of the park." Imogen touched his arm. "I don't say that as blame. I was excited for you, but with things as they were with Dad, I found it hard to watch you excel at every turn while I was stuck in one place."

He had stopped asking Imogen about her work when she had said very tersely that her father had had to cut her piece on him. At the time, her lack of explanations had awakened his suspicions that she had interviewed him to ensnare him. He'd decided she wasn't being completely honest with him and, as it turned out, she *had* been hiding something, just not what he had imagined.

"Henry was a very big deal," his mother was saying with a wistful sort of awe. "People were begging him to go into politics. We used to joke that I was his trophy wife." Her humor turned more poignant. "In some ways, I was. He was at a point in his life he was ready for a brood of children, but he was so busy conquering the landscape he rarely had time for the son he had. I found motherhood quite overwhelming and tried to be happy as a homemaker, supporting Henry, but I felt as though my best years were passing me by." She glanced at Travis again, pleading for understanding. "I didn't *lack* ambition. I hadn't had a chance to fulfill it."

Travis looked into his coffee. His mother had gone on to open a string of boutiques, doing quite well for herself. She had never asked for his help with it. Aside from the odd job around the house, she'd never asked him for anything.

"I felt quite isolated while Henry was pulled in so many directions. It was hard to believe he loved me when his attention was never *on* me. It wasn't until I'd hurt him so badly he couldn't forgive me that I realized how deep his feelings really were."

"But he's forgiven you," Imogen hurried to say. "You were dancing last night. I saw you. It was lovely to watch. You moved well together."

His mother smiled, but it didn't reach her eyes. She was still looking at Travis, gauging his reaction. Seeking a capitulation of sorts from him.

"Infidelity is a deal breaker. If all we'd had wrong between us was my immaturity, I would try again, even this late in the day." Her voice was a little stronger, carrying the tone of maternal wisdom one ignored at their own peril.

An acquaintance approached their table, forcing them to change the subject, and the rest of the meal passed innocuously. Toward the end, however, Imogen seemed to deliberately excuse herself to the powder room, leaving him to have a private word with his mother.

"I like her," she said with a warm smile.

When he didn't say anything, her smile faded.

"Travis, if it's my fault you can't open your heart—"

"It's not," he cut in. Maybe her actions had colored the way he had approached his marriage, contributing to its failure, but… "I don't understand what marriage is even for," he stated with acerbic challenge. "Don't say 'children' when you just told me you felt held back by motherhood. It's not a lifetime commitment. We've both proven that's not true. So why bother with it? It's a social construct that serves no purpose." He set down his mug. His coffee left a bitter taste in the back of his throat.

She was taken aback, blinking once, twice, then said with faint astonishment, "I wasn't talking about marriage. I was talking about love."

"Also temporary," he stated flatly. If such a thing existed at all.

His mother gasped a protest, but she had stepped out on his father because she hadn't believed he loved her. He had, but not enough to keep her faithful. His father had gone on to love someone else, proving Travis's point that the heart was fickle.

Imogen might not be as self-interested and bloodless as he'd thought her, but she hadn't loved him when they married. Not enough to be honest with him. She didn't love him now.

They were finding common ground, though, and he didn't want that jeopardized.

"We're in a good place, Mother. Don't mess with it."

"Are you?" she asked stiffly. "Your father thought that about us and look how that turned out."

Imogen returned to find Travis glaring at his mother, not nearly in the space of reconciliation she had hoped to see between them. It left her feeling defensive for forcing the meeting. Now they had to pack up and move to Henry's for Christmas Eve and morning.

At least the children provided a buffer and a distraction. It wasn't until they had been put down for the night that things became a little awkward.

Vito was liberally pouring wine with his family's

label and they were all sitting around the winking tree, mellow after a lovely dinner, when Gwyn asked Imogen if she was missing out on celebrating with her own family.

"No one left." She explained that she had lost her mother and sister quite young and her father this year.

"Your first Christmas without him. I'm so sorry."

"We didn't celebrate," she dismissed easily. "This has been really lovely. Thank you for including me."

They all looked at her the way other people did when she said she didn't celebrate, like they were trying to tell if it was a religious choice or something.

"Not at all?" Gwyn asked.

"I put up a tree a few times, but..." She shrugged off how futile that had been, sipping her wine, aware of Travis staring at her.

When they went to bed a short while later, he said, "Your father didn't even give you Christmas gifts?"

She paused in undressing. "Please don't spoil what's been a really nice evening." She stepped out of her skirt and folded it lengthwise, adding with some anxiety, "And please don't feel like you have to surprise me with a gift tomorrow to make up for that. It would upset me."

"Why?"

"Because it would be charity."

He took her into his arms, making it impossible for her to keep unbuttoning her blouse. "I hate him, you know."

"*Please* don't waste your energy."

"If you insist."

He kissed her and made love to her tenderly, then woke her with a coffee topped with whipped cream and sprinkled with chocolate shavings.

"The minion is awake and begging to open her gifts. Do you want to open this here or downstairs?" He set her coffee on the night table and held out a small box wrapped in gold with a glittering ribbon.

"I told you—" She sat up to admonish him.

"They looked so good on you, I kept them. I was going to give it to you anyway." He dabbed his finger on her whipped cream and touched it to her nose. "Say 'thank you.'"

"Really?" She rubbed it away with the back of her wrist, but her avaricious fingers were already closing on the box, itching to tear it open. He had insanely good taste in jewelry and she was already grieving the loss after giving back last night's pendant and earrings. They were so pretty.

"Yes, really. Merry Christmas."

For the first time in more than a dozen years, it was. As emotion clogged up her throat, turning her voice husky, she leaned forward to kiss him. "Thank you."

Imogen had spent the last four years blaming herself for the breakdown of their marriage. Travis had been so disparaging in their final conversations, first angry about the credit card, then agreeing immediately that, yes, divorce was a great idea. She had been convinced she'd brought nothing to their relationship.

By the time she'd had a lawyer request the settlement Travis had promised in their prenup, he'd barely been speaking to her. She'd felt small and rejected, unworthy of his love in the first place. It was hardly a surprise he hadn't wanted to stay married to her. Given her relationship with her father at the time, it had been her default to take the blame for Travis not being in love with her.

Their two days of truce and lovemaking and pleasant visiting with his family reminded her why she had fallen for him in the first place. He was wicked smart, keeping up with Vito on investment-banking talk long after her eyes had crossed, but always listened to her opinion even when it turned into a spirited debate. He was a gentleman and, yes, a neat freak, but it was kind of nice that he hung her coat and wiped a bit of flour from her cheek.

And seeing him with his niece and nephew was another side of him altogether, the kind of thing that made a woman's ovaries burst into flower.

She had to keep her expectations realistic, however. It was a point driven home to her when he screwed in his earbuds to watch some work-related slide show on his laptop during their flight back to New York, then made phone calls in the car all the way into the city.

She wasn't so much stung by it as sad. Was it ambition that drove him to shut her out? Or was it a kind of rebound after their closeness the last couple of days? Was she too much for him, as he had claimed that first night in Charleston? How was that any better than not being enough?

I make rash promises I can't keep, just for the privilege of touching you.

She had to remember he wasn't making any promises at all this time. She had to be careful not to imagine he was. Figuring out how to protect herself from heartbreak was a challenge, though, when she was so susceptible to him, feeling his withdrawal so keenly.

"Did you hear me?" he asked, touching her arm.

She had wandered onto the terrace of his building after they arrived back, hugging herself, lost in thought.

"Hmm? Oh, okay." Her breath fogged as she spoke and she nodded, then admitted as his words penetrated, "No. I don't know what you said."

"I have to run to the office." He gave her a look of amusement. "Where were you?"

"Thinking about making a doctor's appointment." As far as protecting herself went, that was a good start.

He frowned. "Did the flight hurt your ear?"

"No. I want to go on birth control."

"I wear—" he started to say, then made a face as he recalled his slip. "Probably a good idea. Thank you." Something enigmatic passed over his expression. He seemed to shake off whatever he was thinking with a distracted nod. "Let me know when you have to be there. I'll arrange the car."

"Thank you. Do you want me to cook tonight?"

"You don't have to."

"I'll see you when I see you, then, and make do with whatever is in the fridge." She set her hands on his chest, preparing to rise on tiptoe to kiss him goodbye.

He tucked his chin. "I meant we can go out for dinner if you'd rather. I'll only be gone an hour."

"Right." She patted his chest. "I've played that game before. I'll see you when I see you," she repeated with good-natured rue and stretched to peck his cheek.

His hands closed on her arms, keeping her from retreating after her kiss. "That sounds like a reprimand."

"Not at all. You have even more demands on your time than you used to. I occupy an even smaller slice of your life than I did then. I accept that." At least, she was trying to. "I'll use the time to look for work. Rowan emailed me. It sounds like she might have something. I have to read it properly."

Nic showed me your piece on Travis. I hope you don't mind. I'd love to know what you would do with my mother's story, given the chance.

Imogen wasn't taking it seriously, but writing a proposal was a good exercise.

He dropped his touch and stuffed his hands in his pockets.

"What you said to my mother... Four years ago was a very busy time for me, expanding, taking on projects that were bigger than anything I'd attempted before. I had no idea what was going on with your father. You're right that I didn't ask, but even so, I wasn't trying to diminish you when I put work ahead of spending time with you."

"I know. And I don't expect you to make me a priority now." She smiled, but her voice felt stuck like a wishbone lodged in her chest and she couldn't resist saying, "But I feel for your mother. This is very different. You and I aren't married and I don't have a child with you, but she did. It must have hurt when your father shut her out. I just wish you and she were on better terms."

"It's not that easy," he muttered, swiveling away to stare grimly at the view. "When I told you that Dad drank after she was gone, I meant he dove into a bottle and didn't come out. He's a teetotaler now, but it was *bad*. I was still in high school, but I was suddenly the parent, getting him to bed, getting him to work. I couldn't leave him alone and go stay with her. I was scared of what he might do to himself. That's why I didn't see her."

"Wasn't there anyone to help? What about your uncles?"

He shook that off. "Dad wouldn't even admit Mother was gone or why, let alone that he couldn't cope. His business was suffering. That's why I had to keep such a sharp eye on things. I don't blame her for his drinking, but I couldn't abandon him when *she* just had. She and I grew apart for all of those reasons." His profile was like granite. "I can't pretend everything is fine with her after that."

Fair enough, she supposed. "How long did it go on? His drinking? I mean, he seemed fine the other night…"

"He's been sober for years. He started going to meetings when I was leaving for university. I genuinely wasn't sure I'd be able to go, but he was really trying, pulling himself together. Then I found out it was because he was seeing Gwyn's mom. She was the janitor in his office. I didn't know what to think of that. I was suspicious and programmed to be protective of Dad. When I did have time to go home, it was to check on him. I wasn't choosing him over my mother.

"I'm not still nursing anger. Well, she said some things the other day that annoyed me, but if she was sick or in trouble, if she really needed me, of course I would be there for her. But on a day-to-day basis, all we have is nostalgia and I'm not a particularly sentimental person."

That was a warning, she was sure. She looked to her feet.

"Was she good for him in the end? Gwyn's mom, I mean."

"He would say so," Travis said with an impatient shrug. "But she got sick almost right away. He spent most of their marriage taking her to treatment and was shattered when she died. Fortunately, Gwyn was there, giving him someone to stay sober for, checking on him often enough I was able to move to New York, but..."

But none of that added up to a good reason to become attached to anyone. She wondered if he had any positive experiences with love. Even his stepsister had been through a rough time that had left nuclear fallout all over him.

"Were you worried about your dad when we were married?"

"I'm always worried about him," he said with a grimace. "One of my coping strategies is to bury myself in work. I'll cop to that." He sent her a look of frustration, one that made her think he might be regretting all he had just revealed. "I did push work between us when we were married. I had set myself some lofty goals and my desire to spend time with you was a threat to them. Today it's the other way around, though." His voice softened. "I'm trying to clear up a few things so we can have more downtime in Hawaii."

"Really?" She was genuinely astonished, but touched. "You want to walk the beach and hold hands at sunset?" It was a tease, but also a tantalizing idea. A wish.

"Among other things," he said, mouth quirking, but he lifted her hand and kissed her knuckle, making her think it wasn't *only* sex he wanted from her.

The idea of him making her a priority was such a sweet and heady thought that she nearly turned all mushy and cried. She wrinkled her nose at him instead and hurried him out the door. "You should get to work, then."

He stole one warm kiss and did.

CHAPTER EIGHT

TRAVIS HAD FIBBED, Imogen thought on their last day in Hawaii. This hadn't been the affair they were supposed to have had. It had been the honeymoon she had longed for.

After a day of meetings in Honolulu and a mixer with his client, they had flown to Kauai and the site of a new resort Travis would build over the next three years.

He had booked them into a bungalow—which was actually a three-story six-bedroom villa with an infinity pool and a short walk down to a stunning lagoon. He had worked half days, taking her with him a couple of times to walk the property, have lunch with his clients and check out the competition.

The rest of the time they had floated in the pool, snorkeled in the lagoon or made love in the airy privacy of their palatial master bedroom. They drank excellent wine and ate fresh tropical fruit and other meals prepared by their day staff. It was bliss.

"I don't want to leave," she murmured when he joined her on their last evening. She stood at the rail of their private balcony wearing only a sarong, watching the sun set.

"Same." He stood behind her and set his hand on the rail near her hip, half caging her against it.

She leaned into his frame, utterly his after a week of near constant contact.

"Did you get your proposal sent?" he asked, kissing her bare shoulder and sending tingles down into her breasts.

She smiled and reached up to caress his jaw. "Are you asking if I got all my work done? I did. Not that I expect anything to come of it, but it was nice of them to invite me to throw my hat in."

"I don't think Nic does things just to be nice."

"Rowan probably does." Nic's wife had been on the hunt for a biographer for a couple of years, although not very seriously. She'd had other priorities with adopting children and other family commitments.

"The proposal makes a nice calling card, but I don't expect to pay the bills with writing. Not right away. I applied for some positions back in New York that I might actually get."

"Like?" His hand stole into the folds of her sarong. He cupped her breast, gently massaging so her nipple tightened and poked at his palm.

"Mmm..." She rubbed her hip against the growing press of his arousal. "Um..." She couldn't think when he did that. "Nothing inspiring," she managed to recall. "Scanning papers for a museum curator. I think the primary skill required is the ability to withstand supreme boredom."

She tried to turn, but he didn't let her.

"Don't lock yourself into something you'll hate." Her hair was up, so he kissed the side of her neck, then took her earlobe between his teeth, exerting just enough pressure to threaten pain, making her hold very still and grow sensitized all over, breast swelling into his hand.

"It feels good to take constructive steps," she said breathily, barely tracking that they were still talking. "I put my name on some lists for rent-controlled apartments, too."

His hand on her breast squeezed a little tighter before he shifted his grip and lightly pinched her nipple, circling and teasing and pulling.

"Let's go to the bed," she murmured, rubbing her butt into the front of his shorts.

"Not yet." His hand slid down her belly in lazy circles, caressing and building her anticipation until he slowly cupped his hand over her mound. He made a sound of satisfaction at finding her naked and slick. "I want to make love to you right here."

She bent easily to the light exertion of his frame against hers, until her elbows rested on the rail. She was already shifting her feet open, letting him touch her more intimately, biting her lip and scanning through slit lashes in the dark.

"Somcone might see."

"There's no one here but us." He shifted to lift the back of her sarong away, then his strong thighs were against hers and he was probing for entrance.

Before they'd left New York, she had seen the doctor again and was fully protected now. She arched to take him in, gasping because she was a tiny bit tender. They made love constantly, but it felt so good every single time that she welcomed the friction against her sensitive tissues.

Even so, he made a noise of concern and moved very

gently, sliding his hand to caress her again where they were joined, exploring, inciting. Digging her nails into his forearm on the rail, she bucked and shivered with a sweet, quick orgasm.

His breath pooled at the top of her spine as he chuckled with satisfaction. "Again," he commanded, arousing her with easy thrusts and strokes. "This is all I think about all day, being in you like this, feeling you shiver and come apart."

"Me, too," she admitted, meeting the slap of his hips with pushes of her own. Her need for this made her desperate and scared. For all the steps she was taking to strike out on her own, she knew it was going to kill her to live without him. It made her greedy and uninhibited, determined to be whatever he needed.

When he covered her and held her tight, pressed deep and stroked her into losing herself, she abandoned herself to the pleasure he gave her, crying out, then whimpering with loss when he withdrew.

His shorts were already gone and he flicked her loosened sarong away with a single tug of one finger. As they stood there naked and bathed in the rising moonlight, he picked her up. Rather than take her to the bed, he took her to the lounger.

They stayed there all night, joined and caressing, kissing and pleasuring, neither wanting to go to the bed and end their last night in paradise.

Travis hadn't realized how much he'd grown used to coming home to Imogen until she wasn't there.

The short January days meant it was usually dark outside when he got home from work, but the main rooms were usually lit with lamps and the fire, and she was invariably cooking something that smelled mouthwatering, offering a kiss before getting back to whatever she was chopping or simmering.

It had been two weeks since Hawaii, and as of today, their affair had officially lasted one week longer than their marriage. He thought they should celebrate by getting out of the city and had reserved a cabin in the Catskills along with asking his pilot to fuel up and file a flight plan.

But the apartment was empty, the kitchen spotless and Imogen's laptop not winking a screen saver but completely off. She had had a lunch date with Rowan, but it was five o'clock.

He texted her and got a prompt reply.

Be there in twenty.

He poured himself a drink, surprised how much he wanted one. He told himself it was relief that she wasn't collapsed in the street again, but there was something about knowing she was on her way *back* that eased a tension inside him.

Did he wonder if there was a man involved in her delay? Maybe, but he consciously pushed that thought aside.

He didn't want to be jealous and dependent. He made a concerted effort *not* to be. It wasn't just leftover teenage angst from watching his father spiral. It was *her*. Along with wallowing in betrayal, he'd missed Imogen after she had left that first time.

That hadn't sat well with him. It was the reason he was trying so hard to keep his boundaries in place now. Hawaii had been incredible but had aided and abetted both a feeling of connection and of reliance. Not his style at all. *He* was the one who was needed, not the other way around.

He moved to look at the view, a place they often stood as they shared a drink, talking about their day. If she wasn't writing for one client or another, she went out on interviews and had signed up for a class to do some sort of website updating, so she would have more skills to peddle.

He found it strangely threatening.

She had also gone back and forth to his accountant's office, finalizing things for her father's estate, growing less stressed by degrees.

"I might actually be able to pay you back for his fee someday," she had said the other day. "Now that Dad's debts have been folded into his estate."

She had been tickled pink when her first earned income had gone into her account from a client of Joli's. It was writing blogs for a car dealership, the amount nominal, but a weekly thing she could count on for the next while.

"Look," Imogen had said, showing him the deposit on her phone. "I can take you out for a very modest lunch tomorrow."

He had opted for her to pick up sandwiches and deliver them to his office. They'd made love on his leather sofa. After she was gone, he had taken out the rings that somehow made their way into his pocket every day. *This could be my life*, he had thought. Imogen could be a fixture in his world, with her self-deprecating humor, delivering his lunch and erotic distractions, littering his home with shoes and hair clips, but filling it with her lilting voice and other signs of life.

For how long? he wondered. Marriage didn't last forever. Nothing did.

The elevator dinged and she came in, flushed and beaming, wearing the green dress he'd bought her the first day she'd been here. It sat tighter against her figure now that she was back to a healthier weight. Her breasts pressed against the neckline and the belt was no longer a loose bracelet around her waist but a pretty flash of gold that emphasized the flare of her fuller hips.

Fetching as she was, the way she kicked off her shoes and practically skipped toward him, looking very damned pleased with herself, was what really kicked up his heart rate. When she threw her arms around his neck and planted a big kiss on his mouth, her bright, golden energy coursed through him like a current.

He picked her up off her feet so her legs dangled and they were eye to eye, his arms around her butt.

"Did you finally win the lottery? Why are you so cheerful?"

"I'm always cheerful. But yes, I kind of did." She was incandescent, holding him rapt as he took in the sparkle of her eyes, the smile that wouldn't leave her lips, the air of sheer magic glittering around her. He wanted to make love to her, but he wanted to simply gaze on her at the same time.

"Where were you?"

"Rowan's. We finished lunch but weren't finished talking, so we went back to their apartment. She offered me a contract." Her eyes bugged out.

"For the biography?"

"Yes! I told her she was crazy, that there are other people who are way more qualified, but every time I tried to talk her out of it, she offered me more money."

"Why would you talk her out of it? That's fantastic. Let's celebrate." He walked them across to the wine fridge, then set her on her feet to bend and take out a bottle of champagne.

"I haven't signed anything. I wanted to talk to you first."

"As long as the compensation is fair, I say it's a terrific opportunity." He opened the cupboard and brought out two flutes. "Quit worrying you're not good enough. You are, otherwise she wouldn't have asked you."

"But I've never taken on anything so big. Nic has a guy working on his father's biography who's done seven already. I asked Rowan if I could cheat off his work. She laughed and said that's why she wants me. That we have the same sense of humor and she feels comfortable talking to me about her childhood. I guess her relationship with her mother was rocky at times. She needs someone she trusts to find the balance between truthful and kind."

He popped the cork and a minuscule cloud wisped from the neck of the bottle before he poured the frothy bubbly into the glasses.

"And she chose you. Well done. I'm proud of you."

Imogen hesitated to clink and he met her eyes. They were swimming in a thick gloss of tears. "Really?"

His heart took a swerve and nearly tipped completely. Had no one ever said they were proud of her? Ever?

"Yes." Emotion thickened his throat and his chest ached. "Very."

They touched glasses with a crystalline ping and sipped. Actually, she seemed to take a bigger gulp, swallowing audibly. Her voice sounded nervous when she spoke.

"There's a small catch if I take it."

If.

The air shifted. The pressure in his chest grew. "What's that?"

"I'll travel to Greece a lot, especially at first. She's fine with my bringing some things back here, but there's a lot to sort through. Letters and photographs. Playbills and other memorabilia. All very flexible. I'll be back for the opening of the hotel in Florida. If you still want me to be there." Her voice thinned as she said the last.

"You're leaving." And here came the train whistle in the distance.

"Rowan is taking the kids back to Greece at the end of the week. She's hoping I'll go with them, since she'll have some time to get me started while she's there. That's why I said I needed to talk this out with you first."

They hadn't made any commitments. He couldn't hold her back unless he was prepared to make one. He pushed his hand into his pocket and the diamond on the engagement ring cut into his palm.

"Once I sign the contract... The advance is very generous. I should be able to find a decent apartment—"

"Not necessary," he heard himself say, staring into the rise of bubbles in his glass.

"You don't feel differently about my being here, now that I have options?"

"No. I want you here." So badly it scared him.

Her mouth trembled into a fresh smile. "Really?"

The emotional intimacy of the moment nearly undid him. He hated feeling this vulnerable.

"Of course," he said gruffly. "Come here." He set aside his glass.

She moved into his arms.

He had to remind himself to be gentle, because the beast was roused. The greedy one who was possessive and ravenous and territorial, needing to mark her as his own.

She matched him, though. Matched him in the way that was terrifying because it turned their lovemaking raw and elemental, and because it told him she was feeling the same desperate need to cleave onto him that he felt with her.

He picked her up and carried her to his bed, leaving their fresh bottle of champagne to go flat.

CHAPTER NINE

Travis woke to her cry.

He rolled, gathering her trembling form into him so her wet cheek smeared across his pecs. He was only half-awake, reacting on instinct, not thinking until he was stroking her hair and murmuring for her to wake up that she preferred to suffer through this.

He couldn't bear it, though. He couldn't bear the wrenching sounds of sorrow, and he couldn't bear the reason she was having her bad dream.

When I'm feeling sorry for myself...

Why? He had given her as much pleasure as he knew how to deliver, binding her to him as indelibly as possible without sewing their skin.

"Travis," she breathed on a sniff and hugged her arms around him, pressing her silky warmth to his front. Shudders of reaction were still working through her spine.

"My fault," he said in a voice that rasped his throat. They'd made love for hours, skipping dinner. "I'll go order something for delivery."

She made a noise that wasn't quite a protest, but the weight of her against him urged him not to move. Her heart rate eased along with her breaths, but she had a sense of despondency about her.

"I feel like this is the beginning of the end," she said in a hollow whisper.

He did, too, but he wasn't ready to face it. That's why he had drowned them both in sexual ecstasy. Cupping the back of her hair, he pressed a kiss to her forehead. "Let's see how things go."

He left the bed.

Imogen had been gone a week, and she missed Travis to the point she woke with a tearstained face and a dream of waiting for him to come to her, which he never did.

I want you here. She had taken such heart from that, but now she had time to reflect, she saw it wasn't words of love or commitment. What they had was unrestrained passion, not something that lasted.

So, even though she pined for him and feared that this job was going to be the undoing of their relationship, she also knew she had to push herself into a position of independence.

Heck, she needed that for her own self-worth and peace of mind. She could never stay with him as his mistress, kept and resented over time, eventually abandoned. She needed this job, this money, this distraction from fretting about their future. She needed to know she had a future regardless of what happened between them.

So she signed the contract and sent him a photo of her signature.

He FaceTimed her. "Congratulations." He looked so pleased for her that she could have cried.

"Thank you— Oh," she cut herself off, noticing the

man at the window. "Sorry. Rafe is waving and giving me a thumbs-up." She waved at him, calling, "Bye!"

"Who the hell is Rafe?"

She faltered under the sudden ice in Travis's tone.

"I told you about him. He's my counterpart, working on Nic's father's biography. He's leaving for London."

"But he'll be back. You'll be working with him."

"Remotely. Travis." She had always thought that jealousy in a man would be flattering, but it just sounded like a lack of trust. "We'll check in via email, to discuss crossover details. That's all."

He seemed to accept that and she promised to come to him in Florida when she returned. He had a grand opening of a hotel he had designed and she was joining him for the gala ball.

She arrived with just enough time to change in their top-floor suite while reading his text that he was downstairs and couldn't get away.

He had left her a gown. It was an airy confection with a flowing skirt in shades that matched the tropical waters off their terrace. The bodice was strapless and snug, sexy and elegant at once.

She hadn't arranged a stylist so only gathered her hair back from her face, letting it fall behind her shoulders in a fluttering mass of auburn and amber.

When she arrived in the ballroom, it was an aquarium of bright gowns and tuxedos. She looked for a podium or the bar, somewhere he was likely to be standing—

Oh. He was looking right at her.

He held a drink and seemed arrested, wearing a look she couldn't interpret. Approval? Hunger? With a blink he took action, setting aside his drink and weaving toward her through the crowd.

Her heart soared as he approached. Growing bigger with each step until she couldn't deny what the enormous feeling inside her was. *Oh, no.*

"I missed you," she said, when she really wanted to confess, "I love you. I've always loved you."

It dawned through her with all the promise of a sunrise, a new day, a fresh start. It wasn't the immature, unrealistic love she had had for him when they were married, though. It was a mature, achingly wise kind of love that knew she couldn't beg for or demand or *earn* his love. She could only offer her heart and hope.

Was it glowing like a neon sign from her smile, beating like a telegraph message in her throat? He must have seen something because he seemed to grow more reserved. Stony.

"You look beautiful." He took her hand and bussed her cheek with the lightest of kisses, lacking the heated frenzy of need that thrummed in her.

The ballooning sensation inside her began to deflate.

"So do you," she said, trying not to falter into doubt. In so many ways, he had helped her find her confidence, encouraging her to pursue this job and believe in herself. She didn't want to think it was suddenly in jeopardy, but there was no safety net of reassurance to fall back on, no declaration of love, of anything, to save her from plunging into insecurity.

She kept her smile on her face and searched his expression, asking inanely, "Is everything going well?"

"Perfectly. I imagine you're tired from all the travel. You only have to make an appearance. Let me introduce you and you can disappear early if you'd like."

He took her cool hand in his and dragged her across to meet his clients. Words were said. Pleasantries exchanged.

"You haven't had a chance to look around?" the owner said, offering his arm. "Let me show you."

Travis offered his arm to the owner's wife and followed them onto the mezzanine. They looked down into the lobby fountain, then moved out to a terrace that overlooked a palm-tree-lined pool and a beach glowing in the moonlight against a starry sky. The design was meant to hark back to the owner's family château with arches and columns, wrought iron and well-crafted stonework. At the same time, his wife was very fanciful and demanded every luxury be afforded to their exclusive guests.

He'd seen it all and talked to these people until he was sick to death of them. He watched Imogen instead. Drank her up and hated himself for having waited to see her one more time before he ended it. Needing this much at least.

"It's stunning. Like a fairy tale castle," Imogen said after the tour. "And now I know your secret," she said to Travis in an undertone, hugging his arm. "You're a closet romantic."

He stiffened, reacting to her, as always. Applying brutal discipline within himself, trying not to.

He had been feeling her absence keenly, which unnerved him. He wasn't a needy man. It was uncomfortable for him to be distracted, wondering where she was, what she was doing. The hollow ache in him had warned of a deeper, more debilitating pain the longer their relationship went on. A harder fall when she left for good.

Then she'd delivered a one-two punch of taking a job that would continue to take her away and mentioning a man. The jealousy, the uncertainty, that had risen in him then had made it clear to him he was in too deep. He couldn't ride a roller coaster with this many plummets and heights. She already held too much power over him.

"Your husband is a genius," the owner stated magnanimously. "I couldn't be happier."

Imogen dropped Travis's arm, turning to correct the man about the state of their marriage, but his wife was busy saying, "You two should join us on the vineyard next week. We're having a house party at our cottage."

"Imogen is fresh in from Greece," Travis interjected. "She's writing a biography. I don't expect to see much of her in the next while as she digs into it."

His words jarred her. She glanced at him with a little frown.

She tried to keep a smile on her face as they returned to the ballroom, walking with the owner's wife now, telling her what she could about her assignment, but she kept glancing back at him.

When Travis drew her onto the dance floor, Imogen said stiffly, "If you didn't want people to think we're a couple, you shouldn't have invited me to join you here."

"I was repeating what you told me in your text," he said flatly. "You said you were going back as soon as you could. How is Rafe?" he added.

She stopped dancing. "What are you doing, Travis?"

"What do you mean?"

"You know." With a little flinch, she looked for an exit. "I'm not playing. Or maybe I am, because you don't really give me a choice, do you?"

"What the hell are you talking about?"

"I'm taking you up on your offer to leave early." She forced a smile. "Please make my excuses."

He looked into her eyes, the raw anguish and shadow of betrayal, and knew this was it. Wind seemed to rush past his ears, as though he was in free fall, but at least he could see the ground. The end point. *Okay, then.* He braced himself.

"I'll walk you up."

He followed her to the alcove where the bank of elevators let out. It was empty and a pair of doors opened the moment she jabbed the button.

"Why did you ask me to come down here?" she demanded as they were closed into a car alone. "Just so you could pull the pin in the most humiliating way possible? Why didn't you tell me to stay in Greece? Why did you tell me you wanted me to stay with you?"

"You're the one hiding that you're meeting a man—"

"Don't you *dare.*" She charged out the opening elevators and down the silencing carpet of the hall. It took two jabs of her card to open the door to their suite, she was shaking so badly.

She barely restrained herself, waiting for the door to close before she rounded on him.

"Accuse me of anything," she said, rage thickening in her throat. "But don't you *ever* accuse me of cheating on you. You're the one who spent the four years since our marriage sleeping with anything that moved."

He rocked on his feet as though she'd clawed his face. "Bit late in the day to bring that up, isn't it?"

"You think because I haven't mentioned it that it

doesn't bother me? I hate it! But I have never once said anything because *I* left *you*. Our divorce was *my fault*. I was the villain." She knocked her breastbone so hard it thumped.

He frowned, but she railed on.

"No, I did not jump into bed with the first stranger I met, the minute I was out of your sight. Go to hell, Travis, for thinking I would." She kicked off her shoes and yanked out her earrings. She threw the jewelry onto the table, glad for the way her earrings caught in her hair. The hurt distracted her from the way she was disappearing inside. Growing hollow and filling up with darkness. "How many women have you slept with since I've been away?"

"None," he bit out, seeming affronted she would even ask. "But whether it was Rafe or some other man or some other reason, we were never going to last. You knew that, Imogen."

"Really?" That took her aback. "Well, I guess if you believe it, then it must be true."

He narrowed his eyes. "Your optimism is appealing, but it's delusional. We both knew, up front, that this was temporary."

"So Rafe is an excuse. You're ready to end it, but didn't have the guts to say so."

"Is there a reason this needs to be ugly? Yes," he said, voice brutally hard and clear as crystal. "I'm ready to end it. I'm sorry if that hurts you, but yes. It's over."

"Oh, you're sorry? *If* you've hurt me? Well, *I'm* sorry every day that I'm even *alive*. I've been conditioned to take the lion's share of blame in every confrontation or conflict. Do you realize that I'm going to walk out of here believing this was my fault? My fault *you* don't want to make a commitment. That *you* aren't capable of love. That *you* don't want *me*. You hurt me, Travis. Every single day, it hurts to be this in love with you and know you don't feel the same. Are you sorry for that?"

He flinched, jaw pulsing. "Yes. And it only proves my point. You should leave and find someone who can give you the love you deserve."

"Wow," she choked, thinking it ironic that she finally believed she did deserve it when he was telling her to look for it elsewhere. "I definitely will."

She hadn't unpacked more than her hairbrush and makeup. It only took a moment to fill and close her carry-on with a snap that sounded very loud in the thick silence. Like a gunshot through the heart.

"I'll get a few things from the apartment, then go back to Greece. Rowan set up the guest cottage for me to come and go." She lifted her head. "Don't expect me to stay celibate this time. Don't expect me to forgive you for the fact you won't. This is really it. This one is on you."

Travis went back to the party and only drank water, even though an urge to drink himself blind prickled his throat. He wasn't his father. He wouldn't be destroyed by a woman.

The next morning, he packed her gown and jewelry on autopilot, taking care of what needed to be done exactly the way he had every other time his life had taken an unexpected dip or turn.

He had told her the truth. This breakup was always going to happen. Maybe he had hurried it with his flare of jealousy, but even though he doubted she would ever cheat, the harder truth was that he couldn't *make* her be faithful. He couldn't *make* her stay.

He might not survive the disaster in the distance, so he had forced the issue today, while he was still able to carry on. He wasn't proud of it. Looking back, he saw he'd done the same thing the first time. His only regret was that he'd left Imogen feeling blamed back then. At least this time they both knew it was his fault.

Which was no comfort at all.

Rather than fly directly to his empty penthouse in New York, he stopped in Charleston to see his father. During Gwyn's escapade, Henry had moved into a gated neighborhood for privacy. Attention had long died down, but his father enjoyed the social community he'd formed there.

"How is it over when it only just started?" his father said after inquiring about Imogen. "I thought she was only going to Greece sporadically, not staying there."

Travis sighed, wishing his father would accept things at face value. This grotto behind his father's house was usually one of the most relaxing places to sit and visit with him, but Travis rose to his feet, restless.

"We knew very quickly the first time that we wouldn't last. We couldn't sustain it this time, either." He pushed his hand into his pocket and found her rings. He was going to ruin them, rubbing them together the way he constantly did, but he pressed them onto his finger and thumb tips, working them against each other. It had become a habit.

"I've been seeing your mother, you know."

"What?" Travis snapped his head around.

His father shrugged sheepishly. "We had coffee a

few days after my party. There were things we had never talked through before. I hadn't given her a chance to tell me her side of it, too busy calling her names and impugning her. I worry I distorted your view of women with things I said back then."

"Dad—"

"Do you know I was drinking before she cheated? I never wanted to tell you that, but I thought you might have guessed. No? It wasn't nearly as bad as after, but I was feeling pressure from work. Untold pressure from those committees asking me to run in state elections. Maybe I wasn't sleeping with other women, but I was spending more time lunching with a bottle and other people than with your mother. I wasn't there for you the way I should have been, before or after." He made a face.

"I'm not here to play blame games, Dad. I've never felt that Mother really needed me, not the way you did. That's the only reason I'm closer to you. We don't need family therapy or anything." He rubbed the back of his neck, thinking that felt like a lie. Maybe he had come here looking for commiseration of some sort. Women. Right?

"Has Imogen cheated?"

"Not even close," he muttered, freshly ashamed that he'd questioned her about another man. She'd had every right to be angry about that. "We're different people, that's all."

"Good."

"How is that good? I want something I can count on, Dad. Someone who's predictable, not..." Whimsical and kind and sensitive. Someone so sensual and engaging he forgot himself.

"Then get a dog."

He shot his father a dirty look. "I don't want to believe we have a future, start a family, then discover we're not going to work. Better to nip that in the bud."

"If you actually aren't compatible, then yes. But what kind of lifetime warranty do you expect, Travis? Do you know what Gwyn said the last time she was here? That she was glad her mom had those years with me. We had plans, you know. We were going to travel. I was counting on *that*. It didn't work out, but I have no regrets. I didn't divorce her because she got sick and canceled our future. You can't count on anything, especially time.

"If you don't love Imogen, fine. Move on. But if you do love her, what the hell are you doing acting like she'll still be there when you wake up and realize you want her? You're wasting time you could be spending making my future grandchildren."

Travis returned to New York the next day. His father's words were turning over in his mind, wearing holes in his skull. Now his empty penthouse was filled with her memory, making it a difficult place to be. He called a Realtor and made an appointment, then stood in the office he had rarely used. He had intended to tell Imogen she could use this room as a home office, to write the biography. He stared at where she had lounged that first day, when he had fantasized about making love to her again.

If only he *had* got her pregnant that night on the yacht.

He pinched the bridge of his nose, wondering if that was what he was reduced to, needing the excuse of an unplanned pregnancy to try again with her. Really try.

Oddly, he was convinced that he would somehow make that work. He was at his best when he was needed.

He looked back on his father's breakdown, a time when Travis had been frustrated and angry but had understood his role. The few times he'd helped his mother, it had been when her lover was away and the sink had backed up, or she needed furniture moved. Gwyn had thought Travis hated her until her life had burned down around her. He'd been furious that it took her so long to involve him, thinking she ought to have known he would come the minute she asked, but she'd been too proud to fall back on him.

Was he waiting for Imogen to pass out in the street again so he could race in and save her? Had he felt threatened when she had ceased to lean on him? Had that been the real issue?

She had told him she loved him, but he'd only seen that she was leaving him despite saying it. She had said that he was hurting her, which had been a blow, one that had made him think letting her go was a kindness.

He hadn't considered that her upbringing predisposed her to have a specific need for love. He'd made no effort to meet that need. He had covered her basic survival with food and shelter—exactly as her piece-of-dirt father had done.

Travis didn't *want* to love anyone, though. He never had. Love was obligation and loyalty at best. At worst, it was an emotional wringer when the people you loved were in pain. Romantic love was a glittering facet of passion, not something true and deep and sustainable.

And yet, what he felt toward Imogen was all of those things. He knew that as clearly as he knew she had left him and it was nobody's fault but his own.

* * *

When Imogen had been a child, inventing stories had been her salvation. Later, when grief had engulfed her, she had filled up notebooks with poetry and song lyrics. Essays and ad copy and current events had all played their part in keeping her sane while her heart throbbed and ached.

Two weeks after her breakup with Travis, she had a new medium to help mend her broken heart, one she found infinitely fascinating because she identified with her subject. Cassandra O'Brien had been rejected by her family the moment her teenage aspirations turned to acting. She had had a rough life making ends meet, riding the feast or famine trials of acting, falling for men who didn't love her the way she longed to be loved—deeply and forever.

By some miracle, she had eventually met her soul mate and wound up here, on this Greek island, living in a house that looked like it belonged in the English countryside. It was a fairy tale and fed Imogen's starved, scorned heart with hope.

She couldn't help sighing over that.

"You sound like you've sprung a leak."

Travis's voice startled her so badly that she gasped and leaped to her feet, knocking her chair back into the wall.

He looked amazing. Rumpled and travel-weary in a button-down shirt with the sleeves rolled back, but a feast for her eyes as he gazed around the small front room of the guest cottage.

"Looks like you've called in Joli's decorator."

"I know. Rafe said this isn't how he works—" *Damn.* She bit her lip.

"Rafe," Travis repeated gravely.

"He peeked in the other day when he came by for some boxes. I don't see him. I shouldn't have brought him up."

Just like that, her eyes were hot and her self-worth was in the toilet. Tears were in her eyes.

This was why it was good they were over, she reminded herself. Not because he had accused her of cheating, but because he made her feel so very imperfect without even trying.

"What are you doing here?" she asked huskily.

"I want to talk to you. Can you take a break?"

"Travis—" She was barely hanging on over here, only getting through her days because the children checked on her and she refused to let them find her with her head in the oven. But there was no way she could withstand another interaction with this man. It could very well be the one that killed her.

She shook her head.

He closed his eyes, flinched. "I deserve that," he said in a serious tone that might have held an edge of agony. "But I came all this way. Give me five minutes. Please."

She looked around. The cottage was not only messy, but too small to contain him and how she felt about him. She couldn't risk permeating it with his memory. It would leave her incapable of living or working here.

"Outside." She cleared her throat and rose, picked her way across the piles littering the floor, each step a dreadful inch closer to more heartbreak. "We'll go to the beach."

He stepped back as she came through the door. She closed the screen and put on her sandals.

"Why didn't you call?" she asked as they made their way through the orange grove.

"Because you would have hung up."

Maybe. "Is something wrong?"

"Very."

She looked up, concerned. "Your dad?"

"You're here and I'm not."

"Travis—"

"I love you, Imogen." A flash of pain sliced across his expression as he said the words. "God," he muttered, rubbing the center of his chest. "I didn't know that would feel so good. I think I loved you when we were married. I think that's why I married you."

She halted, jaw going lax. "But you…"

"Let you go. Slept with other women. I know. I hate myself, Imogen. I hate myself for all of that. For hurting you. For calling you my only mistake. Letting you go was the mistake."

She tried to move her lips, but her hand was over her mouth and she didn't know what to say anyway.

"I don't want to be in love. I hate myself most for the tears that are coming into your eyes as I say that. But I need you to understand why it scares the hell out of me. I doubt you've slept with Rafe—in fact, I'm sure you haven't. But if you have, hell, I deserve that. I should have been true to you the way you were true to me. But it wouldn't change how I feel about you if you've been with a dozen other men. I don't think anything could. That's why I don't know how to handle it, Imogen. You *could* cheat and I wouldn't stop loving you. I would probably stay married to you. How the hell am I supposed to live with giving you that kind of power over me?"

He faced her and drew her hand down, holding both of hers in his. He was very solemn as he looked into her eyes. His were filled with turmoil and remorse and something so tender that the flimsy shields she'd spent the last two weeks trying to recover toppled like a house of cards inside her.

"How do I ask your forgiveness? How do I convince you, after driving you away *twice*, that you should give me another chance?"

Her heart was quavering so hard it turned her voice fluttery and weak. "Tell me again that you love me." Had she imagined it?

"I need bigger words, better ones, for what I feel for you. 'I love you' isn't enough. I've never been the one in a relationship who needs, but I *need* you, Imogen. I need you like air. I need the love you've offered me. I won't take it for granted again, I swear." His hands were tight over hers.

"Oh, Travis." She started to step forward, to throw her arms around his neck, but he disappeared.

He dropped to his knee and there in his palm were her rings.

She stacked her hands over her mouth again, this time to still the trembling of her lips. She was crumpling on all sides, wetness falling from her lashes as she clenched her eyes shut, terrified this was a dream and she was going to wake up alone.

"This time we do it right," he said. "A public engagement. A proper wedding with witnesses who will hold us accountable to our vows. I want to tell the world that you're mine, that I love you. I want you to let me take care of you because I want you in sickness and in health, Imogen. Richer or poorer. We've seen each other's worst. Let's do better this time. Let me have your hand. Please."

It was too perfect. He was saying all the right things and it wasn't *possible*. "I can't believe..." But she offered her hand because even if it was a dream, she wanted to take it as far as it could go.

"Believe it. You do deserve my love, Imogen. I'll do everything in my power to deserve yours." He reached for her hand and reverently slid both rings on her finger, holding her knuckles against his lips a long moment. "I've been wanting to see them on you... Never take them off again. Promise me."

He waited, looking as if he wouldn't rise until she gave him that vow.

"I do. I promise."

He rose and she shook even harder.

"Is this real?"

"It's very real. Feel." He pressed her ringed hand to his chest where his heart pounded inside his rib cage. When he kissed her, his lips were hot and worshipful. Then, because they could never resist turning a chaste kiss to a passionate one, they sank into a deeper kiss, one that tasted of hot blood and excitement, but something more exalted.

As they twined their arms around each other, desire rose, a desire that needed physical expression, but sought the joining of souls as much as bodies.

"We should go back to the cottage," she breathed, pulling back. Then she frowned, eyes widening in apprehension. "What about my contract—?"

"Sometimes we'll have to be apart." He said it with stoic dismay. "I'll come to you as often as you come to me. I don't want you to feel anything less than what you are, Imogen. My equal. My love. My heart. The woman I want to spend the rest of my life with. The woman I want in my life every single day. I love you."

"I love you, too, Travis. I always have."

"I know. You humble me with that. I want to give you everything your heart needs."

"You already have…"

EPILOGUE

Two years later

SOMEONE WAS IN the bedroom, moving toward the bed. It wasn't Imogen. She was pressed against him, fast asleep. *He* was fast asleep, but even so, he was aware of this other presence and there she was. A girl who might have been Imogen at twelve with hair in two braids, the bridge of her nose freckled, her smile a little too big for her face and her teeth set with a hint of overbite. She was pretty, wearing a dress that might have been white or navy or the same red-gold as her brows and lashes.

One day, he found himself thinking foggily, he and Imogen would have a daughter who looked just like her. Maybe a few months from now.

She giggled. He heard it in his head along with her high, sweet voice. "He's a boy. I'm here to tell her not to worry about him. He'll be fine."

Imogen wasn't eating much these days and was worried her empty stomach was hurting the baby. Was she crying? Through his heavy sleep, he thought she might be starting to sob. He started to turn toward her and gather her in.

"Wait," the girl said. "I want to talk to her. I want to tell her I won't be coming anymore. She doesn't need me. She has you now. And Julian."

Who was Julian?

She giggled again. "If she's sad, tell her she'll see me when Lilith comes."

Who was Lilith?

"Go make breakfast. Be quiet. Don't wake her."

Travis snapped his eyes open to the walls of the penthouse. The blink of colored Christmas lights off the downstairs terrace reflected faintly on the ceiling. It was midmorning, Christmas Eve. He was fully dressed on the bed with Imogen. They'd been starting their day when she had been unable to stomach breakfast and started crying, fearful that if she didn't eat, she would miscarry. She was incredibly emotional these days, not feeling well at all, which was why they'd opted not to join everyone in Italy and were having Christmas here, just the two of them. Two and a half.

With his protective buttons pushed to max levels, he had cuddled her on the bed, promising to call the doctor, but they'd both fallen asleep.

Now she was whimpering beside him, face turned into the pillow, but it wasn't the sorrowful, lonely cry he'd heard before. It was a subdued sob, like she was trying to hold back her cries so she could listen.

His scalp tightened. It had been a dream, he assured himself. A bizarre, fanciful dream that had no place in a rational man's mind as anything but.

Still, he was very careful as he rose, letting her continue to sob. It went against everything in him, but he did it, heart battering his chest as he made his way down the stairs.

Such a weird day. It had started out so well, with the doorman sending up Imogen's author copies while she'd been trying to choke down breakfast. He'd teasingly put it under the tree with the rest of the wrapped boxes, earning a cry of protest from her.

She was *not* waiting until Christmas to open that one. For a woman who didn't celebrate Christmas, she was giddier than Toni about the prospect of opening gifts tomorrow. Today had been one of the happiest days of her life until she had become sick.

He picked up the book she had signed to him, the first out of the box. Flipping it over, he saw Imogen's smiling face—so like the girl in his dream, if older and more heart-catchingly beautiful. She had her elbow propped, her hand along her cheek so her rings showed. She wore three now, the original two with a third they'd had custom-made to match. They had decided three was the charm and so far, so great.

Her book was finished and advance reviews and preorders were strong. His latest project had been clinched by his wife's charisma, and they were expecting. Provided she was allowed to travel, they were headed to Hawaii in a few weeks for the latest phase of his project there.

He heard her stirring a few minutes later and put the finishing touches on the breakfast of toast and scrambled eggs he'd whipped together. He had already made her an appointment with the doctor, but she had time to eat first. Hopefully, it would stay down this time.

Her eyes were a little red as she appeared and she came right into his arms, fitting herself against him in the way that was reassuringly familiar. He rubbed her back, still disturbed.

"You were crying. I thought you must be hungry." He wasn't sure if he should mention his dream, but his gaze was drawn to the photo on the side table in the lounge. It was the only one she had of her with her mother and sister. Surely, he'd conjured the image from that.

"Juliana came."

He kept rubbing her back while the hairs all over his body stood up. "It's been a long time since you've had one of those." Not since before he proposed in Greece.

"She said she's not coming back. She says I have you now."

He cradled her closer, disturbed by the melancholy in her voice, but hoping this meant no more crying in her sleep ever again.

She drew back and cocked her head. "What do you think of the name Julian if it's a boy?"

"I love it," he said, voice catching with emotion, echoes of giggles still in his head. "Juliana if it's a girl?"

"I've always thought Lilith for a girl, after Mom."

"I like that, too." He was bonkers, no question, but he didn't care. Not when this woman made him so happy.

He hugged her and she smiled, lifting on her toes to kiss him.

He released her and she eyed the breakfast he'd made. "You're my hero for making this, but if the baby rejects it, that's not on me."

No, it would be on Julian.

Julian, who arrived seven months later with a fine cap of his mother's red-gold hair and a challenging but funny personality that kept his parents on their toes. Travis was so proud and filled with love for the boy, he could barely contain it. He wondered daily how he had ever thought this would be too much for him when he couldn't get enough of family life.

Their daughter, Lilith, came along two years after that. She had her father's coloring and a pair of eyes that Travis knew he'd seen in a dream once. She was incredibly sweet and loving, impossible to resist, not that anyone tried, especially her parents and brother. Her only flaw was a tendency to startle the life out of her father by appearing beside the bed in the middle of the night, then giggling at his reaction.

* * * * *

THEIR CHRISTMAS DREAM COME TRUE

KATE HARDY

For Chloë, my very special daughter.

CHAPTER ONE

So this was it. Natalie's first day as a doctor—a pre-registration house officer, if you wanted to split hairs, but a brand-new doctor was still a doctor. Her hospital ID badge said Dr Natalie Wilkins. This was what she'd worked for. Hard. Against everyone's advice. And she'd finally made it. So what if she was six years older than the other house officers? The important thing was, she'd been offered a six months' post in the paediatric department of St Joseph's hospital.

Not the same hospital as Ethan—

Natalie cut the thought short before it could grab hold and choke her with remembered misery.

Paediatrics was probably the toughest option she could have chosen. Six years ago, she'd thought she'd never be able to walk onto a children's ward again. But she could do it and she *would* do it. Six months here, six months in emergency medicine, then back to paediatrics. Next move: senior house officer. Two years' further training and she'd be taking the paediatric specialist exams. And from there she'd make a real difference. Maybe stop other parents going through—

No. She wasn't going to think about that now. She had work to do.

She headed for the reception desk on the ward and introduced herself to the maternal-looking nurse in the dark blue uniform who was working through a stack of patient files. 'I was told to report here.'

Even though she'd tried to sound cool, calm and professional, some of her first-day nerves must have shown, because the nurse gave her a beaming smile. 'Hello, love. Welcome to Nightingale Ward. I'm Debbie Jacobs, the senior sister—I was off duty when you came for interview. You've got a few minutes until Lenox arrives, so let me show you where everything is.'

'Thanks.'

Fifteen minutes later, Natalie had a key to her own locker in the staffroom, knew where the parents' rooms and isolation cubicles were as well as the general bays, had gulped down her first cup of coffee on the ward, had been introduced to ten people whose names she was sure she'd never remember, and had started a ward round with Lenox Curtis, the consultant.

In at the deep end.

Doing observations, checking medication and treatment plans, venturing her opinion when it was asked for. Hesitantly, at first, but the more she got right, the more her confidence blossomed. By the end, she was able to reassure the anxious parents of a seven-month-old girl who'd been brought in with abdominal pain.

'Maia was always a colicky baby, but she seemed to be getting better. Then she started drawing her legs up again and screaming for two or three minutes.' The little girl's mother was shaking. 'She's been off her food the last day. And then I saw this red stuff in her nappy.'

'A bit like redcurrant jelly?' Natalie asked.

'Yes.'

Natalie examined the little girl gently. The baby's stomach was distended, and Natalie could feel a sausage-shaped mass, curved and concave to the umbilical cord. As Natalie gently pressed the mass, Maia lifted her legs and screamed again.

'All right, sweetheart.' Natalie soothed the baby gently, stroking her face and calming her down. She noted that the soft spot on the top of the baby's head had sunk a bit, showing that the little girl was dehydrated.

'What's wrong with her?' Maia's father asked.

'It's something called intussusception—it's where one segment of the bowel telescopes into another segment and constricts the blood supply. That's why you see the redcurrant-jelly-like stuff—it's a mixture of blood and mucus. But it's nothing either of you have done,' she reassured them both swiftly. 'It just happens. It might be that she has a polyp—a non-cancerous growth—that started it off. Quite a lot of children get intussusception before they're two, so we're very used to treating it here. I'm going to send her for an ultrasound in a minute so we can see exactly what we're looking at—it doesn't hurt and it's the same sort of scan you had when you were pregnant.'

Maia's father turned white. 'Is she going to have to have surgery?'

'Hopefully not. You've brought her in early, so we might be able to sort it out by an air enema—what we do is put a pipe in her bottom and blow air in to gently manoeuvre the bowel back to where it should be. If that doesn't work, we'll need to sort her bowel out surgically, but the good news is she's got an excellent chance of a full recovery.' She smiled at them. 'I'll book Maia in for an ultrasound now, and because she's a bit dehydrated I'm going to put her on a drip so we can get some fluids into her. In the meantime, to make her a bit more comfortable, I need to put a tube into her nose and down into her tummy—that will help get rid of any air that's built up.' It also drained the stomach contents, which made the procedures easier. 'I'll be able to give you a better idea of how we're going to treat her when I've seen the scan.'

'But she'll be OK?' Maia's mother asked.

'She's going to be fine,' Natalie promised. Had the problem been left a few weeks longer, gangrene might have set in, and the outcome would have been very different. But she was confident that this case would be absolutely fine.

And it felt good, so *good*, to help people. To make a difference to people's lives. To make things right again.

'So did you enjoy your first ward round here?' Lenox asked when they'd finished.

'I think so,' Natalie said with a smile. 'It was a bit nerve-racking to start with, but it got easier towards the end.'

He smiled back. 'You'll do fine. Give it a week and you'll feel as if you've been here for ever. And tomorrow you won't even be our newest recruit.'

'You've got another house officer starting?' Natalie asked, interested.

'Special registrar,' Lenox explained. 'We were lucky to poach him from London—he's quite a whiz. His name's Christopher Rodgers.'

Ice trickled down Natalie's spine. *Christopher Rodgers.*

No, it had to be a coincidence. Rodgers was a common enough surname, and Christopher was a popular first name. There was more than just one Christopher Rodgers in the world.

'Though it seems everyone calls him Kit,' Lenox added. *Kit?*

Most Christophers were known as Chris. Kit was the posh diminutive. A much, much less common diminutive.

Kit Rodgers.

From London.

No. It couldn't be him. Surely.

The Kit she'd known had been training as a surgeon, not as a paediatric specialist. Then again, Natalie had been a history teacher and she'd retrained. Kit might have done the same thing...for the same reasons.

Well, she'd deal with it tomorrow.

If she had to.

She managed to put Kit out of her mind when she took Maia for an ultrasound. The results showed the double ring she was expecting. 'Definitely intussusception.'

'Anything else?' Lenox asked.

She looked carefully at the scan. 'It doesn't look as if there's any perforation or significant ischaemia. So I'd say it would be safe to go ahead with the air enema.'

'Good call,' he said. 'Would you like me to talk you through it, or would you prefer to watch me do it?'

'I've seen one done before, though I haven't actually performed one,' she said. 'I'd like to try myself, if that's all right with you.'

'That's fine.' He smiled. 'I think you're going to be an asset to the team—you're prepared to try things rather than hang back. Good.'

He talked her through the procedure. As the pressure-regulated air gently pushed into the bowel, the bowel began to expand and the constricted part finally untelescoped.

'Bingo,' Lenox said with a smile. 'You've done it. Happy about managing the after-care?'

'Yes.'

'Good. You can go and talk to the parents on your own.'

She smiled at him, and went to see Maia's parents. 'You'll be pleased to know the procedure was a complete success, so Maia won't need to go for surgery. We're going to keep her in for a day or so, just to keep an eye on her and sort out her fluids, but she should be fine.'

'Oh, thank God,' Maia's mother said.

'Could she get it again?' Maia's father asked.

'It's extremely unlikely,' Natalie reassured them.

'Thank you so much, Dr Wilkins.'

Natalie smiled, and left them making a fuss over their little girl. So this was what being a doctor was all about. Making a difference. Helping.

She could almost understand why Kit had buried himself in his job.

Almost.

It was good to be home. Well, not quite home, Kit thought. He hadn't actually lived in Birmingham when he'd worked there before. He'd lived in Litchford-in-Arden, a little Warwickshire village halfway between Birmingham and Stratford-upon-Avon, in a picture-postcard cottage that overlooked the village green with its duck-pond and huge oak tree. Close to an ancient church where part of his heart would always lie.

When his world had fallen apart, Kit had fled to London. He'd wanted to lose himself in the anonymity of the city, avoid the pitying glances and the sympathy of people around him. It had worked for a while, but the busyness of the city had never really eased the ache in his heart. He'd never quite been able to block it out, no matter how many hours he worked or how hard he drove himself.

Now he was back. Near enough maybe to find some peace, but far enough away that people around him wouldn't know about the past. And, more to the point, they wouldn't offer him the pity he didn't want—didn't *need*. He was a paediatric specialist, and a good one, on track to becoming a consultant. He'd be good for St Joseph's, and St Joseph's would be good for him. Yes, this was going to work out just fine.

And everything *was* fine until he walked into the staffroom and saw the woman in a white coat talking to another woman in a sister's uniform. His heart missed a beat.

Tally.

Except it couldn't be. Tally was a teacher, not a doctor. And this woman had short, cropped hair instead of Tally's Pre-Raphaelite curls. She was thinner than Tally, too. No, he was just seeing things. Wishful thinking, maybe. And he needed to get his subconscious wishes back under control, right now. Stop seeing his ex-wife in every stranger's face. The past was the past and it was going to stay that way.

And then the woman looked up, saw him and every bit of colour leached from her face.

He wouldn't be surprised if he'd gone just as white. Because it really was her. It was the first time they'd met in five and a half years. 'Tally?' The name felt as if it had been ripped from him.

'Natalie,' she corrected. 'Hello, Kit.'

Her voice was like ice. A voice that had once been warm and soft, a voice that had once slurred his name in passion.

But that had been before Ethan.

'Do you two know each other?' the nurse she'd been talking to asked.

'We went to the same university,' Tally cut in quickly. 'We haven't seen each other in years.'

It was the truth. But very, very far from the whole truth. Obviously Tally didn't want to admit just how well they'd known each other.

Then again, Kit didn't exactly want the whole truth known either. Or the gossip and speculation that was bound to go with it.

Hell, hell, hell. If he'd had any idea that Tally had become a doctor—that she was working here—he would never have come to St Joseph's. He'd have stayed in London. Maybe even gone abroad for a while, got some experience in America or worked for Doctors Without Borders.

A quick glance at her ID badge told him that Tally was using her maiden name. Not that that meant anything. She might be married again now. Though he couldn't see a ring on her left hand, or a tell-tale band of paler skin on her ring finger. Maybe not married, then. Probably living with someone. Family was important to Natalie. She wouldn't be living on her own. She'd clearly moved on with her life.

Just like he had.

And he damped down the 'if only' before it had a chance to echo in his head.

He focused on the nurse and extended his hand. 'Kit Rodgers. Pleased to meet you. I'm the new boy.'

'And I'm Debbie Jacobs. Senior sister, for my sins.' The nurse smiled at him. 'Well, you've plenty in common with our Natalie, then. She's new, too—she started yesterday.' She gave them both a curious look. 'Since you know each other, you two must have a lot to catch up on.'

Natalie's reaction was clearly written on her face. *Not if I can help it.*

'We didn't really know each other that well,' Kit said coolly. Again, not the whole truth, but true enough. By the end, they'd been complete strangers. Living separate lives. And he'd wondered if he'd ever really known her.

'Natalie, maybe you can show Kit where everything is?'

'Um, yes. Sure.' And she smiled.

Oh, hell. He knew that smile. The bright one that pretended nothing was wrong—when, inside, everything was wrong. The one that spelled trouble with a capital T.

This was surreal. Natalie was showing Kit around the ward—and they were both acting as if they were polite strangers. Considering they'd known each other much more intimately, this was crazy.

'So you're a house officer. I didn't know you'd become a doctor. Your parents never said,' Kit remarked.

Natalie stared at him in shock. Her parents? Why would her parents have said anything to him about her change in career? 'You stayed in touch with them?'

He shrugged. 'Just Christmas and birthdays.'

Strange. She couldn't remember ever seeing a card from him on the mantelpiece. Or maybe her mum had kept it to one side when she had been around. Trying to save her daughter from more hurt. Seeing Kit's name in a card, maybe with another woman's name added after it.

And Natalie had to admit, it would've hurt. A lot. Even though, logically, she knew, of course, Kit had moved on. He was probably married by now. A man like Kit Rodgers wouldn't have stayed on his own for long. With cornflower blue eyes, dark hair and a killer smile, he was drop-dead gorgeous. Women adored him. Even when she'd been married to him, women had chased him. He'd never been short of offers, even though he'd always turned them down. Lack of fidelity wasn't one of his faults.

'You know your mum,' Kit continued. 'She always writes a lovely note in with a card.'

He sounded affectionate towards her parents. Though it wasn't so surprising. She knew he'd loved them—and they'd adored him. So had her younger sisters. Kit had the ability to charm just about anyone he met. Of course her parents would have stayed in touch with him.

Though Kit's parents hadn't stayed in touch with her. Also not surprising: they'd always been slightly wary of each other. Kit's family had always made her feel as if she wasn't quite good enough, as if a BA and a PCGE were somehow the second-class option, well beneath the notice of a family of doctors. She'd never really fitted in. Kit's parents and his three older brothers had all been medics, all high flyers. They'd seen her as a distraction, the person who'd stopped Kit achieving his full potential. She knew it wasn't true and she would have shrugged it off quite cheerfully, had it not been the fact they'd blamed her for Ethan.

Natalie pushed the thought back where it belonged—locked away with all the other feelings—and gave him a whistle-stop tour of the ward. 'This is the staffroom. Lockers here, kettle here, tea and coffee here, mugs in that cupboard, biscuits in the tin, milk in the fridge. Debbie has the kitty—and she's the one you tell if you notice we're running low on anything.' Out of the staffroom, back on to the ward. 'Nurses' station, patient board, so you know who's the nominated nurse, parents' phone, parents' room.'

Done and dusted.

'Thank you, Tally.'

'Natalie,' she corrected, annoyed at the amusement in his voice. So what if she'd rushed showing him round? Besides, she wasn't 'Tally' any more. To anyone.

She sneaked a glance at him. He'd barely changed in the last few years. A couple of grey hairs around his temples, a couple more lines on his face. But basically Kit Rodgers was the same. The epitome of tall, dark and handsome. Charming and easygoing with it, too—the female staff in the hospital would be falling at his feet in droves. So would the patients. And their parents. There wouldn't be any difficult cases on Nightingale Ward when Kit Rodgers was around: that easy-going smile was too infectious. Men would identify with him and women would fall for him. He'd manage to get a good response from even the stroppiest parent.

Except maybe from her.

She knew better. She'd keep things cool and professional between them.

He wasn't wearing a wedding ring, she noticed. Not that that meant anything. He hadn't worn one before either. Well, she wasn't going to ask him if he was married. And she definitely wasn't going to ask the question that usually went with that one. She wasn't interested.

Ha. Who was she trying to kid? More like, she wasn't sure she could handle the answer.

'I, um, need to get ready for the ward round,' she said. 'Catch you later.' As in preferably much later. Better still, as in not at all. 'Lenox's office is just there.'

And she walked away, quickly, while she still could.

CHAPTER TWO

NATALIE managed to avoid Kit for most of the morning, and at lunchtime she had the unimpeachable excuse of needing to get her shoes reheeled during her lunch-break. But in the afternoon they were both rostered to the outpatient clinic. Thrown together. No respite.

Well, she could deal with this. Kit was just another doctor. A colleague. She'd keep him neatly pigeonholed there.

'So, would this be your first clinic since you qualified?' Kit asked as they headed to the outpatients area.

'Yes,' she admitted.

'OK. You lead. I'll be here for back-up, if you need me.'

Being supportive? *Kit?* Well. Maybe he'd grown up in the last six years. He was thirty now, after all. And he was the more experienced doctor out of the two of them. Several rungs higher than she was. He was just doing what she'd do if the positions were reversed. Giving a junior doctor a chance to gain experience, with a safety net if it was needed.

But this *was* her first proper clinic. And he wanted her to lead. Take responsibility. 'What if I miss something?' she asked.

He shrugged. 'Then I'll bring it up in conversation

with the parents. But I won't tear you off a strip in front of them or make you look incompetent, if that's what you're thinking.'

She felt her skin heat. 'I wasn't sniping at you. What I meant was, I might get something wrong, put a patient at risk.' She was worried that she wasn't totally ready for this, that maybe in her first clinic she should take a supportive role rather than a lead. 'Are you going to take everything I say personally, for goodness' sake?'

He raked a hand through his hair. 'No. Sorry.'

It had probably been gut reaction. She supposed it must be just as difficult for him, having to work with her and ignore their history. And there had been plenty of sniping in their last few months together. Mainly by her—because Kit hadn't been there often enough and the frustration and misery had made her temper short.

'You'll be fine in clinic. You're qualified, so you obviously know your stuff. If it's something with a tricky diagnosis, something that could easily be mistaken for a different condition, I'll be here to take a look. I'll give a second opinion when you ask for it, and I'll back you up,' Kit said.

Just what she needed to hear. And if only he'd been that supportive all those years ago, when she'd really needed him. Someone she could have leaned on when her strength had deserted her.

But you couldn't change the past. Mentally, Natalie slammed the door on it and locked the key.

The first parent on their list was Ella Byford. She was reading a story to two rather grubby children who seemed to be squabbling about who was going to get the best place on her lap, while rubbing her back in the way that most heavily pregnant women did.

Something Natalie had once—

No. She clenched her teeth hard, just once, to relieve the tension, then reminded herself to keep her personal life out of this. She was a doctor. A paediatrician in training. This was her job. And she was going to do it well. She pinned a smile on her face. 'Hello, Mrs Byford. I'm Natalie Wilkins and this is Kit Rodgers. We're holding the paediatric clinic today. What can we do for you?'

'It's Charlene. Jayden's all right, he's doing fine.' Ella waved a dismissive hand towards her son. 'But Charlene's so *skinny*. She's not doing as well as she should. She's always been small for dates, but she's getting worse.' Ella bit her lip. 'I went to see my GP about her, and he sent me here.'

'Let's have a look at her,' Natalie said. She knelt on the floor so she was nearer to the little girl's height. 'Hello, Charlene.'

''Lo.' The little girl looked at her and scowled.

OK, she could do this. Thin, small for dates. The little girl was quite pale—perhaps she just didn't get to play outside very much, or her mum was rigorous with a high protection factor suncream. Or maybe it was anaemic pallor. Natalie needed to check for icterus—or a yellowish colour—too. Starting with the child's fingernails, palms, mucous membranes of the mouth and the conjunctiva. The conjunctiva would be the tricky part—children hated having their eyes fussed with.

'Can you open your mouth for me and say "a-ah"?' she asked.

'A-ah.' It lasted all of half a second, but it was enough to show Natalie that there was slight pallor in Charlene's mouth but no icterus. It didn't look as if there were any ulcers, but if Natalie saw any other sinister signs in the rest of the examination she'd try for a second look.

'And can I look at your hands now?'

Charlene scowled at her and tried to climb back on her mother's lap.

'Charlene, be nice for the doctor,' Ella admonished her.

'It's not fair. I want to sit on your lap. He *always* does.' Charlene shoved at her brother, who promptly fell off Ella's lap and started howling.

Kit stepped in smoothly. 'Hey. How about I read you a story, Jayden, while the doctor talks to your mum and your sister?' He took two shiny stickers from his pocket. 'And if you can both sit really still while the doctor's talking—and while the doctor's looking at you, Charlene—you can both have a special sticker.'

Why hadn't *she* thought of that? Natalie wondered. And as a distraction technique it clearly worked, because Charlene immediately nodded, climbed onto her mother's lap and sat still, while Jayden plonked himself on Kit's lap so he could see the pictures in the story book. Ella, who'd looked close to tears, suddenly relaxed.

Teamwork. Good teamwork. And Natalie wasn't going to let herself think about the fact that Kit was reading a story to a little boy.

'OK, Charlene. Shall we see if your hands are bigger than mine?'

'Don't be silly. They'll be smaller.'

'Bet they're not,' Natalie said, putting her own hands behind her back.

Charlene giggled. 'They are.'

'Show me, then.'

To Natalie's relief, when she brought her hands round

again, Charlene splayed her palms and pressed them against Natalie's.

'Side by side now. Palm up,' Natalie said.

The little girl, clearly thinking it was a game, did as she asked. Her palms were definitely pale, though at least there was no sign of yellowness.

'And the back, to see if you have princess nails?'

'You haven't got princess nails. They're not glittery,' Charlene said.

Natalie was glad that Charlene's weren't either: it gave her the chance to notice that the little girl's fingernails were concave.

'Can I look at your tummy now?'

'Can I look at yours?' Charlene asked.

'Not this time,' Natalie said with a smile. She definitely wasn't baring any flesh in front of Kit. 'But if you want to play doctors while I talk to your mummy, you can look at a doll's tummy and see what you can hear through my stethoscope.'

Charlene wriggled a bit, but submitted to an examination. Natalie palpated her abdomen gently. She didn't think there was a problem with the spleen, but maybe she should ask Kit for a second opinion. No sign of petechiae, reddish-purple pinhead spots, which would lead to a more sinister diagnosis. And, she was pleased to note, there were no signs of enlarged lymph nodes in Charlene's neck.

As soon as she'd finished, Charlene was wriggling around on Ella's lap again, and Ella pressed one fist into her lower back for support. Natalie gave Ella a sympathetic smile. It must be hard, dealing with small children when you were heavily pregnant and tired.

'She's a handful for such a little scrap,' Ella said, looking embarrassed.

Oh, no. That hadn't been what she'd intended at all. Or maybe Ella was just used to being defensive about her little girl. 'Lively, the medical term is,' Natalie said with a smile. 'How's she eating?'

Ella grimaced. 'She's picky. She won't eat any vegetables—she just throws them on the floor—and she doesn't like anything with meat in it, even if I try to hide it. But I can get her to eat potatoes and eggs, and she drinks milk and fruit juice.'

It was nowhere near a balanced diet, and Ella was clearly aware of it—distressed about it, too, so Natalie decided to take the gentle approach. 'Kids are notorious for that—one day they'll eat something, and the next they won't touch it,' she said reassuringly. 'How about you take me through right from the start, from when she was first born?' She could already see that Charlene had had a low birthweight, something that could predispose her to anaemia. 'Did she have any jaundice afterwards?'

'She was a bit yellow, but the midwife said it was normal.'

Natalie nodded. 'Most babies have it to some extent.' Though Ethan hadn't. He'd been a perfect seven and a half pounds. No problems at all. Prolonged jaundice in the newborn could suggest congenital anaemia. 'How long did it last?'

'A week or so.'

'How was she feeding?'

'I breastfed her for about a week.' Ella grimaced. 'I tried so hard, but I just couldn't manage it. My husband works long hours and it was too much for me. I got so tired—she seemed to be constantly attached to me, just taking little bits here and there, and I never got a break. And I was so sore.'

No support at home, and a husband who wasn't there more often than not. Yeah, Natalie could empathise with that one. Really empathise. She couldn't help glancing at Kit—and looked away again the second she met his cornflower-blue gaze. She just hoped she wasn't blushing. Hell. This was meant to be about her patient, not about her and Kit.

'So I switched her to formula milk,' Ella continued.

And felt she'd failed as a result. It was very clear in Ella's face—guilt, worry that she'd done the wrong thing, that she'd given up at the first hurdle without really trying. 'Hey, that's fine,' Natalie said. 'I know you read everywhere that breast is best, but you have to do what works for you as a family. Don't listen to anyone who tries to make you feel bad or says you did the wrong thing. How did she take to formula milk?'

'OK. I started putting a bit of rice in to her milk when she was two months old, to help her sleep a bit better and stop her being hungry in the night.'

Ouch. That sounded as if Ella had been desperate and had taken advice from the older generation—probably someone who'd gone on and on and on when Ella had been tired, about how Ella had been a baby who had always woken in the night and a bit of rice had never hurt her. Nowadays, the recommendation was to wait until at least four months before weaning.

Careful not to pass judgment, Natalie asked, 'What happened then?'

'She slept through, but she dropped a bit of weight then, and when she was three months the health visitor said maybe we'd be better off with a soya-based formula.' Ella bit her lip. 'But her charts still kept doing down.'

'Do you have the charts with you, by any chance?' Natalie asked.

'Oh, yes. I've got her red book.' Ella dug in her handbag and eventually brought out a slightly dog-eared book with a C written neatly on the front. Natalie flicked to the charts. At birth, Charlene's weight had been a little below average, on the fortieth centile: meaning that sixty per cent of babies at the same age would be heavier than she was. By three months, Charlene had dropped to the tenth centile, from six to twelve months her weight was on the third centile, and the measurement the paediatric nurse had done a few minutes before showed she'd dropped below even that. Charlene's height, too, was below average, on the twenty-fifth centile. But Ella had clearly taken care to have her daughter's height and weight measured regularly, and as Natalie flicked through the book she noticed that all the immunisations were up to date.

'She's a bit of a tomboy,' Ella said apologetically as Charlene stopped fidgeting, wriggled off her lap and headed straight for the toybox, emptying the entire contents out. 'I've stopped trying to keep her clean all day. She starts out with fresh clothes, but if I changed her every time she gets grubby...well. I'd never have the washing machine off. So I just put her in the bath every night and give her a good wash.' She bit her lip. 'I was wondering if she had—' her voice lowered in obvious embarrassment '—worms, or something. If that's why she's skinny. Can you do an X-ray or something to check?'

'An X-ray's probably not going to be very helpful right now,' Natalie said gently, 'and we don't want to expose Charlene to radiation if we don't really have to. As for the other problem—' she'd picked up on how awkward Ella clearly felt '—you'd be surprised at just how common it is. Kids pick them up really easily. Does she talk about itching at all? Or do you see her scratching her bottom?'

'Well, no,' Ella admitted.

'It's unlikely to be worms, then,' Natalie reassured her. 'Though if you really want to be sure, when she's asleep tonight, take a torch and shine it on her bottom. If you see anything white and wriggling, you'll need to nip into the chemist and get some worming treatment—and do the whole family, not just Charlene. You'll also need to keep her nails really short and get a soft nailbrush to keep them clean. What happens with worms is that a child scratches their bottom and some tiny eggs—so small you can't see them—can end up beneath their nails. Kids that age normally have their hands in their mouth half the time so the eggs come out again, and the whole cycle starts again. It's not anything you've done, so don't worry.' She paused. 'Does Charlene eat anything odd?' She was pretty sure the problem was chronic iron deficiency, and pica—eating abnormal things that weren't food, such as coal—often went with it.

Ella shook her head. 'I try and keep her off chips but sometimes it's just easier to give in. At least then I know she's eaten something.'

'What about the toilet? Is she dry at night?'

'Been out of nappies for ages. Just as well—Jayden isn't, and I don't think I could cope with three of them in nappies,' Ella admitted.

Natalie smiled at her. 'That'd be quite a tough call. Tell me, is anyone else in the family very light, or quite short?'

Ella shrugged. 'We're all pretty average, really.'

Not a genetic thing, then. The next thing to rule out was the possibility of a developmental disorder. She doubted it, because she'd heard for herself that Charlene's speech was clear and her words were average for a three-year-old. 'Is there anything you've noticed about the way she behaves, or the way she speaks?'

Ella shook her head. 'She's just a bit lively and a bit of a tomboy.' She frowned. 'You don't think she has that thing where she'll have to go on Ritalin, do you?'

'ADHD? No,' Natalie said, shaking her head. 'I think it's all to do with her being a fussy eater. It means she isn't getting a balanced diet, and her iron stores are too low.' Plus she'd been weaned too early. 'She's probably anaemic and iron deficient. It's not serious,' she reassured Ella, 'and I can give you some iron supplements to help that. She'll need to take them for about three months. But I'll also refer you to a dietician, so she can help you with a few coping strategies to persuade Charlene to eat some meat and a few more vegetables.'

'I do *try*,' Ella said.

'Of course you do. But sometimes you can do with a helping hand,' Natalie said. 'Being a parent's one of the hardest jobs on earth.' Though not being a parent could sometimes be even harder. She shook herself. 'I'd like to take a blood sample and a wee sample, so I can check the chemicals in Charlene's blood and that her kidneys and liver are working as they should be. I'll give you a follow-up appointment for a fortnight's time so I can check her weight and height and how she's responding to treatment.' She paused. 'When are you due?'

'In a month, though Jayden was three weeks early and this one might be the same.'

'Maybe Charlene's dad can bring her in?' Natalie suggested.

'He's busy at work,' Ella said swiftly. 'And he never remembers appointments anyway.'

Unsupportive husband. Oh, Natalie knew all about that.

The sympathy must have shown on her face, because Ella added, 'But I'll try.' With the same defensive note Natalie remembered in her own voice when she'd been the one making excuses.

Natalie took the blood sample—following it up immediately with one of Kit's stickers—and talked Ella through taking the urine sample, then directed her to the reception area to book the next appointment.

'What are you going to order?' Kit asked as Natalie labelled the sample.

'Full blood count, differential, electrolytes, calcium, phosphate, magnesium, iron, ferritin, folate, albumin and total protein, plus renal and liver function.'

He smiled. 'Perfect.'

'I didn't miss anything, then?'

He spread his hands. 'Maybe the involvement of Social Services?'

Natalie stared at him. 'You must be joking. You don't seriously think this is abuse by neglect, do you?'

'Convince me,' Kit said, his voice and face completely neutral so she couldn't even guess what he was thinking.

'In a month's time, Ella Byford will have a newborn, a toddler and an under-four. Her partner clearly doesn't pull his weight with the kids and she's making excuses for him—sure, she's having trouble coping right now and she needs a bit of support, but it's definitely not neglect. Firstly, she's the one who went to her GP because she was worried—it wasn't the health visitor or GP prompting the appointment. Secondly, Charlene's vaccinations are all up to date—which they wouldn't be if she was being neglected. And, thirdly, Ella's been meticulous about recording weight measurements. It's not just the health visitor or GP's measurements on the chart—some of the entries had Ella's initials against them. This isn't a mum who's neglecting her kids, it's a mum who's having a rough time and needs support she isn't getting from her partner.'

The words echoed between them and she couldn't meet his eyes.

But Kit's voice was perfectly level as he said, 'Good call. I agree with your assessment. But,' he added, 'remember that you're dealing with patients. You need to keep your personal feelings out of it.'

The rebuke stung, the more so because she knew it was merited. She *was* bringing her personal feelings into it, and it was the wrong thing to do.

'I'll bear it in mind,' she said, matching the coolness of his tone.

'Good. Next patient, I think.'

They got through the rest of the clinic, and Kit surprised her at the end by saying, 'You did well.'

'Thank you.' Though she didn't meet his eyes.

He sighed. 'Tal—'

'Natalie,' she corrected swiftly. 'My name is Natalie.'

'Natalie.' He gritted his teeth. 'Look, we're going to have to work together for a while. Six months, at least. So maybe we should just... I dunno. Clear the air between us.'

She thought not. Some things couldn't be cleared. Ever.

'We're both due a break. Let's go and have a coffee,' he said.

She didn't want to. How could she possibly sit across the table from Kit and pretend everything was all right? Because it wasn't all right. Never would be.

He sighed. 'Natalie, if we leave this, it's just going to get worse. We need to set some ground rules. And it won't kill you to sit at a table with me and drink coffee.' His mouth gave the tiniest quirk. 'Though I'd appreciate it if you drank it rather than threw it at me.'

'Since when did you learn to read minds?'

'It's written all over your face,' he said wryly.

At the canteen, she refused to let him pay for her cappuccino, and he didn't press the point. He still drank black coffee, she noticed—obviously he hadn't broken the habit from his student days. Or his habit of snacking on chocolate: he'd bought a brownie with his coffee.

'So what made you become a doctor?' he asked when he'd taken his first sip of coffee.

She exhaled sharply. 'What do you think?'

'The same reason I switched from surgery to paediatrics,' he said softly. 'It won't change the past. But I might be able to help someone in the future. Stop them going through…'

He left the words unsaid, but she knew exactly what Kit was thinking. He could have been speaking for her. His voice had even held that same hopeless yearning when he'd said it—knowing he couldn't change the past, but wanting to anyway. And wanting other people not to have to go through what they'd been through.

Natalie willed the tears to stay back. She'd cried all she was ever going to cry over Kit Rodgers. No more.

'You've done well,' Kit said. 'Lenox was telling me how you were the star student of your year.'

Natalie shrugged. 'I studied hard.' And it hadn't been completely new ground. She could remember some of it from the time when she'd helped Kit revise for his finals.

Tally really wasn't going to make this easy. Not that he could blame her. He'd let her down when she'd needed him most.

But seeing her again, like this… It made him realise how much he'd missed her. How empty his life had been without her. And why he hadn't bothered dating very often, let alone having a serious relationship. He'd always claimed once bitten, twice shy, and all that, but now he had to admit there was a little more to it than that.

Simply, nobody had ever been able to match up to Tally.

He understood why she hated him. He'd hated her, too, at one point. Especially the day she'd walked out on him and left him that bloody note saying she wanted a divorce and her solicitor would be in touch. But he'd missed her. Missed the way she'd said his name. Missed her smile, missed her quick wit, missed her touch.

Part of him thought that everything would be all right if he could just touch her, hold her, say he was sorry and ask her to wipe the slate clean.

But he knew that slate could never be wiped clean. And touching her was out of the question. There was a brick wall twenty feet high between them, with an enormous ditch either side filled with barbed wire.

Ah, hell. They were supposed to be clearing the air between them—his idea—and now he was tongue-tied. He made an effort. 'Where are you living now?'

'Birmingham.'

She wasn't giving a millimetre—wouldn't even tell him where she lived. Birmingham was a city of almost a million people, so she could be living just about anywhere within a radius of twenty miles of St Joseph's.

'Me, too. I'm renting,' he said.

No response—no 'Me, too' or 'I'm in the middle of buying a flat'. She was freezing him out. Frustration made him sharp. 'I thought about seeing if there was anywhere to rent in Litchford-in-Arden,' he said, watching her closely.

She flinched at the name of the village.

Good. So she wasn't entirely frozen, then.

'I drove through the village yesterday.' He waited a beat. 'Past our house.'

She still said nothing, but he noticed she was gripping her coffee-mug and her knuckles were white. She was clearly trying not to react, but he wasn't going to let her do it. He'd get over the barrier between them, even if he had to make her crack first. He'd *make* her talk to him.

'There was a...'

But there was a lump in his throat blocking the words. He couldn't say it. It hurt too much, and at the realisation his anger died. What was the point of this? It was hurting both of them, and it wasn't going to solve a thing.

'A child. About six years old. Playing in the garden. I know,' Tally said, her voice shaky as she continued what he'd been about to say. 'I...went back, too. A couple of weeks ago. The woman was weeding the garden.' Her breath hitched. 'She was pregnant.'

Kit could remember Tally, pregnant, weeding their garden. Tending her flowers—she'd made it a proper cottage garden with hollyhocks and lavender and love-in-a-mist. To see another woman doing the same thing, in *their* garden—pregnant, with a child around six years old cycling round the garden—must have burned like acid in her soul.

He'd found it hard enough to handle, seeing someone else living their dreams. For Tally, it must have been so much worse. And he hated the fact that he hadn't been there to hold her, comfort her when she'd discovered it.

But he was here now. He could do something now. He reached out and took her free hand. Squeezed it gently. 'It should have been us, Tally,' he said quietly. 'It should have been us.'

She wrenched her hand away. 'But it isn't. Wasn't. We can't change the past, Kit. We can't go back. Someone else lives there now.'

In their house. The house where they'd made love. The house where they'd made a baby.

The house where their dreams had died. Where their love had been reduced to solicitors' letters. Cold legal words. The end of everything.

'We have to work together,' Tally said, 'but that's as far as it goes. I'm sure we're both mature enough to be civil to each other.'

'Of course.'

A muscle flickered in her jaw. 'I don't think there's anything left to say. We've both moved on.'

Had they? 'Are you married?'

'That's not relevant.'

Which told him nothing. And she clearly didn't want to know whether he was or not, because she didn't ask. He really, really should let this go.

So why couldn't he?

'Tal— Natalie,' he corrected himself swiftly, 'It doesn't have to be like this.'

She pushed her chair back. 'Let's just agree to disagree, hmm?'

And then she was walking away from him.
Again.
And he was left with the feeling that he'd just made things a hell of a lot worse.

CHAPTER THREE

FOR the next couple of days, Natalie successfully continued to avoid Kit. But then they were rostered together again, this time on the paediatric assessment unit.

'Dr Wilkins, I take it this is your first PAU?' Kit asked.

On an intellectual level, she knew the formality was the right way to go—keeping a professional distance between them would be a good thing—but, oh, it stung. Had they really been reduced to this, to titles and surnames, after everything they'd shared? 'Correct, Dr Rodgers,' she responded, equally coolly.

'Do you want to do this as a teaching session, or would you like to lead and I'll back you up?'

He was giving her the choice. Not much of one. Either way, they had to work together. Closely. And she was finding it harder than she'd expected. Every time she glanced up at him she remembered other places, other times, when she'd caught his eye and seen a different expression there. Blue eyes filled with love and laughter. A lazy smile that had promised her some very personal attention once they were alone.

And now he was this cool, remote stranger. Just like he'd

been at the end of their marriage. Reacting to nothing and nobody. Closed off.

'PAU's where we get the urgent referrals, isn't it?' she asked.

'Yes.'

Where her diagnoses really could mean life or death. She took a deep breath. 'Right.' Was she ready for this?

'Or we could lead on alternate cases. Do it together,' Kit added.

His tone of voice on the last word made her look at him. The expression in his eyes was quickly masked, but she'd seen something there. Something that surprised her. Regret, wishing things could have been different?

She pushed it to the back of her mind. Of course not. She was just wishing for something that wasn't there. Kit had shut her out six years ago, and he wasn't about to invite her back into his life now.

They'd both moved on.

Well, *he* had.

'OK.'

'Want me to take the first one?' he asked.

'Whatever you think best, Dr Rodgers,' she said, her voice completely without expression.

'In that case,' Kit said, 'I'm throwing you in at the deep end. You go first.'

Oh, Lord. She hadn't been expecting that. But if that was the way he wanted to play it, she'd show him she could do it—that she didn't need his help.

Their first case was a two-year-old with a fever and a rash. Ross Morley's eyes were red, as if he had conjunctivitis, although there didn't appear to be any discharge. 'He's had a temperature for a couple of days but he seems to be getting worse,' Mrs Morley said, twisting her hands together. 'His hands and feet look a bit red and I'm sure they're not normally as puffy as this. And then I saw this rash…'

'And you're worried that it's meningitis?' Natalie guessed.

Mrs Morley dragged in a breath. 'Don't let it be that. He's my only one. Please, don't let it be that.'

'Rashes can be scary,' Natalie said gently, 'but there are lots of things that can cause a rash like this.' Gently, she stretched the little boy's skin over the spotty area. 'The spots have faded, see? So it's unlikely to be meningitis—though you've done absolutely the right thing to bring him here,' she reassured Mrs Morley. 'If it had been meningitis, he could have become seriously ill extremely quickly. Has he been immunised against measles?'

'Yes. He had the MMR at fifteen months.'

'It's unlikely to be rubella or measles, then.' Natalie swiftly took the little boy's temperature with the ear thermometer—definitely raised. She continued examining him and noted that the lymph nodes in his neck were swollen. 'It could be glandular fever—what we call infectious mononucleosis—or this could be his body's reaction to a virus, most likely an echovirus.' She swallowed hard. 'Or Coxsackie virus.'

She couldn't help glancing at Kit. Saw her own pain echoed in his eyes. And she had to look away and clamp her teeth together so the sob would stay back. Coxsackie B. The tiny, invisible virus that had smashed her life into equally tiny pieces.

She turned back to the little boy and finished her examination. 'His skin's starting to peel at the fingertips.'

'He doesn't suck his thumb or anything,' Mrs Morley said. 'Never has.'

'I think Ross has Kawasaki disease,' Natalie said. 'Peeling skin's one of the signs, plus he has the rash, the redness and slight swelling in his hands, his eyes are red, his lips are dry and cracked, and he has a fever.' Kawasaki disease tended to be diagnosed clinically rather than through blood tests, and Ross Morley's case ticked all the boxes. She glanced at Kit for confirmation.

He nodded, and mouthed, 'Good call.'

She damped down the feeling of pleasure. She was doing this to help people, not to prove something to Kit.

'So what happens now?' Mrs Morley asked.

'We're going to admit him to the ward,' Natalie said. 'The good news is we can treat the disease. We'll give him aspirin and a drip with immunoglobulin drugs to fight the disease. Over the next few days, the fever and the swollen glands in his neck will go down and the rash will disappear, but Ross's eyes will still look a bit red and sore and the skin's going to continue peeling around his fingers, toes and the nappy area. He might feel some pain in his joints and you'll probably find he's a bit irritable, but the good news is that you'll be able to take him home next week and all the symptoms will gradually disappear. It'll take him another three weeks or so after that before he's completely over it, though.'

'Will there be any complications?'

Possibly myocarditis—inflammation of the heart muscle—but although Natalie's mouth opened, the words just wouldn't come out. Couldn't. The lump in her throat was too big.

'There can be complications with Kawasaki disease,' Kit said softly. 'Some children have arthritis afterwards, and some develop heart problems, but we'll send him for a follow-up echo to make sure—that's an ultrasound scan of the heart and it won't hurt at all, plus you can be with him while it's being done.'

Mrs Morley swallowed hard. 'Could he die?' she whispered.

'Most children make a full recovery,' Kit reassured her.

Most children. But myocarditis could be deadly. Sometimes there weren't even any symptoms. In very small children it was difficult to tell the problem—they couldn't tell you if they had chest pain, were tired or had palpitations. You just noticed the difficulty in breathing, which could be caused by just about any of the viruses causing a cough or cold in a little one. The over-fast heartbeat could only be picked up by monitoring. And the average person in the street wouldn't even know what S1 and S4 were, let alone that S1—the first heart sound, when the mitral and tricuspid valves closed—was soft if there was myocarditis, and S4—the fourth heart sound—made a galloping noise, like 'Tennessee', when tachycardia was involved. And then the heart stopped pumping efficiently. Failed. And finally stopped.

Just as Ethan's had. And all she'd been able to do had been to hold her little boy in her arms as his heart had finally given out and the life had seeped from his body. Natalie clenched her fists hard, willing herself to stay strong.

Though she was sure that Kit was thinking of Ethan, too. Especially because she noticed the tiniest wobble in his voice when he added, 'We'll get Ross booked onto the ward, Mrs Morley, and one of the nurses will take you up and help you settle him in.'

'Can I—can I ring my husband? He's at work. I was just so worried about Ross this morning, I couldn't wait for him to get home.'

Oh, yes. Natalie had been there, too. So sure that something was wrong, she hadn't waited for Kit. She'd left a message for him at work and taken Ethan to the emergency department. A mother's instinct was usually right: it was one of the things she'd been taught at med school. Parents knew when something was wrong with their children—they couldn't always put their finger on it, and the words 'he's just not right' were usually justified, on examining the child.

'No problem,' Kit said. 'I'll get our nurse to show you where the phone is. There's a special phone on our ward, too, which we keep as the parents' phone—you can give the number out if people want to ring you for an update, and you don't have to worry about blocking the ward's main line.'

When they handed Mrs Morley and Ross over to the liaison nurse, Kit turned to Natalie. 'Are you OK?'

'Sure,' she lied. 'Why shouldn't I be?' Though she could hear the cracks in her own voice. Ha. At least he wasn't bawling her out for not doing her job properly. He could have picked her up on the fact that she hadn't told Mrs Morley what the complications were. But he clearly understood how hard she found it to say the words. How she could barely breathe—it felt as if someone had put her whole body in a vice and was slowly, slowly squeezing it.

'If you want to take five minutes, have a glass of water or what have you, that's fine,' Kit said.

But that would be showing weakness. As good as saying that she couldn't cope with her job. And she *could*. It had just caught her unawares this time. Next time she'd handle it better. 'No, I'm fine,' she said tightly. 'I'm doing my job. I don't need mollycoddling.'

Perhaps she was being a little bloody-minded. But it jarred that Kit was trying to soften things for her now.

When she'd needed his support, six years ago, he hadn't been there.

'If you're sure.'

She couldn't stand him being so nice to her. Kindness wasn't what she wanted from Kit.

Though she wasn't going to think about what she did want from him.

'Tally. *Natalie*,' he corrected himself quickly, 'paediatrics is a tough option. Especially at this time of year. You're going to come across cases that remind you. Cases that have parallels. And some days you'll find it harder to deal with than others.'

Meaning that he did, too? She'd noticed that he hadn't actually said Ethan's name aloud. Would the word choke him, too?

Kit laid his hand on her shoulder. Squeezed it, giving the lightest of pressure. 'Natalie, if you need—'

No. She didn't need anything from Kit. 'We have a full list. Let's move on,' she cut in quickly. If he offered her a shoulder to cry on now, nearly six years too late, she couldn't bear it. She shrugged his hand off her shoulder, too—a white coat and her sweater weren't enough of a barrier between them. Right now she couldn't cope with feeling the warmth of his touch.

His voice cooled noticeably. 'Of course, Dr Wilkins.'

Somehow she got through the rest of the afternoon. But the more she saw of Kit working—the way he was able to soothe the most fretful child—the more she realised how good he was with kids. They responded to him, to his strength and calmness, someone who was clearly going to take the pain away and make them feel better.

He didn't rush through diagnoses either. He'd read a story if it was needed, or start telling a series of truly terrible jokes—jokes she'd had no idea he even knew—and made a game out of examinations. Let children listen to his heartbeat through his stethoscope. Took time to calm the worries of parents. Explained exactly what he was doing in terms the parents would understand, without frightening the child.

And she couldn't help thinking what a great dad he would have made. How he would have been with his own children, dealing with tantrums and tears without letting them fray his temper. He'd still have kept his fun side, too, flying kites and racing round on a bicycle and playing boisterous games with them.

What a waste. What a bloody, bloody *waste*.

Or was it? Did Kit have another family now? Another son to replace the one he'd lost? A daughter, perhaps, one who looked like his new wife?

Natalie wasn't sure what was worse: thinking about the dad he might have been, or thinking about the dad he might be now—to another woman's children, not hers.

It broke her up inside, though she managed to keep a cool front. Even had coffee with him after their PAU stint, although neither of them spoke much and they kept the topics strictly neutral. Work. Safe areas.

And then she had two blessed days off. Two days when she wasn't going to think of Kit at all. And by Monday, when she was on duty again, she'd be back in full control of her feelings.

'What a waste,' Fran sighed as she filled the kettle in the staffroom. 'He's so gorgeous, too.'

'Waste?' Natalie asked, frowning. What was Fran on about?

Ruth, the other nurse in the room, sighed dramatically. 'Tall, dark and handsome. Drop-dead gorgeous, in fact—the sort who makes your knees go wobbly every time he smiles. And he's a thoroughly nice bloke, too—not one of these who knows how gorgeous he is and expects every female he meets to worship him. He's *lovely*. He takes the time to explain things to parents—and to students. He's not one of these know-it-all doctors who think they're God and nurses don't have a brain cell to rub between them. He actually shows respect for the nursing staff. And he's gay,' she explained, looking equally disgruntled.

Natalie really wasn't following the conversation. 'Who is?'

Fran rolled her eyes. 'Kit, of course. Our new registrar. He's been here a week now. And you've been working with him in clinics and on ward rounds, so don't say you haven't noticed.'

Natalie blinked. 'That he's gay?'

'No, that he's gorgeous. I mean—tall, dark and handsome doesn't even begin to describe him. He's beautiful. And those eyes! Oh-h-h.' Ruth shook her head. 'You're too focused on your work, Natalie. You really need to chill out. Get out more.'

'Get a life. Yeah, I know,' Natalie said, forcing a smile to her face. There had been a time when she'd partied with the best of them. Before her marriage had crumbled into dust. Since then, she'd preferred a quiet life.

'It's such a waste,' Fran said again. 'You know, I can just imagine what it'd be like to be kissed by him. That beautiful mouth, doing all sorts of lovely things...' She gave a blissful shiver. 'Ooh.'

Natalie didn't need to imagine. She knew exactly what it was like to be kissed by him. How Kit's lips could elicit a response from hers. How his mouth could move from teasing to passion within a second, as heat flared between them. How his mouth had taken her to paradise and back.

She gritted her teeth, trying to push the memories back where they belonged—in the past. She and Kit were over. *Over.* Remembering stuff like this was pointless.

'I've got a friend who worked in his last hospital,' Fran continued. 'The nurses were falling over themselves to ask him out. He'd go on most of the staff nights out—he was always a good sport—but he never actually dated anyone. Turned down every single offer.' She looked thoughtful. 'Gina from the emergency department asked him out for a drink the other night. He turned her down—and considering Gina only has to click her fingers and men come running, panting...'

Kit didn't date? But... Natalie damped down the little flicker of hope. No. Absolutely not. She didn't want to start thinking about the reasons why Kit didn't date. Or her own reaction to the news that maybe, just maybe, Kit was still single, too.

If she told them she knew he wasn't gay, she'd have to explain. Which she didn't want to do. But she didn't want them getting the wrong idea about Kit either. 'Maybe he's just concentrating on his career.'

'The way you do, you mean? No, I'm pretty sure it's not that.' Fran shook her head mournfully. 'And it's not because he's an adoring husband because he's not married, either.'

Ruth nodded. 'I reckon he's just not interested in women. I mean, he notices things like shoes.'

'She's right, you know,' Fran said with a sigh. 'Only gay men notice things like shoes, don't they? Straight men don't think about what you're wearing, they think about how to get it off you.'

Natalie couldn't help smiling, but inside she ached. Of course Kit noticed shoes: once upon a time, Natalie had been a major shoe fiend and hadn't been able to pass a shoe shop without drooling over high heels in outrageous colours. Kit had bought them for her, even when they hadn't really been able to afford it.

And the day she'd discovered she was pregnant, she'd bought a tiny pair of white satin pram shoes. Had wrapped them up and given them to him. And when he'd worked it out, he'd picked her up and spun her round and—

'Hello? Earth to Natalie?' Fran said, waving one hand in front of her face and proffering a mug of coffee with the other.

She took the coffee with a rueful smile. 'Thanks, Fran. Sorry. I was miles away.'

'Natalie's definitely not your average woman,' Ruth informed Fran with a grin. 'She actually glazes over at the mention of shoes.'

'Ah, but she understands chocolate,' Fran said. 'She's one of us.'

Natalie didn't mind the teasing. At least it got them off the subject of Kit.

But as if they'd read her mind, Fran asked, 'He's lovely, though—don't you think?'

Uh-oh. This was going in a direction she really, really didn't want to go in. Especially as she'd already learned that Fran and Ruth didn't take no for an answer. They kept asking. If she said she didn't think Kit was lovely, they'd want to know why. And she'd end up admitting that she used to be married to him. And why they'd split up. And Natalie really didn't want her past dragged up and discussed on the hospital grapevine. 'Handsome is as handsome does,' she said with a shrug.

* * *

Kit had been about to walk into the staffroom and grab a coffee when he heard the subject of the conversation.

The nurses on the ward thought he was gay?

Some joke. He'd never been remotely attracted to another man, and he still appreciated pretty women. He just didn't do relationships any more. There was no point, not since he'd lost the love of his life.

The woman who'd just walked back into his life—but had made it very clear that she didn't want to resume where they'd left off. They were barely even friends now. Such a waste, when he remembered what they'd once been to each other.

Handsome is as handsome does.

The scorn that had gone into that remark. OK, so Natalie had good reason to feel that way. He'd let her down in the worst possible way, at the worst possible time. And he hadn't tried hard enough to save the remnants of their marriage, because he'd been focusing on keeping himself together. Burying himself in work, keeping himself so busy that he hadn't had time to hurt. Hadn't gone under. And he hadn't paid enough attention to what was happening to her.

But, oh, that comment rankled. Natalie thought he was shallow?

Maybe, just maybe, he *should* be shallow. Accept all the offers thrown at him. Have wild sex with a different woman every night.

Except that wasn't who he was. Wasn't what he wanted.

As for what he did want... He was just beginning to work out what that was. And it simply wasn't an option.

He turned on his heel and headed back towards his office.

CHAPTER FOUR

ALL those years since the divorce, Natalie had managed not to think of Kit. Not to wish. But now, having to work with him and seeing him every day... It brought it all back. How much she'd loved him. How right it had felt to be in his arms. How her world had collapsed in on itself when she'd realised she'd lost him.

Ah, hell. She had to get over this—and she had to keep working here with him for the next six months, or it'd look as if she couldn't handle her first job as a doctor. As if she wasn't reliable. 'Personal reasons' wasn't a good enough reason to give up the post. It'd make future consultants chary of offering her a post on their ward in case she only lasted a couple of weeks there, too.

She'd worked too damned hard for this. She had to stick it out.

And she was determined to get Kit Rodgers out of her system. Once and for all.

So, for the next month, Natalie managed to keep herself under control. She worked hard, had an occasional evening out with her colleagues—once she'd made sure that Kit wasn't going to be there—and was really settling in.

Until the night of the ward's Hallowe'en fundraiser.

She'd tried to get out of it. 'I'll buy a ticket, sure, but I'll be on duty.'

'No, you're not,' Fran said. 'I've already checked. You're on an early that day. And even if you were on a late...' the look she threw Natalie said that she knew Natalie was perfectly capable of changing her duty if she thought it would get her out of the party '...you'd still catch the last three hours of it. So you're going. No arguments.'

'But—'

'No arguments,' Fran repeated, holding up a hand in protest. 'And you don't have to make your own costume, before you try using that as an excuse. You can hire one.'

Another of her arguments knocked down before she'd even voiced it, Natalie thought with an inward sigh.

'I'm not good at parties.' Not any more.

'You'll be fine at this one. You'll know virtually everyone there, and it's the fundraiser for our ward. You can't not be there.' Fran fished a leaflet out of her locker and gave it to Natalie. 'This is the supplier most people use for costumes. We've been running the night for a few years now, so they give us a percentage of their takings. You'll love it, Natalie. It's great fun, and it raises a hell of a lot of money for the ward. We've got a brilliant band. One of the surgeons fancied himself as a guitarist until he went to med school, one of the midwives sings, one of the Theatre nurses is on keyboards and somebody's brother is their drummer. They play everything, from the old classics through to chart hits. The food's great. And the raffle has to be seen to be believed. You can win a flight in a hot-air balloon, a day at a spa in that posh place that opened just up the road, a rally drive, a—'

'OK, OK. I'll buy raffle tickets,' Natalie said faintly. 'Lots of tickets.'

'Good. But you're still going to the party, even if I have to pick you up and drive you there myself,' Fran warned.

Natalie sank into an armchair. 'You know, when you make nursing director, all the doctors are going to be absolutely terrified of you. With good reason.'

Fran laughed. 'They'll be fine, as long as they buy a ticket to the ball and a pile of raffle tickets.'

Natalie lifted her hands in supplication. 'Have pity on me. I'm only a baby doctor.'

Fran's grin broadened. 'That's a truly terrible pun. For that, you have to buy an extra raffle ticket.'

'I'm not going to get out of this, am I?' Natalie asked plaintively.

'Nope.' Fran ruffled her hair. 'Stop fretting. It'll be good for you. It's a chance to dress up a bit and—well, if you didn't have such short hair, I'd say let your hair down.' She grinned.

'Yeah, yeah.'

But Natalie bought a ticket to the ball and hired a costume: a little black dress with a spaghetti-strap top and a ballerina-length skirt with a jagged hem, teamed with long black fingerless lace gloves. She added a black haematite choker and a chiffon wrap embroidered with spiderwebs, then, for the first time in years, she put on a pair of spike-heeled black shoes.

The kind of shoes she'd worn when she'd been married to—

No. She wasn't going to think about Kit tonight. He was probably going to be there, but there'd be plenty of people she knew at the fundraiser so she could avoid having to spend any time with him.

She hoped.

She didn't usually wear make-up on the ward but that

night she went for the dramatic look, with dark eye shadow and blood-red lips, and long false nails varnished black. She stared at herself in the mirror for a moment, her vision blurring with memories of past Hallowe'en parties when she'd gone as a vampire or a ghost bride. Student parties. And that last one—Kit's first one as a house officer, when she'd been heavily pregnant and Kit had fussed over her all evening, terrified that her waters would break in the middle of the dance floor and making her sit out every other dance in case her ankles started swelling...

Memories.

Memories she'd have to put behind her if she was to have a hope in hell of getting through the evening.

Her stomach was churning with nervousness by the time she got to the party. But as soon as she handed her ticket in to the person dressed as a mummy, she was greeted by a squeal—a voice she recognised behind the mask. Fran.

'You look fabulous, Natalie!' Fran said. 'And those shoes are to die for. Go get yourself a drink and have a good time. Debbie and Ruth are somewhere around—they're both in mummy costumes, too.'

Natalie headed for the bar, and resisted the temptation to buy herself a large glass of wine and down it in one to calm her nerves. She settled for a small glass of red wine and sipped it slowly. And then she didn't get the chance to be nervous any more when Ruth and Debbie swooped on her. 'You look fantastic. Put that drink down and come and have a dance,' Ruth said, dragging her out onto the dance floor.

Kit really wasn't in the mood for a party. He was tired and out of sorts. This time of year was never good for him; there were too many painful memories. Memories he was pretty sure he'd seen in Natalie's face, too. She'd looked strained recently. But he'd promised Fran he'd turn up to the fundraiser. Had it been just an ordinary ward night out, he'd have begged off. Said he had a headache, or something. But the Hallowe'en party wasn't just a party. They were raising money for new equipment for the ward so, as a senior doctor, Kit needed to show his face. Giving a cheque—even a large one—just wouldn't be good enough.

He'd stay for half an hour, and then he'd make some excuse and leave early. It was a shame he'd only been on a late shift, not on nights.

He showered, changed into his hired costume and gelled his hair back. He thought about putting talc on his face to whiten his skin—as he'd done for Hallowe'en parties as a student, when he'd gone with Tally and had needed little persuasion to throw himself completely into the spirit of the occasion—but he just couldn't bring himself to make the effort. Not tonight.

With a sigh, he locked his front door behind him and made his way to the hall.

Natalie knew the second Kit walked in the door, as if there was still some kind of radar system between their bodies. Every nerve-end was screaming to her that he was here, he was here, he was *here*—but she willed herself not to turn round and look at him. She kept her back to where she just knew he was standing, and continued dancing with Ruth and Debbie.

So what if Kit was here? She'd known about it, prepared for it, could deal with it. *Would* deal with it. He wasn't likely to ask her to dance. And if he did, she'd claim she needed to go to the loo or something. And she'd stay there until she was sure he'd moved on to dance with someone else.

* * *

Kit recognised Tally instantly. It was just like the first time he'd met her, twelve years ago, when they'd been at a crowded student party. Everyone else in the room had just faded away for him. There had been only Tally. Then she'd been dressed casually in jeans and a T-shirt, with her glorious dark curls spilling over her shoulders.

Now...she looked fantastic. Not as she'd done that first time: less curvy—too thin, in his opinion, though he supposed it wasn't his business any more—and with her hair cut in a short, gamine style. But she was still as beautiful as she'd been at eighteen. Still drew his eye.

What clinched it for him was the dress. It was perfectly demure, with a neckline barely showing her cleavage and the skirt falling below her knees. But she was wearing high heels with it. Like most of the female staff at the hospital, she wore comfortable flat shoes at work—they spent so much time on their feet, it was only sensible. But Tally had always loved shoes. Sexy, do-me heels. Like the ones she was wearing right now. It made him want to hoist her over his shoulder, carry her out of the room and settle their differences in the most elemental way. Skin to skin.

His body reacted instantly to the thought, and he sucked in a breath. Oh, Lord. He still wanted her as much as he'd done before they'd first become lovers. He'd known within seconds of seeing her that she was the girl he was going to marry. Lust, love at first sight, whatever you wanted to call it: she'd been the one. Nobody else had ever matched up to her.

Why, why, why had he ever been so stupid as to let her go?

Natalie did her best to ignore Kit, dancing with the other staff on their ward and accepting every offer of a dance that came her way. But then, as she was swung round by her partner of the moment, she caught a glimpse of him.

He looked absolutely gorgeous in a white Victorian-style dress shirt, dark trousers, a brocaded waistcoat, a bow-tie and a sweeping black velvet cape. A vampire in the best Bram Stoker tradition, dark and handsome and dangerous. The kind that no woman could resist.

Kit was easily the best-looking man at the ball. Everyone else faded into the shadows in comparison, just like they had, the first time she'd met him. Back then she'd only been aware of his blue, blue eyes and that easy smile that had made her heart do an instant somersault. Tonight he wasn't smiling. He was nursing a drink at the bar and looking grim. But, oh, his mouth. It made her want to reach out and touch him. Take him and make him smile again.

Oh, this was bad. She couldn't possibly still feel that way about Kit. Not after all the bad stuff that had happened between them. They'd been divorced for years. The last few months of her marriage had been the most miserable of her life, and she'd trained herself not to think about him any more.

But there hadn't been anyone in her life since Kit. She'd had offers, but she'd turned them down. Apart from the fact that she hadn't wanted to risk getting hurt again, she'd never felt that instant spark, that magnetic pull, with any other man.

And, from what the hospital grapevine said, there hadn't been anyone in Kit's life either.

Mentally, she stamped on the hopes before they had a chance to grow. It hadn't worked last time and Natalie didn't repeat her mistakes. Ever. She'd just have to avoid him.

Though that was easier said than done, when Kit actually came over to her. Laid one hand on her shoulder. It was the lightest, lightest contact—but it was his bare fingertips against her bare skin, and it made desire shimmer down her spine. Memories of when they'd touched each other much more intimately.

'May I have this dance?'

No, was her head's reaction.

And it must have shown on her face, because he said softly, 'Natalie, if you say no, the hospital grapevine's going to work overtime and there will be all sorts of rumours as to why you've danced with everyone else except me. They'll think you're avoiding me.'

She was.

'And they'll start asking questions.'

Which she definitely didn't want. She didn't think he did either.

'We work together. We're expected to socialise a bit.' Then he gave her a half-smile. One that almost had her knees melting. Oh, this was so unfair. He shouldn't still be able to have this effect on her, not after all these years.

'Dance with me. Just once. To show there are no hard feelings.'

She took a deep breath. If he could be mature about it, so could she. And it was a fast, uptempo song. Meaning she wouldn't have to actually touch him. 'OK.'

And she nearly got away with it. Except the band switched seamlessly into playing a slow number—and, before she realised what was happening, she was in Kit's arms. Dancing with her head resting against his shoulder, the way she'd done so many times before.

Like their wedding day. He'd been wearing a brocade

waistcoat that night too. She'd been in a strapless boned dress, and his arms had been round her just like this. Their first dance had been to a Nick Drake ballad—a quirky choice, but a song they'd both loved—and there had been a smile on her face a mile wide. How happy she'd been. How happy they'd *both* been.

It was like coming home. Natalie was thinner than Kit remembered and he couldn't tangle his fingers in her gorgeous hair any more, and she wasn't even wearing the same perfume, but he remembered the softness of her skin. He remembered the feel of her in his arms, just like this. The way they'd danced on their wedding day, with her head resting against his shoulder in absolute trust that he'd never let her down, that he'd always be there for her.

Though he hadn't been.

He'd messed up, big time. And he'd never been able to get through the barriers she'd put up in defence. She'd shut him out and all that love had just drained away, like the sea at low tide.

Except, for him, it was still there. And now she was in his arms again, it was trickling back up. Threatening to flood his senses.

His head knew he should stop dancing with her, make some excuse and leave the party.

His heart wouldn't let him do it. He just needed to kiss her. Right here, right now. Just once. One tiny, tiny touch of his mouth against her skin. He dipped his head so that his mouth was resting against the curve of her neck.

Oh, bliss.

She still tasted as good as he remembered. He couldn't help tightening his arms round her waist, moving his mouth up the sensitive cord at the side of her neck. She shivered, but she didn't move away.

Kit was lost entirely. He closed his eyes, shutting out the rest of the world so it was only him and Tally. He brushed her earlobe with his lips, then her cheek—oh-h-h, and finally her mouth, so warm and sweet.

It was meant to be just one kiss. One tiny, gentle little kiss. But then her mouth opened underneath his, and he was really kissing her.

It was heaven, having Tally back in his arms, with her hands wound round his neck and her fingers in his hair and her mouth against his. His arms were wrapped so tightly around her that he could feel every movement she made.

He'd missed her so badly.

And now she was back. In his arms. Holding him. He splayed one hand against her back, let the other fall to the curve of her bottom. Lord, Lord, Lord, this was good. What he'd wanted to do ever since the moment he'd seen her again. Holding her close.

Kit had no idea that the song had changed, that the band had gone uptempo again, until someone bumped into them.

The music crashed into his senses and it was like being doused in cold water.

He pulled away from Natalie. He could see the shock in her eyes—no doubt it was mirrored in his. Oh, God. They'd just made one hell of a spectacle of themselves on the dance floor, kissing through God only knew how many dances, and the hospital grapevine was going to go absolutely crazy over this. The rumours had probably already started.

Natalie was shaking. Kit's first instinct was to drag her back into his arms, shield her from all the inquisitive glances with his body, but her barriers were back in place again. Her face was shuttered and she gave him a look that said, Don't come anywhere near me.

To hammer the point home, she took a step backwards. 'We shouldn't have done that.'

Yeah, he knew.

Except he couldn't help wishing they hadn't stopped.

What had they done?

Oh, God. She wasn't going to be able to face **anyone** in this room ever again.

She'd been kissing Kit. *Really* kissing him. **In public.**

Oh, God.

And even though she desperately wanted to bury her face in his shoulder, feel his arms round her again, she couldn't do it. She couldn't go over the same old ground. Yes, she could lose her heart to him—but then he'd let her down again. He wouldn't be there when she needed him. And she couldn't bear it to happen a second time.

'We—we can't do this.' Her voice was shaking, but she forced herself to sound calm. 'If anyone asks, I was tipsy and so were you.'

'Tal—' he began, but she cut him short.

'Excuse me. I'm tired. I'm going home.'

A muscle flickered in his jaw. 'I'll see you home.'

'You honestly expect me to leave here with you?' Oh, no. No, no, no. She didn't trust him, and she trusted herself even less. If he saw her home, they'd end up in her bed. Because that spark was definitely still there between them. Within seconds of being in each other's arms again, they'd been kissing. In public.

In private, she knew that neither of them would be able to stop. That they'd be ripping each other's clothes off, desperate to touch each other's skin again. That they'd make love all night long, exploring and touching and tasting and remembering. Wiping out the bad and replacing the pain with good feelings.

It was so very, very tempting.

But it wouldn't last. Couldn't last. And she didn't want people talking about her, speculating about her love life. 'No way. I'll get a taxi. I'm not having everyone thinking we've spent the night together,' she said between clenched teeth. 'That kiss shouldn't have happened. And we're going to forget it did.'

Ah, who was she trying to kid? No way would she be able to forget it. Her whole body was yearning for him again. She'd missed him so badly. And how she wanted to feel his body curled around hers. How she wanted to go to sleep in his arms, feeling his heartbeat against her body and hearing his breathing go slow and deep and regular as he, too, drifted towards sleep. And then he'd wake her in the middle of the night by kissing his way down her spine, nuzzling her skin and making those tiny little murmurs of pleasure as he explored her body. They'd make love in the small hours and see the whole universe explode...

But it wasn't going to happen. She was going to let her head rule her heart on this one. She was going to be sensible.

'At least let me wait with you until your taxi arrives,' he said.

She shook her head. 'I'm going home, Kit. Alone. I don't want to be with you.' It was a lie, and no doubt he knew it, too. She wanted to be with him. Yearned to be with him. But she didn't want the pain that she knew would go with it.

'You're still not waiting on your own for a taxi,' he insisted.

She rolled her eyes. 'Stop being so overprotective. This is a hotel, Kit. I'm going to be in the foyer. I'll be perfectly safe.'

'You could be waiting for hours. It's Hallowe'en, Natalie. Parties everywhere. Taxis will be like gold dust. No, I'm taking you home.' The temperature of his voice dropped several degrees when he added, 'And, just in case you're thinking that, I'm not going to leap on you. You've already made it perfectly clear you're not interested. I've never forced myself on a woman and I'm not going to start now.'

Kit didn't even need to *ask* women, let alone anything else. They just fell at his feet, instantly captivated. Even when half the ward had been convinced he was gay, they'd found him incredibly sexy.

And tonight she'd just proved his sexuality. Kit Rodgers was absolutely, definitely not gay. Tomorrow's rumour mill was going to be unbearable. Especially if someone saw her getting into his car and assumed they'd gone off somewhere together to finish what they'd started on the dance floor. 'Kit, I...'

He rolled his eyes. 'For your information, I'm bloody tired and I'm not in the mood for a party. But I'll drop you home and show my face back here, just so nobody thinks I've had my wicked way with you.'

Put like that, it made her sound...childish. She squirmed. 'Kit, I...'

'Let's just get your coat and get out of here,' he said coolly.

'I haven't got one. Just this wrap.' Which was hardly sensible attire for a night at the end of October.

Especially, she thought as they left the hotel and stepped into the car park, as it was so frosty outside. She tried really hard not to shiver, but then her teeth started chattering.

Kit gave her a speaking look, removed his cape and slung it round her shoulders.

Still warm from his body heat. It was like having his

arms round her all over again. Oh, Lord. She couldn't cope with this.

'Don't,' he warned, before she could protest. 'You're cold.'

And he'd always had that gentlemanly streak. Good manners.

He opened the passenger door for her, but to her relief he didn't lean over to fasten her seat belt. Good. Because if he leaned over her, she might just be tempted to slide her hands into his hair and kiss him.

Ha. Anyone would think that small glass of red wine had gone to her head.

Then she remembered something. 'Didn't I see you nursing a drink at the bar?'

'Mineral water.'

Oh. Well, of course Kit would be responsible. He'd never drink—not even one glass—and drive. 'Sorry,' she muttered.

'No problem. Where do you live?'

She gave him her address.

'Right.'

He drove her there in silence. Didn't switch on the stereo either, she noticed—and Kit had always been such a music junkie. He'd either had a CD playing or had been humming some song or other under his breath.

He'd sung lullabies to Ethan, the sound of his pure, clear tenor voice bringing tears to her eyes.

She dragged in a breath and huddled deeper into her seat. Bad move, because she was still wearing his cape. Still had his bodily warmth surrounding her. And how much she wanted to feel his arms round her now.

He managed to find a parking space right outside her flat.

'I'll wait until you're in safely.'

His voice was cool, clipped. She didn't bother arguing.

She simply undid her seat belt, opened the passenger door and climbed out. She was about to close the door again when she remembered—she was still wearing his cape on top of her wrap. Quickly, she slid it from her shoulders, folded it neatly and left it on the seat. 'Thank you for the lift.'

'I'll head back to the fundraiser now. And I'll make sure everyone knows your honour is intact. I drove you home because you had a headache.'

Heartache, more like. 'Thank you.'

He waited until she'd opened her front door, stepped inside. Then he drove away. Left her alone. Just as she'd wanted him to. The dark, dangerous vampire leaving his prey.

Though in some ways it was already too late. Kit had stolen her heart all those years ago and had left it in splinters. She'd never be able to give it to anyone else.

She closed the front door behind her. Showered and washed her hair, as if she could wash all the memories and feelings away. But even the citrussy shower gel she favoured couldn't stop her remembering the scent of Kit's skin, warm and familiar, comforting and incredibly sexy, all at the same time.

Hell, hell, hell. She just had to remember they were different people now. Living different lives. Apart, not together.

And that was the way it was going to stay.

CHAPTER FIVE

To Natalie's relief, Kit was on a late shift the next morning rather than an early. She avoided the staffroom and kept her mind firmly on the ward round or doing paperwork, but Ruth and Fran caught up with her at lunchtime and marched her off to the canteen with them.

'Spill the beans,' said Fran. 'Now.'

'I don't know what you're talking about,' Natalie lied.

'That was quite some clinch you had with our registrar last night,' Ruth said with a grin.

Straight to the point. Well, she'd known she wouldn't get away with it.

'Two and a half dances' worth of clinch,' Fran added. 'Only one of them was a slow dance, too.'

Two and a half dances? Lord, had it been that many? It had felt like...seconds.

No, worse than that. It had felt like coming home.

'So we were completely on the wrong track about Kit, weren't we?' Ruth asked. 'He's not gay at all.'

'No,' Natalie muttered.

'And he took you home,' Fran said thoughtfully.

'Because I had a headache,' Natalie protested. Surely

he'd told them that. He *had* gone back to the party, hadn't he? 'I was going to get a taxi.'

'But he went all manly on you and insisted that he take you home.' Ruth looked at her. 'It's all right, don't panic. We know he didn't stay the night. And he wasn't gone long enough for you two to have…' She grinned. 'Well.'

Natalie's face flamed as she got the implication. No. Kit wasn't into quickies. Most of the time he'd preferred slow and easy. Taking his time. Enjoying every second of their love-making.

'He danced with every woman in the room when he came back, though I have to say nobody else got the sort of clinch out of him that you did,' Fran said. 'Or even a peck on the cheek, come to think of it.'

Natalie wasn't sure whether she was more relieved or horrified.

'And he helped clear up at the end,' Ruth added.

Which meant he'd stayed late. Despite the fact that he'd been tired. Because he'd been trying to make sure that everyone had seen him and nobody questioned her about vanishing with him the next day. Guilt throbbed through her. 'Oh.'

Fran raised an eyebrow. 'So *are* you seeing him, then?'

'No. Absolutely not.' That was the honest truth. She wasn't seeing Kit. And she wasn't planning to either.

But neither of them looked convinced.

Hardly surprising, seeing as she'd made such an exhibition of herself last night. Lost control. Forgotten the world, when she'd been back in Kit's arms. She needed an excuse, and she needed one fast. 'Look, I just had too much to drink last night.'

Fran and Ruth exchanged a glance that said they didn't believe her.

Again, hardly surprising. Even though Natalie didn't drink very much or very often, one glass of wine wasn't enough to make her throw herself at someone the way she'd thrown herself at Kit last night.

Had she thrown herself at him? Or had he thrown himself at her? Either way, they'd both gone up in flames at the first touch.

'You knew each other years ago, didn't you?' Ruth asked.

Natalie squirmed in her seat. 'Yes.'

'So is there something you're not telling us?'

More than something. But she didn't want to talk about the wreck of her marriage. 'Please, just leave it. I... It's something I'd really rather not discuss,' she said, rubbing her hand over her face and wishing she was a million miles away.

The strain must have shown in her eyes because they immediately changed the subject. And Fran bought her a frothy cup of hot chocolate and a blueberry muffin. 'An apology for pushing you,' she said with a rueful smile. 'Obviously you two were an item at some point and things went wrong. I'm sorry I embarrassed you or dredged up bad memories.'

Which only made Natalie feel worse: the two nurses meant well and she'd grown friendly with them in the weeks they'd worked together. 'It's not necessary. No offence taken.'

'Good, because I'd hate to make you feel bad.' Fran looked thoughtful. 'He's a nice guy, Natalie. He's lovely to work with. I can only assume he's the same outside work—and you're great, too. I can see the two of you would be good together.'

'Mmm.' Natalie shifted in her seat.

Fran sighed. 'And I'm putting my size fives in it again.

OK, I'll shut up. I won't ask what happened.' Even though she was clearly dying to know—just when had Natalie and Kit been an item, and why had they split up?

'Thanks.' Though it wasn't Fran and Ruth that Natalie was really worried about. It was the grapevine. And Kit's reaction. They were going to have to work together later today—and things were going to be really, really awkward.

Nobody actually said anything to Kit when he came on duty, but he was well aware of the speculative glances. Which meant that people had been talking. Oh, Lord. Natalie would really hate being the subject of grapevine gossip. And when he'd kissed her, he hadn't stopped to think about whether she was seeing anyone else. He'd completely blanked that thought from his mind, right from the start. So, for all he knew, he could've wrecked whatever relationship she was in right now. Caused problems between her and her new love—because no man would take kindly to the news that his partner had been giving someone else hot, wet kisses in the middle of a dance floor. To the point where she hadn't even noticed the song changing from a slow dance to something fast and upbeat.

Then again, Natalie wouldn't have kissed him like that if she were seeing another man. The Natalie Wilkins he knew had integrity. In spades. Which meant she had to be single.

Ah, hell. This was worse than being a teenager going through hormonal changes. He was in a flat spin—and all because his ex-wife had kissed him. His *ex*-wife. He needed to remember that. It was over between them.

Though he wished to hell it wasn't. That he could turn back the clock and change things—even if he hadn't been able to save Ethan, he could have done things differently.

Shared his loss with the one person who'd understood, instead of burying himself in work. Opened up to her. Let her open up to him. They should have helped each other through it, instead of letting it blow them apart.

He leaned his elbows on his desk and rested his forehead on his clasped hands. What a mess.

There was a rap on his open door and he looked up. 'Are you all right, Kit?' Debbie asked, sounding concerned.

'Fine, thanks,' he lied.

'Hmm,' was all Debbie said. Clearly she didn't believe him, but at least she didn't grill him. Just as well. He didn't want to talk about it.

'What can I do for you?' he asked, switching back into professional mode.

'Your clinic's starting in ten minutes. Do you want a coffee?'

'No, I'm all right. But thanks for the offer.' He smiled at her.

He got to hear little bits from the grapevine over the next couple of hours. Natalie wasn't seeing anyone—oh, and just why did he feel so pleased about that?—but everyone was speculating about the mystery man in her past. As the story went, there had been someone in her past who'd hurt her badly, and she'd buried herself in work ever since.

Ouch, thought Kit. That'd be me.

And it seemed she'd reacted to losing him in just the same way he'd reacted when they'd lost Ethan. Work, work and more work. Pushing herself harder and harder so she hadn't had a chance to feel the pain. Running from it.

The grapevine also had a lot to say about the man who'd let Natalie Wilkins get away. What an idiot he must have been, not to see what a lovely girl she was. Beautiful and clever—and nice with it. A real diamond.

Ha. He knew all that. And the grapevine was spot on. He was an idiot. He should have fought a lot harder for his marriage. Turned to his wife instead of his work to heal his broken heart. Pulled together with her, instead of letting the cracks between them grow wider and wider and wider until their marriage had crashed into the abyss.

Irreconcilable differences? Maybe. But they should both have tried a hell of a lot harder to sort them out.

Somehow he got through a clinic, forcing himself to concentrate on his patients instead of thinking about Natalie. He was fine when he was working. The problem was the time in between.

He was walking along the corridor, reading a set of notes, when he literally walked into her and dropped his file.

'Sorry!' He dropped to the floor and scrabbled for the bits of paper. Though it was a relief: it meant he had enough time to get himself under control again. So she wouldn't see the longing on his face.

'Are you all right?' he asked, when he'd got the file back together and stood up again.

'Uh-huh.'

She didn't sound all right. He wanted to pull her into his arms, hold her close, tell her everything was going to be fine—except when he reached out a hand to touch her, she flinched and pulled away.

Clearly she loathed him so much she didn't even want him near her. It felt like a knife twisting in his heart, but he forced himself not to react. Just dropped his hand. 'That's good,' he said briskly, as if nothing had happened. 'See you, then.'

Somehow he found the strength to walk away. Natalie was just a colleague who'd met him briefly in the corridor on the way to see a patient. And he'd do well to remember that in future.

Natalie added enough milk to her coffee so it would be cool enough to gulp down. Right now, she really needed a caffeine hit. When the staffroom door opened, she froze, ready to flee if it was Kit.

But it was Debbie, who took one look at her and frowned. 'Are you all right, love?'

'I'm fine.'

'You don't look it.'

'I'm fine,' Natalie repeated. If she said it enough, maybe she'd even start to believe it.

'If you need a friend to talk to—someone who won't repeat a word to anyone else—you know where I am,' Debbie said quietly.

Natalie gulped her coffee. 'Thanks, but...' She couldn't repeat the lie again. 'It's just this time of year,' she said. 'It's a bit difficult for me. Personal stuff. But I'd rather not talk about it, if you don't mind.'

'Is it to do with Kit?' Debbie asked, her voice gentle.

Oh, yes. Kit and their baby. But she couldn't handle anyone's pity. Been there, done that, cried way too many tears. 'Sorry, Debbie. I can't talk about it. Not even to you. Let's just say Kit and I used to be an item. And it was over a long time ago.'

The senior sister nodded. 'I guessed as much.'

Natalie wrapped her hands around her mug, willing herself not to drop it. 'Is everyone talking about it?' she whispered. 'Last night, I mean?' When she and Kit had been kissing each other stupid on the dance floor?

'It'll die down,' Debbie said with a reassuring smile. 'Just ignore it. Someone else will knock you off the gossip spot by the end of the day. You won't be the only pair who...well. These sort of things happen at a party.'

Natalie flushed. 'I just feel so stupid.'

'Want me to have a word with Lenox and see if we can get you two rostered on different shifts?' Debbie asked.

The tears almost spilled over, but Natalie blinked them back. 'Thanks, Debbie. It's kind of you to offer, really it is. But we're both adults and I can deal with this.'

'Hmm,' Debbie said. 'He looks as bad as you do today. Maybe you two need to talk.'

'Maybe.' But the time for talking had long since gone.

Kit and Natalie were both on the same shift the following day. Early. And they were rostered in the PAU again.

Kit looked like hell. There were dark smudges under his eyes, as if he hadn't slept properly. Join the club, Natalie thought. She wasn't getting a lot of sleep either. And probably for the same reason.

They really had to stop tearing each other apart. Learn to work together, for the ward's sake. And one of them was going to have to make the first move: it may as well be her.

'Want a coffee, Kit?' she asked.

He stared at her for a moment, as if not quite believing that she was using his name rather than a formal title. Then he smiled, and his whole face seemed to light up. 'Thanks. That'd be good. I didn't have time for breakfast this morning.'

'Me neither.' Not strictly true. She'd made some toast

but the first mouthful had choked her and she'd ended up crumbling it on her plate.

He pulled a chocolate bar out of his pocket and offered it to her. 'Want to share?'

Just like old times. Times when they hadn't had time for breakfast because they'd been almost late for lectures. And she'd met him for coffee between lectures—coffee and a bar of chocolate. Hardly a sensible diet. But they'd been so happy...

They couldn't go back. But maybe they could find a way forward. Find some kind of peace.

Their first case was a five-year-old boy with a fever and an abscess on the sole of his right foot.

'Harry was playing in the back garden,' his mum said. She sighed, shaking her head. 'He's such a monkey. I can never get him to wear shoes outside, even in winter. And I've given up hope of him ever wearing a T-shirt that isn't mud-coloured within ten minutes.'

Kit smiled. 'I was the same at his age.' He ruffled the little boy's hair. 'It's not as much fun playing unless you get really muddy, is it, Harry?'

The little boy managed a wan smile.

'So what happened?' Natalie asked.

'He came in, hopping on one foot—said he'd stood on something sharp. I could see the thorn in there, so I got the tweezers and I really thought I'd taken it all out. I put antiseptic on it and everything, and a plaster. But his foot's swollen and tender—and today blue stuff started coming out of it.'

'Can I have a look?' Natalie asked the little boy.

He nodded, and shifted in his seat. Clearly he was torn between being brave and wanting a cuddle with his mum.

Natalie smiled at him. 'If you sit on your mum's lap, Harry, it'll be easier for me to see it,' she said. 'Does it hurt a lot?'

'Yes,' he whispered.

'I'll try very, very hard not to make it feel bad.'

He looked slightly happier. Natalie gently took off his trainer and sock. Now for the crunch—removing the plaster was going to hurt.

'I need your help here, Harry,' she said. 'Do you know any magic words?'

'No.' His bottom lip wobbled.

Kit clearly guessed what she was planning, because he came to the rescue. 'I do. What we're going to do is say a magic word, really fast, and then Natalie can see your foot properly.' He smiled at the little boy. 'Abracadabra.'

'Abracadabra,' the little boy repeated.

'Faster,' Kit urged. 'And again. And again. And—'

The plaster was off. She glanced up at him, nodding her thanks, and returned her attention to the child's foot. Just as Harry's mother had said, it was swollen and tender, and the puncture site was oozing a bluish-green substance. It looked really nasty. 'You've been ever so brave, Harry,' she said. 'In fact, I think you definitely deserve one of my bravery stickers.' She'd copied Kit's habit of keeping a pack of stickers in her coat pocket. 'I just need to do a couple of things first. Do you think you can be brave for just a teeny bit longer?'

He nodded.

'When did it happen?' she asked Harry's mum.

'About a week ago.'

'You did exactly the right thing with the thorn,' Natalie said, 'but I'd say there were some bacteria on the thorn, something that went deeper into the tissues than your antiseptic did, and it took hold. There are a couple of likely candidates—*Staphylococcus* or *Streptococcus*—but I think it's more likely to be *Pseudomonas*. It's a bacterium you often find on decaying wood, and it produces this blue-green pigment called pyocyanin—that's what turned the pus coming from his foot blue.' She stroked Harry's hair. 'We'll get you sorted out and back to normal, honey. But what we have to do now is take a tiny, tiny sample of the gungy stuff so I can send it to the lab and get them to grow it for me, just to make sure I've got the right bacterium. Then I'm going to clean up all the gungy stuff and give you some special medicine that'll zap the bugs for you.'

'Will it hurt?' he asked, his voice wobbling slightly.

'I'll try very hard not to hurt you, sweetheart,' she said. 'But I tell you what. While I'm sorting your foot out, do you want to listen through my stethoscope and hear what your heart sounds like?'

'Can I do Mummy as well?'

'Sure you can.' She tipped her head on one side and looked at Kit. 'Want to do the honours and teach him how it works?'

Kit, obviously realising that she needed to distract the little boy, smiled back. 'Yep. And then you can tell all your friends at school everything you learned today,' he said to Harry.

While he was soothing their patient, Natalie quickly took a sample and labelled it for the lab, then put some local anaesthetic into the little boy's foot. Debridement—removing the infected tissue—was necessary to stop the infection spreading further, but it was messy and it could hurt, even with a local. She worked as quickly as she could, then applied a dressing. 'I'm going to keep him in for a while because we need to give him the antibiotics through a drip for the first couple of days, then we can switch to antibiotics in a liquid form so you can take him home. You'll need to give the medicine to him four times a day and make sure he finishes the course, even if his foot looks tons better, because otherwise the infection might come back.' Not finishing a course of antibiotics also meant that bacteria could develop resistant strains.

'We'll get you booked in upstairs and introduce you to the nurse who will be looking after him. You can stay with him for as long as you want,' Natalie said, 'and there's a parents' phone so you can give the number to anyone who needs to get in touch with you here.'

'But he's going to be all right?'

'He's going to be absolutely fine.' Natalie smiled at her. 'And now I believe someone around here deserves a big bravery award.' She handed the little boy a sticker, then took them up to the ward and introduced them to Fran.

On her return, Kit asked, 'What have you written him up for?'

'Broad-spectrum,' she said. 'Something that will cover staph and strep as well—but I'm pretty sure it's *Pseudomonas*.'

'Good call,' Kit said.

'Well, it was pretty much a textbook case. The colour of the pus—that bluey-green—was a give-away. Poor little mite.'

'You've got a nice way with patients,' Kit said. 'You reassured the mum, told them exactly what you were going to do and threw in a bit of distraction for the bits of treatment that were going to hurt.'

'You did the distraction for me. Both times.'

He shrugged. 'Teamwork. It's what keeps a ward going.'

He didn't say any more, but she could see it in his eyes. *And we make a great team. Always did.*

Yeah. But from now on it would be strictly professional.

CHAPTER SIX

THE morning of Ethan's birthday, Natalie dragged herself out of bed.

How could the sun possibly shine on such a day?

Everything felt like lead. It reminded her of the Emily Dickinson poem she'd studied for her A-levels about reactions after great pain. 'The hour of lead', Dickinson had called it. First—chill—then stupor—then the letting go...

Today Natalie was back in stupor mode. And she'd be there for the next six weeks. Remembering and wishing and keeping a lid on everything. Moving mechanically, getting through the days moment by moment.

She couldn't face breakfast. And there was only one place she wanted to be today. She'd already ordered a spray of white roses from the florist's a few doors down from her flat. Once she'd picked them up, she drove to Litchford-in-Arden. Left her car in the gravelled car park at the side of the church. Then, too numb to feel the coolness of the air, she walked through the churchyard to the memorial stone.

The churchyard still overlooked fields, the heart of England. Bleak right now, with dark ploughed fields and bare trees stretched against the winter sky, but in the summer the fields shimmered with yellow corn, and the air was filled with birdsong.

This was where part of her heart would always lie. Part of the broken shards that would never be whole again.

There was a tiny spot of lichen on the white stone, she noticed with a frown. She set the roses to one side and emptied her carrier bag of the cream cleaner, toothbrush and bottle of water she'd brought with her. Then she dropped to her knees and cleaned the stone meticulously until it gleamed. Ran her fingers over the black carved letters. The date that had splintered her universe.

Ethan Rodgers, aged six weeks. Sleeping with the angels.

Nine words that couldn't even begin to express the pain. The regrets for what might have been. She'd never had the chance to see her little boy growing up. She'd seen his first smile, yes, but no first tooth, no tiny white crescent peering through his gums. She hadn't heard his first 'Mum-mum' or 'Dada', or seen his look of wonder when he'd first realised he could crawl, actually move under his own steam. No wobbly first steps. No splashing in the bath. No mum and toddler swimming class or baby group. No songs, no first day at school, no first nativity play as a shepherd in a dressing-gown with a teatowel on his head.

All the weight of the things they hadn't had time to do seemed to crash down on her. How could emptiness weigh so much?

'My baby,' she whispered. 'Happy birthday.'

It was a day when she should have made him a cake with six candles on it. A day when she should have been planning a party—maybe at one of the play centres where he and his friends could have jumped all over bouncy castles and burnt off their energy before the birthday tea, or maybe she'd have hired a magician to bring forth 'oohs' and 'ahs' with his magic tricks, and delighted laughter as he'd launched into the comedy routine that usually ended with a parent being teased silly.

And all she could do for her little boy now was bring him flowers. Flowers he wouldn't even see.

Shuddering with the effort of holding back the tears, she filled the little push-in vase with water, then arranged the white roses in it.

'Sleep tight, my angel,' she choked, and stood up again.

That was when she saw Kit.

He was leaning against the wall of the churchyard, carrying flowers, just watching her.

Their gazes locked. Blue on blue.

Well, he had as much right as she did to be here. She nodded once, and he walked over to join her at the grave.

'Sorry. I didn't mean to get in your way. I thought you might have gone by now.'

She lifted one shoulder in a half-hearted shrug. 'I've got no sense of time today.'

'Me neither.' He paused. 'Though I suppose when I was in London I always knew you'd have been here first thing, so when I got here in the afternoon we wouldn't have to face each other.'

'You drove here from London?' It was a good couple of hours' drive, even with the motorways.

His face tightened. 'Do you really think I wouldn't care enough to visit my son's grave on his birthday?'

She wrapped her arms round herself defensively. 'Sorry. I didn't mean it like it sounded. Of course you'd want to be here.'

'Oh, hell, Tally. Our baby.' He laid the flowers down and dragged her into his arms.

He was shaking, too. Shaking as much as she was.

Hurting as much as she was.

She slid her arms around his waist and held him tightly. Leaned against him, as he was leaning against her. And he was holding her the way she'd so wanted him to hold her all those years ago. Letting her know she wasn't on her own in this misery, that although things would never be completely all right again, they'd get through it. Together.

When she lifted her head, she saw that his sweater was wet. Wet with her silent tears.

'Sorry,' she whispered.

''S all right.'

One glance told her that he was in just the same state as she was. His eyelashes were damp and his eyes were suspiciously red.

He held her for a moment longer, then let his hands drop.

She loosened her hold on him, too, and backed away. 'I'll let you have some time alone with him.'

'Thank you.' His voice sounded cracked. Just as she turned to go, he whispered, 'Tally?'

She turned back. 'Yes?'

'Don't go.'

He wanted her to stay?

'I think...maybe it's time we talked. Wait for me?'

She nodded. And she noticed that, unlike her, he laid his flowers on the patch of grass in front of the gravestone. Maybe because he felt he didn't have the right to use the little vase where she'd put her flowers?

She knelt down beside him. 'Kit. There's room...if you want to.' She indicated the little vase.

He smiled wryly. 'I don't want to spoil your arrangement. I'm rubbish with flowers.'

'Do you want me to...?'

He nodded and handed her the stems of the yellow roses, one by one. He checked them first to make sure there were no thorns to hurt her, she noticed.

Yellow and white roses. Mingled together. Hers and his. For once, their son had united parents. United in their loss. Their longing. Actually visiting his grave at the same time—something they'd never managed to do before.

Her hands were shaking as she arranged the flowers in the vase. When she'd finished, Kit took her hand and raised it to his lips. 'Thank you,' he said softly.

And she knew he didn't mean just thank you for arranging the flowers. He meant thank you for sharing the moment. For not pushing him away from their baby's grave.

''S all right,' she said, echoing his earlier words.

He didn't let her hand go, she noticed. As he stood up, he drew her up with him. 'Let's go for a coffee somewhere. Not in Litchford-in-Arden, though.'

She knew what he meant. If they stayed here, the chances were they'd come across someone who'd known them when they'd lived there. Someone who'd maybe come to Ethan's funeral, almost six years before. Someone who'd remember and offer condolences neither of them wanted to hear. Someone who'd ask questions neither of them wanted to answer.

'There's a little café in Ashington.' The next village. 'It opened last year.'

He nodded. 'Sounds good to me. Let's take my car.'

She frowned. 'Why?'

'Unless parking's improved greatly...'

She knew what he meant. Parking spaces in the village were like gold dust. They'd be lucky to find one, let alone two. She wrinkled her nose. 'It hasn't.'

'My car, then.'

It felt weird, sitting in the passenger seat next to Kit as he drove them away from the churchyard. Unlike the last time he'd driven her somewhere, at Hallowe'en, there was no tension, no urgent need to run from him. But it was still strange. They hadn't been together in a car like this for years.

It felt even weirder not to rummage among his CDs to find one she wanted to hear. Kit kept his stereo switched off anyway, and she was relieved. If the radio had played some song or other that had meant something to them, she knew she wouldn't have been able to handle it right then.

Kit didn't bother making conversation until they'd collected their coffees from the counter and were sitting at a quiet table in the corner of the café.

'Ethan would have been at school now,' he said softly. 'In year one. He'd be reading and writing, drawing pictures of rockets and fire engines, maybe learning to swim.'

'What do you think he'd be like?' It was something she'd pondered so often. But she'd never shared it with anyone else, not wanting to hurt her parents or her sisters by asking.

'Looks-wise?' Kit shrugged. 'Blue eyes, dark hair. Tall. Beautiful.' He paused. 'He had your smile.'

'And your chin.'

'Personality—I think he'd have been cheeky. Full of fun. Interested in anything and everything.' His eyes darkened. 'Like you.'

'A charmer. Like you.'

He smiled wryly. 'Surface? No, our boy would've been

deep. You wouldn't have let him wrap you round his finger with a smile.'

Ha. Kit had been able to do that. Once.

'You'd have taught him right from wrong, good from bad. Encouraged him to explore. You'd have been a brilliant mum,' he added, his voice cracking.

Tears welled up in her eyes, and she scrubbed them away with the back of her hand.

Kit reached out to hold her other hand. 'Tally. I'm so glad...so glad I can talk about him.' His voice was rough with emotion. 'On his birthday. I...couldn't talk about him to anyone else.'

Not his parents, his brothers? Then again, the Rodgers family hadn't exactly approved of Ethan in the first place. He'd been unplanned. Bad timing: just when Kit had been starting his houseman year and had had enough pressure at work, without the added worry of having a newborn.

She and Kit hadn't made a baby on *purpose*.

But a termination had been completely out of the question. Neither of them had even considered it. Ethan might have been unplanned, but he'd been wanted. So very, very wanted. By both of them, and to hell with what Kit's family had planned for him.

But surely Kit had been able to talk to friends? To his—oh, God, the idea made her ache, but she had to face it—to his new partner? She knew he was single now, but had there been someone else? Had he tried to forget her, forget their baby, in another woman's arms?

She needed to know. 'I thought you'd be married again by now.'

He shook his head. 'There's been no one special.' There was a long, long pause. 'You?'

She shook her head. She hadn't been able to face the pain again. The pain of loving someone…and knowing that she could lose them. Just like she'd lost Ethan and Kit.

'I remember the day you told me you were pregnant. It was March. A day like today, when the sun was shining and the sky was blue and it was freezing cold, and you handed me that little package. It wasn't anywhere near my birthday so I didn't have a clue what it was. And I'd just come off a really, really heavy night shift. All I wanted to do was collapse into bed and sleep.' His smile was bleak. 'And then I saw they were babies' shoes. Little white satin pram shoes.'

'Expensive shoes.'

He lifted one shoulder. 'Since when did *you* ever buy cheap shoes?'

Just when she thought he was sniping, he added softly, 'And they were worth every single penny. I can't think of a better way to find out I was going to be a dad than unwrapping my baby's first shoes.'

Shoes they'd buried him in, later that same year. And the shawl her great-great-aunt had crocheted for him. In the tiny white coffin that had somehow seemed too small to contain their child.

Natalie didn't drag her hand away from Kit's. At that moment it felt right, holding his hand. A connection between them while they shared their memories.

'I remember the first time I felt him kick,' Kit said softly. 'My hand was just resting across you, and suddenly there was this wallop—as if he was saying hello, telling me he was awake, and would I mind moving my arm, please, because I was too heavy. And he used to get hiccups and wake you up at three in the morning with baby gymnastics. He had hiccups at the twenty-week scan, too. We could actually see it on the screen.'

Kit remembered that?

Again, Natalie felt tears film her eyes.

'And the day before he was born, you wanted to go to the beach. We lived smack in the middle of England, miles and miles away from a beach—and it was November, freezing cold, really not beach weather—but you really, really wanted to paddle in the sea.'

The strongest urge she'd ever had, and about the only time she'd ever regretted moving to the heart of England. 'And you looked on the map to find the nearest proper beach. You drove me all the way down the M5 to Weston-Super-Mare so I could walk on the sand and paddle in the sea,' Natalie recalled. It had taken them hours to get there.

'And you couldn't reach your feet over the bump to wipe off the sand when you'd finished paddling. I had to do it for you. And I was terrified you were going to go into labour before I could get you home again and I'd have to deliver our baby myself in the car.'

'My labour didn't start until three o'clock in the morning,' Natalie said. 'And somehow you managed to rub my back and sleep at the same time. Cat-napping. Junior doctor habit.' One she was learning, too.

'Yeah.' He smiled. 'I'd read all the textbooks. I worked out it'd probably be twelve hours before he arrived, so I didn't have to rush you in.'

'Except it took eighteen. And you fiddled with the remote control on the TENS machine and gave me full blast at the wrong time.' She smiled wryly. 'Typical male.'

'I had the bruises for weeks, you were gripping my hand so hard every time you had a contraction.'

Just like he was gripping her hand now.

'I remember the first time I held him,' Kit said softly. 'He was so beautiful. I couldn't believe he was really ours, that he was finally there. That we'd made something so very special.'

'And you slept in a chair that night by our bed.'

'I didn't want to leave you,' Kit said simply. 'I couldn't. My wife, my baby.' His breath hitched. 'My family.'

And they'd had so little time together. So very little time. Six short weeks, and ten days of them had been spent in hospital at Ethan's bedside.

But today they should remember the good bits. 'I remember his first smile,' Natalie said. 'You said it was just wind.'

'And then he did it again and I had to admit it was a real smile all right—of course he'd smile at his mum.' Kit's face softened. 'Remember the way he used to hold our fingers? You on one side, me on the other, just watching him as he lay between us in the middle of our bed. Fast asleep and holding onto both of us. Wearing that little white sleepsuit with the ducklings on it your youngest sister bought for him.'

'Yeah.' Moments when she'd thought her heart would burst with happiness.

'It's not fair,' Kit said, a muscle working in his jaw. 'It's not fair that we didn't get our chance. All the things we never got to do with him. I never gave him piggybacks or took him to feed the ducks or kick a ball around the park. I never taught him to ride a bike or swim or make sandcastles or skip stones in a lake—all the things a dad wants to do with his child.'

'Yeah, it's the might-have-beens that hurt the most.' She'd never had the chance to make him a birthday cake or read him stories or do finger-painting or play-dough with him.

And there was something else that had hurt her deeply. 'You were nearly late for his funeral.'

Kit exhaled sharply. 'I had an emergency at work. I couldn't just leave my patient on the operating table.'

It was good, as excuses went—but not good enough. 'You were a house officer, Kit. A junior doctor, not the lead surgeon. They could've found someone to take your place that morning, of all mornings.'

He didn't try to argue, she noticed. Clearly he knew she was right.

'I got stopped for speeding on the way to the church,' Kit said. 'But the policeman let me off when I explained where I was going and why.'

Maybe, but there was something he'd never explained to her. 'Why did you even go to work on that day? Why weren't you with me?' When she'd needed him so badly, when she'd needed the comfort of his arms round her, the day they'd laid their baby to rest? The day she'd had to walk behind the coffin on her own?

'Because I couldn't handle it,' he said softly. 'I couldn't handle the fact that Ethan was gone. That our beautiful baby had died. The only thing that made any sense to me was work, somewhere I was needed.'

'*I* needed you,' she burst out.

'I know.' He refused to let her hand go. 'I couldn't make things right for you, Tally. I couldn't save Ethan. I couldn't bring him back. But I could make things right at work. I could make a difference *there*.' His eyes held hers. 'I'm sorry I let you down. If I had the time over again, it'd be different.' He sighed and shook his head. 'Tally, we were both twenty-four years old. Hardly more than children ourselves. I was too young, too immature to deal with it properly.'

He had a point. And, deep down, she'd realised that at the time. But it had still hurt like hell. Kit had let her down. He had never been there. She'd been short-tempered, forever finding fault with whatever he'd done on the rare occasions he had been there. So he'd backed away even more, and the vicious circle had gone on and on and on. Pulling tighter and tighter, until finally the life had been squeezed out of their marriage.

'I hurt too much to see what was happening to you,' he said softly. 'I'm sorry. I was wrong.'

Not only him. 'Your oldest brother didn't even come to the funeral.'

Kit exhaled sharply. 'You know why. Melanie was six months pregnant. It would have been like rubbing our faces in it—and even if Julian had come on his own, without Mel, we'd still have been thinking about it. About the fact they were going to have a baby in three months' time, and we were burying ours.'

'And your parents blamed me.' For having Ethan in the first place—and then for him dying. Natalie had overheard that whispered conversation. And she'd never forgotten it. Or forgiven it.

Kit's face registered shock. 'But— No, Tally, that's crazy. He had a virus—Coxsackie B—and there were complications. Cardiomyopathy. He died of heart failure. It wasn't your fault.'

Maybe. But there'd always been that nagging doubt in the back of her mind. Supposing she'd done things differently? 'If I hadn't taken him out somewhere, he might not have picked up the virus.'

'Tally, it really wasn't your fault.' He squeezed her fingers. 'You know as well as I do that viruses are everywhere in winter. Coughs, colds, RSV, Coxsackie B...it's the time of year. You can't move a step without coming in contact with some microbial thing or other. And if you'd stayed stuck indoors with Ethan, maybe a visitor would have brought the virus with them—maybe it was something he *did* get at home. It could have been anyone who called at the door. The postman, the newspaper delivery boy—anyone. It really wasn't your fault. You know Coxsackie B can survive for days outside, even in freezing weather. Maybe *I* was the one who brought it home—maybe I'd come into contact with it at the hospital.' He stared at her. 'Please, tell me you haven't spent the past few years blaming yourself.'

'I... No.' She sagged against the back of her chair. 'Not really.'

'Good. Because it wasn't your fault. It wasn't anyone's fault.'

'That's not what your mother thought. I heard her talking at the wake.'

Kit shook his head, clearly not understanding. 'Why didn't you say something to me? I would've dealt with it. Put her straight.'

'Because you were never there,' she said simply. 'You just left me to deal with everything.'

'Maybe this was a mistake. Trying to talk.' He dragged in a breath. 'This isn't going to help either of us—going over old ground, old hurts. We can't change the past. I would've given my life to be able to save our son, Tally, but I couldn't. If anything, I failed him far more than you did. I was the qualified medic.'

'You weren't a paediatric specialist. Or a cardiologist. And even if you had been, it wouldn't have changed what happened. As you said, nobody could have saved him.' She wrested her hand free. 'Kit. We have to move on. Forget the past. Let's just leave things here.'

'So where does that leave us?'

'We're colleagues. At least until my six months is up.' She took a deep breath. 'And that's it. Kit, I need to go now.'

She hadn't touched her coffee, Kit noticed. Just as he hadn't touched his. He didn't have the stomach for it.

And those moments in the churchyard, where they'd held each other by Ethan's grave, that was past, too. A passing weakness in her eyes. It wasn't the beginning of maybe finding some common ground. It was closure.

The end.

And there was absolutely nothing he could do about it.

'I'll take you back,' he said quietly, and pushed his chair back. In silence, they left the café. Kit drove her back to Litchford-in-Arden. Watched her leave. Then walked back into the churchyard and sat by Ethan's stone.

'I wish I could turn the clock back,' he whispered, running the tip of his finger along the tightly furled petals of the rosebuds. 'I wish I could change it all. Bring you back. Not let you have that bloody virus in the first place. And then everything would be how it should have been.'

But he couldn't change a thing. And nothing he could do would fill the hollowness inside him.

CHAPTER SEVEN

THE problem was, Kit thought as he scraped his barely touched meal into the bin that evening, he still loved Tally. He hadn't contested her request for divorce because he'd been too numb at the time. He hadn't allowed himself to feel, in case he fell apart completely. And it had stayed that way ever since.

Until their lives had collided again.

The moment he'd seen her in the staffroom, he'd known. The moment he'd held her at the fundraiser, he'd been absolutely sure. She was his one and only.

And today, when they'd held each other, had been the first time he'd really cried since the day Ethan had died. Every birthday, every anniversary, Kit had brought flowers to Litchford-in-Arden. And he'd stood by his baby's grave, dry-eyed, wishing the wreckage of his life would somehow fix itself the way he fixed patients.

Right now, the wreckage seemed to be sliding further towards an abyss.

Natalie's words echoed in his head. *We have to move on. Forget the past. Let's just leave things here.*

In her view, they were just colleagues. *And that's it.*

It wasn't enough. Never would be enough.

But right now he didn't even know where to start trying to change things.

Natalie huddled in her chair, her knees drawn up to her chin and her arms wrapped around her legs. It was the first time she and Kit had talked—really talked—since Ethan had died. If only he'd told her how he had been feeling back then. If only he'd shared, let her in instead of shutting her out. But he hadn't, and she'd felt more and more alone. As if she had been the only one in their marriage.

In the end, she hadn't been able to stand it. She'd packed, left him a note, telling him that it was over and she wanted a divorce, and all communications from then on had been through a solicitor. Sighing, she remembered how her parents had tried to tell her that he was grieving in his own way, to give him a chance, but she'd refused to listen. All she'd seen had been that the love of her life hadn't been there when she'd needed him. He'd turned away. Thrown himself into his job. Shut her out.

For better, for worse...in sickness and in health.

Vows she'd meant when she'd taken them. Really, really meant.

Till death us do part.

She'd thought it would be her death, or his. Not their baby's.

Maybe they'd just been too young when they'd got married. Twenty-one. Both still students—Kit an undergraduate, Natalie studying for her post-graduate certificate in education. They had no money, lived in a rented cottage because they couldn't afford to buy anywhere, and their honeymoon was three days in a little bed-and-breakfast in a Cornish fishing village, because it was all Kit's bank account could stretch to and he insisted on sticking with the tradition that the bridegroom paid for the honeymoon.

But they were happy. So very happy. They laughed and loved and were just *together*. It didn't matter if they had to live on beans on toast by the end of the month, or that they didn't go out to flash restaurants. All they needed was each other.

Ethan's death changed all that. They weren't even able to share the good memories. They simply stopped talking. And when she left Kit, he didn't exactly try to get her back. Which proved to her that their marriage was finished. The day their divorce came through, she found out he'd moved to London.

It was all over.

So she'd started a new life. Talked her way onto a degree course in medicine, left her job as a history teacher and started the long haul to train as a paediatrician. The world of medicine was a pretty big one and she had no intention of working in London, so she'd never dreamed that her life would cross Kit's again.

Until the day he'd walked into the staffroom at St Joseph's.

She'd been lying to herself for years. Telling herself that she was over him. That she didn't date because she didn't want to end up in the same kind of mess, trapped in a marriage that no longer had love to hold it together. That she was focused on her career and she just wasn't interested in another relationship.

Ha. What she hadn't faced was *why* she wasn't interested in another relationship.

The truth was, she was still in love with Kit.

The way he'd kissed her at the fundraiser—it had been

like coming home. Like being fully alive again, seeing the world in colour instead of living from moment to moment in a monochromatic world. And she knew it had been the same for him, too. That he'd felt the same spark, the same need. Everyone else in the room had just melted away. They hadn't even heard the music change, they'd been so lost in each other.

But they couldn't go back. They couldn't change the past. And although it would be, oh, so easy to call him, go back to him, start their relationship all over again, she knew it would be a mistake. Because there would come a time when she'd need him—and he would let her down. Just like he had last time. People didn't change, not deep down. She couldn't afford to lean on him again—if she needed his support, she knew it simply wouldn't be there.

So they had to move on. Be professional about the fact they had to work together. In a few months, when her rotation in the paediatric department was over, she'd move to the emergency department for six months. She wouldn't see him again, except maybe if she referred a case to Paediatrics. And then, once her house officer year was over, she could change hospitals. Find another job on another children's ward, in another city, a long, long way from Kit Rodgers. Maybe move back to Bristol, where she'd done her training.

For now they were colleagues. Just colleagues. And that was how it was going to stay.

Over the next couple of weeks, Kit and Natalie were wary of each other at work. They were civil to each other on the occasions when they had to be in the same place at the same time, but both scanned the staffroom before they went in, and if Kit was there Tally would make some excuse about forgetting some paperwork, or if Tally was there Kit would invent a patient who needed to see him.

It was fine, as long as they didn't have to be too close to each other.

Kit wondered if Debbie had said something to Lenox, because he and Tally were rostered apart for a while. Or maybe she hadn't, because then they ended up working in the PAU together.

Kit flinched when he saw their first patient. A small girl, around two years old, carried in her father's arms. The mum was there, too—pregnant. About six months, he'd say, from the size of the bump. Her partner was making sure she was comfortable on the chair, clearly taking as much of the worry from her as he could.

Exactly what Kit had done when Tally had been pregnant with Ethan. Fussed over her, made sure she had everything she'd needed.

Exactly what he *should* have done when Ethan had died, instead of shutting the world and the pain out.

He shook himself. No. He had to concentrate on his job. Not the mess that was his personal life.

The little girl had definite stridor, harsh abnormal breathing that was caused by a narrowing or obstruction of the larynx or trachea. This would be a good case for Natalie—she'd need to work out if the stridor was being caused by croup, a foreign body, epiglottitis, a low level of calcium in the blood or one of the rarer causes.

'You lead,' he said to Natalie.

Natalie introduced Kit and herself to the Leonards, and discovered that little Gail was two years old.

'How long as she been like this?' she asked.

'Since yesterday. She's got this barking cough, and it was worse last night,' Mrs Leonard said.

'I know her breathing sounds scary, but we can do something to help,' Natalie reassured her. 'Small children have narrower airways, so they find it harder to breathe when they have a cough or cold. And coughs are usually worse at night when you've been lying down for a few hours. May I examine her?'

The Leonards nodded.

'And may I ask you something first? You said she's been like this since yesterday.'

'Except it's got worse overnight,' Mr Leonard said.

'Sometimes this kind of breathing's caused by inhaling something—a peanut or a bead, something small that blocks the airways. Is there any chance Gail could have inhaled something?' Natalie asked.

'No. We never have peanuts around the house, and she's always with me,' Mrs Leonard said. 'I'd have noticed if she'd put something in her mouth or up her nose or what have you.'

'That's fine. I just needed to rule it out before I examine her,' Natalie reassured her.

Kit watched her carefully. If she moved to examine the child's throat before ruling out the possibility of epiglottitis, he'd stop her. Epiglottitis, a bacterial infection that caused swelling of the epiglottis—the flap of cartilage at the back of the tongue that closed off the trachea and larynx when you swallowed—could become a medical emergency within seconds, because trying to examine the throat could cause a complete obstruction of the airway. It was something you could only do properly when the child had been intubated, and that needed an anaesthetist.

'Has Gail been immunised against Hib?' Natalie asked.

The *Haemophilius influenzae* bacterium was the cause of epiglottitis. The vaccination programme meant that fewer cases were seen nowadays, but if Gail hadn't been immunised, there was a chance that this was epiglottitis.

'All her vaccinations are up to date,' Mr Leonard confirmed, stroking his little girl's hair.

'Has she had a cough or cold over the last few days?' Natalie asked.

'Yes, a bit,' Mrs Leonard said.

'Have you noticed if she has any problems swallowing?' Natalie asked.

Kit relaxed. She was asking all the right questions, and little Gail wasn't drooling, so the chances were she wasn't having that much of a problem swallowing. It was unlikely to be a case of foreign body inhalation or epiglottitis, then.

'None,' Mr Leonard said. 'She's been a bit off her food, but we've got her to drink a bit.'

'I'll just check her temperature and listen to her chest,' Natalie said. She examined the little girl, and noted the measurements down on the file. 'She doesn't have a fever, and I can't hear any wheezing, so it's not a lower respiratory tract problem. I'm just going to check her throat, but I think she's got croup, which is very common in children of her age group at this time of year. Though she's finding it very hard to breathe and getting a bit tired, so I'm going to admit her for treatment.'

Kit glanced over her shoulder; she'd written, 'Rib recession—query croup—admit.'

'What I wanted to check is that she didn't have a condition called epiglottitis, which has very similar symptoms to croup. But her temperature's fine, she doesn't have problems swallowing and her breathing's very harsh, so we can rule that out,' Natalie continued. 'Croup is caused by a viral infection in her upper airway—most likely the parainfluenza virus.'

This time, she actually glanced at Kit; he knew what she was thinking. There were other viral causes—respiratory syncitial virus, influenza virus type A, rhinovirus…and Coxsackie virus.

The virus they both found so hard to handle.

'It's basically affected her throat,' Natalie explained. 'Do you have any other children?'

'Only Gail. And this little one.' Mrs Leonard placed a protective hand on her bump. 'Croup couldn't affect my baby, could it?'

'It's unlikely, but you might be a bit uncomfortable if you catch the same virus. The virus is transferred through airborne droplets, such as coughing and sneezing, and it's passed from one person to another by touch. It tends to go from your hands to the mucous membranes of your eyes and nose, so make sure you wash your hands a lot. You may also find that Gail gets croup the next time she has a cold,' Natalie warned. 'It may keep recurring, but the good news is that the symptoms aren't so severe once children get to about five.'

'Are you going to give her antibiotics?' Mr Leonard asked.

Natalie shook her head. 'They won't make any difference because it's a viral infection, not bacterial—but as she's having difficulty breathing we'll keep her in for a while and give her some humidified oxygen to help her, as well as some drugs through a nebuliser to widen her airways and make it easier for her to breathe. Croup usually clears up in three or four days, though you'll find that the barking cough lasts a bit longer. I'll take you up to the ward and get her booked in, and you can stay with her as long as you like. Try to keep her as calm as possible—I know it's hard, when you're worried, but if Gail sees you're worried it will upset her more, she'll cough even more and she'll start panicking.'

The little girl was snuggled against her father's chest, and Kit felt his heart contract.

Oh, God. Would it ever stop hurting? Would he ever stop wishing?

'When you get Gail home,' Natalie said, 'you need to keep eye on her. If she has any more breathing difficulty or looks a bit blue round her mouth, nose or nails, you need to call your doctor immediately or bring her back here, because it means she's not getting enough oxygen and she'll need a bit of help.'

'What can we do to help the cough?' Mrs Leonard asked.

'Cough mixture's a waste of time,' Natalie advised. 'The best thing you can do is sit her up to help her breathing—prop her up against plenty of pillows at night. Steam inhalation helps, but you can't really sit a child over a hot bowl with a towel over her head—apart from it being too much of a risk for burns, little ones find it much too scary. The best thing you can do is to sit her in a steamy bathroom—run a shower on hot for a few minutes, or run a hot bath, and keep the door closed so the air's nice and moist.' She smiled at them. 'Obviously I don't need to tell you to keep an eye on her so she doesn't fall in the hot water and get burned.'

'What about food? Should we stick to soft foods?'

'For now, yes, because they'll be easier for her to manage. Keep her meals light, because anything heavy might make her be sick, and get her to drink lots of cool fluids. Now, let me take you up to the ward and introduce you to the nurse who'll be looking after Gail while she's here.'

When she returned, Kit took her to one side. 'You handled that well. You checked the main causes of stridor before you examined her throat.'

'She didn't look toxic, so I didn't think it was epiglottitis—but I wasn't going to take the risk.'

'Good. You'll make an excellent doctor, Tally.'

'Thank you.' Her voice was very cool.

Hell, hell, hell. She was shutting him out again.

And he couldn't get that comment about moving on out of his head. What did she mean by that? Finding someone else? Starting another family—with someone else?

He hoped not.

He didn't want anyone else. And he couldn't handle the idea of seeing her with someone else. Of course he wanted Natalie to be happy—but, please, not with someone else. He couldn't bear the thought of finding out that she was pregnant, and not being the one who had the right to go to antenatal classes with her, see the wonder of their baby at the ultrasound scan, feel the baby kicking in her womb, or share those first precious seconds when a new life came into this world.

What he really wanted was to start again. Make a new life. With Tally.

But that meant persuading her to change her mind about him. And, right now, he didn't even know where to start.

CHAPTER EIGHT

NOVEMBER slid into December, the dark days of the year. The days Natalie always found hardest. The hospital was gearing up for Christmas—the tree in the reception area was decked with tinsel and baubles and coloured lights; there were cards from colleagues and past patients on the notice-board; the pictures of Santas and snowmen drawn by the older children were pinned up on the boards by their beds; and there were mince pies and chocolates and Christmas biscuits in the staff kitchen—but Natalie really couldn't get into the spirit of things.

She'd joined in the ward's 'Secret Santa' and, to her relief, she'd drawn Ruth's name out of the hat—if she'd picked Kit's, it would have been too much. Fran had also talked her into going for a Christmas drink with some of the staff before going to the hospital social club revue. But that was as much as Natalie could manage. That, and a forced smile as people wished her a merry Christmas.

Christmas hadn't been merry for a long, long time.

Probably never would be again.

And as the days dragged on towards the day of the year

she really hated, she grew quieter and quieter. She wanted to be on her own. Just quiet and thinking, and wishing things were different.

Kit knew Natalie had booked the day off. It stood to reason: today was a day when she wouldn't want to be around anyone. But she'd been so withdrawn lately, her face pale and pinched. And he was worried about her.

He rapped on Lenox's door and glanced through the window. At the consultant's nod, he walked in and closed the door behind him. 'Hi. Can I ask a huge favour, please?'

Lenox lifted an eyebrow. 'You want to swap your Christmas duty?'

Kit smiled. 'No, no, that's fine. I don't mind working at Christmas.' It was better than sitting on his own in a rented flat. And much, much better than heading south and spending the day with his family, following old traditions yet feeling out of place. Kit was the only one of his siblings who wasn't married with children—even though he'd actually been the first of the four to get married and the first to have a baby. Catching the occasional glances from his brothers, the looks that said, there but for the grace of God—it hurt like hell. The way his sisters-in-law tried to share their children with him, make him feel part of the family, encouraged the kids to make a fuss of their special uncle... Oh, he hated it.

He made the effort, always played nice, made a point of playing games with them and making sure he could talk to them about whatever the in thing was. But inside his heart always ached. Because it wasn't the same as doing it with his own child. And seeing his nephews and nieces was too much of a reminder of what he'd lost. What he hadn't had the chance to do. Like little ghosts of what Ethan might have been like at that age.

So Kit would much rather spend his time with the children on the ward instead. Helping them to get better. Doing something positive instead of inwardly brooding, hating the fact that his son wasn't there to open his stocking on Christmas morning. Losing himself in work instead of counting the seconds until he could escape for a walk on his own and not have to fake a seasonal jollity he simply didn't feel.

'What can I do for you, then?' Lenox asked.

Now for the tough one. 'I need Natalie's home phone number.'

Lenox shook his head. 'Sorry. I can't give out confidential staff information.'

Well, Kit had expected that. So now he had no choice but to explain. He took a deep breath. 'There's a good reason. I'm worried about her.'

'She's been a bit quiet lately,' Lenox agreed. 'I was going to have a chat with her, check she was happy on the ward or if she was worried about her work.'

'It isn't the job. It's the time of year.' Kit raked a hand through his hair. 'Look, can I tell you something in confidence? Something I don't want going any further?'

'Of course.'

'I should've told you this when I first came here.' Kit stared at the floor. 'Though I accepted the job before I knew Tally was going to be working here. I had no idea that she was even training to be a doctor, let alone newly qualified.' He sighed. 'I used to be married to her.'

'Ah.' There was a wealth of understanding in Lenox's

voice. 'So you need me to look at the rosters and keep you two apart?'

Kit wrinkled his nose. 'No, working together isn't a problem.' Well, it was—but it was *his* problem. He'd just have to deal with the fact that he was still in love with his ex-wife. 'Today's an anniversary.'

'Wedding?'

Bile rose in Kit's throat. 'I wish it was.' Framing these words were so hard. And he really couldn't bear to see the pity he knew he'd see in Lenox's face when he explained. But he had to do it. 'We had a baby. Ethan. He died six years ago today.' He dug his nails into his palms, reminding himself to keep this professional. To keep the emotion out of it. Just explain it in dry medical terms. 'He was six weeks old. Cardiomyopathy—a complication of Coxsackie B. We, um, split up not long after he died.' And that had been his fault. All because he'd shut Natalie out. Hadn't put her first when he should have done.

'I'm sorry,' Lenox said.

All the sorries in the world wouldn't bring Ethan back. And Kit really hated expressions of sympathy. Even when they were well meant, they rang a false note with him. He looked his consultant straight in the eye. Faced the pity. Right now, Natalie needed help. And Kit was going to put her first, above his own feelings. 'I could ring her parents and ask them for her number—but it's a tough day for them, too, and I don't want to drag up bad memories for them. I could wait until my lunch-break and just drop by her flat, but…' He shook his head. 'I just need to call Natalie and see if she's OK.'

'I see.' Lenox looked thoughtful.

'I know it's against the rules. But sometimes rules need

to be bent, to—' Oh, no. Wrong tack. He didn't want Lenox thinking that there was any question over Tally's suitability for the position of house officer or future progression in her career. She was going to make a superb doctor, and Kit wasn't going to put obstacles in her way. 'Look, I'm not saying she'd do anything stupid. She's far too sensible for that. But I just know how she'll be feeling today.' The same way he felt. Empty. Bleak. Still railing against the fate that had ripped their lives apart. Wishing, wishing, wishing to hell that things were different. 'So I need to talk to her, to make sure she's all right. Please?'

The moments dragged by. Finally, Lenox nodded. 'As the circumstances are exceptional, I'll bend the rules this once. And I won't mention what you told me to anyone, even Natalie.'

'Thank you,' Kit said quietly.

Lenox took a file from his cabinet, looked up Natalie's record and wrote the number on a piece of paper for Kit.

'I appreciate this,' Kit said.

'Give her my best when you speak to her,' Lenox said. 'And tell her, if she needs to talk about things at any time, I'm here.'

Just like Kit hadn't been.

And then he noticed the photograph on Lenox's desk. Three children—the eldest sitting, the middle one standing and the baby on the eldest one's lap. Even now, Kit knew that his consultant would be thinking about his children. Realising how lucky he'd been. And Kit would just bet that all three children would get an extra-big hug from their father when he got home from his shift.

He didn't wait for his break, he simply went outside and rang Natalie from his mobile phone. There was no answer, as he'd half expected, but he didn't bother leaving a message on her machine. Maybe she'd gone to spend the day with her parents in Cotswolds.

Though somehow he doubted it. He had a feeling that it would be like Ethan's birthday. A day when she just wanted to be on her own. She was probably at the grave, laying fresh flowers there. But maybe she might share today with him. Ease the burden. Ease the heartache, the empty space inside.

As soon as Kit's shift finished, he drove to Litchford-in-Arden. He reached the churchyard while it was still just light enough to see where he was walking. There was no sign of Tally in the churchyard, but there were fresh roses on Ethan's grave, and a holly wreath.

A wreath for their son for Christmas, when he should have had a big red stocking with a furry white top. There should have been a glass of milk and a mince pie left out for Santa on Christmas Eve, with a carrot for the reindeer and a pile of wrapped presents under the tree on Christmas morning. Talcum-powder footprints, so their little boy would marvel that Santa had walked in from the 'snow'. Home-made decorations hanging on the tree from nursery and school, bells made from egg boxes covered in glitter with a loop of narrow tinsel.

Instead, there were flowers. Stupid bloody flowers.

How come it still hurt so much, every year?

And who was it who kept fostering the lie about time being a healer? As time passed, sure, a scab formed over the wound. But every anniversary stripped it raw again.

Kit didn't disturb Natalie's arrangement but left his flowers, still wrapped, lying on the grass in front of the wreath. 'God bless, my little boy. How I miss you,' he whispered. 'How I miss what we should have had. Our family.' He blinked to stop his eyes stinging, then headed back to his car.

It was a mistake to have the radio on. The classical station he'd tuned into was playing carols. An *a capella* version of 'In the Bleak Midwinter'.

Bleak didn't even begin to describe how he felt right now. Sitting the car in a church car park, in the twilight, on his own.

He switched off the radio and headed back to Birmingham. He parked at the side of the road where Natalie lived, then found her flat. She didn't answer the doorbell, but he'd seen her car parked further down the street. She was there all right, she just wasn't answering. Though he couldn't see any lights. Which meant she must be sitting there on her own, in the darkness.

He'd said to Lenox that Tally wouldn't do anything stupid. Had he been wrong about that? Was the weight of today so much that she'd…?

God, no. It didn't bear thinking about. He'd already programmed her number into his mobile phone; he pushed the button to dial it again. As he'd expected, the answering-machine kicked in. He grimaced as he listened to the message, then waited for the long beep. This time, he left a message. 'Tally, it's Kit. I know you're there—I can see your car. I'm worried about you. Just pick up the phone so I know you're OK and you haven't done anything that will make me kick your door down and drive you straight to the emergency department at St Joseph's. Please?'

No answer.

Fear blazed through him. Please, please, please, don't let her have done anything stupid. And why the hell had he let his pride get in the way? Why hadn't he bridged the gap between them, made her talk, made her understand that he was there for her? Why had he let her struggle on her own?

He hung up, and was about to put his shoulder to her door and break it down when the light came on and the door opened. Natalie stood there, her face white. In jeans, he registered, and an unironed long-sleeved T-shirt. Bare feet. As if it had been an effort for her even to get dressed that morning, a day when everything hurt too much.

'How did you get my number?' she demanded.

He'd invaded her privacy. Bad move. She clearly resented it. And he couldn't blame her. But all he could think about was the fact that she was OK. That she hadn't been driven completely over the edge. 'I bent a few rules because I was worried about you. I was going to come and see you anyway today.' He dragged in a breath. 'You look like hell.' And she was shivering.

'I can't stand today,' she whispered. 'It's the day of the year I just can't handle.'

The misery in her voice broke his heart. 'I know, honey, I know. It's bad for me, too.' At least he'd managed to block most of it out through work. She'd been on her own. She'd had time to think. Time to brood. Time to mourn their loss. He stepped forward and held her close, cradling her against his chest and stroking her hair.

And he was whispering to her, whispering the words he should have said all those years ago. 'It's going to be all right. I'm here. We'll get through this, honey. It's going to be all right, I promise.'

She shuddered against him, but her arms were wrapped tightly round him, as if she'd never let him go. The same way he was holding her. And he never, ever wanted to let her go again.

Somehow—he had no idea how—they were standing inside her flat and the front door was closed behind them. He rested his cheek against the top of her head, breathing in the clean scent of her hair. Thank God, she was letting him hold her. Letting him melt the frozen barriers between them with the warmth of his body.

As if she'd guessed his thoughts, she pulled back slightly and scrubbed at her face with the back of her hand. 'Sorry. I didn't—'

'Don't apologise,' he cut in gently. 'I'm the one person you can cry with today, if you need to. And I'm here, Tally. I'm *here*.'

Her flat was tiny. There were four doors leading off the hallway. He assumed one was her bedroom, one the bathroom and one the living room; through the open door, he could see her kitchen. A narrow, galley-type room with a table at one end. The light was on, so he'd been wrong: she hadn't been sitting in the dark. She must have had the door closed so he'd been unable to see the light.

'Come and sit down. I'll make you a hot drink,' he said softly.

He knew he was taking over. Bossing her about. Knew that in ordinary circumstances she'd be caustic about it and she wouldn't let him get away with it. But today wasn't ordinary. It was the darkest day of the year—not literally, as the winter solstice hadn't yet arrived—but this was the day of the year when it felt as if the sun didn't rise. When it felt as if the sun would never rise again.

Natalie allowed him to lead her into her kitchen, settle

her at the table. He hit lucky with the first cupboard door he opened—Tally had always kept the mugs and the coffee in the cupboard above the kettle, and her habits clearly hadn't changed. He made them both a mug of coffee, adding a spoonful of sugar and some milk to hers before bringing them over to the table.

She took one mouthful, and gagged. 'Ick. Sugar.'

'I know you don't take it normally. But I think you need it right now—I would've made you sweet tea, but I know you loathe it, and coffee's the next best thing.' He looked at her. 'Have you eaten at all today?'

She shook her head. 'I can't face anything.'

He knew what she meant. He'd only seen food as fuel today. Hadn't had a clue what he'd eaten. His sandwich at lunchtime could've been made from cardboard and he wouldn't have been able to tell the difference.

'Ah, honey.' He wanted to pull her onto his lap and comfort her, but he didn't dare go that far. 'Let me make you something. A sandwich.'

She shuddered. 'I can't. It'd be like swallowing ashes.'

'Tally, you have to eat. If you don't, low blood sugar's going to make you feel even worse.' In the old days, he remembered, her preferred comfort food had been cheese on toast. 'I'll make you something.' The activity made him feel better. And how weird it was—he'd never been in this room before, but he knew exactly where she kept everything. Bread in the china crock, cheese and tomatoes in the fridge, sharp knife in the cutlery drawer by the sink.

Just as it had been in their cottage in Litchford-in-Arden.

It didn't take long before the bread was toasted and the cheese was bubbling on top of the sliced tomatoes. He slid it onto a plate, cut each slice into four triangles, and brought the plate over to her.

'Just take a bite. One little bite. For me,' he encouraged.

She made a face, but she bit into one triangle. He watched her eat it, then another. But then she pushed the plate away, leaving most of it untouched. 'Sorry. I just…can't.'

'No worries.' He reached across the table and took her hand. 'I know how you're feeling. Same as me. Hollow inside.' A huge, empty space that couldn't be filled.

'I hate this time of year,' she said. 'I hate Christmas.'

He'd noticed that there were no decorations in the hall, no cards up, no holly wreath on the door. Tally had always decked their hall with boughs of holly, just like in the Christmas carol. She'd always had the cards on display, putting them up seconds after she'd scooped them up from the doormat. And they'd always had a real tree, filling the air with its scent. She'd even put together a stocking for him every year, filled with silly presents to make him laugh. The year they'd been totally broke, their first Christmas as a married couple, she'd wrapped up a packet of teabags in his stocking. Individually. And had made him guess what each little square parcel might contain. They'd laughed and laughed and fallen into bed, not caring.

Today, Natalie's Christmas cards were in a pile on the dresser. Not even a neat pile at that. As if she'd gone through the motions of opening them, but had lost all heart before she'd read half through the greeting.

'Celebrating the birth of a baby, just after the death of mine.' Her breath hitched. 'How can I do that?'

'I know.' He gave her a bleak smile. 'It's never been the same for me either—not since the year we got sympathy cards when we should've been celebrating our first Christmas as a family.'

The last word broke her. She propped her elbows on the table, buried her face in her hands and sobbed.

He couldn't just stay to the side and watch her. Couldn't stay apart. He shifted her chair back from the table, picked her up, sat down on her chair and settled her on his lap. Held her tight, stroking her hair and letting her howl into his chest until she'd cried herself back under control.

At last, she lifted her head. 'I'm—'

'Hurting,' he said, heading off her apology. God, he was the last person she needed to apologise to. If anything, he should be the one making the apologies. He stroked her face. 'It's better out than in.'

Ha. Said he, who'd always blocked out his feelings with work. Except for that moment in the churchyard, six weeks ago.

Her eyes were puffy and her face was hot. 'Hey. Stay here for a second,' he said, lifting her off his lap and settling her back onto the chair. He assumed the first two doors on the corridor would be her bedroom and living room, and when he opened the door to the bathroom he was relieved that he'd got it right.

There was a flannel folded neatly over the rim of the sink. He soaked it in cool water, squeezed it out then returned to the kitchen. Wiped her face, then laid the cool flannel over her eyelids, holding it there to relieve the swelling.

She lifted one hand, curled it over his. 'Why are you being so nice?' she whispered.

Because you're the love of my life and I hate to see you hurting. I want to make you feel better. Not that he was going to tell her that. It wasn't the right time. 'Because I care, Tally. Whatever's happened between us, I still care.'

He still loved her. And he always would.

CHAPTER NINE

SOMEHOW—Kit couldn't even remember moving—he was sitting down, on his own chair this time, and Natalie was sitting on his lap. The damp flannel lay on the table, discarded. Her arms were round his neck, her fingers sliding into his hair. And he was kissing her eyelids, tiny butterfly kisses brushing down to the corners of her eyes, her temples. The lightest, lightest touch. A moth's wing against the candle flame.

And he was burning.

'Kit...'

But her voice wasn't saying 'stop'. It was saying 'go on'. That husky, slurring note he remembered from years ago. From the first time they'd made love, when he'd taken his time exploring her skin. When he'd found out just how and where she liked to be touched, where she liked to be kissed. What made her sigh with pleasure, what made her hyperventilate. What made her come apart in his arms.

There was a sensitive spot by her ear, he knew. And, just as he remembered, she reacted by giving a sharp intake of breath and tipping her head back. Offering him her throat. Her beautiful, beautiful throat.

It had always been so good between them. How could

he possibly resist? And right now he thought they both needed to reaffirm that they were still alive. He drew a trail of tiny, nibbling kisses down her throat to her collar-bone. Lord, her skin was so soft, so sweet.

He found her pulse beating strong and hard. He touched the tip of his tongue to it, marvelling at how her body still reacted to him. Even after all this time they were physically still in tune. Her hands were in his hair, and her fingertips were pushing hard against his scalp, urging him on—not that he needed much encouragement. He moulded his hands to her curves, sliding down until he found the hem of her T-shirt, then slipped his hands underneath and splayed his fingers flat against her bare midriff.

He wasn't sure who was shivering most—her or him. The sweet floral notes of her perfume and the scent of her skin were driving him crazy. He was burning up with need. He needed to touch, see, taste. Needed to be skin to skin with her. Needed her to touch him, to make him feel alive again.

As if she'd read his mind, she untucked his shirt and slid her hands under the soft cotton and along his back, smoothing along his musculature. He exhaled sharply at the first touch. Oh, it felt good, so good. Like sunshine beating down on his naked skin after half a lifetime of walking through the freezing rain.

And he wanted more. More. Much more.

He moved his hands higher, skating along the edge of her ribcage, and felt her gasp. So near, yet too far away. For both of them.

Kit moved his hands higher still to cup her breasts. The lace of her bra was flimsy, but it didn't hide her arousal. Her nipples were hard, and she shuddered as his thumbs grazed them through the lace. Her eyes were open but unfocused, the pupils huge with desire.

A desire he shared. More than shared.

Touching wasn't enough. He needed to see her—now. Taste her. He slid one hand around her back, fumbled with the clasp of her bra and heard her sharp sigh of relief echoing his mental one as the clasp finally gave way. She lifted her arms, letting him peel the T-shirt from her; her bra dropped to the floor at the same time, leaving her naked from the waist up.

Kit arched back for a moment just so he could look at her, drink in his fill.

Lord, she was beautiful. She was thinner than he remembered, her breasts smaller, but she was still gloriously curvy. Her skin was so pale, the perfect foil for her dark hair. He'd loved just looking at her, with those dark curls falling over her shoulders against her bare skin. Yet her new style, the short gamine cut, was just as sexy. Sophisticated.

He cupped her breasts, lifting them, feeling their warmth and weight. He wanted to tell her how gorgeous she was, how much he wanted to touch her and taste her and make love with her, but he couldn't speak—he was too full of longing and need for the words to come out.

Longing and need—and love.

He loved this woman with every fibre of his being. Always had. Always would. He'd been stupid enough to lose her six years ago. Now, please, please, let him find his way to her again. Build the first bridge between them. Show her with his body just how much he wanted her back in his life.

For good.

Slowly, slowly, Kit dipped his head. His mouth traced

the valley between her breasts, and then at last he drew one nipple into his mouth. Sucked. Licked. Teased it gently with his tongue and his teeth and his lips, until Natalie was quivering. Then he did it all over again with her other nipple.

'Oh-h-h.' Her gasp was soft and needy.

She was wearing way too much for his liking. So was he. And he couldn't wait any more. He wanted her now. He stopped playing with her breasts. Cupped her face. Touched his mouth to hers, and poured his soul into the kiss. Oh, please, let her understand how much he loved her, how much he regretted losing her, how much he wanted her back. Right now he couldn't frame the words. But he needed her to know this wasn't just sex. This wasn't just a need to reaffirm life on a day that was filled with sadness. And this definitely wasn't something he wanted to do with any other woman.

Only with Tally.

He kissed her until he was dizzy. And then he realised he wasn't wearing his jacket any more. Or his shirt. He had no idea which one of them had removed them or when—or even where they were—but it felt good, so good, to have Tally's hands on him again. Stroking his pecs, skating over his skin, her hands learning his shape all over again.

The tips of her fingers brushed against the soft hair on his chest, then followed the line down, down over his abdomen. When her fingers dipped just inside the waistband of his trousers, he shivered. Closed his eyes. God, he wanted this so much. Needed this.

He tipped his head back in offering and felt her mouth teasing his skin. He loved it when she kissed his throat like that. He loved feeling her mouth against his body. When she touched the tip of her tongue to the pulse beating frantically at the base of his throat, he knew she must be able to tell what effect she was having on him. How crazy she was driving him.

That, and the fact that she was straddling him. She'd be able to feel his erection pressing against her through her jeans, just as he could feel the heat of her sex against him. She'd know just how much she aroused him, how much he wanted her.

And it felt as if she wanted him just as much.

Please, don't let him be wrong about this.

'I need you, Tally,' he whispered. 'Now.'

'Yes,' she said, her voice equally soft and low.

He stood up, lifting her with him; she wrapped her legs round him.

'Tell me where to go,' he said softly. And, please, don't let it be 'to hell', he begged silently.

'Second door.'

Carrying her to her bed sent desire thrilling down his spine. He'd done this before. On the day she'd got her first-class honours degree in history. The day she'd passed her post-graduate course. The day he'd qualified as a doctor. Their wedding night, when he'd carried her over the threshold of the bridal suite that had been her parents' gift to them. And then again when they'd returned to their cottage in Litchford-in-Arden as a married couple—he'd carried her over the threshold of their home and straight to their bed.

Red-letter days that had been among the best in his life.

And maybe, just maybe, this was a return to those days. A new start. A chance to wipe out the bitterness and glory in the best of their love.

He laid her down gently on her bed. A double bed, he noticed with relief. He was way too old to try finessing his lover in a single bed. He and Tally had shared a single bed every night at university, sneaking in to each other's rooms and flouting the rules of the hall of residence which had decreed no visitors of the opposite sex after two a.m., but that felt like a lifetime ago.

Well, it was a lifetime ago—the days when he used to laugh a lot and all was right with his world because he'd wake up with the love of his life in his arms.

He'd missed her so much. Needed her so badly.

He clicked on her bedside light and closed the curtains.

She had to be crazy, Natalie thought. When Kit had asked her where to go, she should have told him to get out of her flat and out of her life.

But, oh, she'd missed him so much. And she was cold. So cold. Frozen to the bone. She needed his body heat to warm her, take the chill from her heart.

Just any man wouldn't do. She wanted Kit. Kit, who knew all her magic spots and whose mouth and hands could drive her crazy. Kit, who understood the way she was feeling right now—he felt the same way, probably—and could make her feel better.

They'd make each other feel better. Heal the hurt.

As Kit joined her on the bed, Natalie reached up to touch his face. There was a slight roughness under her fingertips, the beginnings of stubble. And he looked sexy as hell, his eyes dark with passion and his mouth slightly parted. Funny, even the shadows under his eyes made him look sexy. Dangerous.

'Ah, Kit.' She cupped his face, sat up, pressed her mouth against his.

His arms wrapped around her, holding her tight, and his mouth opened under hers. Letting her set the pace, she noticed. Not that he wasn't capable of taking over, taking control. But she liked the fact that he was putting her needs first.

And, oh, she was going up in flames.

Slowly, she leaned backwards until she was resting against the pillows and Kit was lying half on top of her, still kissing her. But it wasn't enough. She needed more. Needed to feel him inside her. Needed him to take her to another universe, a universe where it was just the two of them and the stars whirled dizzily round them.

She tilted her hips against him. She could feel just how hard he was, how much he wanted her—and she wanted him just as badly.

'Now,' she breathed. 'I need you inside me. Now.'

It took only seconds to strip each other of the rest of their clothes.

And that was it. No more barriers. Just the two of them. Skin to skin.

He nuzzled her cheek. 'Tally, this might not be as good as you deserve. I'm a bit out of practice,' he murmured.

Why should that please her so much? Selfish. Mean. Bitchy even. But she couldn't help hugging herself mentally. He hadn't tried to forget her in wild sex with a different woman every night. So what they'd shared had been special. It had meant something to him.

She slid her fingers down his spine. 'Doesn't matter.' And it was her turn to make a confession now. 'Know what? So am I.'

Both of them were in a mess. And maybe, just maybe, they could heal each other. Ease the pain. Find a way back to the sunlight.

'Just love me, Kit,' she whispered.

His gaze held hers, a deep, intense blue, then his hand slid between her thighs. Stroking, caressing, his clever fingers teasing her to the point where she thought she was going to spontaneously combust.

'O-h-h. I can't—I can't—Kit, *now*!' she begged.

He stole a kiss then, finally, he eased inside her. Filling her. Oh, Lord, it had been so long. So long. How could she have forgotten that it was like this between them?

He paused for a moment, waiting until her body had grown used to the feel of his again. And then he moved. Taking it slow and easy.

The magic was still there between them. The spark that had started on the dance floor at the fundraiser was now snapping and crackling and turning into a blaze. More than a blaze… A supernova. White heat, light, spinning round her. A feeling she hadn't had in years.

'Kit. Yes. Please. *Yes*,' she sighed, wrapping her legs around his waist and urging him deeper. Oh, it was good. So good. The way his body drove into hers, pushing her deeper and deeper into arousal. Heat radiated through her, from the soles of her feet to the tips of her fingers to the nerve-endings in her scalp.

How could she have forgotten how good this was, how amazing Kit made her feel?

It was like being in an oasis after years of wandering through a desert, lost and empty, Kit thought. And his mouth was filled with the sweetness of Tally's. He didn't think he'd ever be able to stop kissing her. Teasing her mouth, brushing her lips with his, until the tingling was too much to bear and he needed a deeper kiss, a hot, wet meeting of mouths that made his body scream for completion.

He'd almost forgotten how good this was. The warm sweetness of her body wrapped around his. The way his pulse rocketed. The feel of her heart beating against his, hard and fast. Urgent. The surge of his blood as his body thrust into hers. Her hands smoothing down his spine, cupping his buttocks, urging him deeper. Complete abandonment to the heat rising between them. The feeling that he could fly.

He felt Natalie's body begin to ripple around his; as he fell into his own release, he cried out her name. Natalie. His love, his life. His one and only.

When he rested his cheek against hers, it was wet. And he wasn't entirely sure whose silent tears they were.

Tally lay curled in Kit's arms, her head resting on his shoulder, his arm wrapped around her waist and her legs tangled with his. The way they'd always curled up together after making love. Just as if the past six years had never happened. As if they'd never been apart.

And then it sank in. What they'd just done.

Oh, Lord.

This shouldn't have happened. The sex had been amazing—it always had been good between them—but it just wasn't enough. It wasn't enough to keep a relationship together, and they couldn't go back to how things used to be. How things had been before Ethan.

And although Kit had been there for her today—had held her when she'd needed it, washed her face so tenderly when she'd stopped crying, looked after her, made her something to eat—how could she be sure he'd be there the next time she needed him? Hadn't he spent today at work after all, using work to block out his feelings?

Just as he'd done when Ethan had died.

So he hadn't changed. Not deep down.

And he hadn't said a word to her about how he felt. Not a single word. No 'I love you'. Nothing.

What man would refuse when he was offered sex on a plate? She'd virtually thrown herself at him, so of course he'd carried her to bed. She'd been such an idiot. Reading much more into it than was really there. Today they'd both been feeling low. Miserable. And having sex was the best way to reaffirm life, make you feel connected to someone. That was all this had been.

It was a mistake and it needed to stop.

Right here, right now.

Slowly, Natalie disentangled her legs from Kit's. Moved his arm from her waist. Wriggled out of his hold and shifted as far away as she could from him.

He turned to her, frowning. 'Tally? What's the matter?'

Did he really not know? 'We can't do this. We're divorced.'

He looked mystified, as if he didn't see what the problem was. 'There isn't a law against it.'

'That's not what I meant. This is all wrong.' Her mouth felt dry with misery. 'We're trying to turn back the clock, pretend nothing's happened, and we can't. This was a mistake. We—we shouldn't have done this.' Her breath shuddered. 'I think you should go.'

'Tally...' He reached out to her, but she shrank away.

She didn't trust herself. If she let him hold her, she knew what would happen next. They'd never been able to get enough of each other's bodies. One touch, and they'd be making love again. And although her body was desperate to be close to Kit's again, her head was shrieking all kinds of warnings. This was all wrong, wrong, wrong. It had to stop now.

'Please. Just go.'

He flinched, as if she'd just slapped him. Hard. And then his face went completely blank. 'If that's what you want,' he said, his voice carefully neutral. 'Perhaps you wouldn't mind looking away while I find my clothes.'

Tally closed her eyes in shame and misery. His clothes. God only knew where they were. Where hers were. Tangled in a heap, strewn all over her flat? She and Kit had been so desperate for each other, neither of them had cared where their clothes landed when they'd stripped each other. He'd carried her to bed, and they'd both been so crazy with desire and need, nothing had had mattered any more.

And now they were going to have to face the consequences.

What a mess. What a bloody, bloody mess. They'd made love. And he had been so, so sure they'd broken down some of the barriers between them. That maybe, just maybe, there was a chance for them to right past wrongs. Talk it through. Understand each other. And then they could wipe the slate clean—forgive each other and start again.

Tally clearly didn't feel the same way.

The words 'I love you' had died on Kit's lips before he could say them. They'd withered away from the look on her face, when she'd shrunk from his touch.

This was a mistake.

Yes, there'd been a mistake all right. And clearly it had been all his.

Grimly, he climbed out of bed and found his boxer shorts and trousers in a heap on the floor. Dragged them on. He went hunting for his shirt, jacket and tie, and finally found them in the kitchen. Discarded on the floor. Crumpled and uncared for.

Yeah, he knew how that felt all right.

He finished dressing. Shoved his tie in his pocket. Slipped on his shoes. Tally hadn't reappeared—well, her clothes were all over the place, too, and she was probably too embarrassed to come out from her bedroom naked. Then again, there were such things as dressing-gowns. And her wardrobe was in her bedroom. The fact she hadn't emerged at all told him she was staying in bed, not wanting to face him. Clearly she didn't want to face what they'd just done. Didn't want to talk to him at all.

Well, that was fine by him. Right now he didn't particularly want to talk to her either. Gritting his teeth, he walked out of her flat. Closed the door behind him. And as the lock clicked, he heard all his hopes shatter.

CHAPTER TEN

Kit spent a sleepless night. Every time he closed his eyes, he saw Natalie flinching away from him. And it made him ache like hell. Did she really think he'd ever do anything to hurt her?

OK, yes, he could admit he'd got it wrong in the past. He hadn't been there for her when she'd needed him most. He'd shut her out—shut everyone out, really. But he'd grown up. Changed.

All he wanted was a second chance.

And she wasn't going to give it to him.

By morning, Kit's head was throbbing. Especially as he'd remembered something. Something he really needed to talk to her about. Something she really, really wasn't going to like. But they would have to be responsible and face it. Together.

He took some paracetamol to deal with his headache and headed for the ward. Thankfully, Lenox had switched the rosters so Kit was working in the PAU and Natalie was doing a ward round with the consultant. Just as well: he didn't think he could face working with her today. Not after the way she'd rejected him so absolutely yesterday.

'Is everything OK?' Lenox asked quietly before Kit headed for clinic.

No. Far from it. But Kit summoned a smile. 'Nothing to worry about,' he lied.

'Good.' Lenox didn't look entirely convinced, but to Kit's relief the consultant didn't press it.

Kit's first case was Nina, a teenager whose mother was convinced she was having a heart attack. 'She's got this pain in her chest,' Nina's mother said.

Nina, Kit noted, was white-faced with pain, but clearly didn't want to admit there was a problem. 'I'm all right, Mum. Stop fussing. And I'm going to get into trouble for missing school.'

'Can you tell me anything about the pain?' Kit asked.

'I'm all right,' Nina said, clearly not liking the fuss. 'My chest feels a bit tight, that's all.'

'You were nearly crying in pain when you sneezed this morning,' Nina's mother cut in.

Tight chest, pain. Oh, yes. Kit knew all about that—except his was mental rather than physical in origin.

A problem with Nina's heart was a possibility. He needed to rule out a few things. And, since she wasn't going to be that forthcoming, he'd have to prompt her to describe the pain. 'Is it a sharp pain, or a feeling as if someone's squeezing you?'

'A sharp pain,' she said.

So far, so good. 'Do you have pain anywhere else?' he asked, carefully making sure he didn't lead the teenager to an answer about pain radiating down her arm. If she said it of her own accord, he'd order further investigations—an electrocardiogram being the first one, to check the rhythm of her heart.

'No. It just hurts here.' She indicated an area a hand's breadth down from her collarbone on the left side.

Probably not a heart attack. 'How's your breathing?' he asked.

She shrugged, then winced as if the movement had caused her pain. 'Fine.'

'Any history of asthma—either you personally or someone else in the family?'

'No, nothing like that.'

OK. Time to rule out a few more things. 'May I listen to your heart?' he asked.

She nodded, and he checked her heartbeat: no sounds he didn't like. No murmurs, no unusual noises. That was a good sign. 'Breathe in for me. And out. And in. And out.' No crackles or wheezing either, so it wasn't a respiratory infection or asthma. He was beginning to have a pretty good idea of what the problem was. 'I think the problem might be with your ribcage. May I examine you?' At her nod, he gently worked his way down her ribs. 'Here's the first rib—just under your collar-bone. Second. Third.'

'Ow!'

Bingo. Just what he'd been expecting. And in exactly the right place, too.

'OK, Nina. It's tender around your second and third ribs, so I'm not going to press any further. What you have is a condition called costochondritis—that's an inflammation of the cartilage that connects the inner end of your ribs with your breastbone,' Kit explained, indicating on himself exactly the places he meant. 'Because of the swelling, it will tend to hurt when you move, or when you cough or sneeze.'

'Is it serious?' Nina's mother asked, looking worried.

He smiled at her. 'The good news is, no. It can be scary,

because most people's thought about a sharp pain in the chest is that it's a heart attack. About one in ten people get this kind of inflammation, and it's more common in young adults like Nina. It'll clear up of its own accord in a few weeks—in the meantime, you'll need to take painkillers to help you manage it,' he said to Nina. 'Have you taken anything for it yet?'

'Mum gave me some paracetamol but they didn't do a lot,' she said, grimacing.

'Start with ibuprofen,' he said. 'As well as being a painkiller, it's an anti-inflammatory so it'll help to bring the swelling down a bit. If it doesn't seem to do much, make an appointment to see your GP for something a little stronger. It should clear up in a couple of weeks, but if it doesn't you might need a corticosteroid injection to bring down the inflammation and ease the pain. I'll be sending your doctor a note to say I've seen you and what my diagnosis is, but in the meantime you need to get plenty of rest and try to avoid any sudden movements.'

Right now, Kit thought, he'd welcome a physical pain he could deal with. Because the pain in his heart was killing him. Emotional pain. And there was nothing—absolutely nothing—he could take for it.

When he finished clinic, he went in search of Natalie. She was with a patient. 'Sorry for interrupting,' he said to the woman Natalie had been talking to. 'When you've finished, could we have a word in my office, Dr Wilkins?'

She looked strained, but nodded.

He headed for his office to catch up on paperwork following his clinic. The seconds dragged by, and still she didn't appear. Did that mean she was really busy, or did it mean she was avoiding him?

Just when he was about to save his file and go back to the ward to track her down, there was a knock at his door.

'Come in.'

To his relief, it was Natalie.

'Thanks for coming. Would you mind closing the door behind you?'

She looked faintly worried. Oh, for goodness' sake, did she think he was about to leap on her? 'Leave it open if you feel more comfortable. It doesn't really make any difference.'

She blushed. Good. She'd taken the point, then. She left the door open—as if making a point of her own—and took the chair he'd indicated.

'We need to talk,' he said softly.

'I don't think so.'

He raked a hand through his head. 'Tally, I really need to talk to you about something. But not here.' Even if she'd closed the door, he still wouldn't have broached the subject here. Not when there was such a likelihood of being interrupted. 'Have lunch with me. Not in the canteen—somewhere quiet.'

'Quiet?' She raised an eyebrow. 'We're hardly going to find somewhere quiet at this time of year. All the restaurants are full of people having Christmas parties, and all the cafés are full of Christmas shoppers.'

Yes, and he didn't want to have to yell what he wanted to say in the hubbub of a crowded room. 'OK, just you and me in the hospital gardens, then. I don't want to discuss this in front of other people.'

She frowned. 'Discuss what? There's nothing to say. We both agreed that yesterday was a mistake.'

He was too weary to argue. 'Tally, don't fight with me.

Please. Just meet me at...' he glanced at his watch '—a quarter to one by the main entrance. It won't take long.'

For a moment, he thought she was going to refuse. Then she sighed. 'All right. I'll see you at a quarter to one.'

Kit spent the rest of his morning catching up with paperwork—and he was relieved that he had something he had to concentrate on, so he could shut out the turmoil in his heart. Just for a little while.

At twenty to one, he was waiting outside the main entrance. He was glad it wasn't raining. He really, really needed the fresh air. Five minutes later—dead on time—Natalie walked out to join him.

'Let's walk,' he said softly, gesturing towards a bench underneath the bare trees in the far corner of the hospital gardens.

They walked in silence to the bench—a silence that grew tighter and tighter as they walked—and sat down.

'So what's this about?' she asked.

'Last night. We got...' Ah, hell. He'd practised the words in his head. But however he tried to put it, it sounded bad. 'We got carried away.'

'And it was a mistake,' Natalie cut in immediately.

She really, really wasn't going to like this. Especially because it looked as if it hadn't yet crossed her mind. 'Neither of us was thinking clearly. There might be consequences.'

She shook her head. 'I'm not with you.'

He sucked in a breath. Countdown to Tally going nuclear. 'We didn't use any contraception.'

She looked at him in utter horror as the penny clearly dropped. 'Oh, my God!'

He winced. 'If it makes you feel any better, I don't sleep around so you don't have to worry about catching an STD from me. I've had two relationships since we split up. Both of them were a fair while ago.' And neither of them had lasted long. He hadn't wanted them to: although the women concerned had both been lovely, sweet and kind, neither of them had been Natalie. Neither of them had made him feel the way Natalie made him feel. And it wouldn't have been fair to string them along.

'I don't sleep around either.' Her face was white. 'Last night was my first time since…'

His stomach dropped as he realised what she meant. Last night had been the first time she'd made love since having a baby.

There really hadn't been anyone since him.

They'd decided to wait until her six-week postnatal check-up before making love again after Ethan's birth. They'd touched each other, but not had full intercourse. And Natalie had missed her six-week check-up because Ethan had been in hospital. Afterwards, there had been a cold wall between them, and she'd moved into the spare room. Sex had been completely out of the equation. And then she'd walked out on him.

There had been nobody since him. So did that mean there was hope after all? Or was he just deluding himself, finding excuse after excuse not to face the fact that it was completely over between them?

Natalie folded one leg over the other and drummed her fingers on her knees, clearly calculating the date of her last period. 'We're probably OK. My last period started a week ago. You know as well as I do there's only a short window for fertility—days ten to fourteen—and the average couple trying for a baby has a one in four chance of conceiving during that window.'

True enough—but only to a certain extent. 'There's no such thing as a safe time, Tally. Ovulatory patterns aren't always consistent. Even if your monthly cycle's regular—' and it always had been, in the years they'd been together '— you get the odd month when things aren't the same. This might be your odd month. You might be pregnant.'

She gritted her teeth. 'We can't have made a baby, Kit. Not on the anniversary of Ethan's death. We *can't*.'

It wasn't so much making a baby that was freaking her, then—it was the timing. Even so. He was going to do the right thing. 'We probably haven't,' he reassured her. 'But if we have, I'll—'

'Just do what you did last time,' she cut in. 'Bury your head in the sand. Shut everything out except work.'

Ouch. He deserved that. But it wasn't entirely fair. 'You're the one who moved into the spare room, Tally. The evening Ethan died.' And he'd needed her to hold him so badly. Except she'd closed the door on him, claiming she had a headache and needed some sleep. He'd tried to put her needs first instead of being selfish and demanding that she return to the marital bed. He'd given her some space.

And what a mistake that had been. The beginning of the end.

'Then you left, without even talking to me about it first. You just wrote me a note saying you wanted a divorce, packed your bags and walked out on me.'

She glared at him. 'You didn't exactly try hard to get me back. Did you call me at my parents'? Did you say you loved me and wanted me to come home?'

No and no and no. Though he had loved her. Deeply.

'You didn't contest the divorce.'

'I was grieving, too,' he pointed out. 'I couldn't cope

with what was happening to us. And neither of us was offered grief counselling at the time. Neither of us dealt with it properly. We probably still haven't, if the truth be known.' He raked a hand through his hair. 'Tally, I admit was young and stupid back then. Things are different now.'

'Are they?'

'Yes. We're both older. Wiser.'

'That's as maybe. It doesn't change a thing.' She stood up. 'I'm going back to work.'

If she refused to discuss it, there wasn't much he could do about it. He could hardly force her to sit down and listen. Even if he did, she could tune him out. Do the mental equivalent of sticking her fingers in her ears and calling, 'La, la, I can't hear you.' He shrugged. 'As you wish. But, Tally, if you're pregnant, I'll stand by you. It's not optional.'

Her jaw tightened. 'I don't *want* you to stand by me.'

Oh, no. No way was he going to let her have his child and be shut out of both their lives. He'd lost one child. He couldn't bear to lose a second. 'If you're pregnant, it'll be my baby too.'

Then he saw a tear slide down her cheek. And he felt like the lowest form of life. She was crying—because he'd pushed her too hard. Made her deal with something she really wasn't ready to face.

Or maybe he hadn't pushed her far enough.

Right now he had no idea what was the right thing, what was the wrong thing. He just had to act on his gut instinct, and hope it wasn't steering him in the wrong direction. He reached out and took her hands. 'Tally. Talk to me,' he said softly. That was where they'd gone wrong last time. They hadn't talked, hadn't shared, had tried to deal with it alone instead of together. Maybe this was their chance to get it right.

'I can't.' She shook her hands free. 'Leave me alone, Kit. Please. I can't handle this.'

He heard the note of panic in her voice. Oh, hell. If he pushed her much further, she might break down completely—which wouldn't help either of them. It was time to back off, give her some space. Though this time he'd be careful not to leave it too long. He didn't want that wall going back up between them. He dragged in a breath. 'OK. I won't push it. But let me know if... I need to know, Tally.'

'If—and it's unlikely,' she pointed out, '*if* there's anything to tell you about, I'll let you know.'

And then she was walking away.

Kit watched her, biting his lower lip. It had been a mess to start with, and now it felt as if things were ten times worse. How the hell was he going to fix this? How was he going to prove to Natalie that he'd changed, that he wouldn't let her down again? How could he prove that he loved her?

So many questions. But, right then, he had no answers.

If anyone on the ward noticed over the next few days that Kit and Tally were avoiding each other as much as possible, they didn't say anything. Kit noticed that Lenox had switched the rosters round so he wasn't working with Tally—at her request maybe? He didn't know. And he couldn't ask. All he knew was that he went up in flames every time he saw her. He couldn't sleep, couldn't think straight.

And he really couldn't carry on like this.

If she wasn't going to give him another chance, then he

had to leave. After Christmas, he'd start applying for another job. Something that would take him a long, long way away from Tally. Maybe a secondment abroad.

A baby. They might have made a *baby*. Natalie hadn't even stopped to think—she'd just needed Kit. Needed to make love with him.

She'd acted like a sex-crazed lunatic. And then she'd thrown him out. Talk about giving mixed signals. No wonder he was avoiding her—he probably thought she was crazy.

Maybe she was.

All she knew was that she couldn't sleep. That she was aware of every time he walked onto the ward, whether she could see him or not. And that she really, really wasn't handling this well.

And if her period didn't start on Christmas Day…

No. It just didn't bear thinking about.

A few days later, Kit was walking down the corridor to his office when he heard a soft voice he knew well in one of the side rooms. Natalie was reading a story to one of their patients—Kyra, a six-year-old who'd recently been diagnosed with acute lymphoblastic leukaemia and was in for chemotherapy treatment. She'd become a favourite on the ward, and even those who weren't rostered as her designated nurse or doctor stopped by her bed for a chat or to read her a story.

Kyra was on her third week of the intensive first phase of treatment, and she'd been very brave throughout. Her parents had taken her to their GP with a high temperature, and the GP had noticed how pale the little girl was. When Kyra's mother had mentioned how easily Kyra seemed to bruise and how tired and lethargic she'd been, the GP had been on red alert and taken a blood sample before referring her to the ward. By the time she'd got to Nightingale Ward, Kyra had developed petechiae—flat, reddish pinhead spots on her skin—and on examination her lymph nodes, liver and spleen had been enlarged.

The blood tests had showed an elevated white cell count. Lenox had ordered a bone-marrow biopsy, which had confirmed presence of 'blasts', immature white cells that overcrowded the bone marrow and stopped it producing normal blood cells.

The cytotoxic drugs Kyra was taking to destroy the leukaemia cells had caused her hair to start falling out and she often felt nauseous, but she always had a smile for any visitors.

And she'd particularly taken to Tally. Kit was aware that Tally often lingered after her shift or skipped her lunchbreak to read to Kyra, and today was clearly no exception. She was reading a story about Christmas wishes.

Ha. He knew what his wish was. One that definitely wouldn't be granted.

'Dr Tally, are Christmas wishes special?' Kyra asked.

'They are. And sometimes they come true just when you think they won't,' Natalie said. 'Are you going to make a Christmas wish?'

'Yes. That I'll be home for Christmas and my mummy will smile again.'

'That's a lovely wish,' Natalie said.

'Will it come true?'

There was a long pause. 'We'll see what Santa can do.'

They were all hoping that Kyra could go home, even if it was only for Christmas Day. The intensive treatment took between four and six weeks and, depending on whether the bone-marrow biopsy showed the leukaemia was in remission or not, she might need to have a lumbar puncture with an injection of methotrexate directly into her spinal fluid. If that didn't work, radiotherapy was a possibility, and perhaps also a bone-marrow transplant, depending on how she responded to treatment. They all had their fingers crossed that she'd go into remission and stay there.

'What about your wish, Dr Tally?' Kyra asked.

Kit knew that he was eavesdropping on a private conversation. That he should walk on. Right now.

But he couldn't have moved if his life had depended on it.

Did Tally have a Christmas wish?

'I've got two wishes,' Natalie said softly. 'One of them isn't really a proper wish because I know it can't happen.' She coughed. 'So my real Christmas wish is that everyone on the ward has a very, very happy Christmas.'

One of them isn't really a proper wish because I know it can't happen.

Kit could guess what it was. That their baby hadn't died. But if Ethan hadn't died, the chances were that their marriage wouldn't have died either. They'd still be together now. So did Tally regret it just as much as he did? And did that mean that his own Christmas wish—that they'd have another chance at happiness—had a chance of being granted?

Maybe, Kit thought. Maybe.

And a flicker of hope lit the shadows around his heart.

A few minutes later, there was a knock on his door.

'Come in,' he called.

Natalie leaned round the edge of his door. 'Have you seen Lenox anywhere?'

Kit shook his head. 'It's his daughter's nativity play this afternoon. He won't be back until tomorrow. Anything I can help with?'

Natalie looked at him for a moment, as if weighing him up, then nodded. 'Kyra. What are the chances of her going home for Christmas Day?'

'Not high.' He sighed heavily. 'Yes, it'd be a lovely gesture and it would probably perk her up no end. But you know as well as I do that the drugs she's on reduce the number of blood cells produced by the bone marrow, meaning that she's at much greater risk of picking up an infection. All it needs is for someone visiting her to be going down with a cold, and she'll become one very sick little girl.'

'But if her parents could make sure she didn't come into contact with anyone who had a cold or even the faintest sniffle, couldn't she go home? Just for a couple of hours? Let her feel as if it's a normal Christmas?'

'A couple of hours would be better than a whole day,' Kit said. 'Let me have a look at her file. I'll review it—and if I think the benefits outweigh the risks, I'll plead your case with Lenox.' He might not be able to make Tally's Christmas wish come true, but maybe he could give their patient a special present. Her Christmas wish. A chance to go home.

CHAPTER ELEVEN

LATER that week, Lenox was speaking at a conference in Bristol, leaving Kit as acting consultant for the day. Kit came in for his shift an hour early so he could run through the handover from the night staff. And when he heard a hacking cough and noisy breathing in the corridor outside his office, he sighed. It sounded like another case of bronchiolitis. This would be the sixth in two days. At this time of year the illness—a lower respiratory tract infection condition where the very small airways in the lungs became inflamed—was virtually an epidemic among children under the age of one. Right now Nightingale Ward had a whole bay of infants being barrier-nursed with 'RSV+' written on the boards outside their rooms to show that their nasal swabs had shown positive for respiratory syncitial virus.

It was always very upsetting for the parents, seeing their babies being fed through a nasogastric tube and with an oxygen mask on. He'd been there himself, knew how bad it felt. How hopeless you felt, how frustrated that you couldn't do anything to save your baby any pain. All you could do was sit beside the bed or crib, maybe hold their hands and talk to them so they knew you were there with them. And it never felt as if you were doing enough.

Kit walked out of his office, about to introduce himself to the parents and add a bit of extra reassurance that although all the tubes and wires looked frightening they really didn't hurt—feeding the baby through a nasogastric tube meant that he or she didn't get tired, the oxygen made it a lot easier for the baby to breathe, and the pulse oximeter meant they could keep an eye on the baby's pulse and oxygen saturation levels—when he realised that it wasn't a patient coughing. It was Natalie.

'You sound terrible. What on earth are you doing here?' he asked, folding his arms. 'You should be at home, off sick.'

'I'm OK.'

She could barely get the words out. Had to take a dragging breath between words. And her voice was little more than a whisper.

Ah, hell. Sometimes he really hated her stubborn streak. 'Tally, go home.'

'On duty.' Breath. 'Not…' Pause. 'Your place…' dragging breath '…to tell me…' Pause. 'What to do.'

How the hell did she expect to get through her shift in this sort of state? His mouth compressed. 'Actually, it is. Lenox is giving a paper, so I'm acting consultant today. And you definitely shouldn't be here. Apart from the fact you're not well enough to work, this is a paediatric ward. Kids have lower immune systems than adults in any case, and the last thing they need is to get this virus on top of the one they've already got. Especially patients like Kyra.'

He noticed her flinch at the word 'virus'. Thinking of Ethan, no doubt. Or maybe feeling guilty at the fact that she hadn't put their patients first. Especially as they'd had that conversation about why Kyra might not be allowed home for Christmas, the risk of her contracting a virus being too high.

'Come with me,' he said, taking her arm.

'What?'

'Don't argue with me, Tally. It's hard enough for you to breathe as it is, without you getting agitated and making it worse. Just come with me.' He marched her into his office, locked his door and pulled the blind. 'Take your white coat off, and lift up your top. Now.'

She made a noise of outraged protest.

Oh, for goodness' sake! Did she think he was making some kind of clumsy, unsubtle pass at her? She should know him well enough to realise that wasn't his style. If he wanted her to take her clothes off, he'd just let the heat between them work for him.

Though he had no intention of doing that either. Last time they'd done that, it had made things even more awkward between them. There was no point in making it worse still.

He waved his stethoscope at her. 'It sounds as if you've got a chest infection, Natalie. Knowing you, you won't make an appointment with your GP to get it checked out—and this time of year you'd be lucky to get an appointment anyway. So you may as well get checked out here. On the ward. By a qualified doctor.'

She flushed, clearly realising she'd misread his intentions. Good. Perhaps now she'd listen to him—where her health was concerned, at any rate.

'Now, lift up your top so I can listen to your chest.'

She said nothing and submitted to the examination.

'Breathe in. And out. And in. And out.' He frowned. 'OK, I'm going to take a listen at the back. Breathe in. And out. And again.' He paused. 'OK, you can put your top down again now.'

She looked near to tears, and he had to fight the urge to drag her into his arms and tell her everything was going to be all right. 'Your chest is clear—no wheezing or crackles—so it's viral and not bacterial. I'm not going to write you a scrip for antibiotics because they won't clear this up any faster, but you're really not in a fit state to work. Look at yourself. You've got no colour, there are dark smudges under your eyes and you're having trouble breathing.' He gave her a grim smile. 'I'll spare you the nasal swab on condition you go home right now and stay in bed for a couple of days.'

'OK.'

The fact she was so docile about it really had him worried. She must be feeling seriously rough. He made a snap decision. 'You're not fit to drive yourself. I'll take you.'

'You're on duty. Can't. I'll get a taxi.'

Each word was clearly an effort between coughs, and her breathing was laboured. He really, really didn't like this. She probably would get a taxi—but she'd be going home to an empty flat, where he very much doubted she'd look after herself properly. He'd already noticed how bare her fridge had been, when he'd made her the cheese on toast. And she'd lost weight over the last week, too. What with the upset of this time of year and the pressure he'd put her under, she probably hadn't been eating properly, and her immune system had lowered to the point where she was an easy victim for a virus.

'Tally, don't argue. I'm taking you home.' He buzzed through to the nurses' desk. To his relief, the senior sister answered. 'Just the woman I need. Debbie, can you do me a favour, please, honey?'

'Sure.'

'Can you get onto the bank team for me? I need a locum for Natalie for the next week.'

'Has she got that awful chest bug that's going round?'

'Yes. And she's really not fit to drive, so I'm taking her home. I'll be an hour, tops. Call my mobile if it's urgent. If I'm not driving, I'll answer; if I am, I'll pull into the next safe place and call you back.'

'OK, Kit.'

'Thank you, Debbie.' He replaced the phone and looked at Tally. 'Coat, handbag—anything else you need from the staffroom?'

She shook her head.

'Right. We're going. Now.'

He set off at his usual pace and she matched him stride for stride, but halfway down the corridor he noticed she was coughing badly. Clearly the effort of walking was making her breathing more laboured and her cough worse. And when she clapped her hand to her mouth he stopped, delved in his pocket and brought out a clean handkerchief. 'Spit.'

'Nuh.' She grimaced as best as she could with what looked like a mouthful of phlegm.

He sighed. 'Tally, if you're coughing up stuff, don't swallow it because it will make the infection worse. You know that—you're a doctor.' And didn't they just make the worst patients? he thought grimly. 'The hankie can go in the wash, or the bin. I don't care. Just spit the stuff out.'

She scowled, but did as he asked. And he slowed his pace so breathing was easier for her. Waited for her in the staffroom while she got her stuff from the locker. Shepherded her to the car park and helped her into his car. Drove her back to his flat.

'Wrong...' cough '...way,' Tally whispered.

'Don't talk. Concentrate on breathing. Take it nice and slowly.' He parked outside his flat.

'Wrong—' she began.

'Tally, I said I was taking you home,' he cut in gently. 'I didn't say *your* home. You need someone to look after you right now. And that someone would be me. So I've brought you to my flat, and I'm going to keep an eye on you until you're better. Don't argue.' He opened the door, ushered her in, then marched her straight into his bedroom. He switched on the bedside light, closed the curtains, then rummaged in his wardrobe for a T-shirt to act as a makeshift nightie. Neither of them had bothered wearing anything in bed in the years they'd been together, but right now he knew that Natalie needed her dignity. His T-shirt would do just fine. 'Put that on and get into bed. I'll be back in a minute.'

'But—'

'Just get into bed, Tally,' he said, and left the room.

Natalie felt too ill to argue; her energy had completely deserted her. The only thing she wanted to do right now was curl up in a ball and sleep for a month. She stripped and pulled Kit's T-shirt on, then climbed into his king-sized bed and pulled the duvet up. The virus had temporarily wiped out her sense of smell, but she knew Kit's scent would be all around her. She was lying in his bed, between sheets he'd slept in. Wearing his T-shirt. And it was almost as if he were holding her, comforting her.

She rubbed the back of her hand across her eyes. She was not going to cry. Whatever was the matter with her? She wasn't normally this pathetic.

She heard a rap on the door. Kit. Preserving her modesty. Ha. Considering how many times he'd seen her naked...

And it made her want to cry even more. Because he was cherishing her. Thinking of her feelings. Putting her first.

'OK,' she rasped.

He was carrying a tray, which he slid onto the cabinet beside the bed. 'Hot honey and lemon. Your throat's sore, yes?'

She nodded.

'There are some throat lozenges here. Don't take more than one every three hours. But I've done you a jug of lemon barley water to keep you going in between. It's weak, so it won't hurt your throat, and it's iced so it'll stay cool during the day. Sip it slowly—if you gulp it, you'll bring it back up. If you run out, I've left the bottle out on the kitchen worktop. Help yourself. Ice is in the top drawer of the freezer.' He looked at her. 'But I'd rather you stayed put and got some rest. If you must, you can lie on the sofa and watch TV or a film, but you do *not* get up properly, understand? You take the duvet with you and you stay put.'

Bossy. She couldn't remember Kit being this bossy. Except maybe when she'd been pregnant with Ethan and he'd turned into a paid-up member of the food police, making sure there were no raw eggs or unpasteurised dairy foods in anything she ate.

Weirdly, she liked it.

The virus must have addled her brains. She was an independent woman, perfectly capable of doing things for herself. She didn't need anyone to look after her.

'I've made you some lunch,' he added.

Lunch. She glanced at the tray. A sandwich with the crusts cut off and covered in cling film so the bread wouldn't go hard with curled edges before she could eat it. A bowl of grapes. A tangerine, which he'd peeled and segmented—and he'd even removed all the white pith. And he'd rustled up a box of tissues from somewhere.

He was making a serious fuss of her.

Now she really wanted to cry.

'If there's nothing there you fancy, have a rummage in the fridge.' He looked at her for a moment. 'I'll be straight home after my shift. But if you need anything, you know the ward's number. Call me.' He gestured to his bedside table. 'The phone's right here.' He took her hand and squeezed it briefly. 'Now, get some rest, OK?'

He scooped up her clothes, and she frowned. 'Where?' she croaked.

He must have guessed the rest of her question because his eyes crinkled at the corners. 'I'm putting your clothes in the washing machine—just in case you had any mad ideas about waiting until I'd gone back to work, then getting dressed, calling a taxi and going back to your place.' This time there was a definite quirk to his lips. 'Even *you* can't go anywhere in soaking wet clothes.'

She pulled a face at him.

'I'm looking after you until you're better, Tally, whether you like it or not.'

She knew when she was beaten, and leaned back against the pillows.

'Rest,' Kit said. He smiled at her, and left.

It was a while before she heard the front door click— obviously he hadn't been joking about putting her clothes in the wash. Ha. If she'd felt better, she wouldn't have let him bully her into going to bed in the first place. She'd never been the sort to let a cold get the better for her. But right now she didn't have the energy to move, let alone go back to her flat.

Kit rang her twice to see how she was—once during his morning break and once during his lunch-break. And when Natalie heard his key in the door later, she was shocked to realise just how much she was looking forward to seeing him.

This was bad. Really bad. They weren't together any more. And she'd blown any chance of reconciliation when she'd panicked the night he'd made love with her again. When she'd thrown him out. When she'd refused to discuss anything with him the next day. When she'd freaked at the idea of having made another baby with him after they'd forgotten to use contraception.

She really didn't deserve his kindness now.

He rapped on the door. Observing her privacy and respecting it, she noticed.

'Come in,' she croaked.

'How are you doing?' He came to sit on the edge of the bed and laid his hand on her forehead. 'Hmm, you've got a bit of a temperature. I'll get you some paracetamol.'

''M OK,' she said, lifting her chin.

'No, you're not. Stop being brave. Some of these bugs are really nasty and I bet you feel terrible.' His hand slid down to cup her face for a moment, and his thumb brushed her cheek—as if he were soothing a fretful child.

'It's a bit like when you first started teaching—you pick up the bugs that go round the school. When you first start in paediatrics, you're exposed to viruses you wouldn't come across in normal circumstances, and more of them, so you're more vulnerable at first. Don't think of it as a weakness. You're doing the right thing by staying put, because you're not spreading it.' He stood up. 'Right. Paracetamol. And I'll get you a fresh drink.' He looked at her tray. She'd made an effort with the sandwich but she hadn't managed to force much of it down. 'Does it hurt to eat?'

'A bit,' she admitted.

'OK. I'll do you something soft for dinner.' He handed her the carrier bag she hadn't noticed him bring into the room. 'You never sit still, so I imagine boredom's starting to kick in. This should keep you going for a little while.'

He'd bought her a whole slew of magazines. One with puzzles in—he'd clearly remembered she liked the crosswords where you cracked the number code to work out the letters—and several glossies. Light, frivolous reading, the kind she hadn't indulged in for years because she'd been busy studying or working: the perfect thing for convalescence.

She heard what sounded like a knife on a chopping board—what *was* he doing?—and then he came back in, carrying another tray. This one contained a fresh jug of lemon barley water and a vase of flowers. Bright, cheerful orange gerberas.

He'd bought her flowers.

Just as he had when he'd been a student. They'd never been expensive or flashy, but he'd bought her flowers every Friday night without fail. Until the day Ethan had died, when he'd stopped doing anything at all.

Tears pricked her eyelids.

'Hey, they're meant to cheer you up. You're supposed to bring flowers to people who aren't well, to make them feel better,' he said, making light of it.

'Sorry.'

'No worries.' For a moment she thought he was going to reach out and touch her again. Hold her. And how she wanted him to.

But then he took a step back. 'If you want a shower, I've

put a fresh towel for you in the bathroom. My dressing-gown's behind the door. Help yourself to whatever you need.'

A shower.

Oh, Lord.

She was glad Kit's last comment had been made as he had been walking out of the room, because she was sure the memories must show on her face. Memories of sharing a shower with Kit. Squeezing into a tiny cubicle together, giggling because the fit was really too tight—and then not caring anyway, because once they'd started soaping each other it had quickly turned from laughter to passion.

They hadn't been able to keep their hands off each other.

Kit had lifted her against the tiles—and the momentary shock of cold tiles against her back had vanished with the heat his body had stoked in hers as he'd entered her.

Bad, bad, bad. She really had to get sex off the brain. Maybe a shower would wash a bit of common sense back into her head.

Kit heard the water running. Good. A shower would probably make Natalie feel better. The steam in the room would definitely help her to breathe more easily. He really ought to persuade her to sit with her face over a bowl of hot water and a towel over her head to keep the steam in and inhale the moist air for a few minutes.

He damped down the urge to join her in the shower. To stand under the running water and soap her all over, sluice the suds from her body, then make love with her until all their problems were forgotten.

It would be, oh, so easy.

Though they'd done that, and it hadn't worked. If

anything, it had made things even worse between them. He really needed to keep his hands to himself.

He shook himself and continued cooking dinner.

When he brought the tray of soup in to Natalie, she was propped up against the pillows, her hair still slightly damp from the shower. She smiled wanly at him. 'Hi.'

'Hi.' He sat down on the edge of the bed and settled the tray on her lap. 'I suppose this ought to be chicken soup, really, to help fight a virus. But I thought this might give you a lift—the colour as well as the taste—plus it's easy to swallow.'

Bright orange, it almost glowed against the plain white porcelain.

She took a sip, then frowned as she recognised the flavour. 'Carrot and orange?'

'Your mum's recipe, yeah. I've always liked it.' Tally herself had taught him to make it. Back in the days when they'd shared things like that—cooked each other meals, ate together, got distracted from doing the washing-up.

He stood up again, needing to put some space between them before he did something stupid. 'I'll be back in a bit.'

He returned a few minutes later with a plate of fluffy scrambled eggs, with roasted courgettes, mushrooms and peppers on the side. 'Thought I'd do you something soft, something that's easy on a sore throat.' She'd finished half the soup, he noted. Good. It was progress, of sorts.

'Where's yours?' she rasped.

'I'll eat later.' He didn't quite trust himself to eat with her. It'd bring back too many memories. And right now he needed to put her feelings first, not his.

When he came to collect her empty—well, half-empty—plate, her eyes were suspiciously red. 'What's wrong?' he asked. 'Didn't you like it?' Surely her tastes hadn't changed that much in the last six years?

'Not that. You're being so nice to me. I'm being wet. Sorry.'

A tear spilled over the edge of her lashes; he wiped it away with his thumb. 'You're not well, honey. Of course I'm going to be nice to you. What did you expect me to do, have a major fight with you?'

She dragged in a breath. 'Where are you sleeping tonight?'

Her voice was slightly quavery, he noticed. Was she worrying that he expected payment in kind for looking after her? 'On my sofa.'

'You're too tall. Be murder on your back.'

He shrugged. 'It's a sofa bed, Tally. Granted, it isn't as big as this is, and I wouldn't like to sleep on it permanently, but it won't do me any harm to sleep on it for a few nights. Until you're better.' He smiled. 'Don't worry, I'm not going to leap on you.' Even though there was nothing he'd like more than to have Natalie back in his bed. Back in his life. 'I just want you to get better. You need to rest. And this is the best place for you right now.'

She didn't answer, but scrubbed away another tear.

He sighed. 'Look, I may not be your husband any more and I know things went badly wrong between us—that I made a mess of things this time round, too—but I hope we can somehow find our way to being friends. Because I still care about you.' A lot. And he wanted to be a lot more than just her friend. But friendship would be a start. And a hell of a lot better than the cold war that had raged between them since the end of their marriage.

He took her tray away before he said something he knew he'd regret later. Now wasn't the time to pressure her.

But when she was better, maybe they'd be able to talk. Thrash things out. Come to some sort of compromise. Maybe—please, God—even agree to try again.

Natalie wrapped her arms round herself, willing the tears to stay back. Kit was looking after her—just like she'd needed him to be there when Ethan had died. Cherishing her. Putting her first. He was no longer the closed-up, shuttered-down man he'd become when they'd lost their baby. This was the Kit she'd fallen in love with. Strong and caring and dependable.

The Kit she'd never stopped loving.

And that was what scared her most. That she was falling for him all over again.

But she couldn't allow that to happen. Because this time, when it went wrong, there'd be nothing left.

CHAPTER TWELVE

KIT busied himself doing the washing-up. There had been a time when he and Natalie would have done this together. Like on lazy Sunday mornings when one of them had got up for long enough to stick some croissants in the oven to heat through and make a pot of coffee, then brought a tray back to bed. Where they'd skimmed through the Sunday papers, licked buttery crumbs off each other's fingers, and ended up making love.

Natalie would pull on one of his shirts—oh, how he'd loved seeing her in nothing but one of his shirts—and they'd pad barefoot to the kitchen, just long enough to wash up. Then they'd go back to bed again. They'd gloried in their time together, revelling in each other's bodies and the way they could make each other feel.

Even the memory made him hard. Made him want her, badly.

Sharing his space with Natalie again was strange. Familiar, yet at the same time not. They'd both changed over the last six years. Had different experiences, things they hadn't shared. There had been a time when they'd been so close they'd virtually read each other's minds. Now it was almost as if they'd met for the first time.

If Ethan hadn't died, things would have been so very different, Kit thought. They wouldn't be living separately in a tiny rented flat, neither of them putting down roots anywhere. They'd be living in a proper family house, maybe with two or three children, a house filled with warmth and love and laughter. After his shift at the hospital finished, he'd be coming *home*—not just to the place where he happened to live while he was in this post.

Right now Natalie was lying in his bed. Ill. Letting him look after her. So maybe her trust in him hadn't gone completely. Ah, how he ached to be there with her. Just lying beside her, being close to her, would be enough for him. But it wasn't fair to push it. Not while she was sick. He'd back off. Wait until she was better. And then maybe he could start to woo her properly.

He buried himself in paperwork for the rest of the evening, breaking off only to check if Natalie needed anything. The last time he checked, she was asleep. He stood in the doorway and watched her for a moment. Asleep, her face had lost the wariness he'd noticed when she was around him. And although she looked older now, he could still see the girl he'd fallen in love with twelve years ago.

The girl he still loved.

If only he could persuade her to give him another chance.

He padded into the room, took out clean clothes for himself in the morning, switched the bedside light off and closed the door behind him. Then he made up the sofa bed and sprawled out on it, though it was a long, long time before he could sleep.

The following morning, Kit woke with another headache. Lack of sleep, he guessed. Apart from the fact he'd had problems falling asleep the previous night, the sofa bed really wasn't that comfortable and he'd woken several times during the night. Though he'd make light of it if Tally asked. No way was he going to make her sleep on something so uncomfortable while she was ill. He showered quickly, dressed, then put out a fresh towel for Tally and restored order to his living room.

Assuming that he'd probably woken her, even though he'd tried to be quiet, he tapped lightly on the bedroom door.

''M awake,' she croaked.

He opened the door and peered round. 'Morning. How did you sleep?'

'Well. You?'

'Fine,' he fibbed. 'Want some breakfast?'

'Uh…' She grimaced.

She'd always been one for toast in the mornings. And toast would really hurt her right now. 'I could do you some porridge. Or fruit and yoghurt, if you'd rather have something cool.'

'Fruit would be good. Thanks,' she croaked.

'Go have a shower.' He rummaged in his wardrobe and found her another T-shirt. 'There are clean towels in the bathroom. I'll bring you a drink and some breakfast when you're ready.' Forestalling her protest, he added, 'I forgot to empty my washing machine yesterday. Your clothes are still soaking. So you'll have to stay put today as well.'

'Bossy,' she grumbled, but to his relief she did as he asked.

Her eyes widened when she saw her breakfast tray. 'Strawberries?'

So what if they were expensive, out of season? He knew she loved them. And raspberries. And blueberries. And orange juice that he'd squeezed into a glass only moments before. 'Vitamin C. Good for you.'

She wrinkled her nose. 'Flawed research. Doesn't really help colds.'

He grinned. He should've guessed that she'd say something like that. When they'd been students, she'd always read his journals and fenced with him on some subject or other. Helped him to see different sides of an argument, where to question and where to accept. 'You don't have a cold. You have a virus,' he retorted.

'Same difference.' But she smiled at him. A real smile, one that reached her eyes. Warm. The first time there'd been real warmth between them for years. 'Thank you, Kit.'

'My pleasure.' He smiled back. And left, before he could say something to stir up the antagonism between them and ruin it all.

Just before Kit left for his shift, he brought in a tray with a sandwich and a fresh jug of lemon barley. 'I'm on a late, so I bought you some pasta for dinner. Ravioli. All you have to do is take it out of the fridge, pierce the lid and nuke it in the microwave for a few minutes. Leave the washing-up. I'll do it later,' he said.

She was asleep when he came home—a little later than he'd intended, but there had been an emergency on the ward and he always preferred to stay around afterwards for an hour or so in case of a relapse. He really hadn't been avoiding her.

The kitchen was spotless. Tidy. Hmm. He'd left the breakfast things to air-dry. Everything had been put away neatly. Clearly she'd ignored his orders to do the washing-up—if she *had* eaten, that was. He checked the fridge, and the pasta had gone. Good. If she was eating, it meant she was definitely on the mend.

On the one hand, it pleased him.

On the other, it didn't. While Natalie was ill, she was staying with him—and he had the chance to get closer to her again. When she was better, he'd have to take her home, and they'd be back to living separate lives. It would be all too easy for the distance between them to grow again.

He showered and crawled into his uncomfortable bed. At least he was on an early tomorrow. Maybe they could talk the next evening.

The next morning followed the pattern of the previous one. Kit brought Natalie a hot drink and breakfast, made a fuss of her, brought in a lunch tray and disappeared on his shift.

And it really warmed her heart that he cared that much.

She was feeling better. Better enough to go home, really—although she was still coughing, her breathing had eased a bit. And she really didn't want to spend today in bed—it wasn't as if she was an invalid or seriously ill.

Kit had dried her clothes and left them in his bedroom for her. He'd ironed them, too, she noticed with a smile—and Kit loathed ironing. As a student, he'd always walked around in creased clothes, claiming there was no point in ironing things that would only get crumpled within a few minutes of wearing them. When they'd moved in together and he'd had to start wearing something respectable to work, Kit had agreed to wash their kitchen floor and clean the oven—her two most hated jobs—if she did the ironing.

They'd shared everything.

Until Ethan's death.

And then it had been as if they'd been stuck in different compartments. Aware of each other's existence but barely communicating.

Natalie showered, dressed and then pottered through into the living room. So this was where Kit was sleeping. Funny, although the room wasn't empty—there was a sofa bed, a television, a stereo and a desk housing a computer—the place didn't feel like Kit's home. It didn't feel lived in. There were no pot plants, no cushions, no little personal touches.

Except for the small framed photograph next to the anglepoise lamp on his desk. Her fingers shook as she picked it up and stared at it. Ethan. His first official photograph. Natalie remembered the photographer coming onto the ward every morning to take pictures of the newborns. She and Kit had already gone through two rolls of film by that point, but they'd had the photograph taken anyway. The one that came with a mount from the hospital. A big photograph for their wall, then smaller sizes to send to proud grandparents, aunts and uncles. Tiny ones that slipped perfectly inside a wallet or purse or credit-card holder. This was the photograph that she'd pasted inside Ethan's baby book—a book she'd kept meticulously during her pregnancy, with the scan pictures and measurements and all the family history. The book she'd planned to share with their son when he was older and curious about himself as a baby. Except she'd never had the chance.

She blinked away the tears. One thing that had never been in doubt was Kit's love for his son. He'd been so proud of their baby. The only time he'd left their bedside that first day had been to get the phone trolley so they could ring round the family with the news. And for long enough to order an enormous bouquet for her. It had arrived with a card handwritten by him that she'd never been able to throw away, even after the divorce. It was still in her keepsake box. Telling her how much he loved her, how proud he was of her.

She shook herself. That was the past. Over. She replaced the photograph on Kit's desk and spent the rest of the morning flicking channels on the television. Kit didn't even have a shelf of books in the house—strange, because he'd always been a great reader. There weren't many CDs either—though maybe he was using an MP3 player instead now. Something that would let him store a lot more music in a smaller format.

This place felt very temporary. Did that mean Kit was planning to move on soon? Was the job at St Joseph's just a stopgap while he waited for a paediatric consultant's post to come up somewhere?

Not that it was any of her business. Not any more. Not her place to ask either.

Natalie realised she'd fallen asleep in front of an old black-and-white film when she heard the front door open. There was a rap on the bedroom door, followed by a soft query. 'Natalie?'

'In here,' she mumbled, sitting up.

Kit walked into the living room, took one look at her and sighed. 'You were feeling better, you got up and now you feel atrocious. Right?'

'Mmm.' She hadn't expected to fall asleep. Or to feel this groggy and disoriented. It was only a virus, for goodness' sake. It shouldn't make her feel this awful.

He spread his hands. 'Now, as a doctor, you would tell your patient with a knockout virus to stay put until they feel better—and then spend one more day in bed to make absolutely sure they are over it. Especially because if they get up too early they risk a relapse. And then they should take it easy and not rush straight back to a demanding job. Right?'

'Yes,' she admitted.

'Good. Then I suggest you take your own advice. Go back to bed,' he said. 'I'll bring you a drink.'

'I'll make it,' she protested. 'You've been—'

'On duty,' he finished for her. 'I know. But the difference is, I don't have a virus. I'm perfectly fit and healthy. So it's not a problem.' To her shock, he actually ruffled her hair. It was the briefest of contacts, but it reminded her of the old days. Kit had always been physical with her. Connected.

'Go back to bed, honey,' he said softly. 'The more you rest now, the quicker you'll get better.'

And the quicker she'd be out of his hair?

No, that wasn't fair. He could have just left her at her own flat. In fact, he needn't even have taken her there himself. He could have put her in a taxi and just washed his hands of her. Instead, he'd brought her here, to his own flat. He'd looked after her, made sure she was eating properly. And she was being an ungrateful whiner. 'Thank you,' she muttered, feeling guilty and out of sorts at the same time.

She dragged herself back to bed. When Kit came in with a hot drink for her a few minutes later, she noticed that he looked strained.

'Are you OK?' she asked.

'Yeah, course.'

But his voice was clipped, tense. Something was definitely wrong. She hazarded a guess. 'Bad day at work?'

He shrugged. 'It was all right.'

Oh, no. She knew that tone. Remembered it well from the last few weeks of their marriage. Kit was upset about something, but he was keeping it locked away. Shutting her out. Again. Just when she'd been beginning to think that maybe he'd changed…

Well, she wasn't going to let him do this. Whatever it was, he needed to talk about it. Bring it out into the open and put it in perspective. She patted the empty space next to her on the bed. 'Sit. Tell me.'

For a moment he stared at her, and then he nodded. Kicked off his shoes. Sprawled next to her. 'OK, since you asked, I've had a hell of a day. If I tell you about it, it's going to upset you. And if I don't tell you about it, you're going to think I'm being like I was after Ethan died. Closed. And I'm not, Tally. I just don't want to...' He shook his head in frustration. 'I don't want to say something that's going to hurt you.'

Her first thought was that he'd met someone. That he didn't know how to tell her that he'd fallen in love and was going to get married again.

Then she shook herself. No, of course not. Apart from the fact that he wouldn't have brought her here if he was seeing someone else—Kit had never been the duplicitous sort—they were no longer married. It was none of her business if he'd found someone else.

Though she was pretty sure he'd been talking about work, not his personal life. His eyes were shadowed with pain.

And he'd said it would upset her.

Oh, God. Please, don't say it was little Kyra. Please, don't say she'd stopped responding to the cytotoxic drugs. 'Kyra?' she whispered. 'It's not Kyra? I didn't give her my virus? She's hasn't...' Oh, no. Please, no. She couldn't force the words out.

'No, so don't start worrying. She's doing OK, and she seems to be responding well to the treatment.' He gave her the briefest of smiles. 'And, thanks to you, she gets to go home for two whole hours on Christmas Day. I had a chat with Lenox about it and her Christmas wish will come true.'

'That's good.'

But something had happened, something to upset him. She wanted to make him feel better, soothe him the way he'd soothed her when she'd felt so rough earlier in the week. She stroked the hair back from his forehead. 'Tell me what's wrong,' she said softly. 'It's better out than in.'

'It's...' His mouth worked but no sound came out. Then he closed his eyes. Looked defeated, as if he didn't have the strength to deal with whatever it was any more. Well, that was OK. She was there.

'Tell me,' she said softly. 'Share. Lighten the load.'

He swallowed. 'We had a baby on the ward today. His mum brought him in with a virus. At first I thought it was another of our RSV cases. The baby had the usual symptoms for an upper respiratory tract infection—poor breathing, a bit of cynosis round the mouth. But I had a bad feeling about it.'

A doctor's gut reaction. Yeah. She was beginning to develop that, too.

'The heart rate was way too fast. I listened, and there was an S4 gallop.'

She knew what that pointed to. 'Myocarditis?' she asked, her voice low.

'Yeah.'

She took his hand and squeezed it. 'Is this your first case since Ethan?'

He shook his head. 'Far from it. But it gets to me every time. I think I'm being professional about it, and I'm absolutely fine on the ward. Nobody would ever guess what it means to me. But as soon as I'm off duty...it all comes back. Every single second. Ethan's face, the way his breathing got worse and worse, the moment he fell asleep for ever. The moment the sun burned out.' His expression was bleak as he opened his eyes and looked at her. 'When's it ever going to stop hurting, Tally?'

'I don't know.' Instinctively, she slid her arms round him. Pillowed his head on her breasts. Stroked his hair and just held him close. His arms wrapped round her, but this time there wasn't the usual sexual frisson between them. This time, she was holding him. Comforting him. And for once he was actually leaning on her. Letting her in. Sharing his pain. Accepting that you didn't have to be strong and in control of your feelings all the time.

It wasn't for long—'I'll go fix dinner,' he muttered, clearly thinking he'd been weak in her eyes, and was embarrassed about it—but it was a start.

Maybe there was hope for them yet.

CHAPTER THIRTEEN

THE following evening, Kit came home in a much better mood.

'Had a good day?' Natalie asked.

He smiled. 'Yeah. We had one of the best cases ever on the ward today.'

She patted the bed. 'Sit down and tell me about it.'

He looked at her for a moment, as if about to refuse, then kicked off his shoes and sat down next to her, leaning back against the pillows.

Just as he'd done in the days when he'd been a house officer and she'd been heavily pregnant, too tired to wait up properly for him but not wanting to go to sleep until he'd got home from his shift.

'We had this little boy in. Billy. Three years old and a right little scamp. Anyway, he's been limping for the last three months.'

Natalie frowned. Why was Kit smiling? How could this be a good case if a child was ill? Hurt?

'Lenox knew he was coming in today and asked me to see him for a second opinion because the case had him puzzled—actually, young Billy would've been a good case for you.' There was a glint of mischief in Kit's eyes. 'Quick *viva* for you. What causes limping?'

'A stone or something sharp in the shoe, badly fitting shoes or maybe a foreign body in the foot.'

'Nope. Remember, this child has been limping for three months—and his mum brought him within a couple of days of the limp starting.'

It went without saying that Billy's mum had checked his shoes for a stone. And if the cause had been a foreign body—a thorn, or even the after-effects, like poor Harry a few weeks ago—it would have been picked up as soon as he'd come in for examination. And ill-fitting shoes could be crossed out for the same reasons. So that ruled out the three most obvious causes.

Something developmental maybe? 'He's been limping for just three months? His mum didn't notice anything before, not even the slightest hint of problems with walking?'

'Nope. Not a thing. And she's very observant,' Kit added.

Natalie thought aloud. 'It's unlikely to be hip displacement, then.' She frowned. 'Is Billy in any pain at all? Has he complained of any aches, anything hurting, a pushing or a squeezing pain?'

'Apparently not.'

'Is he accident prone?' she asked.

'A bit.' Kit looked interested. 'Why?'

'It might be an undiagnosed greenstick fracture that had mended badly.'

Kit nodded. 'Good call—and I'm impressed that you're thinking outside the box, not just limiting yourself to the obvious. That gets you an extra mark, Dr Wilkins. But the X-rays show absolutely nothing wrong.'

'How about mild cerebral palsy, but nobody had picked up on it yet simply because it was so mild?' she suggested.

'He wasn't a late walker, there are no signs of CNS lesions and there are no other symptoms.' Kit laughed. 'There's definitely nothing wrong with his speech, I can tell you that—he chatted nineteen to the dozen to me. Oh, and he was a full-term baby.'

Which ruled out most of the possible indicators of cerebral palsy. Natalie folded her arms and drummed her fingers on her elbow. 'Unlikely to be CP, then. How about Duchenne muscular dystrophy?'

'Good try, but nope.' Kit shook his head. 'OK, I'll tell you a little bit more. Billy's had every test you can imagine. Bloods—that's hormone assays as well as full blood count, U and Es and what have you—X-rays, ultrasound... And they've all been negative.'

Natalie was beginning to see why Lenox had been puzzled. There was no obvious cause for a limp. And if their extremely experienced consultant couldn't work out what the problem was, how on earth did Kit think that a house officer who was still wet behind the ears would come up with a diagnosis? If it wasn't physical, then maybe... 'Is it psychosomatic perhaps?' she asked. 'Maybe something had happened at home to upset him? Maybe it's a form of attention-seeking?'

'No. We're talking about well-adjusted little boy who lives in big, noisy, happy family—a family who loves him to bits, I might add.'

The kind Natalie had grown up in. The kind she'd wanted for her own children. 'Uh-huh.'

'I thought maybe his tendons had retracted in the back of his leg, and that was what caused the limp. How would you deal with that?'

'Refer him to a surgeon to have them released,' Natalie suggested.

'Or botox injections to relax them,' Kit said. He grinned. 'You know, I never thought just the threat of a needle could cure a limp so fast.'

She frowned. 'I'm not with you.'

'I'd explained it to his parents while he was playing—what I thought the problem might be and how we could manage it. But I always like to talk to my patients, too—they may be small but they still have a right to know what's happening to them. So then I sat down next to the toy box and explained to Billy that we were going to have to give him an operation or maybe a very special type of injection to help stop him limping. And then he piped up, "Will an injection cure Grandpa Henry, too?"'

'Who's Grandpa Henry?' Natalie asked.

'His mum's dad. Who just so happens to have a limp—he has arthritis.' Kit laughed. 'Apparently, young Billy had just been copying his grandfather.'

'No.' Natalie stared at him in disbelief and amusement. 'You're kidding.'

'I'm serious. There was absolutely nothing wrong with him. He was just copying his grandfather and seeing how it felt to have a limp.'

'For three *months*?'

'Yep. I couldn't quite believe it either. He kept it up for three whole months.'

'The little...' Natalie laughed, shaking her head. 'What did his mum say?'

'She wasn't sure whether to be relieved that he wasn't going to have to go through an operation or whether to throttle him for worrying her sick!' Kit's lips quirked. 'Poor woman. She was so embarrassed. Lucky for her, I have a sense of humour. So does Lenox. And I'd never yell at a parent for wasting our time anyway. Often the parents are the first ones to pick up that there's a problem. And I'd much, much rather it was a false alarm than for things to progress beyond the point where we can treat them.' He smiled again. 'My money's on young Billy becoming a famous actor in about twenty years' time. He could be the new Brando—a method actor who really becomes the character. You know: gains weight if he has to for the role.' He chuckled. 'Or, in this case, walks with a limp for three months.'

Natalie smiled back. 'Certainly sounds like it.'

'It's not all tragedy in paediatrics. Yes, we get sad cases—there will always be some we can't help.' He was clearly thinking of their son, because his face clouded for a moment. 'But there are many, many more we can help get better. And then there are the ones that go down in legend. The ones where you only have to mention the patient's name and the staff have to try really hard to keep a straight face.'

She loved this side of Kit—when he really opened up to her and told her what he enjoyed about his job. Like the days when he'd first qualified. He'd never broken patient confidentiality, but he'd come home and chatted to her about his day. Just as she'd told him about hers. And she wanted to keep him talking now. 'What sort of cases?'

'I think my favourite one was when I was doing a stint in the emergency department as their paediatric specialist. This little boy came in—apparently, he was a bit accident-prone anyway, and his file was enormous. He'd been in with a foreign body up his nose, in his ears—even swallowed at one point. He found his dad's superglue and managed to glue his fingers together. He'd fallen over so many times that his mum was terrified she'd be on an abuse register. You name it, he'd done it. But that particular day he showed up with a potty stuck on his head.'

'A potty?'

Kit grinned. 'I know, I know—the classic case is a saucepan stuck on a kid's head. But his mum had already sussed that one out and kept a child lock on her saucepan cupboard to make sure he didn't try being a robot or something and get his head stuck in a saucepan.'

'But how on earth did he get his head stuck in a potty?' Natalie asked.

Kit chuckled. 'Apparently, he tripped over the cat and landed headfirst in his brother's potty.'

'Ow. Please tell me it was an empty potty,' Natalie said faintly.

Kit's grin broadened. 'Nope. Think worst-case scenario. His mum was just cleaning up his little brother before she emptied the potty. They were in the bathroom when she heard this wail, and rushed out to see her eldest with some rather unusual headgear.'

'Oh, no! That's awful.' Natalie was torn between sympathy and laughter.

'Let's just say her face was a bit red when she explained. Poor woman. She probably sees the funny side of it now, but at the time she was frantic—obviously she needed to get the potty off her son's head and get him cleaned up, too, but it was stuck. He wasn't too happy either—he was yelling and creating the whole time, and we just couldn't get him to calm down.'

'Well, it can't have been too pleasant for him. And I can't even begin to imagine the smell. How did you get it off?' Natalie asked.

'We had to put a warm damp cloth over the top of the potty. It was plastic, so obviously the material would expand with heat and we'd be able to get it off, but we had to be careful with the temperature—if the cloth was too hot it'd make the plastic melt and make the situation even worse. We replaced the warm cloth every ten minutes or so and smeared cold baby oil right up under the rim, as far as we could reach. Eventually, the contrast between the warmth of the cloth and the coldness of the oil did the trick—the potty expanded and we managed to get it off.' He grimaced. 'It took an hour, and the poor little scrap was left with oil and poo all over his hair. We cleaned him up before we sent him home. But that's one episode I bet he never lives down!'

'It's something his mum can remind him about whenever he's being a really stroppy teenager and she wants to take him down a peg or two,' Natalie said.

'Definitely.' He smiled at her. 'So are you enjoying paediatrics?'

'Yes. I'm doing an emergency department rotation next, but I want to come back to paediatrics.'

'It's really rewarding,' Kit agreed.

'Do you ever miss not going into surgery?' The question was out before she could stop it.

He shrugged. 'Not really. I mean, yes, there's a real adrenaline rush in surgery. You're working against the clock, and you're taking risks—calculated risks, but there's still a possibility your patient won't make it out of Theatre. Everything depends on your skill, and that of your team. But there isn't the same...I dunno.' He wrinkled his nose. 'I think it's the contact, really. I like seeing my patients. I like it when they come back for a review and I can sign them off, and I can see how much they've changed since the last review. I like getting to know them, seeing the tots turn into bouncy little people with minds of their own. Or the shy young children blossoming in their teenage years. No, I don't regret the change at all.' He tipped his head on one side. 'How about you? Do you regret giving up teaching?'

'Yes and no. I liked working with the kids, teaching them to really think about what they were looking at and how to structure a proper argument. But I'm glad I do this now.' Natalie admitted. 'There's something special about being able to help people, make things right again.'

'Yes,' Kit said softly. 'There is.' And then he climbed off the bed. 'I'd better go and sort dinner. See you in a bit.'

Natalie would quite happily have foregone food for more time with him. Time they'd spent laughing—the first time in years they'd laughed together. Talked about what they were doing and how they really felt.

But maybe she was just hoping for too much.

The following day, Natalie was feeling much brighter. She was up, showered and dressed before Kit got up, and had the coffee on and the table set ready for breakfast before she even heard him go into the bathroom.

Kit blinked in surprise as he walked into the kitchen, his hair still wet from the shower. 'Wow. What's this?'

'You made a fuss of me while I was ill. This is the least I could do,' Natalie said, pouring him a coffee and switching the toaster on.

'Thanks.' He sat down and took a sip. 'You sound a lot better. Your voice is almost back. And you've got some colour in your cheeks again.'

'I *am* better. I'm going back to work today,' she said.

He shook his head. 'Don't rush it. You've got two days off anyway.'

She raised an eyebrow. 'How do you know?'

'Checked the roster.' He lifted a shoulder casually. 'You must be dying to have your own space back again.'

Ouch. Whatever she said could be taken the wrong way. If she said yes, he'd think she was desperate to put space between them. If she said no, she'd be throwing herself at him. He'd slept on his sofa-bed every single night since she'd stayed here—even the night after he'd talked to her about the baby with myocardia. The night she'd half expected him to come to her bed, seek comfort in her arms.

He hadn't.

Which meant he really did see her just as a platonic friend now. Not his life partner.

'It'd be nice to have my wardrobe back,' she said, trying for lightness.

'I would've gone to your place and brought you some things back, if you'd said.'

'I know. But you've already done enough for me. Thanks, Kit. I appreciate it.'

He didn't meet her eyes. 'That's what friends are for, isn't it?'

Yes. But they'd once been more than friends. A lot more.

'I'm on a late today. I'll drive you back to your place when you're ready.'

It sounded as if he wanted his space back, too. 'OK. I'll just strip the bed—'

He lifted one hand to stop her. 'Leave it, Natalie. I'll sort it out later.'

She didn't bother with the rest of her breakfast, and it

didn't take her long to pack. 'Maybe you should drop me at the hospital. I can pick up my car,' Natalie said.

'No need. I moved your car the other day.'

How?

As if she'd spoken the question aloud, he said, 'I drove it to your place, then caught a taxi back to the hospital.'

She flushed. 'Thank you. Um, I'll reimburse you for the taxi.'

'No need.'

She hated this sudden awkwardness between them. But right now she couldn't think of any way to change it.

He drove her back to her flat. Saw her to the door. 'Take care of yourself,' he said with a smile. A smile that was just that little bit too bright. And which meant he was shutting her out again.

'Thanks for everything.'

'No worries. See you at work.'

And that was it. He was gone.

Well, what had she expected? That he'd stay for coffee? She knew he was on duty shortly. And, knowing Kit, he wanted to drop in to the intensive care unit and see how the baby with myocarditis was doing.

Natalie let herself into her flat. Weird. This place didn't feel like a home either—even though, unlike Kit's flat, hers was full of family photographs and pot plants and books and flowers. It just felt...empty, without him. Which was stupid. He'd never lived here. He hadn't even spent a whole night here—they'd had sex and she'd thrown him out.

There was a heap of mail on the doormat. Christmas cards, she thought, her heart aching as she scooped them up. No doubt full of round-robin letters from friends she only heard from at this time of year. Letters full of 'proud mummy' moments—moments she'd once dreamed of writing about in her annual catch-ups.

Christmas just *sucked*. And if she put the radio on it'd be some Christmas song or other, either a bouncy one saying how wonderful life was or a sad one wishing their loved ones would be home for Christmas.

Her baby hadn't made it home for Christmas.

She sighed, put her mail on the table and made herself a strong cup of coffee. This was crazy. She had a job she loved, family she loved, friends. She ought to be delighted with the way her life was right now. Why on earth did she feel so lonely, so empty?

Though she knew the answer. It was because Kit wasn't there. He'd dropped her off only a few minutes ago and already she missed him.

Maybe she should call him. Tell him how she felt. Ask him to give their relationship another try.

But he'd already suggested that and she'd knocked him back. And although he'd looked after her when she'd been ill, he'd made it very clear it was on a friends-only basis.

So just where did they go from here?

Right now she didn't have any answers. Just a cup of coffee and an ache in her heart and a wish that things were different.

CHAPTER FOURTEEN

IT FELT odd to Kit that evening, coming home to find his flat dark and empty. Although Tally had only stayed for a few days, he'd grown used to having her there. He'd enjoyed coming home to her.

Though he'd noted that as soon as she had felt better, she hadn't been able to get away fast enough.

Kit sighed inwardly. He wouldn't see Natalie again until after Christmas now. She was off duty tomorrow, and he was off duty for the two days after that—days when he'd go south to pay a fleeting visit to his parents to drop off the family's Christmas presents and pretend to his brothers that of course everything in his busy-busy-busy life was fine—and then it would be Christmas. Tally was bound to spend the holidays at her parents' home. She'd always been very family oriented.

And then it would be the new year.

Time for a new start.

Kit was beginning to think his would have to be in another hemisphere, let alone another hospital.

'Kit!' Nicole Rodgers smiled at her son as she opened the front door. 'I wasn't sure if you were coming.'

'I promised I would.' Even though he really hadn't felt

like it. 'I wouldn't let you down. And I'd be the meanest uncle in the world if I didn't bring the kids their presents in time for Christmas morning—especially as it's too late for the last post before Christmas.'

She squeezed his arm briefly. 'I know it's a tough time of year for you. Too many memories.'

'I'm fine,' Kit protested.

'You don't look it.' She ushered him into the kitchen and switched the kettle on. 'You look as if you haven't slept properly for weeks.'

Kit didn't answer. How come his mother was suddenly so perceptive?

'So how's the new job?' she asked.

'Fine.'

'Right, and that's why you sound so underwhelmed. What's the problem? A consultant who wants to keep all the responsibility and can't delegate?'

'No, Lenox is great. I love working on the ward. It's a good team.'

His mother busied herself making tea. 'So it's a nurse who won't take no for an answer, then?'

When he didn't reply, she sighed. 'Kit, I know you were badly hurt by what happened with Natalie. But you can't live in the shadows for the rest of your life, thinking of all the might-have-beens. You have to make a new life. Move on.'

Move on. What Natalie herself had suggested. Kit sighed. 'That's easier said than done.'

'You need to get out and meet people,' Nicole said authoritatively. 'You can't just work, work, work all the time. What you need is to find someone to share your life with. Join a club.' She put a mug of coffee in front of him. 'Or a dating agency—one of those places that caters to people who are too busy to find themselves a partner. They'll match you up with someone who has interests in common with you. There's no stigma in that sort of thing nowadays.'

Kit stared into his coffee. 'That isn't what I meant.'

'Then what do you mean, darling?' she asked.

He might as well tell her straight. 'I'm working with Natalie now.'

Nicole frowned. 'What, she's one of these teachers who work on the paediatric ward with children who are in long term? I thought she was a history teacher?'

'Not any more. She's a house officer on my ward.'

'Good Lord.' Nicole pulled out a chair from the scrubbed pine table. 'I mean, I always knew she was clever—but how?'

'Same way as I did, I guess,' Kit said dryly. 'Five years at university, and then a year in pre-reg.'

Nicole gave him a look that said very clearly, Don't give me that smart-alec response. 'And she's specialising in paediatrics?'

'Mmm-hmm.' Kit pre-empted his mother's next question. 'For the same reason I switched specialties, I guess.'

Nicole paused before asking delicately, 'And how are you both coping with this? Working together?'

'OK.'

To Kit's surprise, she reached out and squeezed his hand. 'You never really got over her, did you? If you ask me, I'd say you're still in love with her.' At his half-shrug, she asked, 'Does she know?'

'No.'

'Do you know how she feels?'

'No.' Which was the problem. Sometimes he thought it was going to work out, that they'd have another chance—

and then they were back on opposite sides of the fence. He wasn't sure whether he was just trying to see something that wasn't there, or whether Natalie was running scared, or what.

All he knew was that he was miserable. Bone-deep miserable. And he missed her.

'You need to talk to her,' Nicole said gently. 'The way you should have done years ago.'

Kit frowned. 'Let me get this straight. You're telling me to talk to her, not to run like hell in the opposite direction?' He shook his head. 'Tally always thought you disapproved of her. That she wasn't academic enough for you.'

Nicole looked surprised. 'No, not at all. I just thought you were both too young to get married. You were both still students, remember. I thought you both needed to grow up a little, see more of the world before you settled down.'

'And Ethan?'

Nicole sighed and took a swig of her coffee. 'I admit, when you told me you were expecting, I thought it was bad timing, even though I know he wasn't planned. You were only just in your houseman year and up to your eyes in your job—you really weren't ready for the responsibility of a family.'

'So you disapproved.' Kit stared at the table. It looked as if Natalie was right about that, then.

Nicole shook her head. 'Ethan was my first grandchild. Who couldn't love their grandchild to bits? And he looked so very much like you as a baby.'

The last words sounded choked. Kit glanced at his mother, and was shocked to see her eyes filling with tears. As an oncology specialist, Nicole Rodgers was completely unflappable and cool at work. Kit had always thought her a bit that way at home, too, since he'd met Tally's family. Nicole had never been as warm and demonstrative as

Tally's mother. Though Kit had sometimes wondered if it was to do with the fact that she had four sons, whereas Tally's mother had three daughters.

He reached over and squeezed her hand. 'Mum, I...' Ah, hell. Now he was choking up, too.

She blinked the tears away. 'I know. My loss was nothing compared to yours. But I was sorry when you and Natalie split up. I wish now I'd gone to see her. Talked to her. Made her realise that although I was only an in-law, I was still there for her if she needed me.'

'But you didn't stay in touch with her,' Kit said. Not the way he'd stayed in touch with Tally's parents.

Nicole shook her head. 'I didn't think she wanted me to. And I wasn't going to push in where I wasn't needed.'

'So if,' Kit asked carefully, 'I could persuade her to give me a second chance...'

'I'd welcome her back with open arms,' Nicole said, 'if she could make you happy again.'

Kit smiled. 'Let's just say I'm working on it.' His smile faded. 'And if it doesn't work out, I might need to work abroad for a bit.'

'I hope,' Nicole said, 'for all our sakes, that doesn't happen.'

On Christmas Day, Tally woke at stupid o'clock to find a familiar dragging feeling in her abdomen. Her period had arrived. Like clockwork. She'd got her Christmas wish, then. She wasn't pregnant.

So why the hell did she feel so miserable about it?

As for her other wish...well, that was just a pipe dream. It wasn't going to happen.

She went into work early—she thought she may as well,

seeing as she was awake and didn't have anything better to do with her time. She helped the nurses to sort out the Christmas parcels for the children on the ward; money collected by the Friends of the Hospital had paid for all the patients to have a small gift. Debbie told her, just before the ward round on Christmas morning, that the most senior male doctor on the ward donned the Santa suit and walked round the bays, saying 'Ho, ho, ho' in a deep, jolly voice and giving each child a parcel. And all the nursing staff got a Christmas kiss under the mistletoe.

'Sounds like fun,' Natalie said, forcing her voice to sound bright and cheerful.

'It makes the day at bit easier for the parents,' Debbie said. 'It isn't much of a Christmas, torn between a family at home and a child in here. Wanting to be with both, and wearing themselves out in the process.'

'Mmm,' Natalie said, not trusting herself to say any more, and busied herself with preparation for the ward round.

Kit glanced at the roster board and did a double-take. He'd had no idea that Natalie would be working here on Christmas Day. He hadn't even looked at the roster sheets, because he'd assumed that she would spend the day in the Cotswolds with her parents and her sisters.

Ah, well. They'd just have to be civil to each other. It was Christmas after all. Though he had no intention of kissing her under the mistletoe. One touch of her mouth against his and he knew his self-control would be in shreds. They'd already made enough of a stir at the Hallowe'en do—the last thing he wanted was to give the hospital grapevine another juicy morsel.

The Santa suit was in Lenox's office. Kit climbed into it, added the beard and went in search of the presents.

* * *

'Ho, ho, ho. Merry Christmas, children.'

Natalie blinked hard. That most definitely wasn't Lenox's voice. And she hadn't been expecting to hear Kit: she'd assumed that he would be going south for Christmas. Spending the holidays with his family.

She still hadn't quite taken it in by the time he walked over to Debbie and held the mistletoe over her. 'Merry Christmas, Sister,' he said, giving her a resounding peck on the cheek.

Debbie laughed, and gave him an equally smacking kiss in return. 'Merry Christmas, Santa.'

Kit repeated the act with every nurse on the ward. And the auxiliary staff. And the mums.

Which left just Natalie.

He came to a stop in front of her, his blue eyes glittering. 'Merry Christmas, Dr Wilkins,' he said softly.

'Merry Christmas, Santa.' Her voice was actually shaking.

The briefest, briefest touch of his lips against her cheek, and he was gone.

Even so, it left her knees weak.

Avoiding the curious looks of the nurses, Natalie escaped to the staff kitchen for a much-needed cup of coffee.

'I thought I might find you here.' Kit walked into the kitchen a few minutes later and made himself a cup of coffee.

'I didn't realise you were on duty today,' she said.

'Snap.' He pulled back the hood of the Santa outfit and removed the beard. 'I thought you'd be at home with your family.'

She shook her head. 'Christmas is a time for kids. We've got staff who have children—I'd rather give them the chance of spending the day with their families instead of coming here and missing out.'

Meaning that she didn't have anything to miss out on? Yeah, he could identify with that.

Kit stared at her. She looked as miserable as he felt. Maybe…?

Well, he had nothing left to lose. He'd ask her. It might mean that his notice period over the next few weeks would be awkward in the extreme—but, then again, it was Christmas. A time he'd once thought held magic. If he didn't ask, he'd never know. And if he held back now, he might just be missing out on the rest of his life.

'I overheard you talking to Kyra about your Christmas wish.'

Her eyes widened. 'That was none of your business.'

He ignored the comment. 'Are you going to tell me what it was?'

'That everyone on the ward has a very happy Christmas.'

Which was what she'd told Kyra. He didn't buy it. At all. 'I meant the real one,' he said softly.

'No point. Because it's not going to happen.' She leaned back against her chair. 'I'm glad I saw you, actually. You asked me to let you know if… Well. The answer's no. I'm not pregnant.'

She was striving for coolness. He could see that. But her lower lip wobbled. Not for long—but long enough to give him hope. Was she disappointed that they hadn't made a baby? That they hadn't had a second chance?

He pulled up a chair next to hers. 'Want to know my Christmas wish, Tally?'

She wouldn't meet his eyes. 'No.'

'I'm going to tell you anyway. I should have told you this a long, long time ago.' He reached out, took her hand and held it between his. 'I wish I could have saved our son.

I wish I could have saved our marriage. I wish we had more children now—that we were a proper family. The way we wanted it to be, back when we were eighteen and we realised that we'd found the one we wanted to be with for the rest of our lives.'

Natalie was trembling, but he wasn't going to let her go. Not yet.

'But you can't change the past,' he said softly. 'I couldn't save Ethan. Our marriage blew apart. And now we're both on our own. Lonely.'

A muscle flickered in her jaw, as if she was trying not to cry. It looked as if he'd hit the nail on the head.

Please, God, let this work.

'So I have another wish.' He swallowed hard. 'What I wish, more than anything else in the world, is that we could have a second chance. That we could try again and make a real go of our relationship. Make it the marriage it was supposed to be.'

Slowly, slowly, she met his gaze. 'You want us to...?'

'Get back together. Get married again.' He took a deep breath. 'Yes. I never stopped loving you, Natalie. Even though I tried to block it out with work. I tried dating—but it never worked because they just weren't you. You're the love of my life and nobody will ever match up to you. Ever. And last week, when you stayed with me...it was the first time in years that I felt as if I were coming home. Because I was coming home to you, not just to an empty space filled with memories and regrets.' He took a chance. 'And I think it was the same for you. Wasn't it?'

Her breath hitched. 'You shut me out. You wouldn't talk to me. I needed you and you just weren't there.'

'I know. It's something I'm not proud of. Something I

regret from the bottom of my heart. I'm sorry. And all I can do is ask you to forgive me—because it won't happen again.'

She looked torn. Tempted and scared at the same time. 'How can you be so sure?'

'Because I'm a different person now, Tally. I'm older. Wiser, I hope. I deal with things in a different way now. You might have to prod me occasionally—I'm not perfect and I'm never going to be—but swear I'll try never to shut you out again. And if you just talk to me, we can make it work.'

'What if…?' Her breath hitched.

'If we're not blessed with another baby?' He drew her hand to his mouth and kissed each finger in turn. 'That's OK. Because we'll still have each other. And if we *are* lucky enough to have another child, he or she won't take Ethan's place.' He could guess her other fears. They'd be similar to his own. 'It's very, very unlikely our baby will have the same problems as Ethan. But if something bad does happen—well, we'll get through it together. I won't run away into my work. I'll face it with you. Hand in hand. And we'll get through whatever bad stuff life throws at us—just as we'll celebrate the good stuff, too. Together.' His hand tightened round hers again. 'Take a chance on me, Tally. Take a chance on *us*.'

'Put all the bad memories behind us and start again.'

'Yeah. It's going to take time, I know that. And we'll have bad days as well as good, days when we'll fight. But we'll get through them because we'll be together.' His eyes held hers. 'I love you, Tally. I never stopped.'

'Neither did I.' A tear trickled down her cheek. 'Do you really want to know what my Christmas wish was?'

'What?'

'The same as yours.'

He lifted one hand to wipe the tear from her cheek. 'Then let's make it come true. For each other.'

She shook her head. 'Your family won't approve.'

'I think,' Kit said, 'you might be surprised. I talked about you to my mother when I went back to Surrey on my off-duty.'

Natalie looked worried. 'And?'

'Same problem as me. You didn't talk it through together. Do you know, she still carries a picture of Ethan in her purse?' His fingers tightened on hers. 'She thought we were too young to get married and needed to grow up a bit, but she liked you. She's just...not very good at showing it. I dunno. Maybe it's because she had four sons and no daughters. She didn't know how to respond to you.'

'Maybe,' Natalie said softly.

'And she regrets not coming to see you after Ethan died and telling you that even though she was just an in-law, she was there if you needed her. She didn't want to push in because she thought you didn't want her.'

Natalie looked stunned. 'I had no idea.'

'Neither did I. I think maybe my family needs to learn a bit about talking. And sharing.' He smiled at her. 'You were a teacher. A good one. Would you consider taking on a new pupil?'

She opened her arms to him. 'Yes.'

Neither of them heard the kitchen door open. Or the wolf whistles. Or noticed Debbie shooing the nursing staff out again. All they could focus on was each other. And the feeling of coming home. For good.

EPILOGUE

Eighteen months later

KIT sat on the side of Natalie's bed, cradling their newborn daughter. 'She looks just like you,' he said with a smile.

'She definitely has your chin, though.' Natalie stroked the baby's soft dark hair. 'Carolyn Nicole Rodgers.' They'd decided to name their daughter after both their mothers. 'Our little girl.'

Kit looked at his wife, picking up the sadness in her voice. 'Hey. She's not a replacement for Ethan. Nobody will ever take his place, even if we have sons in the future. He'll always be our firstborn, and we'll tell Carolyn all about her big brother.'

Natalie's eyes were dark with worry. 'Kit, you don't think…?' She broke off, shaking her head, as if trying to dismiss it.

He guessed what she was worrying about immediately—the question that had flashed into his own mind, too—and set about reassuring her. 'Firstly, Carolyn's a summer-born baby. She's unlikely to come into contact with the same viruses in the summer that you get in the winter. Secondly, even if she does pick up Coxsackie from somewhere, it won't necessarily lead to cardiomyopathy in her case. It doesn't always cause it. Ethan might have had a heart problem anyway, and we just hadn't had a chance to pick that up. Carolyn is going to be absolutely fine. I checked her over myself.' His mouth twitched. 'Of course, if you want a *second* consultant's opinion, we could wait for Lenox to do his round.'

Nicole smiled. 'He's been a consultant for a lot longer than you have.'

'Cheek! I'll have you know I'm perfectly competent.' Kit leaned over to kiss his wife. 'She's doing well, Natalie. Everything's going to be fine. Because our Christmas wish has come true.'

'We've been lucky,' she said softly.

'And we're only going to get luckier. Because we're together.'

CHRISTMAS IN HIS BED

SASHA SUMMERS

To those whose first love is still their only love.

1

BEING BRALESS WAS as close to rebellious as Tatum had been in almost a decade. So was reading her third romance novel in a row, barely emerging from the nest of quilts she'd dragged to the comfy rocking chair in front of the now-dying fire. No makeup, no expectations, no worries. Day one of her new life was good.

When she was done reading, she could dig through her suitcase for her vibrator and some quality alone time. Or she could stay up reading all night long.

For the first time in her life, there was no one to stop her from doing whatever she wanted. And knowing that was…*awesome*.

She glanced at the old cuckoo clock over the mantel. Right now her ex-husband, Brent, and the new Mrs. Cahill, Kendra, were probably sipping umbrella drinks on some beach somewhere—if he'd actually taken a vacation. But knowing Kendra, she wouldn't have given him a choice.

She burrowed into her quilts and added the book she'd finished to the pile at her feet. Her evening would be far more satisfying than a night with Brent and his tiny penis. Penis size aside, he had no stamina and had never taken an active interest in giving her pleasure. Tatum had always waited for him to head to the shower before finishing things off right with her handy-dandy purple-swirly love machine. She called him Chris, after her favorite movie actor. Brent and Chris had never met. Brent had no idea Chris existed.

She drained hot chocolate from her large Santa mug and stood, padding across the wooden floor in her socks and slippers to restart the Nat King Cole album. Maybe it was wrong that she was in such a good mood, newly divorced and absolutely alone on Christmas. But she was. She wanted to be happy. And right now, Nat King Cole, stimulating romance novels and copious amounts of hot chocolate were all she needed to be happy. And, maybe later, Chris.

She picked up the last book on the side table, reading the back blurb and its tantalizing promise of "eroticism on every page" with a sigh. But a slight movement from out the large picture window caught her eye. She froze, a prick of fear running down her spine.

A man stood on her front porch railing. A big man. So tall she couldn't see his head or shoulders as he reached for something on the roof.

She edged closer to the fireplace and the brass poker resting against the wall. She might be alone, but she wasn't helpless. She gripped the poker and made her way closer to the window.

But the man wasn't armed with a weapon. He had a large coil of Christmas lights hanging around his shoulder. Christmas lights. She didn't drop the poker, but her swing-first-question-second instinct wavered. Something about a man hanging Christmas lights brought the threat level down.

She lowered her weapon, watching as the man moved along the porch railing with ease, threading the heavy strand of lights on unseen hooks. He was fast. But why was he there, working so hard to decorate her house? He must run one of those decorating services. Maybe he was at the wrong house? She should stop him before he got too far.

She wrapped a throw around her shoulders and pushed through the front door, still holding her poker. A blast of cold air cut through her sweats and the thermal underwear beneath. *Shit, shit and double shit.* She'd forgotten how frigid North Texas could get. She hurried across the porch, but stopped a few feet from the man on the railing.

His leather jacket rode up as he worked. And his stomach… She swallowed. *What a view.* He stretched, exposing more actual man flesh than she'd seen in oh so long. And it was amazing. The kind of amazing even the best romance novels would have a hard time capturing.

Cut. Hard. All man. Every cleft and ridge of his six-pack was on display. His jeans hung low enough to reveal the edge of his hips. Just looking at him made her light-headed. Stunned. Excited. Achy.

Something deep inside her turned molten and fluid.

Her fingers twisted in the throw around her shoulders as her gaze followed the impressively dark happy trail that disappeared beneath the waistband of his jeans. What sort of surprises would be found underneath the skintight, faded jeans that clung to this man's hips? She swallowed, her imagination offering up all sorts of possibilities. She was oh so tempted to touch that stomach.

Which was wrong. And completely unexpected. She'd never *ever* do something so irrational but…

But all that muscle and strength, the dark lines of a

tattoo peeking wickedly from under the edge of his shirt, had her utterly captivated. What would it be like to touch a man like *this*? Better yet, what would it be like to have *him* touch *her*? A shiver racked her body. Brent had very specific preferences in bed—namely her lying still beneath him, quiet, aching for something more. Wanting something...more. *More...like this.*

She pressed her hand against her stomach and the delicious flare of liquid heat that coiled inside her. Maybe all that reading was getting to her.

This man wasn't supposed to be here; he might even get in trouble for being here if he was hired to holiday-fy another house. She stepped closer, surprised to hear him humming a Christmas carol. The sound was deep and rough, an undeniable turn-on.

"Excuse me?" she said. "I think there's been a mistake."

No response. But one arm went higher, revealing more of the tattoo on his side. A feather? A quill? Covering a long scar along his ribs... And more muscles.

"Hello?" she tried again, a little louder.

He was on one foot then, reaching for something on the roof.

She stepped forward, considering the best way to get his attention. She blew out a deep breath. This was ridiculous. What was the matter with her? She reached out and tugged on one of his jeans belt loops.

"Hold up," he called out. "Almost...got...it." The strand of Christmas lights came on, casting the porch in hues of red and green.

She held her breath as he leaped down, eager to see what the rest of this man looked like. But the clear blue eyes that greeted her were a total surprise. The kind of surprise that left her breathless—and shocked.

No.

"Spencer?" Her voice was high and tight. Even now, after years, she knew him. Instant recognition—instant reaction. Her heart twisted sharply at the all-too-familiar blue eyes regarding her in astonishment. And her body was racked with something he'd inspired whenever he was close to her: desire.

Spencer Ryan. The very last person she wanted to see right now.

He stared at her, frozen. Why was he acting so surprised? It was her house. A house she'd practically run from years ago, because of him. *She* had every right to be here. *He* did not. She welcomed the anger warming her belly. Anger was good. Much better than…the other feelings bouncing around inside of her.

His gaze sharpened, searching hers. She tried to ignore that familiar pull tightening the pit of her stomach. "Tatum?" His voice was low, husky.

"Yeah… Hi," she croaked. *This is bad.* So, *so* bad. Like she needed another bump to her already dinged confidence. Nothing like coming face-to-face with the man who had humiliated her, destroying her heart and her fragile ego eight years before. Yes, it was the holidays and there'd been a *chance* she'd run into him. But she'd hoped she wouldn't. Definitely not her first night home. Not when she wasn't ready to face him. And certainly not with crazy hair and no bra.

She tore her gaze from his, wrapping her arms around her waist. All the muscle and sexiness was Spencer? What the hell had happened to him? *This* Spencer barely resembled the clean-cut boy she'd held hands with in the halls of Greyson High School. Now he was big, almost intimidating—with shaggy black hair, a thick stubble covering his angular jaw and a new wariness about his clear blue eyes. Those eyes.

She forced her gaze away. She would not think about his eyes. Or his body. Or those abs. And that tattoo... Her pulse was racing just standing there. He was all hot in his gloriously ass-hugging jeans and broad-shoulder-hugging jacket while she wore a blanket.

"It's been a long time," he said, finally smiling. He hesitated briefly before pulling her against him in a warm embrace.

She stiffened. She didn't want to hug him. He might look good—who was she kidding, he looked frigging amazing—but she knew what he was capable of. What sort of pain he could inflict. She knew that but... His hand pressed, open, against the base of her back. Even through the layers of fabric, she could feel the contours of his fingers and the warmth of his palm. And it—he—felt good.

Then she took a deep breath and inhaled his scent. She swallowed, trembling. Dammit. He smelled the same, teasing her...flooding every cell with a steady throb of want. "It has." She didn't know where the overwhelming urge to hold on to him came from, but she fought it. It shouldn't matter that it had been too long since anyone had held her close. She wasn't going to melt in *his* arms.

She pushed away from him, stepping back quickly.

His smile faded as he eyed the poker in her hands. "Prepared for battle?"

She blinked, looking at him, then the poker. "What?"

"Or is it some new fashion accessory I don't know about?" He shot another pointed glance at the poker, crossing his thick arms over his broad chest. If she wasn't pissed as hell at his sudden and irritating reappearance in her life, she might admire the shift of muscle in his forearms. But she was. She was pissed.

"Where I come from, a woman alone protects herself from strange men hanging off their porches." She sounded unruffled and together—revealing none of her inner turmoil. "Especially when it's in the middle of the night."

He glanced at the open door behind her, then back at her.

"I'm a little tired for company and, since it is late, it's best if you go," she said over her shoulder, heading back inside and out of the cold—away from him. Her voice wasn't shaking. She didn't look like she was retreating. Even if that was sort of what she was doing. But she sort of had to because she couldn't seem to get a handle on the way she was reacting to him.

But he didn't move. He just stood there, a strange expression on his face. "I'm sorry I scared you." He held up his hands. "If I'd known you were here, alone, I would have said something first."

"Before you decorated my house?" she asked, holding the doorknob.

He planted his hands on his hips and shook his head. "Yeah, about that. It was made perfectly clear by the lady in charge that this needed to be done now or suffer the consequences."

What the hell did that mean? "The lady in charge? Sounds like your wife takes the holidays as seriously as your mother."

"*No* wife," he clarified, placing an odd emphasis on the word *no* before chuckling. "I was talking about the head of the neighborhood association."

"Why would they bother you with that?" she asked, more and more confused.

He pulled his keys from his pocket, watching her intently. "Guess Brent didn't tell you I was renting the place?"

Her lungs emptied painfully. "No, no, he didn't," she muttered, reeling. Brent hadn't told her a lot of things.

"Six months now. After the last tenants left? You didn't notice my stuff? In the master bedroom?"

"I didn't know," she murmured. "I'm staying in my old room." Was this Brent's idea of a joke? Not that she'd told him much about Spencer. But he knew enough. He knew Spencer Ryan had been her first love and that he'd broken her heart.

And now he was living in her house. The place she needed to regroup and recover.

"You remember how the town gets around the holidays?" he asked, seemingly unaware of her discomfort. "That hasn't changed." He shrugged. "I've been on assignment for over a week and I'm running out of time. So that's why I was hanging lights. Now. At night. In the cold."

He was decorating her house…because it was also his house? It wasn't some horrible mistake. But what the hell was she supposed to do? It wasn't like she was going to let him stay. No matter what time of the night it was. But she couldn't think of a single coherent thing to say.

He shivered. "It's a damn cold night." He grinned.

"I guess this means I have to let you in?" she asked, seriously considering shutting the door in his grinning face. He thought this was funny? Did he not remember the last time they saw each other? The things he'd said? She thought she'd never recover.

"That'd be the neighborly thing to do." He brushed past her, elbowing the door shut behind him.

"Right. Neighborly," she tried not to snap. Why was he surveying the room?

Why did he have to have that ass?

Her anger died a little. It was really hard to hate him while thoroughly appreciating the way his jeans hugged the muscles of his thighs. And his ass. That was definitely worth a long, thorough inspection. She swallowed, forcing her eyes up before he saw her. But he was still looking around the house, curious. "What are you looking for?"

He turned, his blue gaze pinning hers, and shook his head. "Nothing."

Obviously he was lying. It was clear he was looking for something. But what. His gaze was far too…intense and probing. And more than a little unsettling. More than a little…affecting. But words wouldn't come.

"Home for the holidays?" he asked, his voice deep and rough.

She mumbled, "Yes." Then added, "And no." Why was she answering him? Why wasn't she telling him to leave?

His crooked grin caused her heart to thump heavily in her chest. Not the most reassuring response. "That's cryptic." He shook his head.

Maybe it was, but she didn't feel the need to say more. Yet she couldn't seem to manage, "Get out now," so she stood there, her awareness increasing and the silence stretching out. He sighed, that gaze never leaving her face. She couldn't seem to look away. Or think. A cold shower was definitely in her future. Or Chris. Lots of Chris time.

He was saying something, but her mind was too busy processing *everything* to hear him. Oh, God. In less than thirty minutes she'd gone from content to distressed. And it was all Spencer's fault. Again.

"I'd offer to stay across the street at my mom's but she's got a full house, with the holidays and all." His words were soft, echoing in her ears.

She frowned at him, wrapping her arms around her waist. "One of us needs to find a hotel."

"I haven't slept in a few days, Tatum. I'd appreciate one night in my own bed. I'm not here much—the empty fridge and pantry can confirm that. I'll stay out of your way." He did look tired. His blue eyes were bloodshot and there were bags under his eyes. "I don't even snore."

"Spencer—"

"I can move into your room," he offered.

He was sleeping in her parents' room. Which was good—she wasn't ready to go there. Any and all memories of her mom could wait behind that closed door for a few more days. "No," she said. "I w-wouldn't sleep in there."

"I'm sorry about your mom," he said, grabbing her attention.

Tatum nodded. She hadn't visited Greyson since her mother's death three years before. "It's strange to be here and have it so quiet." She shrugged, not wanting to share with him.

But Spencer had known better than most about her mother and her fits of temper. When she'd been on a real tear, her mother could be heard all up and down Maple Drive. Her mother's anger and bitterness had been one of the reasons she'd gone to live with her father her senior year of high school. Spencer had been the other.

"You look good, Tatum." His voice pitched low, all gravel.

She was acutely aware of the way his eyes leisurely swept her from head to toe. When his attention returned to her face, his jaw was locked. Was that disapproval on his face? Or—her heart was thumping—was it something else? She didn't know how to read the tension that rolled off of him. But it was unnerving as hell. His gaze narrowed, piercing hers. What was he trying to figure out?

"Tatum?" Her name. His voice. She felt a shudder run down her back.

"No, I don't." Her words spilled from her lips. She looked like hell and she knew it. "*You* look different," she admitted. *Different* was an understatement. Even if her response to him was the same: hyperaware. When he was close, she'd *felt* it. Right now, she was feeling all sorts of things that made her nervous and excited and tense. *Dammit*.

He cocked a questioning eyebrow her way.

She shrugged. "There's...more of you." Including abs and tattoos and the lovely dark happy trail disappearing beneath his waistband. She needed to stop talking—and thinking—immediately. Instead, she stared at his chest, encased in a skintight gray shirt and leather jacket. What was absolutely terrifying was how badly her fingers itched to explore him. *No. No exploring. Evicting. Immediate evicting.*

He laughed. "More of me?"

His laughter rolled over her, leaving her tingling in all the right places. *Dammit.* It was cruel that he'd turned out even more beautiful than she remembered. And completely unfair. He'd broken her heart, made her doubt her judgment and left her unbelieving she was worthy of love.

How dare he stand there, teasing her, acting like he wasn't the bad guy. She knew better. It wasn't like he was just some dangerously good-looking man making her house all festive while waking up every one of her lady-part nerves. If only that were the case.

"Tatum?" he whispered, coming to stand in front of her. "You okay?"

She nodded. Her attention wandered to his mouth, leaving her breathless. Would his touch feel the same? His lips had branded her skin, magic against her lips... No, she wasn't okay. If she was, she wouldn't be dragging up memories better left buried.

Besides, he didn't deserve to touch her. To kiss her. And she needed to stop thinking of that. Of him—naked. Of what she wanted to do to him—naked. This was Spencer. And the two of them would not be getting naked together.

Even if he is way more exciting than my vibrator. The thought sent another shudder through her.

"You cold?" His voice was gruff and rumbling—shaking her to the core.

"No," she managed, her tongue thick and her throat tight. She wasn't cold. For the first time in a long time, she was feeling delectably hot. The only problem with this scenario was *he* was the one making her feel this way.

She stepped around him, hoping to quiet the desire surging through her veins. Her overstimulated reaction to him made no sense. She didn't like him. *Maybe this is what happens when you go for more than a year without sex?* "But I need something to drink and you need to... to go to bed," she said, glancing at him. "One night," she added, knowing she was a coward. But it was after midnight, cold, and she wasn't heartless.

"Okay. One night. I'll crash here tonight and look into

staying somewhere else while you're in town." He was staring at her again. "If you're sure Brent won't mind?"

She nodded. *Brent so won't mind.* She headed into the kitchen, deliberately avoiding his gaze. She could sleep under the same roof; she could be an adult. But she wasn't going to talk about her marriage or her divorce with him.

He followed her. "Why is it so cold in here? Pilot light go out again?" he asked, rubbing his hands together. "Brent couldn't get it to work?"

"The heat won't come on." She pointed at the fireplace over her shoulder. "But at least I got the fire going, even if I did burn my thumb and singe some hair." She held her thumb up.

She hadn't expected him to cradle her hand in his or hold up her thumb for a thorough inspection. She wanted to yank her hand away and scowl at him… No, she didn't. Which was worse.

His gaze locked with hers. "Some homecoming." His hold went from reassuring to overwhelming. "I am sorry about tonight. Not the way I'd imagined seeing you again." His words shook her. The rhythmic stroke of his thumb along her wrist turned her insides fluid.

Not the way I'd imagined seeing you again.

She blew out a deep breath. "It's…it's fine." Her words were a raspy whisper but she managed to pull her hand from his. No touching. Touching was bad. And more space was good too. She stepped back, wrapping her arms around her waist. "I…I can call a repairman in the morning."

He glanced at her hand, then back at her, his eyes narrowing. "I'll fix it before we go to bed."

We *go to bed.* She swallowed, staring at the floor so her face wouldn't betray her thoughts. "Thanks."

"What's going on?" he asked softly.

"What do you mean?" She knew what he meant. But her life was none of his business. And, dammit, she was having a hard time thinking straight with him standing there staring at her that way. She needed to stay cool. And keep him at arm's length. So she busied herself in the kitchen, pulling out the milk, a saucepan and some cocoa packets.

He followed her, standing too close. "You're here alone, basically in the dark, without heat. Alone."

She put the kettle on the burner, her hands and her voice unsteady. "Did you have to say that twice?" she asked.

"I guess that's the thing I'm most hung up on," he confessed.

He was standing behind her, his warmth rolling over her. "It is?" She glanced back at him, the questions in his gaze enough to turn her back to cocoa making. "I assure you, you don't need to be hung up on *anything* that has to do with me, okay?" She tried to sound flippant but it didn't work.

"Old habits die hard. I know how to read you. I always have." There was an edge to his voice.

"Maybe. When we were kids," she agreed. But they definitely weren't kids anymore. And even if he had known what she was thinking—wanting—before she had, didn't mean he did now. That was a long time ago. "Right now I want cocoa. And peace and quiet." She spun around to face him, shoving the mug into his hand. "Good night."

"Trying to get rid of me?" he asked, glancing at the mug she'd placed in his hands before leveling her with the weight of his gaze once more.

"I didn't realize that was unclear."

He chuckled.

She was very proud that she didn't smile at him. Because his smile was hard to resist. He was hard to resist. Because, honestly, she would happily replace her swirly purple battery-operated love machine with this new manlier version of Spencer. She choked on her sip of cocoa. *Please, God, don't let him figure out what I'm thinking. And wanting.*

"Brent's not here." He paused. "You're alone." He swallowed, his gaze searching her face as he leaned forward, placing his mug on the counter, his large hands on either side of her—effectively pinning her against the counter.

"So?" She didn't deny it. She was alone. She was relieved her out-of-control hunger for him had somehow escaped his notice. But now that she was so close, that wouldn't last for long. Her heart was slamming against her ribs and breathing was becoming increasingly difficult. Because breathing drew in his scent, his tantalizing, captivating, enticing scent.

"And there's this." He pointed at her, then himself—stepping so close that his breath fanned her hair. "There's still a hell of a…connection between the two of us." He practically growled the words. Her body tightened, expectant, at the sound of his undeniable hunger.

For her.

His attention wandered to her mouth, leaving no doubt what he wanted. He felt it too. Of course he did.

She could sway into him, give in… But she should fight it. Even if his lips were so close. "Yes." It took a lot of effort to form a coherent answer.

"Yes?" he repeated, his nostrils flaring as his gaze locked with hers.

"Yes. I am alone." Her voice wavered.

He shook his head, the muscle in his jaw hard as rock. "That's all?" he asked. "I won't touch another man's wife." He ground out the words. "But, dammit, I want to kiss you so bad it hurts."

Kiss me. She stared at him, gripped by a crushing, desperate ache. *Touch me.* "I'm no man's wife. But I don't want you to kiss me," she whispered.

2

SPENCER STARED DOWN at her, his nerves strung so tight he worried he'd pop.

Tatum was here.

And all he could think about was touching her, tasting her. Silk. Warmth. Pure temptation. And even though he had no right to touch her, to think of her tangled up with him, he couldn't stop himself. His body responded to her without reason, as if they hadn't been living separate lives for years.

Her quiver revealed her lie. She wasn't immune to him.

"I don't believe you," he argued.

She drew in a wavering breath. "I don't care what you believe." There was an edge to her voice. She wasn't immune to him—but she was going to fight it.

Her green eyes clashed with his and he smiled at her. This was Tatum. The girl who'd stolen his heart, the girl he'd lived for. The girl he'd crushed, shredding his own heart in the process. He'd missed her every day for the last eight years.

He reached up, smoothing an errant curl from her forehead. "Your hair is longer."

She didn't say anything as he threaded the curl between his fingers. The curl coiled around him, clinging to him the way he envisioned her clinging to him.

"So is yours," she whispered.

A woman alone protects herself. He'd heard her. *No man's wife.* For the first time, nothing was stopping them. Except maybe the defiance in her gaze.

He saw the way she looked at his mouth, the way her lips parted and her hands tightened on the counter's edge. There was a restlessness about her he'd never seen in her before. She was nervous… That was obvious. Hell, he was nervous. But it was more than that. It was their past. What he'd done was reprehensible. Could she still hate him so much that she couldn't bear to be close to him?

Or did she hate that she still wanted him?

From the look on her face, it'd be all too easy to assume it was the latter. Because that was what he wanted. Badly. The way she was looking at him now, flushed and dazed, focused on his mouth… He hadn't been this hard since he was sixteen.

He stepped forward, erasing the small space between them. His thumbs ran along her jawline, tracing the soft skin of her neck and the shell of her ear. She closed her eyes, her lips parted, her breath escaping on unsteady gasps. He watched her response, her arousal driving him crazy. "How long?" he asked, his tone soft.

Her green eyes fluttered open. "How long?" she repeated, breathless.

"Since you've been…kissed." He bit out the last word. "How long has it been since a man's loved your body?"

"My body is none of your business." But the tremor in

her voice told him he wasn't imagining this. Her hands gripped the counter edge as if she was holding herself back. She wanted him, even if she didn't want to accept it.

"And it's a damn shame," he murmured, longing to pry her hands from the counter, to feel her fingers slide through his hair. Before he was through, she'd be holding on to him.

He smiled as his lips brushed her startled mouth—featherlight, a whisper of a touch. She shuddered as his nose traced the length of her neck. "You smell just as sweet," he murmured. He sucked her earlobe into his mouth, her little sigh making the hair on the back of his neck stand up straight. "You taste the same." It was true. And it was torture. When he pressed her back, pinning her hips against the cabinets, the feel of her curves against him almost brought him to his knees.

His mouth brushed hers once, still teasing. He tilted her head back, nipping her lower lip. Her lips were so damn soft. He pulled, sucking her plump lower lip until her lips parted. The tip of her tongue...stroking the curve of his lip. *Damn.*

He groaned, leaning into her, sealing her mouth with his and sliding his tongue into the hot recesses of her mouth. Her hand tangled in his hair, anchoring him firmly so she could deepen their kiss. And she did, the touch of her satin tongue making him groan. Her sudden hunger spurred him on. He gripped her hips, lifting her onto the kitchen counter. She wrapped a leg around his waist and pulled him close—arching into him.

His kiss wasn't gentle; his tongue demonstrated exactly what he wanted from her. And the soft moan, her grip on his hair, told him she wanted it too. His hold on her hips tightened as he ground against her. He tore his mouth from hers, groaning against the hollow of her throat at the building friction between them. She cried out when his mouth latched on to her neck. He devoured her, holding her tightly, wanting more.

It had always been this way with her. All that mattered was the feel of her, her response, the way she touched him.

But as quickly as she reached for him, she withdrew. Her hold went from clinging to pushing against his chest. "Spencer," she gasped. Fighting this—fighting him. He heard her deep, unsteady inhalation as she attempted to put some space between them.

Space he didn't want. He stepped back, breathing hard.

"Spencer," she repeated. Her voice was low and husky.

He looked at her. God, he wanted her. He hurt from wanting her. He was breathing heavy and losing control. He knew it, but he couldn't apologize for it. She drove him crazy, made him lose his head. She always had.

"If we're doing this… It's one time." Her eyes bored into his. "Only once."

He frowned, cupping her face in his hands. "Once?" He'd been half expecting her to tell him to leave. Now she was telling him they were going to have sex. But only once?

"I don't want to think…" She paused, her voice unsteady. "I want to feel alive…to feel *something*."

Her words cut through him. He didn't know what had happened with her marriage. Had she been mistreated? Heartbroken? She wanted one night, nothing more. And could he handle that, with the history they had, the feelings he still harbored? He knew one thing: refusing her was impossible.

Her green eyes bored into his, waiting, searching—and hungry.

Still, he had to be sure. "Tatum, I'm not sure—"

She pressed her fingers to his lips. "If the answer's no, just say it. Otherwise, I'd rather we didn't do much talking."

He raised an eyebrow. Because talking meant thinking. And she'd already made it clear she didn't want to overthink this. He *should* tell her no and walk away. Instead, he was going to give her what she wanted, what he wanted. "I'm not saying no." He tilted her head back, making sure she was listening. "You want me to kiss you, Tatum? To touch you?" he asked.

Her eyes widened. "Yes." The quiver in her voice shook him, stirring a possessiveness he hadn't felt since they were young and in love. He swallowed back the wash of memories—and regret—and focused on the job at hand.

She wanted to feel alive. He'd give it his all. And enjoy every damn minute of it.

His hands cupped her face, his thumbs tracing her lower lip before he pressed his mouth to hers. His lips parted hers, sealing their mouths and mixing their breaths. When she trembled, he smiled, wrapping his arms around her and pulling her tight against him. She was soft and warm, moving against him and gripping his shirt. He kissed her until she was clinging to him, her body molding to his, her tongue making him dizzy. Whatever she wanted, he'd give her.

He paused long enough to turn off the stove and swing her up into his arms. She twined her arms around his neck, her fingers slipping into his hair as he carried her into the living room. He set her on her feet long enough to toss the couch cushions onto the floor in front of the fire, then knelt in front of her.

His hands settled at her waist, working the fabric of her top free from the waist of her leggings. Her skin contracted beneath his fingertips, quivering. He looked up at her as his mouth brushed across her bare abdomen. She gasped, her fingers running through his hair. His lips skimmed her stomach, her waist. Her fingers tightened, tugging. He was mesmerized by the wonder on her face and the feel of her skin. Soft as silk. His hands slid up her sides and around her back, his fingers exploring every bump of her spine.

Her hands moved, settling on his shoulders to fist in the fabric of his shirt.

He lifted her hands, kissing each finger before pulling his shirt off. Her reaction was unexpected. He wanted her to touch him, hoped she would. Instead, she stared at him, slowly dropping to her knees. Her breathing was erratic, so rapid he worried she'd hyperventilate. Her hands stayed put, pressed flat against her thighs.

"Breathe, Tatum," he whispered.

She nodded, staring at his chest.

"You okay?" he asked.

She nodded, still staring at his chest.

Tatum had never shied away from telling him what she wanted. There'd been times he'd had to put on the brakes. But now she seemed hesitant. "Want me to put my shirt back on?"

She shook her head. *"No,"* she croaked.

"Talk to me," he encouraged, taking her hand. How many times had they ended up twined together, too caught up to know where one ended and the other began? It had been natural between them, easy. But now she seemed uncertain and it tore him up inside. "Tell me what you want. What you like."

She looked at him, blinking rapidly, but said nothing.

He pressed her hand against his chest. Her gaze fixed on her hand, her lips parting as her fingers traced the valley between his pectorals. "Whatever you want, Tatum…" He couldn't finish his sentence. The way she was looking at him made it impossible for him to say a word.

Her breathing echoed in the quite room, her attention focused solely on his bare chest and stomach. He was spellbound by the fascination on her face.

One second she was sitting there, facing him, her touch tentative. The next he was lying back on the pile of pillows, her hesitation replaced by desperate curiosity. He watched her expression, aware of every move her hands and fingers made. She bent over him, her long golden hair spilling onto his stomach as her lips and tongue explored the super-sensitized flesh of his nipple.

He reached up to thread his fingers in her hair, absorbing every caress and stroke. She took her time, exploring every inch of him with her soft hands and mouth. Her teeth nipped his side, her nails ran the length of his arms, and she kissed and sucked her way down his abdomen. He could barely breathe. Her tongue dipped into his belly button and he arched into her, groaning as her warm mouth brushed across his skin. "Dammit, Tatum."

She unfastened his pants, clasping the waist of his jeans and tugging his boxers off with them. She sat back on her heels then, staring at his prominent erection. No way could she miss the way he was throbbing, aching, for her. He shuddered as her fingers lightly stroked the length of him. But the noise she made, a strange broken cry, drew his focus back to her.

She tugged her shirt off, standing to remove her pants. She wavered on unsteady legs, so he sat up and helped her frantically peel off the two pairs of leggings and more socks. When she was as naked as he was, he had to touch her. He buried his face against her side, pressing a kiss against the swell of her hip, before pulling her down with him. Her lips found his, their tongues touching and stroking. He slid his hand through her hair, holding her close, savoring the taste of her as every curve and angle of her body fitted against his.

He didn't know how much more he could take. He needed her, needed to be inside of her, now. But that wouldn't be fair. He'd barely touched her. He wanted to touch her. And clearly, she needed to be touched. He wanted to make her fall apart, to lose control, to find a release. Again and again.

His hand cupped her breast, drawing her nipple deep into his mouth. She made that strange little cry again. He looked at her, at the way she bit her lower lip.

"I want to hear you," he murmured. "I want to know when you like something."

He rolled her nipple between his fingers and thumb, watching her. His tongue flicked the tip. She groaned, crying out when his mouth latched on to the other nipple.

He lifted her arms over her head, kissing along her sides, sucking the skin until he knew he'd leave marks. His hands were busy too, stroking the curve of her hip, the underside of her breast, the soft skin of her inner thigh. When his fingers traced the slick flesh between her legs, she made that strangled cry.

"Don't hold back, Tatum," he demanded, stroking the nub of nerves at her core. "Not with me." His finger parted her, sliding deep. He groaned at the feel of her, closing his eyes at her tight heat gloving his finger. He moved, stroking her skin, filling her. His thumb set an urgent rhythm against the taut bud, his finger doing the job his body ached to do. And the sounds she made... Pure torture.

Her hands gripped his shoulders as she arched into his touch. He cupped her breast, gently running his teeth over the tip as he added another finger. She was so tight around him. He groaned, burying his face against her breast and gritting his teeth against the need to bury himself inside of her. "You feel so good." He all but growled the words.

She cried out, long and ragged. He watched her face as her body contracted around his fingers. She grabbed his arm, holding his hand in place as she rode out her climax. It was the sexiest damn thing he'd ever seen. She was beautiful. So damn beautiful. And he wanted to see that look, that stunned, frantic release, on her face again.

She opened her eyes, gasping. "That was so...*so* much better than a vibrator."

He was so surprised, he laughed. And then she was laughing too.

3

Tatum stared at the boxes of decorations she'd pulled from the attic. They'd been buried, covered in junk and a layer of dust. But now the wreath hung over the fireplace, its colored glass balls aglow from the white lights inside. The Christmas village was arranged on the side table and she'd unpacked the train that would go around the Christmas tree. These were the things her father had delighted in... Seeing them made her think of him and happier times.

Now all she needed was a tree.

The repairman had arrived first thing. Nothing like working heat and electric, Christmas decorations, carols and a solid night's sleep to help dispel some of her moodiness.

Or the mind-blowing orgasm courtesy of Spencer. But last night had been wrong. A huge mistake. He'd caught her when she was vulnerable and needy... And it had been the single most erotic moment of her life.

Not that it would ever—*ever*—happen again. She'd been arguing with herself all morning. What had she been thinking? Why had things gotten so carried away?

And then she'd remember the feel of him, the things he'd done to her, and all her arguments faded away.

She'd been gasping, still clinging to him, when his cell phone chirped. His posture had changed instantly, his forehead creasing. "Shit," he'd muttered.

"Something wrong?" she'd asked, wishing she was still in touch with her inner teenager enough to ask him to stay and give her another orgasm—or two.

"Work," he'd groaned, nuzzling her breast again.

Her fingers had slipped through his tangled black hair. "If you ignore it, will they go away?" *Please tell me they'll go away.*

He'd chuckled, then groaned again, his breath brushing her nipples and his hand stroking along her belly. "I wish. They call, I go. *Dammit.*"

She tugged the plaid throw over her nakedness, watching him dress with a mixture of appreciation and disappointment. In that moment, disappointment won. She hadn't wanted him to go. From the bulge in his pants, she knew he didn't want to go. And when he'd looked at her, there was no denying how badly he wanted to stay. He'd kissed her, once, so hard and deep she moaned. Which made him mutter *"Dammit"* again before stomping out.

She'd lain on her nest of pillows hoping he'd reappear. But he hadn't come back and she'd eventually crawled into her bed, buried in quilts and oh so lonely.

She'd woken up with the echo of his fingers on her skin. She could still feel him, taste him... All morning she'd thought of things she wished she'd done. It wasn't the regret she was expecting, but it was still regret. He'd been her own personal playground and she'd only been allowed on one ride—a ride that had been cut short.

After living in a state of denial, her body was ready

to give in, let go and thoroughly enjoy what Spencer was willing to offer her. Too bad she'd said once.

Of course, they hadn't actually slept together so...

No. God no. What was she thinking?

"Tatum?" She heard the singsong voice through her front door. "Are you decent? It's Mrs. Ryan, dear, from across the street."

She blushed. Spencer's mother. "Coming," she called out, smoothing her red tunic into place and running a quick hand over her hair and the long beaded necklace she wore. Appearance was important. First her mother, then Brent had insisted she always look her best. And now that Spencer's mother was on the front porch, she was glad of it.

She pulled open the door to find Mrs. Ryan and Lucy Ryan, Spencer's cousin. Lucy was the one person she'd kept in contact with from Greyson—the one person Tatum had always counted a true friend. But after Lucy had come to visit her and Brent, their emails and phone calls grew further apart. Brent hadn't liked Lucy and made it clear he didn't approve of their friendship. And, sadly, Tatum hadn't fought to preserve or defend their friendship.

"Tatum!" Lucy squealed, her gray eyes widening at the sight of her.

"Lucy? Oh, Lucy," she answered, laughing when Lucy hugged her tight.

"I hadn't heard from you in a while." Lucy's voice was muffled. "It's so good to see you."

"I'm sorry," she murmured. "I guess I've sort of been in hiding."

Lucy let go of her and Mrs. Ryan hugged her gently.

"Well, you're home now and that's all that matters," the older woman said.

"We brought you cookies," Lucy said, offering her a huge basket overflowing with cookies, breads, some wine and fruit.

"Well…thank you," Tatum said, taking the basket. "Come in, please."

That was when she saw Spencer coming up the path. It hadn't been her imagination. He really was the hottest thing she'd seen in real life. And watching him stroll up her path, all bad boy and muscled body… The phantom heat of his fingers inside her body had her throbbing for his touch and aching for more. Sticking to "once" was going to be hard.

Especially if one of them didn't move out.

"Hurry up, Spencer," Lucy called. "It's cold."

Spencer took the steps two at a time, striding into the living room before Tatum could react. He hugged her, casually, his scent flooding her nostrils. "Morning, Tatum," he said tightly, his blue eyes staring into hers.

She nodded, reeling from the effect of his quick embrace.

"Well, come sit, tell us everything," Mrs. Ryan said, patting the couch beside her. "I haven't seen you in… Goodness, how long has it been?"

"Almost eight years?" Lucy asked, sitting on the couch beside her aunt.

Tatum nodded.

"You look just the same." Mrs. Ryan smiled. "I always thought we'd see you in a magazine or a movie someday."

"Oh…no." Tatum shook her head. "Would you like something to drink—"

"No, Aunt Imogene is literally bursting to ask you

questions about everything that's happened since you left," Lucy cut in.

Imogene Ryan's eyes went round. "Lucy," she chastised.

"It's true," Spencer added.

Tatum laughed, sitting in the rocking chair. She tried not to pay attention to Spencer as he knelt in front of the fire to add more logs. Tried not to think about how he'd stripped her down on the floor where her feet now rested... "Ask away," Tatum answered unsteadily.

"What have you been up to?" Mrs. Ryan asked. "I know you finished out high school in California with your father, but after that? Lucy said you went to college there?"

"UCLA," she said, shrugging. "Got my accounting degree. I get numbers." *People, not so much.*

"Ugh." Lucy winced. "No, thank you."

"Okay, Miss PhD," Tatum teased. "I met Brent there. We were married for three years. I was his wife, his accountant and his events planner...and we've been *officially* divorced for eight months."

"I'm so sorry," Mrs. Ryan said.

"I am too," she agreed. "Wish I'd had the sense to get out sooner." She smiled, trying to make light of the situation. But it was true. She'd worked hard to be what Brent wanted, keeping his books sound, his house tidy and his parties memorable. When he hired "more seasoned professionals" to do his books, the slight daily contact they had was gone. Things had disintegrated by their second anniversary. So why had she held on?

She felt Spencer's gaze on her and glanced his way. He was studying her, looking for something. But what exactly? Instead of worrying about what he was thinking or feeling, she'd be wise to remember he'd been the first one to replace her with another woman.

Whatever spark remained was purely sexual. Which was fine.

"Good riddance," Lucy chimed in. "His loss."

"That's sweet of you to say," she laughed, even if it sounded a little forced.

"It's true," Mrs. Ryan agreed. "You'll find the man that deserves you, don't you fret."

So not fretting. Worrying over her romantic future wasn't on her top-ten-things-to-worry-over list. She didn't know who she was or what she wanted—now wasn't the time to fall in love. No, that was the main reason it had fallen apart with Brent: he defined too much of her. That, and he'd been screwing the most successful real-estate agent in their wealthy, gossipy group of friends.

If anything, she didn't want a relationship right now. She needed to figure things out, needed to live a little and try new things—for herself.

Like sex. Last night had been a revelation. She *wanted* lots of hot sex. But she only knew one person she was attracted to. She glanced at Spencer again.

Could she get up the nerve to really consider such a thing? Roommates with benefits? *And* ask him if he was interested. The potential for rejection gnawed on her insides.

But last night. She drew in an unsteady breath, flooded with a tangle of want-inducing images, sensations and sounds. They *were* already sleeping under the same roof. Neither of them was involved. And, hell, they were both adults.

He could say no. She swallowed, tearing her gaze from him.

"What are your plans?" Lucy asked. "Whatever they are, tell me you're staying."

She nodded. "Come home, regroup, get a job...start again."

"Sounds like a good plan, dear," Mrs. Ryan said. "Oh, I know. I'll check in with George Welch, see if he knows of any openings in his office. He has the largest accounting firm in the county."

Tatum held up her hand. "You don't have to—"

"No, she doesn't. But it's what she does," Spencer said. "With or without your blessing, trust me."

Tatum smiled at him, then Mrs. Ryan. "Thank you."

"Free today?" Lucy asked. "I'd love to spend some time with you."

"I'd love that too," she agreed. "Up for shopping? I have no food." She paused, looking at the huge goodie basket on the table. "Well, I do now. But I'm thinking a Christmas tree might brighten things up."

"You *do* decorate?" Mrs. Ryan asked. "I'm so glad. I know your mother... Well, I'm glad."

"I do," she said. "And I want this Christmas to be extra special."

"You've got a great yard, Tatum," Spencer said.

"You had ideas for a theme, didn't you?" Lucy asked.

"Spencer, you're going to have to find a place to stay now that Tatum is back. I'm sure the last thing she wants is a roommate. Especially in your line of work. I tell you, a police officer is never off duty. Constant interruptions. Calls in the middle of the night. Never a dull moment," Mrs. Ryan said and wrinkled her nose for emphasis.

Law enforcement. It made sense. Spencer's father and grandfather had both been cops. Why shouldn't Spencer? It also explained why he left for work in the middle of the night and why he'd been on assignment for so long. She'd been too lost in a lust-induced haze to find out what he did for a living—about his life now.

Spencer sighed. "I'll figure something out."

"I feel bad to cause problems, especially this close to the holidays," Tatum jumped in. She did feel bad, which she didn't like, for forcing him out of his home, even if it was her house. And if—*if*—she did decide to proposition Spencer, it would be a hell of a lot more convenient if he was here.

Spencer's gaze met hers. "There's nothing to feel bad about."

Had his eyes always been so blue? So…unrelenting?

"I love it when people put up trees outside." Lucy steered the conversation back toward decorating. "Ooh, or those giant light-up nutcrackers?"

"Nutcrackers?" Mrs. Ryan didn't look pleased with the suggestion.

"My car's too small for that," Tatum said, eyeing the space in front of the window and remembering her father's pleasure in big, flocked trees that made a mess but looked bright and cheery glowing with colored lights.

"I can take you," Spencer offered. "To get a tree, I mean. Or two. One for inside, one for outside."

"He's got the truck," Lucy agreed. "It can fit all three of us, right?"

She caught the arched eyebrow he turned on Lucy before he answered, "Yes."

"Can't you shave before you go out in public?" Mrs. Ryan sighed heavily. "You'll have to excuse his appearance. I can't stand it when he's undercover, putting himself in harm's way. Not only is it dangerous, but he looks like a…a gang member." She waved at her son.

Tatum grinned. All she saw was a powerfully built man, a man with an amazing body and equally amazing hands. "He did surprise me last night." She felt delightfully wicked as she added, "I was a little shell-shocked when he left."

Spencer looked at her, blue eyes narrowing. "Oh, it was mutual, believe me."

The look in his eyes made her tingle. She'd been more than satisfied, even if he hadn't. But was he still interested? She hoped he was. She cleared her throat, her voice tight as she asked, "Next time, maybe we can finish our conversation?"

She saw him swallow, the flare of his nostrils, the absolutely gorgeous ridge of his jaw locking. His nod was stiff—but it was enough to have her throbbing.

"Oh, to be a fly on the wall for that conversation," Lucy murmured.

She and Spencer looked at Lucy in unison, making Lucy grin widely.

"Well, I have to get those pies in the oven for the women's auxiliary auction Saturday night." Mrs. Ryan stood. "You'll come, won't you, Tatum?"

"I'd like that, thank you," Tatum agreed.

"There are so many wonderful parties and events this time of year. *And* a wedding. A wedding you will be shaving for, Spencer?"

Spencer sighed, then nodded.

"Well, that's something, I suppose. Have fun today. Now that you're back, Tatum, I expect to see a lot more of you. You'll feel at home again in no time."

"I will, thanks," Tatum agreed.

"Good." Mrs. Ryan kissed her on the cheek. "Spencer,

make sure you get the rest of Tatum's lights done today, as well. The roof looks a little bare."

Tatum might want to strip Spencer down and explore every inch of him with her hands and mouth, but she could decorate her own house. "I can probably—"

"I'll do it," Spencer assured her. "And we'll have time to finish that conversation."

So many delicious images raced through her mind that every inch of her tightened with anticipation.

"Sounds like that's settled. You make sure the job is done right, Spencer," Mrs. Ryan said, shooting her son a stern look.

"I'll make sure," he said, staring into the fireplace, his jaw tight.

"I'll see you tomorrow, dear," Mrs. Ryan called out, waving goodbye as she headed back across the street to her house.

"She hasn't changed a bit," Tatum said, smiling at Lucy and Spencer. "You're lucky to have her."

Lucy hugged her. "Oh, Tatum… I just realized… I'm sorry about your dad. And your mom. Well, that's it. You're going to be a Ryan this Christmas, no arguing. No way you're going to spend it alone, you hear me?" She hugged her tighter. "This Christmas does need to be extra special."

Tatum blinked back her tears. She'd lost her mother and grandparents years ago. Her father had passed last year. And now, without Brent, she had no one to celebrate with. "Thanks, Lucy. But I don't want to invade—"

"Invade," Spencer said. "You'll appreciate coming home to a quiet house." He smiled at her, his blue eyes so blue.

"Off to the tree farm?" Lucy asked. "Or would you rather go shopping?"

One look Spencer's way told her exactly what she wanted, even if it wasn't one of her choices. But she could wait. Anticipation was a good thing. Until then, she'd have to find a way to occupy herself. "Let's start with a tree."

"I'll get the truck," Spencer said, heading out the front door.

"What's it been? One day?" Lucy asked as soon as they were alone. "How naked did you get last night? And don't even try to deny it. You two—in the same room—wow. I need a fan and some ice water to cool down."

She should argue, but she'd never been good at lying. "I admit, he's… I'm…overwhelmed."

Lucy laughed. "Yeah, well, you're not alone. He almost poured orange juice in his coffee this morning."

"He did not," she argued, delighted to know their time together had him just as rattled as she was.

"Yep," Lucy said. "Aunt Imogene texted him to come straight over after work, ready to tear into him for not having the house done. I don't think he's had a break in a few weeks but his mom gets all crazy over the holidays. All he said was he'd gotten distracted. By you. Then he stormed off for a shower. I can only imagine what that meant." Lucy giggled but didn't ask questions. One of the many reasons Tatum had always loved Lucy—she didn't pry.

But Lucy's words ramped up her excitement level. If he'd found last night distracting, she couldn't wait for tonight.

SPENCER HELD HIS breath as Tatum bent forward to inspect the bin of wood-chip angels. She had great legs. Long, trim, encased in tall black boots. The sight of her round ass hugged by skintight leggings almost made him groan. It definitely made his pants uncomfortable. He shoved his hands in his pockets.

"These are adorable." She straightened, holding up one of the ornaments.

"They're to go on your outside tree," Lucy explained. "To give it that rustic look. If that's what you're going for?"

Tatum turned the ornament in her hands, her expression assessing. "I have no idea what I'm going for, but I like them."

"Start with a tree," he offered.

She looked at him, nodding. Her gaze fell to his mouth. "Whatever you say," she said.

She was teasing him. Driving him out of his damn mind. Later, he'd remind her she said that. All he could think about was getting her back to her place and into her bed. Instead, he barked out, "This way," and led them outside. If he was lucky, the chill in the air would help him gain some control over his libido. The last time he'd felt this kind of desire, he'd been nineteen and she'd been his whole world. He glanced back at her, talking and laughing with Lucy. He was older, more grounded now…but somehow being around her made him forget that.

Last night had been a revelation. Leaving her had been one of the hardest things he'd ever done. Yes, he'd wanted to finish what they'd started, but it was more than that. They'd had unfinished business for a long time. Now that she was back, and they were the way they still were, he hoped he'd finally be able to apologize. And, if she'd give him the chance, explain why he'd done what he did—why he'd broken both of their hearts. His had never fully recovered.

One hour and two trees later, they were pulling in front of Tatum's house. He was glad Lucy had volunteered to squeeze in the middle. He'd spent most of the day being aware of Tatum's every move. He wasn't sure how he'd react if he was being pressed up against her. His wayward body had no problem revealing just how much he wanted her. Walking through a Christmas tree farm with a hard-on wasn't exactly socially acceptable but there hadn't been a damn thing he could do about it. Now that they were back at her place and he knew what he had to look forward to, he was in for a long, uncomfortable evening.

Spencer followed them down the path, watching the light fall of snowflakes settle in Tatum's hair. She was shivering. Didn't she have a heavy coat? Guess it didn't get too cold in Los Angeles. It took everything he had not to pull her close and warm her up.

As Tatum opened the front door, Lucy said, "If you decide you need extra hands, call my brothers Dean and Jared. They're off tomorrow. I figure Zach is going to be pretty out-of-pocket since this is his first Christmas as a married man. And with Patton's wedding coming up—"

"Zach is married?" Tatum asked, stunned. "Is Patton finally marrying Ellie? She was so stuck on him." She hung her keys on a hook by the door.

"Patton and Ellie ended a while back," Spencer said. "Cady, Patton's fiancée, she's a force of nature. One my brother didn't stand a chance against."

"It was one of those whirlwind sort of things," Lucy agreed. "The wedding's New Year's Eve at a fancy mountaintop resort in Colorado that Zach manages. Romantic, right?"

Her open disbelief had Spencer grinning from ear to ear. "Really?"

Spencer nodded. "I know. Patton. Whirlwind. Marriage. Romance. Who'd have thought?" His big brother Patton was hardly the hearts and flowers type. Hell, neither was Zach. But somehow they were both content to be tied to one woman.

Tatum nodded. "He was always sort of…stuffy. And reserved. No offense."

"None taken. He was. Hell, for the most part, he still is." Spencer laughed.

Lucy giggled. "You should see him, Tatum. He's adorable. Never in a million years did I think Patton could be so crazy in love. And show it. But Cady's got him hooked."

"It's nauseating," Spencer agreed. But that wasn't really true. He was happy for his brothers—hell, he envied them. Both of them had the love of a good woman, women who completed them.

"And Zach?" Tatum asked.

"Bianca," Lucy said. "Sweetest girl I have ever met. I think we were all worried he'd bring home some world-traveling, socialite type with his career and all. But Bianca is wonderful, grounded and kind. You'll meet them both soon, being an honorary Ryan this year."

He saw the look on Tatum's face, the yearning pressing in on him.

"I remember being so jealous of you growing up," Tatum said, hooking her arm with Lucy's. "A big family, get-togethers, big parties." Her gaze met his. "There was always something happening at your house, Spencer.

Lots of laughter. And they're all still here? Your whole family?" Tatum asked. "That's—"

"Smothering?" he interjected, laughing.

Tatum laughed.

"Sometimes," Lucy agreed. "But when you've got multiple trees to decorate and a mother who wanted this done yesterday, having extra hands—"

"Is pretty damn convenient," Spencer agreed.

"So, tomorrow, we'll get you set up before the big Holiday Lights kickoff?" Lucy asked. "I'd offer to stay and help tonight, but I promised to watch Mrs. Medrano's grandson."

Which was a relief. He didn't know how he was going to get Lucy to leave, but there was no way he and Tatum wanted a chaperone tonight. He grinned, anticipation warming his blood. "I'll get the house lights done. And the tree up." He glanced at Tatum, noting the flush to her cheeks and hoping it meant she was just as eager. "What else do you want to tackle tonight, Tatum?"

The look she shot him made him bite back a hiss. Damn, but her face gave everything away. And damn if he didn't like the way her mind was working.

"Shopping," Lucy prompted.

Tatum nodded, tearing her gaze from his. "Yes. Food... I should go to the store. You're doing so much to help me out, the least I can do is feed you. And your family tomorrow."

"I'll get started here," he agreed.

Lucy checked her watch. "I have an hour. We can shop, I'll drop you off and head to Mrs. Medrano's?"

"Thank you," Tatum said. "Thank you both for today. It was great to get out, to have...fun doing normal things, you know?"

He needed to remember she'd been through a hell of a lot. She seemed happy, but then, Tatum had always been the smiling, upbeat sort—even when she was hurting on the inside. He wanted her to *be* happy. If Lucy wasn't standing here, he'd tell her as much. She deserved to be happy. And if chopping down a tree and putting up some lights made her happy, he'd do it.

He was also more than willing to take off all her clothes, spread her out on her bed and love her body until she was shouting his name. He knew that would make him very happy. He shoved his hands back in his pockets.

Lucy hugged her. "It's Christmas, Tatum. You're home. You should be happy."

Tatum's smile touched his heart. He'd missed her. He'd missed that smile.

"Now let's go get you some food so you're not starving," Lucy said. "Need anything?" she asked him.

"Nope."

Lucy nodded and headed out the door.

Tatum smiled up at him. "You sure you don't want anything?"

"You know I do. But we've got all night," he promised, his gaze shifting to her full red lips. "And I plan on taking advantage of that."

She shivered. "Who said last night's offer was still good?"

He smiled. "It's still good."

She opened her mouth, then closed it. Her green eyes narrowed before she whispered, "I'll hurry."

He nodded, taking in every nuance of her reaction. The dilated pupils, flushed cheeks, parted lips, the quickening of her breath… When their eyes locked, he wanted to lose himself in her—to bury himself deep and never come up for air.

"Tatum?" Lucy called from the front porch.

She blinked, smiled up at him and headed out the door.

He stood watching them run across the snow-covered lawn to Lucy's waiting car.

Loving Tatum had been as easy and natural as breathing. They'd been inseparable, snatching every spare moment together. How many nights had he scaled the side of the house to meet her on her roof? How many nights had they lain there, staring up at the stars and sharing their plans? Plans he'd severed for her. To protect her. Even though driving her away had made every day for the next two years an exercise in survival. He swallowed, watching Lucy's car pull away from the curb.

Now they had time, time he wanted with her. So he needed to get the damn lights up.

He worked quickly. First things first, he dragged her tree inside, ready to decorate. Then he worked outside, finishing the roof and dormer windows, wrapping the rest of the porch railings and hanging lights around the front windows. He stood back, looking up at his handiwork.

"You're a Christmas light superhero." Tatum's voice reached him.

He glanced back to see her, holding two large bags of groceries. "Got it?"

"There's two more," she said. "If you can grab them, Lucy can head to Mrs. Medrano's. I think I made her late."

"I think Mrs. Medrano can be five minutes late for her weekly bingo game," Spencer said, hoping to reassure her. "But I'll get the groceries."

"Thanks." She hurried toward the front door.

He opened the back door of Lucy's car.

"You okay?" Lucy asked him.

He frowned at her. "Why wouldn't I be?"

"Don't get all defensive. I'm not being your shrink—I'm being your cousin. The one that knows how devastated you were after your breakup and Tatum left, remember? So I'm worried about you, sue me." Lucy sighed. "What is it with men acting like they have no emotions? Like it's some weakness or something. News flash—women like men that emote. Not cry their eyeballs out, but emote."

Spencer laughed. "Okay, I'll try to remember that." He paused. "I'm good. I'm glad she's back."

Lucy nodded. "I thought you might be."

He scooped the two bags of groceries from the back. "Have fun tonight."

"You too," she said, giggling. "I'm pretty sure you're not going to need this, but here. In case you need my sofa to sleep on." She held out a key.

He hoped she was right, that he wouldn't need it, but he took it anyway. "Thanks." He slammed the car door and headed back to the house. It looked good. No one on the neighborhood decorating committee could complain now—his mother included. He pushed through the front door, gently shoving the door shut behind him. He put the groceries on the counter and placed the eggs and milk in the refrigerator before he saw Tatum's shopping bags sitting—unpacked—on the counter.

"Tatum?" he called out.

No answer.

He headed down the hall, toward her room. "Tatum?"

He knocked, pushing her door open to find it empty. That was when he heard the telltale sound of water running. She was in the shower? He went back out into the hall and paused. The bathroom door was cracked. He'd take that as an invitation.

He opened the door, greeted by a cloud of steam, and pushed it closed behind him. Her red tunic lay on the floor. Her leggings, boots, a lacy black bra and a scrap of fabric he assumed was her underwear led the way to the glass-enclosed shower.

"You hoping I'd wash your back?" he asked, his throat tight.

She glanced over her shoulder, smiling sweetly. "To start, maybe."

"To start?" he asked.

"You said we had all night." He heard the waver of her voice and knew she wasn't as brave as she was acting.

He nodded and stripped quickly, leaving his clothes in a pile on the floor before stepping into the shower behind her. He stepped forward, shuddering as he pressed against her. There was no way she could miss just how much he wanted her. The length of him was throbbing, pulsing against the soft curve of her ass. He leaned in, his chest flush with the wet skin of her back. He groaned as he pressed an openmouthed kiss against the base of her neck.

She shivered.

He reached around her, pouring body wash into his palm and lathering his hands. His palms slid up her arms and over her shoulders. He took his time, kneading her skin with strong fingers. She sighed, her head falling against his shoulder as he massaged the length of her back. He washed her, his hands slipping and sliding over every inch of her. He didn't linger in one place, but used his touch to heighten her awareness…and his. His hand slid between her legs, barely cupping the soft skin before sliding up her stomach to cradle her breasts. Her nipples were tight peaks, begging for his touch. He almost caved, pushed her against the wall and slid home. But he didn't. Not yet. She felt so damn good, the lather of the body wash making her slippery in his hold. When his hands clasped her hips, he ground against her.

Her hand came around, gripping his lower back as she arched into him. She turned her head, looking at him with unfiltered hunger.

She turned in his hold, pressing herself against him and twining her arms around his neck. Her teeth nipped his lower lip, her fingers curling in his hair to pull his head toward hers. He didn't hold back. His tongue slid between her lips while his mouth sealed hers.

She broke away, gasping. "My turn." She poured body wash onto her hands.

He stood still, watching as she explored his body with her hands and eyes. She turned him, kneading his back and shoulders, thighs and hips. Her teeth grazed his hips, her tongue traced his spine, and her hands came around him, clasping the length of him with slippery hands. He shuddered, giving in to the onslaught of sensations her hands and mouth unleashed. She turned him once more.

He hadn't expected her to be on her knees, to have her soft hands clasp the rigid length of him and bring it to her mouth. But the silk of her lips slipping over his tip, the wet heat of her mouth encasing him, made him groan out loud. With one hand she braced herself on his thighs, and the other gripped him firmly in place, letting her set a rhythm both sweet and torturous. Every stroke of her tongue and caress of her lips had him teetering closer to the edge. Did she know how close he was? He pressed his hands against the side of the shower, steadying himself.

"Stop, Tatum," he ground out. He had to stop her. Had to get control. But, when it came to Tatum, he had no control.

"Stop?" she asked, breathless. "You're not enjoying it?"

He heard the vulnerability in her voice and ached from it. He groaned. "I am. Too much."

"I don't want to stop," she answered, drawing him deep into her mouth. Her hands slid up the backs of his thighs to grip his hips and he was done for. His climax hit hard. Wave after wave of pure, raw pleasure rocked through him. His moan tore from his throat and echoed in the steam-filled shower.

When he opened his eyes, she was standing before him—a huge smile on her face. He was gasping, his heart hammering and his lungs scrambling for air. She seemed pretty proud of her handiwork.

His hands slid down the side of the shower stall to cup her face. He wiped the water from her forehead and tilted her face back to kiss her. "You're gorgeous," he said, pressing a kiss to her forehead.

"I probably look like a drowned rat," she argued, kissing him back.

"A gorgeous drowned rat," he continued, pulling her against him. He groaned at the slip and slide of her skin against him.

"Spencer." Her whisper was low, pleading.

He held her back, staring down at her. "Bed?" he asked, turning off the water without waiting for her answer.

He helped her out of the shower, wrapping a thick white towel around his waist before rubbing her down.

She laughed at the thorough job he made of it, but she was dry and rosy when he was done.

Her fingers traced his side. "What kind of feather is this?" she asked, tracing the tattoo.

"An eagle feather," he answered, twisting the water from her hair.

"Why an eagle feather?"

He glanced at her. "An eagle is a protector. He's powerful in battle. Alert and watchful. I needed to feel that way after Russ was killed." Instead of feeling like a failure.

He and Patton had worked side by side with their little brother but neither of them had ever suspected Russell of being corrupt. Even after the night Russ was mowed down, Spencer had a hard time coming to terms with the truth. His little brother had been the bad guy.

Tatum was staring up at him, her fingers stroking the intricately detailed design and easing the crushing weight of his memories.

"I'm sorry about Russ." There was no doubting her sincerity. "He was a character, always the jokester."

She was right. Russ had always been the class clown—the one everybody loved. Being charming was a very useful way to divert suspicion.

"To lose your brother and father in the same year..." She paused, sliding her arms around his waist. "I'm sorry you had so much grief all at once, Spencer."

He stared down at her, loving the feel of her in his arms. *Missing her.* How many times had he picked up the phone to call her, only to hang up? "Things were tough for a while," he admitted. "But you get up every day, you find a way to keep going."

She nodded. "You have to." Her voice was thick.

There was a sheen to her eyes. She knew all about grief. She'd lost everyone she'd ever loved. If he could chase away her suffering he would. So he kissed her, a long, slow kiss that instantly stirred his desire. "I'm glad you're back, Tatum."

"I'm thinking my stunt in the shower might have something to do with that," she teased.

"I'm not complaining," he murmured.

Her green eyes searched his before she said, "My body feels awake when you're around. *I* feel awake." Her fingers stroked across his chest and down his stomach.

"It's a damn good thing because I'm not planning on getting much sleep tonight." He scooped her up in his arms and carried her out the door and down the hall to her bedroom.

4

Tatum watched the lone drop of water run down Spence's neck. Even his neck was muscular. He was one hard, rippling mass of sheer power. And yet, wrapped in his arms, she felt only safe and secure—almost treasured. And there was no denying the hunger he had for her. She wanted him crazy for her, the way she was crazy for him. She bent forward, licking the drop of water from his skin.

She landed in the middle of her bed, the cool air hitting her exposed skin—right before his hands clasped her hips and tugged her to the edge of the bed. She was still reeling when his tongue stroked over the tight bundle of nerves between her legs.

"Spencer," she hissed, her hands fisting in the blankets beneath her.

"Turnabout is fair play," he murmured, his warm breath brushing along the inside of her thigh.

His tongue was magic, teasing her until she was out of her mind. His fingers joined in then, stroking deep inside of her. He moved with a purpose, setting a rhythm that was both blissful and maddeningly taunting. It built, her need, until she couldn't hold on.

"Please, Spencer," she gasped, so close. "Oh, please." She reached for him, her hands holding on to his wet hair. His rhythm stayed the same, but the pressure... His mouth, his fingers pushed her over the edge. Her body spiraled, her lungs emptying of all air as she gave way to sensation. Her grip tightened on his hair as her climax found her. She lay, shuddering and stunned, as he kissed his way back up her body.

She was still reeling when his lips pressed against hers. She felt him, hard and ready, against her thigh. Her gaze met his, the heat of his hunger making her quiver once more. He was big...bigger than Brent. And she wanted him, all of him. Now. "I'm ready," she whispered, her fingers gripping his arms.

"Protection... In my pants, in the bathroom."

"I'm protected." Her hands tightened on his arms.

"I've waited so long, I can wait a while longer," he murmured against her lips.

"Why?" she asked, wrapping a leg around his hip.

He smiled down at her, his hands cradling the side of her face. "Maybe I want to drive you crazy for me."

"You have," she answered, her heart in her throat. She could feel him, so close. "I want you, Spencer."

His eyes fluttered closed before he gripped her hips and lifted her, opening her for him. When his eyes met hers, he moved into her, slowly filling her. She gasped, her hands resting on his chest as she concentrated on relaxing. Her body strained to accommodate him, the pressure building and emptying her lungs. She closed her eyes, sucking in a deep breath.

"Tatum," he growled, stilling. "Look at me." His hands tightened on her hips.

She did. The look on his face was almost pained. He

thrust deep, so deep, never breaking their gaze. She cried out, unable to stop herself. It was too much. Too good. Too intimate. She wanted more. He thrust again, his raw groan forcing a soft cry from her lips.

He kissed her, his tongue caressing her own. She moved beneath him, losing herself to the feeling of him deep inside of her. The weight of him, the power... All she could do was hold on.

Her hands slid along his back, gripping his hips. The quiver and contraction of his muscles beneath her fingers, the pause at each thrust, his ragged breathing—he was barely holding on, for her. When all she wanted was all of him. She didn't want restrained or controlled. She wanted to let go, for him to let go. To give in to the passion that would undoubtedly drown them both.

"You feel so good, Tatum...so damn good," he growled. He moved deep, almost leaving her, and slid home again. Over and over, he had her so close. His mouth latched on to her neck, her shoulder, her nipple. He drew her breast into his mouth, his tongue flicking, his teeth nipping. She arched into him, everything but him fading away.

He moved faster then, lifting her and holding her in place as he powered into her. She was out of her mind, overwhelmed, balancing on the precipice of pleasure and pain. Her hands slid down his back, feeling the flex and shift of his muscles. His body was incredible. He was incredible.

One look at his face was all it took. Her pleasure slammed into her. Her body bowed off the bed, the sharp edge of pleasure giving way to a powerful climax. She was drowning in sensation. But he wasn't done.

He kept moving, harder and faster, driven. She watched

him, gasping for breath, instantly aroused by the sweet friction. "Spencer…" His name slipped from her lips, thick and husky.

His arms were columns of steel, bracing him over her as his eyes bored into hers. His face crumpled and he stiffened, shouting out his own release. She wasn't prepared for the hard climax that gripped her, making her yell out as she held on to him. Still he gripped her tightly to him, pinning her.

They collapsed in a tangled heap, panting on her quilts. He was heavy, sprawled across her. But she ached when he moved to her side. She didn't want this to end. She wanted to stay here, lost in pure passion and sensation. His arm drew her tight against his side before pulling the quilts over them and bundling them closely together.

"Warm enough?" he asked against her hair.

She nodded, loving the waver in his voice. Even now, savoring the delightful aftershocks of their lovemaking, she wanted him. It didn't matter that her body was humming, satisfied.

He chuckled.

"What?" she asked.

"You still have pom-poms on your shelf," he said, pointing at the shelf across the room.

"You live here," she said, breathing a little easier now. "You could have boxed them up."

He shook his head. "It's your room. The last tenants hadn't touched this side of the house. I didn't, either."

"Can I ask why this house?" she asked, looking up at him.

"My apartment building burned and it was empty so… I didn't like seeing the place sit empty." He shrugged.

"Sorry about your apartment." How horrible. And now she was going to make him move again.

"Thanks. It sucked." He paused. "I'm not home a lot. I didn't lose anything important. Like pom-poms or trophies."

She laughed, slightly embarrassed that her room hadn't been touched. She'd just assumed the house had been packed up for tenants—Brent had assured her that was the case. "I haven't had a chance to weed things out or decorate yet." She looked up at him. "I've spent more time naked with you."

"Again, not complaining," he said, smiling down at her. "Just a little déjà vu. Being here, in your bed, when the room looks the same."

"We never did this, never slept together," she argued. "Before."

"I know. But we spent a hell of a lot of time right here doing plenty of other things." His arms tightened around her.

His words poked at the hurt he'd caused so long ago. She'd left the middle of her senior year of high school and had only the haziest memories of her time in California high school. What she did remember was pain. Losing him had felt like losing an arm. She'd felt confused and broken.

It was only when she met Brent that she put every thought and memory of Spencer in a box, tightly latched, in the far recesses of her mind. That box needed to stay locked up. "So what have you been up to?" she asked, desperate to turn their conversation into neutral waters. "Besides busting bad guys and taking care of your mom, have you taken up any hobbies? Like woodworking or… beer making?" she asked. "You know all about me."

"I know the bare minimum," he said, tucking an arm under his head and looking down at her.

"Nothing more to tell, I guess." It was true—and pathetic. The last few years had made her a Stepford wife. Whatever thoughts she'd had or plans she'd made had been replaced by things Brent needed to get ahead in his career. She didn't want to admit that to Spencer. Especially when they were wrapped up, naked, in bed together.

His fingers slid through her hair as he spoke. "Mostly school, then the academy. I've worked my way up to detective, alongside Patton. Been in the narcotics unit for a few years now. Greyson's still pretty small, but shit happens now and then. The real action is when I'm working with the joint task force. Being so close to the Oklahoma border, with as much wide-open land as there is, we do have a lot of drug on the move."

"You're happy?" she asked, curious. She understood loving your work, but was that really enough? Spencer had always wanted a big family, like the one he'd grown up in. She'd wanted that with him… But that was a long time ago.

He nodded, reaching out to tuck a strand of her hair behind her ear. "Mostly."

"No women?" she asked.

He grinned. "Oh, there have been women."

She smacked him on the arm and sat up, tucking the sheet around her. "Relationships?"

He shrugged. "None that stuck. My job comes first. Hours aren't exactly family friendly." He broke off, staring at her. "I figure I'll know when it's the right time. Or the right girl."

"So you're not attached?" she asked.

"If I was, I wouldn't be here, Tatum." He paused. "You know me."

She thought she had. And then he'd proved her wrong. "Not really," she said, suddenly nervous.

"You do. You know me better than anyone." He frowned.

Maybe once. But now it didn't matter. She didn't want to get serious when she was about to suggest what she was about to suggest. "I have a proposition for you." What she wanted was crazy and selfish and indecent, no denying that. And without Spencer it wasn't going to happen. But she really hoped he was agreeable to her proposal. "I want to…borrow you," she said, her voice lowered.

"Borrow me?" he asked.

She swallowed. "Your body. It was just Brent, and he was…well… I just wanted… I was wondering if you'd be willing to help me… Learn to be sexy. Appealing… in bed."

His blue eyes continued to stare at her, intense and searching.

"No strings. I'm not ready and you sound like you're not interested in getting tied down, which is great. But I feel like I've missed out… On sex—good sex. I want to be sexy…seductive." She stopped, clasping her hands in her lap. Maybe she should have kept her mouth shut. Saying it out loud, she sounded ridiculous.

He lay there, still staring at her. His breathing had accelerated, but she didn't know what that meant.

"You can stay here. Roommates with benefits." She swallowed again, her nerves forcing her to continue. "You and me, two consenting adults, spending as much time naked as possible. With an expiration date of midnight Christmas Eve."

He frowned. "Why Christmas Eve?"

"I'm supposed to fly to a friend's on the West Coast Christmas day," she explained.

His eyes narrowed slightly. "Two weeks?"

"Twelve days," she clarified.

"Like the Christmas carol?" He smiled.

"With less birds and more sex, sure," she agreed, laughing.

"What do you mean you need me to help you feel sexy or appealing?" he asked.

She shrugged, wishing she hadn't shared that piece of information.

"Come on, Tatum, it's a fair question. I think you did a damn fine job seducing me in the shower. As far as I'm concerned, you're sexy as hell."

"Oh." She smiled.

His hand came up to stroke her cheek. "Only Brent?"

Another piece of information she hadn't meant to share.

"And he let you go?" His voice was rough. "Stupid shit."

So did you. But she pressed her lips tight. "I guess men are different. You *like* me to make noise, to touch you—to respond."

He frowned. "I'm pretty sure all men like that." He twined her hair around her fist and pulled her down to kiss him. "If it feels good, I want to know. Plus, it's hot."

She shuddered, leaning into him. "Is that a yes?" she asked.

He took his time inspecting her face and body. She heard the change in his breathing when his gaze fell to her breasts. And sighed as his hand cupped her, his thumb grazing the hardening peak.

"Spencer?" she asked, feeling exposed and aroused. She didn't know what she wanted more, his answer or his mouth on her body.

SPENCER LOOKED AT her face. She was so easy to excite, so responsive. To see her come alive under his touch was a powerful aphrodisiac. He couldn't get enough of her. Her body was meant for touching. And she was offering herself to him for twelve days. Twelve days of no-strings-attached sex. With Tatum.

"You think twelve days will be enough?" he asked, stroking her nipple with the pad of his thumb. She hardened beneath his touch, and she had the exact same effect on his body. He'd come twice in the last hour and he was already ready for round three.

She clasped his wrist, holding his fingers in place against her breast. "Guess we'll find out?"

He nodded, bending to kiss her. "I guess so." He kissed her until she was breathless, until her arms were wrapped around him and her fingers twisted in his hair. "I'm hungry," he said against her mouth. "I need food. If you think you can control yourself?"

She laughed, the gentle curves of her body brushing against him and threatening his resolve to wait. "I'll try." She sighed. "At least I went to the grocery store. I can feed you."

"Good idea. Don't want me to waste away." He kissed the tip of her nose.

"Not for the next twelve days, anyway," she added, slipping from the bed.

"Ouch," he teased. "Only want me for my body, huh?"

"Yes," she answered, laughing. "But I admit, I'm hungry too." She slipped into her robe, pulled the sash tight and headed into the kitchen.

He followed, in nothing but his boxer shorts. She was staring at him with such appreciation he couldn't help but grin. He ran a hand through his hair and crossed his arms over his chest. "What?"

"Just enjoying the view," she admitted.

He cocked an eyebrow. "I'm in favor of matching outfits."

She shook her head, laughing. "What sounds good?" she asked, unpacking the grocery bags.

"Whatever's quick and easy?"

"Omelet?"

They fell into step, working side by side. He watched the way she moved, how graceful and easy she was in the kitchen. "You know your way around the kitchen," he said, washing off the tomatoes.

"Lots of cooking classes. They were cheaper than hiring a caterer every time we threw some fancy dinner for one reason or another. And I liked cooking," she said with a smile, chopping up some mushrooms and tomatoes with quick, sure strokes. She stopped long enough to turn on some Christmas music, then tossed some onions in a skillet. By the time dinner was ready, his mouth was watering from the delicious aromas scenting the air.

They sat on the floor in front of the Christmas tree, enjoying their meal. He rested against the couch, propped on some pillows, savoring his beer. He watched her, her green eyes fixed on the tree. The firelight turned her eyes deep emerald and the gold of her hair shone. She hummed along with the instrumental carol playing, the only other sound the snap and pop from the fire. The night couldn't get much better.

She glanced at him. "So, Spencer, what do you want for Christmas?"

He chuckled. "My present came early this year." What more could he want?

Her brows rose, stunned. "Me?"

He laughed. Did she not realize what a treasure she was? She might be in this for the sex. He saw this as his second chance.

She shook her head. "You must have wanted something, before I came along and offered you endless sex."

He sat quietly, thinking about it. "If I did, I can't remember." It was a sobering thought. She'd only been here two days and he was already so caught up in her. Maybe this proposal was more dangerous than he realized. He took a sip of his wine. "Are you going to the charity auction?" he asked.

"I told your mom I'd go," she answered. "Guess it's time I stopped being a hermit and returned to the land of the living. I admit I'm not looking forward to the questions and comments, but I guess it's unavoidable."

"Questions and comments?" he asked.

"I thought about having a shirt made up that says something like, 'I'm divorced, I've moved back home and I'm fine.' But I wasn't sure how that would go over." She shrugged. "Most people mean well. But admitting I've already been replaced is embarrassing."

No one could replace her. He knew—he'd tried. "I never liked Brent." He smiled, watching her smile in return.

"You never met him."

"Don't have to. I don't like him." He finished off his omelet, watching her shake her head, poking at the food on her plate.

She'd always had a good attitude—that was one of the things that had drawn him to her. Even living in a less-than-happy home, Tatum had a loving heart. Living across the street, he and his brothers had heard the yelling. Jane Buchanan, Tatum's mother, had been a hard woman. Hell, most people called her The Witch Buchanan. When her husband left, Tatum had to deal with her mother's demands and unrealistic expectations on her own. Nothing Tatum did was ever good enough. Even though she'd been involved in every school club or organization, she had few real friends. No one wanted to come to her place and she was rarely let out of the house.

He'd been the one to climb onto her roof and pull her out. He'd been the one to hold her close and listen to her, support her. The connection between them had been so powerful, so out of control, it had bordered on obsession.

When her mother's behavior grew dangerous, Spencer had done the only thing he could. He couldn't stand to see her so bruised, her body and her spirit. Her father wanted her in California, away from her mother. But Tatum stayed—for Spencer. Breaking up with her took her away from her mother and the judgment of their small town. And him. She was free to start over, to flourish and have a parent that adored her, new friends and accomplishments.

"You could go with me?" he asked. "To the charity auction, I mean."

Her eyes went round. "No. No, that would make it a million times worse." She shook her head. "People would talk, assume we were involved again—"

"That we're sleeping together?" he asked, reaching for the tie on her robe. The silky fabric parted, revealing the full creamy curve of her breast. His fingers traced the swell, brushing along the tip until she pebbled beneath his fingers. He smiled.

She blew out an uneven breath. "You're teasing me."

"And loving every minute of it." He nodded, his hand falling from her. "I'll do the dishes."

She shook her head. "I won't argue."

After the kitchen was clean, he headed back to find her propped on some pillows, staring into the fire. He gazed at her, mesmerized. Twelve days of this… Christmas really had come early.

"Is that for me?" she asked, reaching for the glass of wine he'd brought her.

He nodded, sitting beside her and covering them both with her plaid throw. "What about you?"

"What about me?" she asked, looking up at him.

"What do you want for Christmas?" he asked.

"Hmm, besides having sex without something that requires batteries? I'll have to think about that."

"Go through a lot of batteries?" he asked, partly teasing. Did Brent have some sort of physical defect?

She looked up at him. "Possibly."

Just imagining her enjoying her battery-powered friend had him rock hard. "You're not going to need batteries for a while," he murmured, brushing her lips with his. "Unless you want to liven things up."

She stared at him, her cheeks turning red. "Liven things up?" she repeated softly.

"Play. Experiment," he whispered, his fingers stroking the side of her neck. "Whatever you want."

"I…I don't know."

"We'll have to work on that." His mouth latched on to her lower lip.

She shuddered. "What about you? What do you want?" Her teeth nipped his lower lip.

He hissed, pulling her onto his lap. He untied her sash and pushed the robe from her shoulders, exposing her breasts. She filled his hands, silky soft, making him ache to possess her. "Damn, Tatum, I don't know where to start," he said, his voice low and broken.

She reached down between them, freeing him from his boxers. "Let's start here," she murmured, wincing as she slid onto him. She was so hot, so tight. If he wasn't careful he'd be done before she was.

He groaned, his head falling back on the couch. "Here's good." He blew out a breath, focusing on something neutral, to keep his head. But the feel of her, like a glove...

She started slow, but soon her nails were biting into the skin of his shoulders and the feel of her ass bouncing against his thighs was too hard to fight. He looked at her, their eyes locking. He wasn't prepared for the ferocious ownership he felt. Or the desire to protect her, to cherish her. Maybe it was the hunger in her eyes, the unabashed want she had for him. But whatever it was, he knew he was in trouble. Even buried deep, he wanted more of her. His hands tangled in her hair, pulling her lips to his. He caught her cry in his mouth, wrapping his arms around her as her body shook with her release. He held her, letting her take him over the edge with her. He went, every muscle clenched tight, his body wrung dry and his lungs emptying until he was spent.

She rested her head on his shoulder, her wavering breath fanning across his chest. She'd always felt right in his arms, like she was made for him. And that was what scared him. Leaning back, he cradled her against him, worrying that these twelve days might just break his heart all over again.

5

Tatum stretched and rolled onto her side. But when she opened her eyes, she realized she was alone. She sat up. "Spencer?" she called out.

No answer. A peek at the clock told her it was eight fifteen. Sleeping in was a rarity. But after last night… She smiled, stretching with a soft squeal before collapsing back on the mattress. She stared up at the ceiling, enjoying images from last night to warm her up. Spencer. Spencer's hands and mouth and his incredible body. Last night had been… Her breathing grew a little unsteady and her heart rate picked up. How she could want him again—so fiercely—when she enjoyed him not three hours ago was a mystery. But she did.

"Spencer?" She threw back the blankets and slipped into her robe, smiling at the delectable soreness left from last night. Once her slippers were on, she headed into the kitchen. But no Spencer.

There was a brown paper bag on the counter, her name sprawled across it. She grinned as she opened the bag and found a large breakfast burrito wrapped in foil inside. And a note.

She pulled out the note and carried her burrito to the kitchen table. It read,

On the first night of Christmas, my lover took from me: sleep. But I'm not complaining. Be back with the family around 9:30 a.m.

She smiled, tucking his note in her robe pocket, and unwrapped her breakfast. On the counter, a small pot was on, heating coffee he'd obviously made and left for her. Sex all night, hot coffee and yummy food, and a sweet note. She could get used to this roommate-with-benefits thing. She munched away on the burrito and poured herself a cup of steaming coffee.

A flutter of movement caught her eye, drawing her attention to the view out the window over the kitchen sink. It was snowing, thick, heavy flakes falling steadily onto the already carpeted expanse of her backyard. Snow didn't last long in Texas. Ice and slush were more prevalent. If she'd been little she would have hurried to get dressed so she was the first person to touch the snow. She'd make snow angels and build a small snowman and make snowballs to have ready—Lucy would've come over for a snowball fight. But then the Ryan boys would sneak up on them when they were halfway through their snowman, annihilating it and burying them under a hailstorm of well-packed, well-aimed snowballs. She and Lucy would end up soaked and shivering in front of the fireplace, waiting to thaw before going out to finish their snowman.

Not this time.

The clock told her she didn't have much time. She finished off her breakfast, swallowed down the strong coffee and hurried to make stew for later. Once that was done, she fished out her baby-pink ski gear from her high school ski trip. She dressed, tugging on the faux fur–trimmed puffy coat and a knit hat with its matching pink pom-pom on top before pulling on her snow boots. She might look ridiculous, but she was warm. In no time, she was in the backyard, preparing her snowball arsenal for the arrival of the Ryan boys. She finished just in time for the telltale sound of voices in the front yard.

Tatum sneaked around the side of the house. "Lucy?" she whispered as loudly as she dared.

Lucy saw her, her eyes going round as Tatum waved her over.

Spencer, Dean and Jared had no idea what hit them. She and Lucy unleashed years of pent-up frustration, pummeling the three until their dark coats were crusty with snow. The few snowballs they managed to throw couldn't compare with the intense rain of freezing cold missiles she and Lucy kept lobbing their way.

When the last snowball was gone, she and Lucy set off at a dead run for the house—knowing their luck was done. As they pulled the door shut behind them, the resounding thud of at least a half a dozen snowballs hitting the door reverberated through the entry hall.

They were laughing too hard to care.

"You are a genius," Lucy said. "That was..."

"Epic," Tatum finished. "Though I suppose the nice thing to do now is make them some coffee?"

Lucy rolled her eyes. "When did they ever do anything to warm us up?"

Tatum couldn't help but remember all the wonderful things Spencer had done last night. He'd warmed her up. She was getting warm just thinking about it—and him.

Lucy was waving her hand in front of her face. "Earth to Tatum. I so don't want to know what you're thinking right now. Let's make coffee."

Five minutes later, her kitchen was filled with three shivering, irritable men holding steaming cups of coffee.

Lucy continued to giggle off and on.

But Tatum was too caught up in the bright blue gaze of Spencer, intense and brooding.

"Not the welcome I was expecting," Dean said, grinning over his coffee mug at her. "But the coffee helps."

"Oh, come on," Lucy said. "How many times did Tatum and I end up face-first in snow while you three ran off laughing?"

The three of them mumbled, knowing she was right. They gave up, grinning in defeat.

"Exactly," Lucy continued.

"Well played," Jared said, toasting her with his mug. "Might need another cup, though. My boots are full of snow and I can't feel my toes."

Tatum laughed. "Sorry."

"Somehow I don't believe that," Spencer said, his eyes pinning hers.

She couldn't say a word. The heat in his look was blazing, chasing away any of the chill that clung to her. When his gaze traveled along her neck, she could almost feel his touch on her skin.

"So how's life been treating you?" Dean asked, breaking the hold Spencer had on her. "I hear you're single. I'm happy to volunteer my services as your rebound guy."

Tatum looked at Dean, stunned. Was he serious? Dean had always been the hot guy, the ladies' man with the biting humor and the restless spirit. While there was no doubting he was nice to look at, he was—and always would be—Lucy's annoying brother.

Jared nudged his brother. "Seriously subtle, bro."

"Wow, Dean, just wow," Lucy said, shaking her head.

"Pissed I beat you to it?" Dean asked Jared, ignoring Lucy altogether. He grinned at Tatum. "Think about it, Tatum, if you're looking for a way to get back in the game—" He pointed at himself, cocking an eyebrow. "I'm just saying—"

"I think we all get what you're saying," Spencer barked. "But if we want to get the house ready for tonight, you'll have to hold off on your *sweet-talking* for now."

Tatum glanced at Spencer, taking in the tightness of his jaw and the slight narrowing of his eyes. What was surprising was just how much she liked his irritation over Dean's flirting.

While the others finished off their coffee, she ran back to her room to get her glove liners. It was cold and she wasn't as used to it as they were. If she was going to be any help she'd need—

She turned to find Spencer filling the doorway. "Spencer?" The way he was looking at her...it was hard to breathe.

She found herself pressed against the wall, his lips parting hers, his tongue seeking entrance and his hands holding her face. Her fingers threaded through his thick hair, pulling his head down to hers. There was nothing gentle about his touch or his kiss. It was possessive—claiming her, making her quiver and ache.

He pulled back, his eyes searching hers before he left her panting against the wall. She stood, trying to calm the frantic beating of her heart, as she heard the door open and close.

She was still pulling herself together when Lucy poked her head into her room.

"He leave you all hot and bothered?" Lucy asked. "'Cause he looks like a ticking time bomb. I thought you two would have, you know, done the deed by now."

Tatum felt the heat in her cheeks as she tugged on her glove liners.

Lucy giggled.

"We should go help," Tatum said, unable to stop the smile on her face.

Even with the glove liners, Tatum's fingers went from tingling to numb. The others had no problem wrapping the large tree in white lights. She and Lucy hung all the wood-chip angels, adjusting the lights so the whole tree was illuminated. When the only thing left was the star for the top, Jared and Dean held the ladder while Spencer teetered on the top step.

"Be careful, Spencer," she called up to him, wincing as he balanced on one foot to place the star.

"Will do." His voice reached her.

"Some things never change." Jared chuckled.

Jared was right. On the surface, it all felt very familiar. Except it was so very different now. She and Spencer had been young and crazy in love—strong and deep. Well, it had been for her. They weren't in love—how could they be? They didn't know each other anymore, not really.

This wasn't about love; this was about want. And she wanted Spencer more than she'd ever wanted…anything. She wasn't going to spend hours wondering about his thoughts or feelings. She was going to spend hours exploring his body and her sexuality. This *was* different.

Maybe it was reckless to invite Spencer into her bed when there was still such a strong connection between them. Maybe it was a mistake. Maybe she'd regret it… later. Right now, the thought of touching him, kissing him—having his hands on her—was all that mattered. Her body needed him in a way she didn't fully understand.

"Looks great." Mrs. Ryan joined them, gripping a large pot. "I made mulled cider, to help chase away the chill."

"Smells good," Dean said.

"Thanks, Auntie," Lucy joined in.

"Thank you so much, Mrs. Ryan. I know I'm freezing, so this will definitely help," Tatum agreed, ready to get inside. "It will go great with the stew I made."

"You go on in," Spencer called down. "We'll finish up out here."

"I'll carry it," Tatum offered, taking the large pot from Mrs. Ryan and heading up the path.

"I'll be in, in just a minute," Mrs. Ryan offered, making the three men groan. "Oh, shush, I only have a few ideas."

Lucy hooked arms with Tatum and headed inside.

"The cider was totally a ploy." Lucy laughed. "It's hard to argue with her when she's bringing you something to eat or drink. She'll probably have them out there another hour."

Tatum glanced back at the group, the three men stooping to hear whatever Mrs. Ryan was telling them. "Smart woman."

Lucy nodded. "Don't get me wrong, she loves to take care of people too. Especially her family."

The word *family* had become somewhat bittersweet to Tatum in the last few months. Most people took their loved ones for granted. But knowing she didn't have anyone was a very eye-opening experience. If and when she was ever lucky enough to find someone to love, she'd make sure they knew it every single day.

"I'm sorry about the divorce…about Brent being a cheating dickwad." Lucy's words ended her introspection. Her friend put the pot on the stove and hugged her. "God knows you've had more than your fair share of hurt."

She nodded again, hugging her friend. "Wanna know something funny? It was hard to accept he'd cheated on me. But when I figured out who it was with, I was devastated." She stepped back, pulling soup bowls from the cupboard. "Kendra is a couple of years younger than me, but not much. It's just…she and I weren't so different. I'd done everything he said he *wanted* to make him happy." She shook her head. "It turns out he really wanted a smart, career-minded woman—exactly what I had been when we married. Apparently Kendra is also terrific in bed." She shook her head. "Don't ask. Apparently Brent wasn't the first husband she tried to steal. Just the wealthiest."

"Miss him?" Lucy asked.

Tatum shook her head. "No. And I don't miss who I was when he was around." She smiled. "It's sort of liberating."

"And now you're free to explore other options—like Spencer."

She definitely wanted more exploring time with Spencer. Tatum pulled silverware from the drawers to set the table. "What about you? Are you seeing anyone?"

Lucy wrinkled her nose. "Nope. I'm not sure if it's the psychologist thing, having two brothers that happen to be cops, or the working for the police department, but guys seem a little…hesitant to date me."

Tatum looked at Lucy. She knew men looked at her friend—there was plenty to look at. Lucy was petite with killer curves and sassy pale blond curls. While they were both blonde, Lucy had a confidence Tatum had never felt. She remembered feeling invisible next to her in the halls of Greyson High School. Unless she was with Spencer. With Spencer, she'd felt special, beautiful and important.

"Their loss," Tatum murmured. "Maybe we need a girls' night? We can see what kind of prospects are out there."

"Maybe." Lucy shrugged. "Right now I'm happy to focus on my career."

They chatted a bit longer, laughing over some of Lucy's more memorable bad dates until Dean, Jared and Spencer joined them in the kitchen and sat at the table.

"Where's Mrs. Ryan?" Tatum asked, ladling the stew into bowls.

"She only brought the cider to soften us up," Jared explained.

"She wants us to redo the lights," Spencer said.

Tatum looked at them. "Are you serious?"

The three of them nodded.

"Too many holes." Spencer took the bowl she offered, smiling up at her. "I'll just add a few more strands and it'll be fine."

Once everyone had stew and bread, she sat beside Spencer. His hand rested on her thigh, making her jump. She saw his grin out of the corner of her eye.

"We're driving tonight, so you're on your own," Dean said between bites.

"Driving?" Tatum asked, trying not to think about Spencer's hand moving slowly up the inside of her thigh.

"The whole town gets officially lit up tonight," Jared

said, reaching for more bread. "Some of us have been volunteered to drive the judges through town."

"You volunteered?" Lucy's surprise was evident.

"Well, maybe we were told to. After that snake-in-his-drawer thing, the captain wasn't too happy, so…" Dean let the sentence hang there.

"You put a snake in your boss's desk?" Tatum asked, spoon halfway to her mouth.

"It was a grass snake." Jared shrugged.

"But he didn't think it was funny," Dean said.

"So they're driving tonight," Spencer finished.

"You didn't have anything to do with this, did you?" Tatum asked, arching a brow at Spencer.

He shook his head. "I tend to find ways to stay on the boss's good side, not his shit list."

They all laughed.

"Dean's a regular," Jared agreed.

Dean shrugged, his hazel gaze finding hers. "Guilty is as guilty does. And speaking of guilty, you have a chance to think over my little proposition?" He smiled.

Spencer's hand tightened on her thigh.

Lucy almost choked on her stew before sounding off. "First, yuck, she's my best friend and you're my brother. And, two, even if she did decide she wanted to take you up on your offer, do you really think she'd do so with an audience?"

Dean shrugged. "I'm all about full disclosure."

"How about we keep a little less disclosed," Spencer said, tearing into his bread and glaring at his cousin.

"Anyway…" Lucy glanced back and forth between them. "I'll be out in the cold, handing out maps for the light tour. I think I'd rather be driving around judges—at least you have heat."

Tatum shivered. "I couldn't do it." If she was this cold now, she could only imagine how frigid it would be when the sun went down. "I can bring you emergency hot chocolate?"

Lucy laughed. "That's okay. We set up in front of the fire station and they keep the hot chocolate and coffee coming. You can join me if you want? Didn't want you to be all alone tonight."

Tatum didn't miss the small smile on Lucy's face. Or the way Spencer's hand squeezed her thigh ever so slightly. "Oh, I have plenty to keep me busy. I haven't even started unpacking. Or cleaning out my bedroom. It seems strange for a divorced woman to be sleeping in a room with pom-poms."

Dean chuckled.

"Why not move into the master bedroom?" Lucy asked.

It made sense. It was her house now. But she wrinkled her nose at the thought. "I know I'm not ready to go through my mom's stuff. One thing at a time. Besides, I refuse to kick Spencer out until after the holidays. I'm not that heartless."

There was a slight silence, Dean and Jared exchanged an odd look, and Lucy was grinning. She didn't risk a look at Spencer.

Lucy nodded. "You've got time to make this place your own."

Her own. But did she really want to stay in Greyson? One of the reasons Gretchen, her college roommate, had invited her to San Diego for Christmas was to talk about an employment opportunity. Gretchen's family owned a finance and investment firm and, according to Gretchen, there was the *perfect* opening for Tatum.

Now was the time for trying new things, pushing her comfort boundaries and not passing up once-in-a-lifetime career opportunities. Even for great friends and amazing sex.

OVER THE YEARS, Spencer had wanted to punch Dean on more than one occasion. His cousin was good at finding his weakness and poking the shit out of it—until Spencer had enough. And right about now, Spencer had reached his limit with Dean's outrageous flirting and open admiration of Tatum.

She was sitting beside him, her scent pure distraction. It took everything he had not to run his fingers along the side of her neck, to bury his nose there and press a kiss to the hollow of her throat. He wanted to make her breath hitch and her hands tighten in his hair...

"Don't you think, Spencer?" Jared was asking.

He had absolutely no idea what Jared was talking about. But all four of them were looking at him, waiting for his answer. He had no choice. "About?"

Jared frowned at him. "New Year's?"

Nope. That didn't help at all. He waited, hoping like hell Jared would keep talking.

"Your brother's wedding?" Jared looked concerned.

Lucy went on. "According to Zach, we can stay after."

He glanced at Lucy, waiting. Why were they—

"Tatum's invited and I'm trying to convince her to come. If anyone needs some R & R, it's you, Tatum. Come on, we'll have the best time," Lucy pleaded.

He looked at Tatum. She was red-cheeked, clearly uncomfortable. Did she not want to go? Or...or was she thinking about the fact that their twelve days would be up by then? It might prove awkward to be in such close quarters after having such an intimate arrangement. But by then things wouldn't be as…urgent as they were now. Maybe. Possibly. If they were, having her there would be a good thing.

But beyond his hunger for her, he knew she was alone and no one should be alone during the holidays. "You should," he agreed.

"See," Lucy said, squeezing her arm.

"Let me think about it," Tatum said.

He glanced at the clock. It was almost two. He wanted to get the house done so he could take her on the lights tour. And then bring her back here and make her scream his name. He pushed back from the table, his abrupt movements making everyone jump. "Going back out," he said, standing.

Dean and Jared looked at each other, then him.

"I'm not done," Dean argued.

"Five more minutes isn't going to hurt a thing," Jared said.

"I didn't say you had to come with me," Spencer said. "Thanks for the stew, Tatum. It was delicious."

She smiled up at him, her green eyes bright. "You're welcome. Thank you for getting my—our—house up to judging standards."

Our house. Her words jolted him. "My pleasure," he said, winking at her before he hurried out of the kitchen. He liked what she'd said a little too much.

After finding more strands of white Christmas lights, he set about filling the holes his mother had found. And he tried his hardest not to let Dean and Jared lingering inside a hell of a lot longer than five minutes or the smile Dean wore when he did finally show up rub him the wrong way.

Ever since they were kids, Dean liked to get a rise out of him. This was no different.

"Damn, she's a good-looking woman," Dean said, taking some of the lights from him. "Why the hell did you dump her again?"

Spencer glared at his cousin.

"Gotta kill you, man. To see all that, back here, out of your reach." Dean sighed. "I feel for you."

Jared laughed.

Spencer continued to glare at Dean. "She take you up on your offer?"

Dean smiled. "Not yet."

"Then maybe she's not out of my reach," Spencer finished.

"Being roommates sure makes things cozy," Jared said, glancing at his brother.

They had no idea. "We'll see what happens," Spencer said.

"Right." Dean uncoiled some lights. "Or she might be over ancient history and want to try someone new. Like me."

"You can try." Spencer forced the words out, knowing his irritation was obvious but unable to do a damn thing about it.

But Spencer was the one staying tonight. He was the one who knew how to make her come apart at the seams and shatter in his arms. He knew how beautiful she looked when she climaxed. He turned back to the tree. But all he could think about was Tatum, the feel of her mouth on him...

"People are still talking about Wednesday night," Jared said. "Everyone's nervy."

Spencer hadn't given much thought to work. Clint

Taggart was bad news. It was about time the department had given him more than a warning or improvement plan. Spencer believed in backing his squad, but he didn't hold with putting the team in jeopardy. Which was exactly what Clint had done.

"You think Clint's going to follow through on his threat?" Dean asked.

Spencer shook his head. "If he wants to bring trouble to my door, I'll be ready and waiting."

Jared snorted. "Dumbass got himself in the situation, period. He doesn't know how to keep his mouth shut."

Which was true. Clint talked too much and too loudly. Which was a concern when you worked with undercover cops. As far as the department knew, no real damage had been done. Clint had drunk too much at a bar and mentioned a few names. Lucky for them, the bartender had been a source more than once and called Spencer. But, because Spencer had picked up Clint, Clint blamed Spencer for what happened next: Clint losing his job. And, before he left, Clint had threatened to beat the living daylights out of Spencer the next time their paths crossed.

"I'm not losing sleep over it," Spencer said.

"He was pissed. And pissed people do stupid things. Like sharing confidential information to get even." Jared looked at him.

Spencer paused, frowning. "I don't like Clint but I don't think he'd sell anyone on the team out."

Dean shrugged. "Guess we'll see."

They didn't talk much after that. Spencer couldn't shake the unease in the pit of his stomach. He took risks every day. He didn't need some asshole with a grudge getting him killed out of misplaced anger.

"Looks good to me," Jared said, standing back.

"She can't say there's a light shortage," Lucy said, as she walked outside to join them. "I've got to change and head to the fire station."

Spencer kept his impatience in check, trying not to think about Tatum waiting for him inside. His cousins helped him collect his tools and clean up the yard before they climbed into Jared's big black truck.

"You know she's over you, right?" Dean asked, grinning at him.

Spencer flipped him off, making both his cousins laugh as they drove away. He drew in a deep breath of cold air and made his way up the walkway. He stomped the snow off his boots on her porch and slipped inside. "Tatum?" Spencer called out. Unless she was waiting for him in the shower again. That would warm things up.

"Kitchen," she answered.

He headed into the kitchen. She had a large mixing bowl on the counter and a cookbook propped up. "What are you making?" he asked.

She turned, a smudge of flour on her nose. *"Pizzelle."*

"Oh, *pizzelle*," he said, then arched both brows. "What are *pizzelle*?"

She crossed the kitchen and threw her arms around his neck. "Yummy wafer cookies I have snowflake molds for. I thought I could make some for tomorrow night's fund-raiser?" She touched his nose. "Your nose is red." She was so pretty his heart thumped.

"It's cold out there," he said, pressing his hands to her cheeks.

She jumped, covering his hands with hers. "Your hands are freezing! Where are your gloves?"

"I took them off to mess with you." He winked.

"I like it when you mess with me," she answered.

His eyes narrowed, the corner of his mouth cocking up. "I like it too."

"Wanna help me make cookies?" she asked, swiping some cookie dough from the bowl and offering it to him on the tip of her finger.

He shook his head, sucking the dough off her finger and biting the tip. "I need to warm up."

She nodded, unzipping his coat and tugging it off. She draped it over the back of the chair before unwinding the black scarf from around his neck. She laid it atop the coat and pulled a chair out. "Sit."

He did, smiling as she turned and straddled his leg to pull his boot off. He had the most inviting view of her ass, hugged in tight jeans. When the second boot joined the first, he grabbed her around the waist and pulled her back onto his lap. His hands slid under the long black sweater she wore, the thrill of her flesh contracting beneath his fingers making him ache instantly.

His hands slid up, pausing when he encountered only smooth flesh. "You forgot your bra, Miss Buchanan."

"No, I didn't, Officer Ryan." She arched into his hands.

He groaned, burying his nose at the base of her neck. "You're soft as silk."

She shivered, the rapid thrum of her heart evident beneath his palm.

"You can't go out in public like this," he groaned as his fingers worked her nipples into hard peaks.

"I'm going out?" she asked, breathless.

"Can't miss the lights," he said, resting his forehead between her shoulder blades. He could wait. He didn't give a damn about the lights. But he wanted her to get out, to remember happier times and how good Greyson could be. "It's a tradition. I wanted to drive you."

She looked back over her shoulder. "I thought we were about sex. And sneaking around."

"Okay, forget the lights," he said, his hands cradling her breast more firmly. Not that he was going to let the subject drop altogether. Just for the next hour or so.

"Now I'll feel guilty. You should go." But she stood, faced him and straddled his lap. Her arms wrapped around his neck as she kissed him. He let her lead, let her lips part his and her tongue stroke the inside of his lip. He shivered, his arms winding around her waist and anchoring her in place.

"You want me to go?" he rasped.

Her green eyes sparkled as she stared at him. She nodded, then shook her head. "First, we need to warm you up," she purred, leaning forward to nip his earlobe.

He shivered as she sucked his earlobe into her mouth. She slipped from his hold and stood, pulling her shirt up and over her head and tossing it at him.

He caught it, soaking up the vision before him. "You're a beautiful woman."

"You don't have to say that," she said, an almost embarrassed tone to her voice.

He stood then, looking down at her. "It's the truth, Tatum. You're beautiful."

She blushed, tearing her gaze from his as she took his hand and tugged him toward the bedroom. The creamy line of her back demanded he touch her. They made it to the hall before he pressed her against the wall, running the tip of his nose along the base of her neck and the ridge of her shoulder blade. His hands cupped her breast as he trailed wet, hot kisses down her back. She sagged, leaning into the wall as he gripped her hips and ground against her. She arched into him, robbing his lungs of air.

"Dammit," he bit out, pulling her back against his chest and steering her into the bedroom.

She spun around, her parted lips latching on to his mouth. When his tongue slipped between her lips, he ground his hips against hers and bore her back onto the mattress.

"Spencer," she breathed.

His fingers were quick and deliberate, sending her clothing to the corners of her room. But the sight of her breasts quaking, her nipples tight peaks and her skin flushed shook him to the core. His hands were shaking as he fumbled with his clothing. By the time he'd climbed between her legs, he had no control left.

He pinned her hands over her head and pressed the tip of his rock-hard—

"Tatum?" a voice called out. A familiar male voice.

They froze.

"Left my phone."

"Is that Dean?" she whispered, the rosy hue of her skin draining as panic set in.

Yes, it was Dean.

And chances were the asshole had left his phone here on purpose so he could horn in on Tatum without an audience. Right now, so close to being wrapped in the heat of her body, he could give a rat's ass if his cousin found them like this. It would serve the smug-faced bastard right. "I'm guessing you didn't lock the door?" He smiled down at her, shifting his weight to remind her they'd been occupied.

She shook her head, breathless as she pushed against his chest. "Spencer," she hissed.

He wanted to argue but she was already sliding out from under him and pulling on her robe. "Stay here. I mean it," she whispered. Without looking back at him, she was gone. He flopped onto his back and stared at the ceiling, his heart hammering in his ears and his dick. The sight of her pom-poms made him smile.

TATUM TUGGED HER robe tight and walked into the living room. Dean stood, his cheeks red from the chill outside. When he saw her, his brows rose and his eyes widened. Yes, she was in her robe—with mussed hair when less than thirty minutes ago she'd been put together and civilized looking.

"You okay, Tatum?" He frowned as he looked down at her. "You look like you've been crying."

She felt her cheeks flame under his inspection. Crying was the last thing on her mind. "Oh? No…no, I'm fine."

"I know you've had a rough time of it," Dean said. "If I need to go kick some ass, I'm happy to do it."

"I appreciate the offer. But there's no one I'd want you to waste your time on." As long as Spencer stayed in bed. If he walked out…that might change.

His smile grew. "Then there's no one worth you wasting tears on, either."

His concern was sweet, even if the manly appreciation in his hazel gaze was a little overwhelming. All Dean was offering was a shoulder to cry on. While Spencer was lying in her bed…offering her his body. But nothing else. Not that she wanted anything else from him. From anyone, for that matter. She didn't. No complications, no expectations. No pain.

Losing Spencer all those years ago had taught her never to let go of her whole heart. Maybe that was why her divorce from Brent hadn't destroyed her. In a way, she should thank Spencer. But, with all the sex he was getting, she supposed she was.

"Tatum?" Dean asked, looking concerned.

She needed to snap out of it. "Sorry. You're right. No tears," she agreed.

"Good." Dean winked at her, making her giggle. "And if you need distracting, give me a call."

"I'll keep that in mind." She shook her head. "Did you find your phone?" she asked. She half expected Spencer to emerge any second—naked—just to stake a claim.

Dean held up his phone. "All good. I'm calling you now, so you'll have my number."

"Okay." Not that she'd call him. She and Spencer had a sex-only understanding. But Lucy was her best friend. No way she'd mess that up by dating Dean. Besides, as gorgeous as he was, she wasn't attracted to him like she was to Spencer. "Have fun tonight."

"See you later, Tatum," Dean said, before he left, pulling the door closed behind him.

Tatum counted to twenty before she locked the door and hurried back to her bedroom. She was amazed by how quickly her heart rate picked up. Her body seemed to rise, tighten, already sparking with the fire that gripped her moments before. Finding Spencer propped up on the pillows, the sheet resting low around his waist, was oil to her flame.

"He gone?" he asked, tossing a small heart-shaped pillow at her. "You two solve all the world problems or make your cookies while you were at it?"

She smiled. "I wasn't gone *that* long."

He cocked an eyebrow. And she leaned back against the wall, enjoying the view. His black hair was mussed, his jaw and chest dusted with a dark shadow. She could see the outline of one thigh beneath her sheet and the heavy length of his arousal. She swallowed, forcing her gaze back up to his. His blue eyes were blazing, and she stumbled over her next words. "Anticipation is a good thing."

"Not as good as being buried inside of you," he said, his voice rasping.

She exhaled slowly, a slight roar in her ears. He'd said that out loud, for her to hear. And from the look on his face, he meant it. Every muscle in her body tightened, clenching with pure need. "He's gone," she murmured.

"Come here," he said, not moving.

Something about the rigid line of his jaw made her pause. He wanted her. Badly. And it was empowering. She took her time crossing the room, aware of him watching her hands as she fiddled with the tie of her robe. "It's getting late," she said.

"No, it's not," he argued.

"You said the lights were a tradition." She stepped closer, transfixed by the way his body seemed ready to pounce.

"I'm in favor of making new traditions," he said, low and husky. "Believe me."

"Like making cookies?" she asked, teasing.

"Like getting you naked."

She swallowed, excitement coiling in her belly. She could do this. She could be sexy and provocative. His barely restrained hunger gave her all the encouragement she needed. She untied the sash of her robe and let the fabric slide from her fingers. She stood at the side of the bed, just out of his reach.

But she wanted him to touch her. She wanted him to

reach for her. So she shrugged out of the robe and waited. His eyes devoured her. Even without his hands on her, she felt the bold heat of his caress. She was so exposed like this. And in his eyes, she hoped, beautiful.

His hands fisted in the sheets at his side as she ran her hand along the column of her neck and across her shoulder. Her breathing picked up as her hand dipped lower, her fingertips sliding between her breasts and across her stomach.

The expression on his face hid nothing. He was a man on fire. For her. He tossed the sheet aside and slid to the edge of the bed, pulling her between his legs and pressing her tight against him. His mouth latched on to the tip of her breast, his lips and tongue stroking and licking until her nipple pebbled in his mouth.

Her fingers twined through his thick hair, holding him in place. When his teeth grazed her sensitized skin, she moaned. His lips moved along the swell of her breast and down her side. His tongue traveled around her hip. Somehow she ended up falling forward, her hands tangled in sheets. Spencer was behind her, exploring the plane of her back with his hands and mouth. He kissed the dip behind her knee. Nipped the curve of her ass. One long finger traced a slow path up the inside of her thigh.

With a growl, he clasped her hips in his hands and wrapped around her to suck her earlobe into his mouth. She felt him, the muscles of his chest against her back. The thick tip of his hard shaft against her, seeking entrance. She curved back, opening for him. And when he slid deep, she was done for. His hand slid across her stomach and between her legs. Calloused fingers worked their magic, the rough abrasion wreaking havoc on her tender, swollen flesh.

He shifted, standing at the bedside and pulling her back onto him. Strange noises spilled from her mouth, broken and low. Every time he moved, his hold tightened. It was the sweetest invasion, complete and absolute. Pushing her until she knew she'd split apart. And when his fingers found her again, she did. The desperate cry that tore from her startled her.

And then she was turning. Spencer's rhythm barely paused. From stomach to back, he was inside her, still relentless. Still wonderful. There was a slight sheen of sweat on his chest. His jaw was clenched tight. And he was staring down between them, watching as he moved in and out of her. His hand traveled down, his fingers stroking her again, and she was crying out her release again.

When his eyes met hers, he tensed, thrusting once, then again, before he climaxed. He slumped forward, pressing her into the mattress and blanketing her with his strength and warmth. She lay there gasping, her body still tingling with delightful twinges.

Spencer was equally breathless, hissing as he slipped from her to lie at her side.

She glanced his way to find him looking at her. "What?"

He shook his head, his gaze never leaving her face. It was the look on his face that made her heart slow…before tripping over itself in an unsteady rhythm when the corner of his mouth curved into a crooked grin. She wanted him to make her body hum with pleasure, but that was *all*. Her heart was off-limits. She frowned.

His grin grew. "How about we grab a couple of burgers and go check out the lights?"

"I've got things to do," she mumbled, deciding time alone, dressed and conversation focused were a bad idea.

He shook his head. "Well, you're going to have to feed me before I can *do* anything." His fingertips skated along her collarbone.

She smiled in spite of herself. "I wasn't talking about you." She shook her head. "I was talking about..."

He rolled over, rising up on one elbow. "About?"

"Unpacking."

"Unpacking?" he prodded. "What about tomorrow?"

"I have the women's auxiliary auction tomorrow night," she said, unable to ignore the curve of his bicep.

"What else?" he asked, his finger trailing between her breast and along her ribs.

"Nothing," she said, growing distracted by his teasing touch.

"So you can unpack tomorrow," he said, leaning forward to suck her nipple into his mouth. His tongue was wicked, erasing her argument completely. "And we can get those burgers and check out the lights. By then, I'll have enough energy to do whatever you want."

That was an offer she wasn't going to refuse.

6

SPENCER WAS CONTENT. Tatum sat in his truck, singing along with the Christmas carols on the radio and holding a steaming cup of hot chocolate in her hands. He drove five miles an hour down Cedar Bend Lane, uncaring that they were wedged, bumper to bumper, among the opening-night crowd. At the rate they were going, it would take an hour before they were done. And he couldn't be happier.

Not that their adventures in the bedroom an hour ago hadn't been amazing. They definitely were.

"Wow," she said, tapping the window at one especially lit-up home. "Check out those animatronics. Do you get extra points for that?"

"Depends on the judging committee. There was a big fallout a few years ago, the younger home owners wanting a voice on the judging committee and all."

"Sounds like serious stuff." She smiled, cocking her head as they drove past another house with a psychedelic lighting scheme. "I wouldn't give this one high marks… So what happened?"

"It was close, but the committee did have some turnover and there's a more *even* distribution of judges."

She glanced at him, sipping her hot chocolate. "I heard that."

"Heard what?"

She raised an eyebrow. "Sarcasm. What does 'even' mean?"

"Let's just say the whole age thing was fixed. But the overall mentality of the committee remains the same." He smiled at her. "I've never seen a first-time winner."

"Hmm." Tatum turned to look out the window. "That sounds like a challenge. If I'm still here next year, I'll have to pull out all the stops and see if I can steal one of those revered winner signs for my yard."

He heard the "if." He didn't like it. Not that now was the time to talk about what she meant. Not yet, anyway. As they pulled up to a large white column-fronted mansion with a double lot, he slowed. "Betty Brewer's grandmother still lives there."

She stared. "She's still alive?"

He chuckled, nodding. "Betty says her grandmother will live forever just to drive the rest of the city crazy."

"I remember her and her causes. The city-hall clock being a minute off. The need for school buses to have their brakes regularly oiled—to reduce noise pollution. Wasn't she one of the loudest voices in the fight to make this a dry county?"

"Damn happy that one didn't work out," he said. He loved the dimple in Tatum's left cheek. Loved the way her eyes creased when she smiled.

"I take it she hasn't mellowed with age, then?"

He shook his head. "Last city-council meeting she

wanted to discuss trash pickup times. Too early disrupts her sleep, too late and it's unsightly."

"She needs a hobby." Tatum laughed. "She and my mother got along famously—they played bridge together a couple of times a week. I remember visiting her house twice. The second time I bumped into an end table and knocked a tiny crystal lamb onto the floor. Its leg was broken. I felt terrible but Mrs. Brewer was *so* angry we had to leave. I wasn't allowed to come back after that and my butt was sore for days." There was no bitterness in Tatum's voice.

"How old were you?"

"Um…around six, I guess," she said, shrugging.

She might brush it aside, but the story reminded him of just how difficult Tatum's upbringing had been. Especially after her father had left. How many family dinners had been disrupted in their own home? His mother would sit there wincing as Mrs. Buchanan's shouts grew louder, staring at their father until he stood up, stomped across the street and warned Mrs. Buchanan that her behavior was crossing a line. Some nights, Tatum had come over to have dinner with them. And on one of those nights, he'd fallen completely in love with her.

"Does she win every year? Mrs. Brewer, I mean?" Tatum's question pulled him from the past.

He took a deep breath and eased his iron grip on the steering wheel. "Her house was disqualified from judging last year because she'd hired a decorating company."

"That's against the rules?" Tatum glanced his way as she took a sip of her hot chocolate.

"Only if it's not a local company."

"So I won't be disqualified? Since you and your cousins are from here?" she asked, turning her gaze back out the window. "I should do something for them—Jared and Dean, I mean. It was nice of them to lend a hand on their day off."

"Dean would love that," he muttered.

Tatum's shoulders were shaking. The sound of her giggle startled him. "So, it's okay for me to do something nice for Jared?"

"He's not trying to get you into bed."

She laughed then. "Dean might be trying to get me into bed but it's never going to happen. Lucy would kill me."

He almost rear-ended the car in front of them. "Lucy?"

"You don't sleep with your best friend's brother," Tatum said, watching him curiously.

He stared at her.

She was still giggling. "What?"

"Nothing," he growled. She was teasing him. He was acting like a child and he knew it. He had no right to be jealous—she'd laid out their arrangement clearly. No strings. No attachments. Just mind-blowing sex with an expiration date.

"What happened to Betty?" she asked.

"Betty?" he repeated. "Betty Brewer went off to college, married some guy and is living in Austin. She visits now and then with her kids."

"That's nice." This time there was an odd sound to her voice—high and tight.

Kids. God, he hadn't even thought about that. Did she and Brent have kids? Surely that would have come up by now. "Big commitment, having kids. Don't think I'll be ready for a while."

She glanced at him. "No?"

He shook his head.

"But you do want kids?" she asked.

He nodded. "Well, yeah, eventually."

"Be sure," she said, that tone edging her voice again.

"I'm sure."

"Just make sure you don't change your mind. Especially *after* you get married," she said.

He swallowed. No kids, then. Because Brent had changed his mind. He should be sorry for her but all he felt was relief. "You still want kids?" Tatum had always wanted a big family, one full of love and laughter—to make up for her childhood.

"Yes. I do." The longing in her voice made his heart hurt. She looked out the window, tapping on the glass. "*This* house is gorgeous. Oh, it's…magical."

Spencer made a point of keeping it light from then on. He wanted her to laugh, to smile and relax. That meant keeping talk of Brent and her mother to a minimum. When the drive was through and they were pulling up in front of the house, he could hardly wait to get her inside.

Tatum turned to face him. "I had fun tonight. Thanks."

He smiled. "Good."

"I'll see you tomorrow? At the women's auxiliary fund-raiser?" she asked, her hand falling to the door handle.

He tried not to let his disappointment show as he nodded. He'd envisioned a long night in her bed. How the hell was he supposed to *sleep* under the same roof?

She opened the door and slid from the truck. "Then I'll say good-night now." She slammed the door and headed inside before he'd turned the truck off.

Spencer sat there, staring at the front door. Maybe he should take a drive, clear his head, get a beer—anything to help him forget he was going to bed—alone.

TATUM STARED OUT the front window. She saw him sitting in his truck, looking at the house. Beyond the steady stream of headlights and the happy sparkle of her Christmas lights, he was there. Waiting.

She was testing him and she knew it. She'd sent him away and he was listening to her. Even if she hadn't really wanted to stay away, not really. What was she doing?

She crept closer to the window, watching him run a hand over his face, shake his head and back the truck out of the driveway. He headed down the road, his brake lights glowing red before he turned right.

"Fine," she gasped. "Good. Time to bake anyway."

She changed into some thermal leggings and a large sweatshirt, the feel of her own fingertips on her skin making her pause. Her fingers felt soft, not rough like Spencer's. She tugged her hair into a ponytail, irritated, and headed into the kitchen. She would not spend the rest of the evening pining for Spencer. Nope. She was going to do something…that wasn't Spencer. She smiled, blasted some Christmas carols and set to work.

She could make something else tempting to offer up at the bake sale tomorrow night. But what? Something about baking, which Brent approved of only when they were entertaining, brought out her rebellious side. She'd whipped up a batch of gingerbread, two blackberry-cranberry pies, some fudge, and finished two dozen *pizzelle* when her phone started ringing.

"Hello?" she asked.

"You up?" Spencer asked.

She smiled, running a finger around the inside of a bowl. "Clearly. It's a little late for a phone call."

"I knew I wouldn't sleep." His voice was gruff.

"Why?"

"Thinking about you."

She swallowed, walking from the kitchen into the front room. She glanced out the window. His truck sat there. "You're sitting in the dark?" She giggled. "Are you trying to have phone sex with me?" There was no way she could do that. It was too…odd. Listening to him telling her what he'd do to her. She felt incredibly warm. She'd touch herself and imagine it was him. Could she do that? Could she let the sound of his voice guide her until she—

"No."

She drew in a deep breath, willing her heart to return to a more sedate pace. "Oh."

He chuckled. "Don't sound so disappointed."

"Who said I was disappointed?" she lied. She'd rather he dragged his butt inside and had actual sex with her. "I'm tired. I'm going to bed."

"Tired meaning you'll be naked in bed waiting for me?" He paused. "Or tired meaning I'll see you tomorrow?"

She waited, knowing what she'd say but not wanting it to be too easy for him. *Oh, to hell with it.* "I'll see you in five minutes."

She ran to the bathroom, brushed her teeth, tossed her clothes on the floor and slipped the rubber band from her hair. She was running to her bed when she heard the door open. She squealed, hopping into the bed and burrowing beneath the covers. "That wasn't five minutes," she called out.

He was smiling when he entered the bedroom. "*I never said five minutes.*" He started shrugging out of his clothes.

She slid to the edge of the bed, the quilts tangled about

her. Her fingers traced a long scar that curved around his side. "What happened here?"

He kicked his pants aside. "A knife. Two guys fighting over a woman in a bar. First week on the job. I was so green. And this is what happened. A tetanus shot and twenty-two stitches."

"Ouch." She looked up at him, catching another white line along his shoulder. "And here?"

He glanced at it. "A broken bottle. Woman didn't like me breaking up a fight. I didn't think she had it in her. Guess I was wrong. Eleven stitches and a staph infection."

She winced. "The one under your jaw?" she asked.

He traced the scar. "My brother Russ." He smiled. "According to him, I'd been in the swing too long."

Russ. She saw the flash of pain on Spencer's face and pressed a kiss on his tattoo. "What happened to him?" she asked, looking up at him.

He shook his head. "I can't. Not now."

She nodded, covering his tattoo in slow, openmouthed kisses.

He dropped his boxers.

And she stared at the rest of him. She couldn't seem to pull enough air into her lungs.

He stooped, pressing his open mouth to hers. In seconds, the quilts were gone and she was wrapped in nothing but Spencer. His arms, his lips and his tongue. She tugged him closer, running her fingers along his tapered waist and the clenched curve of his buttocks. He was man—muscle and power—and she wanted him. She parted her legs, panting, and arched into him.

"Impatient?" he rasped, his jaw tight.

She nodded. *Impatient* was an understatement. She'd been wanting him since she'd climbed out of his truck. Even making pie and gingerbread, she wanted him. So, so bad. "You weren't supposed to leave." Her words were bracing, too needy. She didn't like it.

His eyes searched hers, the tightening of his features unnerving her. "I won't."

God, she hated how much she loved the sound of that.

He thrust forward, filling her, joining them. His groan sent a thrill down her spine, forcing her nipples into tight peaks. When he moved, she knew it wouldn't take long to climax.

But he moved slowly, taking his time with her. There was a tenderness about him that made her nervous. She wasn't sure why he insisted on looking at her, why he whispered her name when she'd close her eyes or bury her face in her pillow. He seemed intent on…connecting.

His hand cupped her cheek, tilting her face and pinning her in place. She couldn't look away, couldn't fight the way his blue eyes claimed her. He cupped her breast, caressing her nipple and forcing her into pure pleasure. His steady, deep, rhythm had her falling. Her body contracted, her cry spilled out into the room, but all she could see was him. His face crumpled, hardening as he gave up the control he'd been exerting. He stiffened, fusing them together as he throbbed with his release. He kissed her, his groan shaking her to the core.

He rolled them, pulling her on top of him—crushing her in his thick arms.

Her body was humming, pleased and relaxed. But her eyes were burning with tears… Which was the last thing she needed. Spencer didn't need to see her that way. Emotional. Vulnerable. *Dammit...* It wasn't fair. She'd kept herself together when most people would have fallen apart. So why now?

Because I'm alone. Her heart thudded. Even now, wrapped in Spencer's arms, she was alone.

"You good?" His voice was low. His hands stroked down the length of her back, over and over.

She nodded, her tongue too thick to speak. She was not going to cry. Being alone wasn't a bad thing. She needed to stand on her own two feet—to figure out what she wanted.

He hugged her, sighing. "Sorry if I interrupted your baking."

She shook her head, swallowing the lump in her throat.

"Smells amazing," he murmured, his fingers combing through her hair.

She closed her eyes, absorbing his touch. Maybe that was the problem. Sex was one thing—affection was another. She pushed off of him, pulling the quilts up.

"Cold?" he asked.

She nodded, refusing to face him. "Tired," she murmured, flopping down on her side, her back to him.

He curved around her, his arm holding her against him. She sniffed as quietly as possible, wishing she was strong enough to move his arm and send him away. But she wasn't. She wanted him to hold her. She wanted him to press kisses against her temple, like he did now. She wanted him to stay. Which was a very big problem.

She lay there, listening to his breathing even out and his body go limp. There was far too much comfort in the weight of his arm and the whisper of his breath against her ear. What would happen when this was over and she was in a big, empty bed—aching for what she now knew existed? Before she could only imagine. Now she knew. How could she ever go back to Chris and his batteries?

7

"You're taking all of this?" Lucy asked, eyeing the double-stacked cake plate and Tupperware container full of her *pizzelle*.

"Too much temptation sitting around." Tatum smiled. "Tonight is the whole reason I made them."

"Spencer let you out of bed long enough to cook? That's considerate," Lucy teased.

Tatum laughed. "We're not that bad." Which wasn't true. Every time he was in the same room she wanted to touch him. And touching him quickly turned into more… *serious* touching.

Lucy snorted. "Whatever. Are you two really trying to keep this thing a secret?"

Tatum glanced at her friend. "This thing?"

"Tatum, there's obviously something going on between you two."

"It's called sex," Tatum argued. "*Nothing* else." She had to keep reminding herself of that. Waking up to him, his tongue stroking between her legs and his fingers sliding deep, had been the perfect way to start the day. The hot coffee and kiss before he left for work had been pretty damn wonderful too.

But after, when she sat in her bed, alone and cold, her melancholy returned. She almost gave in to it. Why not sob into her pillows? Wail a little? But she couldn't do it. It was too much like…giving in. Instead of thinking about what might happen after, she needed to enjoy every second of the before—the now. She'd crushed her pillow to her chest, immediately distracted by Spencer's scent clinging to the cotton pillowcase. She hugged it, breathing him in until she was smiling, and leaped from the bed. A cup of coffee and a long, hot shower had her perking up. So did putting on something pretty. When Lucy arrived with tea and some yummy little finger sandwiches and cakes, Tatum was feeling downright optimistic and full of enthusiasm.

"It's nice to have someone to hang out with," Lucy said, sipping her tea.

"Especially like this." Tatum grinned. "I feel like we should be wearing fancy hats and using my grandmother's china."

"Next time, definitely." Lucy grinned. "You going to be okay with Spencer going up for auction?"

Tatum frowned. "For auction?"

"You can buy one of our first responders for work around the house or something."

"Something?" Tatum asked.

"Last year a bunch of the elementary teachers put their money in to get a fireman to visit the school. Of course the whole station got into it. They spent the day there, making copies, playing with the kids, showing off the fire engine."

"And the money goes for?" Tatum asked.

"It's split. Half goes into the library and its literacy programming. The other half goes to the youth soccer association here. You know what a big organization it is here. They make sure there are scholarships and equipment, field repairs and referees for the games—that sort of thing."

Tatum nodded. Growing up, everyone had played soccer in Greyson. "So improving young minds and young bodies. Sounds like something that's easy to support. I'm sure he'll bring in a lot of money."

"Uh-huh." Lucy smirked.

She sipped her tea, then set it on the table. "How awkward is this going to be?"

"Very," Lucy said. "You're back. After…well, you know. People will be watching you two. And wondering."

Tatum stared into her tea. She did know. She could remember every horrible word he'd said, the horrified looks on the faces of her friends and classmates—

"Tatum, don't go there," Lucy said. "You don't know… He…" She shook her head, sat back in her chair and sighed. "He has regrets. Big regrets."

Tatum jumped up, busying herself with tidying the kitchen. "The past is in the past." She shot Lucy a smile. "I'm not stupid enough to let myself fall in love like that ever again. It wasn't healthy to be so connected with a person." She shrugged. "All I want is great sex."

Lucy looked doubtful.

"It's totally great sex," Tatum assured her.

"I don't want to know," Lucy laughed. "I just want you to be happy. Both of you. And I know he hasn't been really happy since you left."

Lucy's words bothered her. Surely that wasn't true.

Too many years had passed. She wanted him to be happy—even if it wasn't with her.

Tatum waved a hand at the containers of treats. "Let's load this up and see if your aunt needs any help."

"She and Spencer are probably already there," Lucy said. "Aunt Imogene is on pretty much every board in Greyson, so she's there in some official capacity or other."

They loaded Tatum's baked goods into her backseat. Lucy slid her sheet cake in and sighed, hands on hips. "You're making me look bad."

Tatum laughed as they climbed into her little beige SUV and headed to the other side of town. She drove slowly, the ice making her tires slip more than once. But going slow had other advantages. For one, she could enjoy every dazzling holiday display. For another, she could prepare for the night.

There wasn't much appeal in being surrounded by her past—especially the painful parts. But confronting them, making peace, was the only way to move on. And since she was sleeping with the person who'd actually hurt her, she figured handling the ones who'd simply watched the whole humiliating event wouldn't be too hard.

"Looks packed," Lucy said as they parked. "Ready? You certainly dressed to make an impression."

Tatum glanced at her red dress. It was modest. A sweetheart neckline, fitted sleeves and a full skirt. Lucy was wearing slacks. "Is it too much? I thought I was being festive."

"It's not too much. I just mean you're going to make tonight hard on Spencer." Lucy giggled as she climbed out of the SUV.

Tatum buttoned up her long black coat, collected her baked goods and followed Lucy up the bricked path to the large door of the Auxiliary Hall. Christmas music poured out the front door, mixed with jingle bells and laughter.

"Sounds like the party's already in full swing," Lucy said as they walked inside.

Tatum followed, placing her desserts on one of the long covered buffet tables that lined the hall. She tried not to make eye contact with anyone, tried not to let her nerves take root. But she couldn't exactly be antisocial at a social event.

"Can I take your coats?" Jared asked.

"Thanks." Lucy shrugged out of hers.

"Tatum?" he asked.

"Thank you." She slipped hers off and laid it over his arm.

He grinned, shaking his head. "Dean and Spencer are already at it, so you know."

"At it?" she repeated, cocking a brow.

"Arguing. Over you." Jared chuckled as he walked off.

She barely had time to process Jared's comment before Lucy clapped her hands over her mouth, a strangled giggle spilling through her fingers.

Tatum grabbed her arm, following Lucy's gaze. "Oh my God," she said before bursting into laughter.

Something about a man in an ugly Christmas sweater was funny. But seeing two really manly men in skintight pom-pom-covered sweaters—Spencer's was rigged with blinking lights—was beyond hilarious.

"Ugly Christmas sweater competition," Dean explained. His navy blue sweater sported two of the scariest elves Tatum had ever seen. Their huge yellow button eyes, arched brows and creepy grins were certain to give kids nightmares. The fact that they were peeking around a sequined

Christmas tree with pointy ice crystal ornaments only added to the whole disconcertingly ominous picture.

"You're going to make kids afraid of Santa's helpers," Lucy said, smacking her brother. "Parents will be investing in therapy instead of building blocks."

"What do you think?" Dean asked Tatum, pointing at his sweater.

Tatum grimaced. "I'm sort of creeped out."

Dean laughed.

"Runner-up," Spencer said. "But I'll give you an A for effort."

Tatum took in Spencer's sweater. Dark green with wide red stitching at the collar and cuffs, a googly-eyed reindeer head smiled at her. Not only did the deer's red nose glow brightly, but its antlers were decorated with pom-pom ornaments and lights that blinked rapidly. And when he turned around, the reindeer's rear end was visible. Its white tail swayed side to side, like a dog when it's happy.

"Nailed it," Spencer said.

Tatum dissolved into laughter again.

"You haven't seen Zach yet," Lucy argued. "Now that he's got Bianca's help, he might just give you a run for your money."

Spencer waved her words aside, his attention shifting to Tatum—a little too obviously for Tatum's liking. If he kept looking at her like that, people would know there was something going on between them. It didn't help that every time he looked at her like that, she immediately started thinking about what was going on between them. How incredible he was with his hands. And his mouth. His amazing rock-hard body. If she kept blushing, she'd be giving the whole town something to talk about.

"Where's your sweater?" Dean asked.

"Didn't get the memo," Tatum said, tearing her gaze from Spencer's. "Besides, you two... I can't compete with...*this*."

"Damn straight," Dean agreed.

Tatum tried not to let the sea of faces distract her. She recognized quite a few, but there was no animosity. Maybe a little open staring. If she could relax a little, she might find she was among friends. After years of self-doubt and second-guessing, she needed to stop looking for reasons to let her insecurity rise up to gnaw at her insides.

"You look beautiful," Spencer whispered.

When he'd made his way to her side, she wasn't sure. But his heat—his scent—was pure distraction. The kind she didn't want right now.

"You shouldn't look at me like...that." She glanced up at him.

His smile was too damn gorgeous, his blue eyes searching hers. "Like what?"

She blew out a deep breath, flushing beneath the weight of his gaze. "Like...that."

"Like I've seen you naked?" His voice was low—a tingle-inducing growl.

"Spencer," she hissed, her lungs emptying.

But Spencer was looking beyond her then, a very different smile on his face. She studied him, yearning for the affection and pleasure on his face. Not that she wanted him to look at her that way. No. But the idea of *someone* looking at her like that, someday, held a very definite appeal. She knew without looking that his brothers had arrived. His brothers, their wives...his family.

She forced her attention elsewhere. How much time had she spent staring at Spencer Ryan while she was in

Greyson? A lot. Too much. And even though his sweater was something of an attention grabber, she should not be staring at him right now. Not here, surrounded by people who'd last seen her sobbing hysterically because of him. The sharp twist of her stomach made her move away from Spencer and toward the table covered in baked goods.

"Can I help?" she asked Mrs. Ryan.

"Oh, Tatum, don't you look lovely?" She paused, then said, "Yes, dear, thank you." Mrs. Ryan patted her cheek. "If you don't mind uncovering those wedding cookies... and shifting that tray from the table's edge."

Tatum did, straightening the other items for sale.

"Drink?" Dean arrived, offering her a glass of white wine. "You look like a Christmas present. All ready to be unwrapped."

She snorted her wine.

He laughed, handing her a napkin. "Sorry."

She shook her head, patting her chin and mouth. "I'm not really sure how to respond to that. Thank you?"

He nodded, toasting her with his glass.

"Stop being sleazy, Dean." Lucy grabbed her arm, tugging her across the room to the newest arrival. "Come meet Cady and Bianca."

"Cady, Bianca, this is Tatum." Lucy made the introductions.

"I've heard so much about you," Bianca said, hugging her. "You're lovely."

Cady exchanged a quick smile with Bianca, her large eyes sweeping Tatum from head to foot. "It's nice to meet you." She nudged Patton.

Patton's hug was awkward and brief. "Welcome back, Tatum."

"Thanks, Patton."

"Hey, Tatum," Zach said, hugging her. "Glad you're home."

"It's nice to be back," Tatum said. "Congratulations to both of you. Well, all of you." She ignored the hollow ache in her stomach at the clear adoration both Zach and Patton had for their partners.

"Oh, hell no." Zach's surprised laughter drew all eyes. "You didn't?"

Spencer was behind her, grinning from ear to ear. His reindeer's nose blinked brightly.

"I told you I was going to own it this year," Spencer said. "Where's yours?"

Bianca sighed, rolling her eyes, as Zach shrugged out of his coat. He looked like he was wearing a Christmas tree, complete with needles, tinsel, ornaments and, yes, lights.

"That can't be comfortable," Spencer said.

"As long as I win," Zach said, draping an arm along Bianca's shoulders.

Bianca leaned away. "You're poking me." She giggled. "And making me itch."

"Sorry, babe." Zach took her hand in his. "Way to sport the evil possessed elves there, coz."

Everyone laughed then.

It was good, to be included—to laugh. There was an easy camaraderie among the men that managed to include the rest of them. And while Tatum tried to keep her distance from Spencer and Dean, Lucy made sure to stick to her side.

Somehow having a wingman made her reintroduction to Greyson easier.

When the dessert auction was done and the dancing was under way, Tatum helped the other women tidying up the kitchen. How her profession became the focus of conversation, she wasn't sure. But the three of them were spouting off all sorts of options.

"I think you should open your own office," Lucy was saying. "You've got the qualifications. I know a lot of women would welcome working with someone other than George Welch."

"Would you handle small business accounts?" Bianca asked.

"Yes," Tatum said. "I could—"

"Then I would hire you," Bianca cut in. "My cousin Celeste and I. That leaves more time for her to bake fancy tea cakes and for me to make the perfect floral arrangements for special occasions. We'd love to hand over our books to you. And I like the idea of women supporting women. A professional sisterhood, if you will."

"See," Lucy said, stacking up Tupperware dishes and covered cake plates.

"It's an idea," Tatum agreed.

"What other options do you have?" Cady was sitting on the counter, her shoes on the floor. "What's your plan?"

"Cady's all about a plan," Bianca murmured.

"What's wrong with planning?" Cady asked.

"I don't have one." Tatum shrugged. "Not yet. Only one real job possibility, in California."

"California?" Lucy asked, pausing.

Why were the three of them looking at her like that? "Yes. San Diego."

"San Diego is so expensive," Cady said.

"And there are earthquakes," Bianca joined in.

"It is a little far away." Lucy forced a smile.

Tatum glanced at each of them, surprised by their immediate objections. "Maybe the job will pay really well. And, yes, there are earthquakes occasionally, but there are tornadoes here. It might be a trek, but that's why there are airplanes. San Diego would be a great place to visit."

"Yes, of course." Lucy's quick response was forced.

And as the others made their way back to the table the Ryans were occupying, Tatum lingered by the refreshments. While she appreciated Lucy's determination to keep her involved, she didn't want to intrude.

Intrude. She heard Spencer's voice and glanced his way.

He was smiling at her, a brow cocked, as if he knew what she was thinking.

Her eyes narrowed and she crossed her arms over her chest, staying put.

He placed his beer on the table and stood, making his way to her—sending a rush of pure delight through her.

"Dance?" he asked.

She shook her head. That would be a very bad idea.

"I can behave."

"Maybe I can't." She looked at his mouth.

She was rewarded with the jump of his jaw muscle. "I say we make this evening more interesting."

She shook her head again.

"Me or Dean," Spencer said. "He's coming this way."

"Fine," she said, letting him lead her onto the dance floor. Tatum grinned at the blinking reindeer nose before he held her in a loose embrace.

"I'd hold you closer, but I wouldn't want to short out," he said.

She giggled, gasping as he spun her around. She had no idea he could dance. High school dances had been an excuse to hop around or slow dance, nothing like this.

But he knew what he was doing. While she was hanging on and trying to keep up.

"Take up ballroom dancing?" she asked, stunned.

"A mom-required event." His gaze fell to her mouth. "Just hold on to me."

Her insides quivered. "I am."

The song blurred into another, a slow rendition of "What Child Is This?" It was a perfect slow dance song, the perfect excuse for him to pull her closer. "You might short out," she murmured, all too aware of the effect his nearness was having on her. And she knew what she was doing to him too.

A quick assessment told her there weren't many couples on the dance floor.

"It's fine." His voice was rough, pulling her eyes back to him.

"No, it's not," she whispered even as his fingers splayed across her back, his palm pulling her close.

"We're just dancing," he assured her.

She forced her gaze down, the flicker of his sweater lights making her grin. Maybe she was taking this a little too seriously. Maybe his response to her wasn't visible.

"I admit, I like holding you," he murmured softly. "You feel good."

"Your lightbulb is poking me in the stomach," she lied, adding, "It's hot." It wasn't, but she was getting there.

He eased his hold on her. "My lightbulb, huh?"

She giggled. "Yes, your lightbulb."

"It's been called a lot of things, but…"

It took her a while to stop laughing. By then the music was over and he was leading her to their table. Lucy squeezed over so they could share a chair.

"Almost sweater time," Jared said, pointing at Dean and Zach by the steps leading to the stage.

"Time to kick some butt." Spencer was all smiles as he headed to the stage.

She tried not to stare at his ass. Horrible sweater aside, his black trousers made up for it.

"I talked to the one real-estate office in town and a dentist, Dr. Maria Klein." Cady slid two cards across the table to her. "Here. They'd love to speak to you about becoming their accountant. And Mrs. Monroe." Cady touched Tatum's hand, then pointed out the black-haired matron. "She said she'd be happy to use you. She owns a shop on the main square selling…" She looked at Patton.

"Kitchen stuff." He shrugged.

"Which you should know, Cady dear, since the two of you should have registered there already. It went out in the invitations." Mrs. Ryan sighed. "You two."

Cady grinned at her future mother-in-law. "I'll drag him there tomorrow."

"Joy," Patton muttered.

"Come on, Aunt Imogene, be happy this is happening," Lucy said. "Patton was fine with Cady's idea of eloping."

Mrs. Ryan groaned and covered her face with both hands.

"One of the hotels Zach manages had a wedding cancel at the beginning of the month. Cady and Patton stepped in, making everyone happy." Bianca smiled.

Patton didn't look very happy, but Tatum didn't say a thing.

"You are coming?" Cady asked. "It's New Year's. In Aspen. At some swanky hotel. So you should come. Dance, laugh, have fun." She glanced at Spencer, then back at her.

It was hard to miss the other woman's message. But

by then, her time with Spencer would be up. Attending his brother's wedding, surrounded by family and close friends, would be beyond awkward.

"Come on, Tatum," Lucy whispered. "We can be roomies."

But she was saved by the static of the microphone and the emcee's announcement. "Good evening, ladies and gentlemen. We have our ugly sweater contest first. The winners of our silent auction. And then the big event, our bachelor auction."

SPENCER COULDN'T BREATHE. He was in serious trouble and he knew it. Watching her, every smile, every laugh... He wanted to take her hand so Dean would back the hell off. He wanted to take her hand so everyone knew she was spoken for. Even if she wasn't.

His hand tightened around his beer bottle.

Her long blond hair spilled over her shoulder as she leaned forward to listen to what Lucy was saying. Her neck arched, pale and graceful. He knew how that skin felt beneath his lips, how she tasted.

He took a swig of his beer.

"Congratulations," Patton said, sliding into the empty chair at his side. "A plastic trophy and a day helping Mrs. Graham around her house."

He glared at his brother. "Jealous?"

Patton shook his head, his crooked grin quick. "Hell no."

Spencer laughed. "How's the wedding thing going?"

It was Patton's turn to glare. "Don't go there." He paused. "She looks good."

Spencer knew who they were talking about. "She does."

"Cady likes her."

"What's not to like?" he asked.

Patton didn't say anything.

"What if I more than like her?" Spencer asked softly.

Patton smiled a real smile. "You always have."

The truth in his brother's words was freeing—and terrifying.

Patton cocked his head, meeting his brother's gaze. "If she can forgive you for what you did, you're probably the luckiest son of a bitch of all time."

Spencer nodded, taking another swig.

"You two talk?"

"No." Talking was the one thing they hadn't done. His gaze returned to her. She reached up, absentmindedly brushing her hair from her shoulder and resting her hand on the table. She'd painted her nails red...

Patton chuckled.

"What?" Spencer asked.

"Just wondering if I was that obvious?"

Spencer sighed, setting his beer bottle on the table. "You were. And you are."

Patton shrugged. "Cady's trying to get her to stay."

"To stay?" Spencer asked.

Patton looked at him, frowning. "Some job in San Diego?"

He knew she was going to visit a friend. But a job? A job in California—a job that would take her away. Again. He picked up his beer, draining the bottle. He had no right to ask her to stay. Hell, he didn't even know if he wanted her to stay.

Which was a lie. He knew.

"Spence?" Patton asked.

"Time for her to do what she wants." He smiled at his

brother, ignoring the cold, hard lump settling in the pit of his stomach. He did want her to do what she wanted. He'd just hoped it would be here.

It wasn't like he'd spent time envisioning a future for them. Even if he had, if he did, no one knew that but him. He wouldn't influence her again. Whatever choice she made would be hers this time.

8

Spencer yawned, beyond tired as he steered his truck down the dark streets toward home. Nothing like working forty-eight hours straight. A long forty-eight hours. Between Clint's disappearance and a pop-up meth lab tip, he'd driven over most of the county and turned up nothing but an abandoned barn and cold trails. He'd busted two teens selling pot at a corner store but lost another in the park.

At least he hadn't spent much time at his desk. Nothing like sitting underneath humming fluorescent lights to make a man doze. Being up, out, adrenaline pumping, kept him sharp and focused.

He hadn't been slated for the shift, but when his coworker's wife had gone into early labor, he'd volunteered to cover the man's shift. Unlike the vast majority of the Greyson force, he was single.

Had Tatum noticed he was gone? Missed him at all? He blew out a deep breath. Dammit, he'd thought about her a hell of a lot over the last forty-eight hours.

There'd been a time when she would have confided in him. Now he was learning about possible jobs in California. She was thinking about leaving? And he finds out through Patton. Through Cady. Someone Tatum had met that night knew more about her than he did.

He shouldn't be hurt. Or angry. So why was he? He'd agreed their relationship was purely physical. In her mind, there was no reason to tell him she might be moving on. At that point, she'd be done getting in touch with her sexual side. And done with him too, apparently.

But his heart was confused by the whole no-strings plan. Spending a little time away from her had been good. And bad. He'd done some thinking—about her. And, after so much sex, the last two days had been hell. And his body was aching to pick up where they'd left off.

He pulled into the driveway and turned off the engine, the heat escaping into the frigid night.

Two cars were parked along the curb. Lucy's and Bianca's. Meaning his plans for stripping her down would have to wait. Upside, he might get a few hours of sleep. He was whistling as he climbed the steps.

"You look like shit," Lucy said as he stepped inside.

"Thanks," he grumbled, his eyes sweeping the room. There was a board game on the floor and empty wineglasses. And Tatum was in pajamas, smiling at him. What would happen if he threw her over his shoulder and took her to bed? He was tempted to try. "Don't let me interrupt."

"You look tired," Tatum said. God, she was beautiful. "We'll keep it down."

He nodded. "Shower. Bed. Sleep." He saluted them and walked down the hall to his bedroom, smiling at the sound of their voices and their laughter before he closed the bedroom door.

He liked her pajamas. He liked the smile she wore for

him. He groaned, wiped a hand over his face and headed for the bathroom. He stood under the hot water until it ran cold, then stumbled into bed. The red numbers on his side-table clock told him it was nine. The garage light illuminated his room, casting an eerie white glow. But he was too tired to get up and close the blinds. He threw his arm over his eyes and passed out.

He woke to faint knocking. At two in the morning? He glanced at his phone. No calls. He was disoriented, exhaustion weighing him down. He opened the door to find Tatum in a silk robe.

"I've missed you," Tatum whispered.

He could be dreaming. She filled his dreams often enough. Maybe he was dreaming.

But then he was engulfed in her sweet softness and he didn't care. Her lips found his, her tongue slipping between his lips at the very moment she pressed her silk-covered curves against him. He groaned, grabbing her with both hands. In an instant, he was throbbing and ready.

Definitely not dreaming.

Her lips teased his throat, his shoulder, her tongue explored the hard contours of his chest—torturing his nipples and his patience. She slid down, the caress of silk on his bare skin incredibly erotic. When his boxers were around his ankles and her lips latched on to his rock-hard erection, he shuddered, leaning against the wall at his back.

He stared down, his fingers in her blond hair and tugging her back.

Her fingers continued to stroke him as her gaze locked with his. "Hi," she said, before bending forward to suck him deep into her mouth.

"Shit," he hissed, her hand cradling him as her tongue slipped around his length. Her lips were like velvet, hot, sucking, drawing him forward. In seconds, she had him on the edge.

He gripped her shoulders and pulled her up. His kiss wasn't gentle, his teeth and tongue showed her just how hungry he was for her. When he tried to ease his hold on her, she pressed closer, welcoming the invasion of his tongue. Her little gasps, the tight hold on his hair and rake of her nails on his neck, had him all but dragging her to the bed.

She wasn't wearing anything beneath her robe.

Her nipples were so hard he couldn't resist. Before she answered, he'd sucked the puckered flesh into his mouth, cupping the fullness of her breast with his hands.

She writhed, her long, toned legs parting as her hands sought some anchor.

He threaded her fingers with his, stretching her arms up over her head as he drove into her.

"Oh, God, Spencer…" Her moan was raw, desperate.

"Miss me?" he ground out, her tight heat challenging his control. He wanted her to miss this, his ownership of her. He wanted her body—and more.

"Yes," she rasped, breaking off as he powered into her again.

Long, slow strokes that filled her up and left him trembling.

Her fingers opened and closed, gripping his hands as his mouth pressed along the length of her neck. He nipped the flesh beneath her ear, drew her earlobe into his mouth and never broke the deep, hard rhythm he set.

"Spencer!" she cried out, her body beginning to shudder as she tightened convulsively around him. He watched, loving her climax—the total abandon in her release.

He held on, never breaking rhythm, never slowing. He hovered over her, his chest brushing again and again over the taut little peaks. His mouth returned to her breast, his tongue laving and flicking until she was gasping again.

His hands clasped her wrists, pinning her in place while giving him more leverage. "I could do this all night," he murmured.

She shook her head, already close to coming again. "Please..."

"Please what?" he asked.

"Touch me." Her voice shook. Even in the shadows of the room, he knew she was staring at him.

He released her hands. His fingers slipped between them, his thumb working over the throbbing nub between her legs. And just like that, she was burying her face in his pillow to scream.

He let go then, out of his mind as he thrust. When his orgasm hit him, he bit out a curse, long and loud—holding her hips steady.

He fell to her side, breathing as if his life depended on it. But once he'd left her, all the anger and frustration he'd held at bay came crashing down. "Why didn't you tell me about California?" he asked, still gasping.

"What?" she asked, equally breathless.

Shut up. "The job, in San Diego." He paused, turning on the bedside lamp. "You made it sound like a vacation."

She blinked, looking so damn adorable with her tangled hair and flushed cheeks that he almost dropped it. "I didn't think it mattered," she said, her brow creasing. "Or that you'd care."

He stared up at the ceiling, his heart thumping heavily.

"Spencer?" she asked.

He didn't say anything. What could he say? "I care." Which were probably the last words he should say.

The silence grew painful. But he couldn't take it back. It was the truth. He cared. He loved her. So damn much. He'd loved her his whole life. He closed his eyes, his hands fisting in the sheets.

She pulled the blanket up and over her but didn't say anything. He lay on his side, waiting. But when she did look at him, she broke his heart. Her green eyes were full of unshed tears and her lips were pressed flat. Even though she was stiffening, pulling away from him, he saw the flash of vulnerability—and reached for it. He rolled over her, keeping her close before she completely shut him out.

"Let me go, Spencer." Her voice trembled.

He brushed his nose against hers, staring down into her huge green eyes. "We need to talk."

"No, we don't," she argued softly.

He shook his head.

"No complications, remember?"

"Just sex?" he asked, an undeniable edge to his voice.

"Yes," she replied, nodding and blinking rapidly.

"Fine," he said, bending his head to kiss her. It wasn't fine. It hurt like hell. And pissed him off. Why wouldn't she let him apologize? Let him beg for another chance? Yes, he wanted her. He'd always want her, but that didn't change his feelings. So he poured his frustration, his pain and anger, into his kiss. He kissed her until her arms wrapped around his neck, until she rolled over him and straddled him.

When he slid home, he gripped her hips and held on. It took seconds for him to come undone, for her to find her release. But he held on to her long after they were done. If sex was what she wanted, he'd give it to her. Until he figured out how to change her mind—and he *would* figure out how to change her mind—sex was the only time she was his.

"CADY'S ALREADY GOT a client list for you," Lucy said, pulling up the strap on her plum evening dress.

"She's...something," Tatum said, grimacing at her reflection. "This one is a no."

"She's assertive. And bossy." Lucy's friend Celeste had joined them for shopping. "I can say that because I've known her for years but I love her anyway."

Tatum laughed. "I appreciate her interest. It's just surprising. She doesn't really know me. I could be a terrible accountant, bad with people..." She shrugged.

"She's very girl-power. She knows you've been through a painful divorce," Celeste said, almost apologetically.

Tatum smiled. "It's not a secret. I know I'm not the last woman to lose her man to another woman."

"That's pretty much all it takes for Cady. You've been wronged, by a man, she's going to help out."

Tatum accepted what Bianca said, but there was one nagging suspicion. "So it's not to keep me here? I sort of get the feeling that she...all of you want me to stay here?"

"This *is* your home." Lucy sighed. "And, yes, I admit, I want you to stay," Lucy said. "It's hard being the only girl in a family of boys."

"You should marry one of her brothers, Tatum." Celeste was all smiles. "They're both incredibly good-looking."

Lucy shook her head emphatically.

"They are good-looking," Celeste argued.

"Couldn't do it. I grew up with them." Tatum reached for the next dress on the rack. "More brother than not.

Even if I've never had a brother. Jared used to put worms in my pudding. And Dean was always trying to look under my skirt or down my shirt. But he did punch a guy for me once." She laughed.

"I remember." Lucy grabbed Tatum's hand. "We were, what, twelve?"

Tatum nodded. "Twelve was such an awkward time. I got my braces and my boobs. This boy in my class was teasing me—"

"And Dean socked him in the face," Lucy finished, her face turning thoughtful. "Huh. I'd almost forgotten about that. I'm just not sure what he's trying to do. Piss off Spencer or get you to date him."

Tatum shook her head. "He's just being Dean. He's teasing." She thought about his rebound-guy offer and grinned. He wasn't serious.

"He and Spencer have had this competitive thing forever." Lucy sighed. "Boys."

"I'm confused. How is Spencer involved?" Celeste asked.

Somehow, he's always involved. But she didn't say anything. Her emotions were too raw at the moment. And she didn't know what to make of them. Or how to face them.

"Spencer and Tatum were pretty serious in high school," Lucy explained.

"A lifetime ago," Tatum murmured, the onslaught of conflicting emotions hurting her head. She let the lightweight material of the blue Grecian dress slide through her fingers, absentmindedly.

"High school romances," Celeste said. "First love. Oh, the memories."

"I never dated in high school." Lucy frowned. "Not high school boys, anyway."

While the others kept talking about past relationships and high school, she tried on the blue dress. Talking about either meant talking about Spencer. She was doing plenty of that already. Lucy had promised to take Celeste dress shopping for Cady and Patton's wedding and dragged her along too. And while Tatum wasn't sold on going to the wedding, she figured spending a day out was better than analyzing what had happened the night before. With Spencer.

"You look gorgeous," Lucy said with a sigh. "It just hugs in all the right places."

"Drop-dead gorgeous," Celeste agreed. "Unlike this." She spun around in a pea green jersey dress stretched taut over her sizable chest.

They all laughed.

She did feel pretty in the dress. And, whether or not she went to the wedding, it couldn't hurt to have something new in her closet. Memory-free. Especially when it made her feel like this. "I think I'll get it." She tugged her clothes back on. "I'm going to do a little Christmas shopping while you finish up."

She carried out her dress and wandered along the racks and aisles of holiday items. She hadn't meant to wander into the lingerie section, but that was where she ended up. And an especially sheer black lace number with a built-in push-up bra and matching lace thong caught her eye. That was undeniably sexy. And since she'd clearly established that they were all about the sex, this would be a perfectly acceptable purchase. She took it, strolling past the jewelry and accessories, her eyes drawn to a large variety of silk scarves on the back wall. Even though the saleslady had no idea what the four silk scarves were for as she packed them next to her sexy lingerie, Tatum couldn't help but blush. She was buying stuff to tie up her... Spencer.

She took her time, poking through shops along the square. She bought Lucy her favorite perfume, added a baking cookbook for Mrs. Ryan and picked a lovely set of embroidered sheets off Cady and Patton's bridal registry.

As she was coming out of the shop, she spied a candy shop across the street. If she remembered correctly, Spencer's favorite candies were jelly beans. The small ones with the superstrong flavor. Some of her favorite memories were of them eating jelly beans in the dark on her roof and tossing all of the buttered popcorn–flavored beans into the dark. She paused, so caught up in the past that she was *there*. His laugh. Her head pillowed on his shoulder. His kiss on her temple. He'd been smaller then, with fewer muscles, but his love had been as constant as the stars above her. She'd trusted him, them. They'd spent hours there on summer nights, talking, just hanging out together. He'd always held her hand, always. She could almost feel his hand on hers now.

I care.

What did that mean? Did she want to know? What if it meant opening up old wounds? She'd bled enough from the past.

Before there was the bad, there had been so much good. She'd let one week of hell—and a moment of utter humiliation—tarnish something that had helped her through so much. He'd been a pillar in her life, a support, something she'd clung to when her parents fell apart. When her grandparents died. Her mother. How many times had he rescued her, built her back up when her mother had torn her to shreds?

There'd been love and laughter too. With jelly beans

and tickle fights, and making out until they both needed to cool down. Maybe reliving that wouldn't be so bad? But reliving the good always led to the end. One day Spencer had been her world, the next he didn't love her anymore. She still didn't know why.

Maybe the why shouldn't matter anymore?

She made a beeline for the shop, purchasing a large bag of assorted flavors before heading back to the clothing store.

They had mani-pedis before Celeste headed to Tucker House to set up for the bridal shower, and Tatum and Lucy went back to Tatum's place to change. By unspoken agreement, their conversation steered clear of all things men and focused on career.

Lucy had been working as the police psychiatrist for a couple of years, working under a veteran psychologist she didn't always see eye to eye with.

"It's the old-boy network, you know? If he likes a guy, he's more likely to send them back out—even though there's no way in hell they should be on the streets." Lucy sighed, leaning forward to apply eyeliner in the large mirror hanging on the closet door.

"I'm sort of glad my career choice doesn't involve weaponry," Tatum teased. But she was serious. She'd lost so many people in her life, the idea of being surrounded by life-and-death situations on a daily basis held no appeal. Another reason not to get attached to Spencer. "Seriously, I respect what you do. I don't think I could."

Lucy shook her head. "Ditto. I could never work with my husband. If I had one." She giggled. "I only met Brent twice, but he seemed like a hard man to please."

"He was very opinionated. His way was always the right way. The work was no big deal, I know my stuff and I did my job. Honestly, we were better at being coworkers than a married couple. Especially in the bedroom."

Lucy's brows rose. "Do tell. Was he crooked?"

"He was small. He was a straight-missionary, lay-there-quietly and no-cuddling-after sort of guy."

Lucy frowned. "Well, that's just sad. But didn't you sleep with him before you were married?"

"He wanted to be traditional. I was fine with it. I thought it was sweet."

"My sex life sounds better than yours," Lucy offered.

"I thought you weren't seeing anyone?"

"I'm not," Lucy said. "Still better."

Tatum burst out laughing.

"I am sorry, Tatum. I know..." She paused. "I know Spencer hurt you. If he hadn't, I think you two would already be married."

"Probably," she agreed. The few times she'd let herself go there, it had been pretty idyllic. A dream versus a reality. "But that doesn't mean we'd be happy."

"Why wouldn't you be?" Lucy argued. "You were. So was he."

"If he'd been happy with me, he wouldn't have dumped me." She cleared her throat. "Not that I want a relationship right now—I don't. At all. But later, much, *much* later, I'm hoping that whole third-time's-a-charm thing applies to me."

Lucy hugged her. "Me too, Tatum. Me too."

At least Spencer hadn't made it awkward this morning. Okay, waking up to an empty bed was hard, but she hadn't had to worry about facing conversations or feelings, doubts or worries where Spencer was concerned.

Instead of overanalyzing things—again—she'd sat up and taken a look around what had been her parents' bedroom. Spencer, or someone, had done some major work in the space. The horrible wallpaper was gone. The shag carpet pulled up to reveal wood floors. It was lovely. As was the master bath.

Which made her wonder what the rest of the house could look like.

"Change of subject, but I've been thinking about the whole home-office thing—"

"You have?" Lucy interrupted.

"The house needs some work." Tatum nodded.

"If you and Spence decide to keep your hands off one another for a day, I'd be happy to come over and help you with the house."

"I was hoping you'd say that." Tatum smiled. "I've never really had the chance to make a space my own. I think it could be fun." And it would increase the house's resale value.

"Are we talking the whole house? Not just turning your bedroom into a fully functional office space?" Lucy's smile grew at Tatum's nod. "I'm so excited."

Tatum stood in the middle of her bedroom, staring at the lavender walls, the tacked-up pictures and remaining high school memorabilia. She'd started pulling things down and boxing them away but it was depressing as hell. An emotion she was trying to avoid.

"This room makes more sense as an office." Lucy opened the blinds on the two windows. "Behind this is an exterior door?" She tapped on the floor-to-ceiling bookshelf.

Tatum nodded. Her mother had it sealed from the outside, but surely that wouldn't be too big a fix? She could put in a stone path directly to the office so it was separate from the rest of the house. And the large windows offered a gorgeous view of a greenbelt. In a few months, the fields would be covered with vibrant bluebonnets, touches of red and yellow and pink.

Tatum said, "I can almost see it."

"That's the first step, then. Visualization is a solid step toward implementation." She giggled. "We need to go to the hardware store and look at paint samples too. I think a sleepover might be required. S'mores, wine, architecture magazines. Maybe a movie too?"

"I like it," Tatum replied. "Just promise me no chick flicks and I'm in."

Lucy nodded. "How about action flicks with shirtless hot guys?"

"Deal."

9

Spencer shifted the large Crock-Pot he'd picked up for the happy couple and opened the door of Tucker House.

"You look wiped," Zach said, giving him a one-armed hug.

"Skeleton crew means extra hours," he said, hugging Bianca. "You look pretty."

Bianca smiled. "Thank you, Spencer."

"Where's the happy couple?" he asked, assessing the crowd. Chances were he could put in an appearance and sneak out. He needed sleep. He'd been called in to work and left Tatum sleeping, warm and soft in his bed. Leaving her was that much harder knowing he had five days before their twelve days were up.

Hell, he could sleep later.

"Library, I think," Bianca said.

He nodded, shifting the box again, and headed toward the library. The last year had been all about weddings and everything leading up to it. He was getting pretty damn comfortable with the B and B that housed many of their events.

The first person he saw was Patton. And he looked

like he could use a drink. Spencer deposited his gift on a table already stacked high with presents and went to the bar. But bumping into Tatum, having her fall into him, almost made him drop the two longnecks he was carrying.

"Sorry," she said, her hands resting on his chest.

His arms had wrapped around her, to stop her from falling to the floor. "Nice catching up with you."

She rolled her eyes, smiling broadly. "Was that a pun?"

He shrugged. "Maybe."

"It was pretty bad." She looked at his arms, still anchored around her waist. "I'm good."

He leaned forward. "The best," he whispered in her ear. He let go of her, but not before he'd felt the shiver that racked her.

Her eyes fastened on his, then on his mouth. *Good.*

He winked at her and headed toward his brother, hoping he looked cool, calm and unaffected by the brush of her curves and sweetness of her scent.

"Beer?" he asked Patton, offering him the bottle.

"Way to make an entrance." Patton took the beer and drank deeply.

"You look like you're having a great time, bro," Spencer retorted.

Cady looked at Patton and laughed. "You want to cut and run?"

"Only if you're coming with me," Patton said.

She took his hand in hers. "Nope. You're stuck right here. But I promise I'll make it up to you later."

"Hey, hey." Spencer made a show of covering his ears. "Little brother here."

Patton laughed.

Cady was looking at him, curiously. "So, little brother, I have a question for you."

"Here we go." Patton took another sip of his beer.

"Shoot," Spencer said, searching the crowd for any sign of Tatum.

"You love her?" Cady asked.

He looked at his almost sister-in-law. "Straight for the jugular, huh?"

"That's Cady," Patton murmured.

"And you adore me." Cady smiled up at her fiancé.

Patton nodded, looking at Cady in a way that made Spencer slightly uncomfortable. "I sure as hell do," he said in a gruff voice.

"I'd tell you to get a room, but…" Spencer teased.

Cady glared at him. "Patton says she's the one."

Patton groaned.

"He does?" Spencer glared at his brother. "Did he tell you I messed it up?"

She nodded. "You were pretty much the biggest asshole ever, from what I've gathered. But things like confessions and apologies make a difference. So does hearing 'I love you.'"

He swallowed. "She doesn't want a relationship."

Patton and Cady both looked at him.

"She's saying that because she's scared," Cady assured him. "Wouldn't you be? Both the men she committed to dumped her."

He didn't say anything.

"Is she what you want?" Patton asked.

He nodded.

"What are we talking about?" Zach joined them. "It looks serious."

"Your brother and Tatum," Cady offered.

"Okay." Zach nodded. "I need a drink."

Spencer laughed. "Conversation's over, don't worry."

He smiled at Patton and Cady. "Congrats, guys. I'm really happy for you. And I appreciate your concern."

He excused himself and wandered into the billiard room, populated entirely by men. He took off his jacket and waited for the next game to start. But sitting in the large leather recliner in the corner, a warm fire crackling, the sounds of the party muffled by the thick wooden doors, wasn't a good idea. He was nodding off when the doors opened.

"Told you," Dean said, slapping Jared on the shoulder.

"Hiding out?" Jared asked.

Spencer shrugged. "Figured I'd wait to play."

When the table cleared, they jumped up, racked up the balls and rolled up their sleeves. On the second round, Dean was chalking his pool cue when he said, "Let's make this interesting."

Jared chuckled. "I was waiting."

Spencer frowned. "Now what?"

"I win, I get to kiss Tatum under the mistletoe. You win, you do," Dean suggested.

Spencer's frown grew. "No."

"I could just do it," Dean said. "This way I'm giving you a chance to stop me."

Spencer sighed. Knowing Tatum, she'd let him kiss her on the cheek. Dean was already getting what he wanted: Spencer's reaction. "Fine." He forced the word out.

Spencer lost.

As Dean grinned at him, Spencer shrugged him off. His cousin didn't need to know that he wanted to punch him in the face.

"Come on, boys, they're about to cut the cake," his mother said, poking her head in the door. "Honestly, it's your brother's engagement party not a pool hall." She ducked back out, leaving the door wide.

But Spencer lingered, putting the table back to rights before reluctantly heading into the library. It took seconds to find her. Her hair fell over one shoulder, one hand holding a glass of white wine, the other resting on her lap. She was talking to an older gentleman, her hand lifting to emphasize the point she was making. The man said something in return and they both smiled.

She was beautiful.

"Hey," Lucy said, nudging him. "You're staring."

"Yep," he said. Because she was beautiful.

"Stop," she said, giggling.

"Do I have to?" he asked, glancing at her with a smile.

"How's work?" she asked.

"I won't be visiting your couch anytime soon." He sighed. "But there's still no word on Clint Taggart. Gotta feel for his wife and kids."

"How long has he been gone?" Lucy asked.

"Five days. Maybe six. His wife thought he'd gone on assignment. She didn't know he'd lost his job." He finished his beer. Not knowing had to suck. "Anything new with you?"

"Nope. Spending most of my free time with Tatum." She paused. "Like you. Only without the sex and nakedness."

He almost choked on his beer.

"No judging here. Two consenting adults. All good." Lucy took a sip of her wine.

"Um. Thanks?" he said. "When did all the women in this family decide they could say whatever they wanted whenever they wanted?"

Lucy looked up at him. "You've been talking to Cady, haven't you?"

He shook his head. "Everyone has an opinion."

"Because we all want you happy," Lucy said.

His attention returned to Tatum. She was looking at him, her green eyes wide. She smiled at him and his heart thudded in his chest.

"Oh my God!" Cady's voice drew his attention. "This is too much, you guys," Cady continued, jumping up to hug Bianca and Zach.

Patton was reading the card, surprise clear on his face. "Two weeks in Italy?"

Spencer chuckled. "I got them pots."

Lucy laughed. "I got them towels. But they're very nice towels."

"Sheets," Tatum added as she walked over, laughing. "Embroidered, Egyptian cotton."

"Nice," he said, beyond pleased that she'd joined them.

"But Italy, wow." She shook her head.

"I know," Lucy agreed. "Talk about a honeymoon."

"Excuse me," Tatum said, slipping from the room.

He watched her go.

"Go on," Lucy said, pushing him toward the door with a smile.

TATUM SMILED AT the bartender as he filled her glass. "Thank you." She sat at the bar, scanning the empty dining room. Everyone was in the library. The quiet was a nice change.

"Not a fan of crowds?"

She heard Spencer's voice and smiled into her glass. She'd known he'd follow her. Wasn't that why she'd let him know she was leaving? "It was getting a little stuffy in there." She glanced at him, sitting on the bar stool next to her.

"Spencer." He held his hand out.

She hesitated, her brows arching. "Tatum?" So he wanted to play games? *Fine. Bring it.* Anticipation settled hot and sweet in the pit of her stomach.

"You sound like you're not sure." The gravel of his voice drove her crazy.

"Sorry, I...I thought we'd met before?" She waited but he just smiled at her. "Guess I had you confused with someone else." He was too good-looking, too intense. He looked at her like she was naked. She felt naked.

He shook his head. "I'd remember you."

She smiled slightly, buzzing with pure lust.

"Who?" he asked, his gaze fastened on her mouth.

"Who what?" she asked.

"Who did you think I was?"

She smiled. "This guy I'm sleeping with."

"Lucky guy," he said, still staring at her mouth.

Lucky her. Spencer was an incredible lover. "I was hoping he'd come tonight," she said, breathless.

"Why?" he asked. His gaze crashed into her.

"I've been thinking about him," she managed. She could do this. "He...he's really good with his hands."

He slammed his beer bottle down on the counter, making the bartender look up from his ledger at the end of the counter. She turned toward Spencer, away from the bartender, nervous enough without an audience.

"Just his hands?" he asked.

She shook her head. "And his mouth."

Spencer slid off his stool, standing so close heat rolled off of him. His hand rested on her knee, sliding beneath the wool of her skirt. His fingers slid higher, finding the edge of her stockings. He closed his eyes, his jaw locking hard. His fingers slid around, finding the silky straps of her garter belt. "Wear this for him?" he asked, so rough she shivered.

She nodded, knowing their behavior was reckless but beyond caring. She'd never ached like this before, never worried she'd lose control so easily. "Think he might like it?" she asked, slipping forward on the stool, forcing his hand higher.

His breath tickled her ear. "I need you. Now," he growled, pressing her hand along the zipper of his slacks. Her fingers stroked his rigid length, making him swallow.

His fingers dipped higher and then he froze.

She wasn't wearing any panties.

"Dammit all to hell, Tatum," he muttered.

She moaned softly, turning her face into his neck as her fingers explored his impressive girth. She stroked him, again and again, wishing he was buried inside her—

"Don't," he growled, grabbing her hand and tugging her off the bar stool.

"Here." She pressed a room key into his hand.

The shock on his face was pure victory. For a split second she thought he'd kiss her now. She wanted him to. Even knowing someone could walk in any second. She walked from the bar, knowing he'd follow, knowing he was just as eager to get to the room as she was.

When they reached the door, he fumbled with the lock. Once the door swung open, his hands were on her. She heard the door slam as he pressed her against the heavy wood. He stared down, yanking her skirt up around her waist to reveal her satin garters and no panties. His broken curse, almost a plea, made her weak.

"Look at me," he growled, his knee nudging her legs apart.

She did, her breath escaping in short gasps.

He kissed her, his tongue invading her mouth as two long fingers sunk deep inside of her. She rocked back on her heels, tilting to take more. His thumb found her, stroking her, driving her mad. Her head fell back against the door as her body surrendered. Her hands clutched his arm, riding his hand, his fingers, lost to the stroke of his thumb. She was trembling, convulsing around his fingers. She shook her head, drowning in him.

He kissed her, latching on to her lower lip.

His thumb grazed her sweetly tortured flesh and she climaxed. She buried her face against his chest, muffling her scream as best she could.

When her trembling eased, his fingers left her.

She opened her eyes to watch him back up, slipping his tie free. He was gasping, his chest heaving as he stared at her exposed body. She steadied herself and moved forward, unzipping her skirt and letting it fall on the floor. She tugged her sweater off, striding toward him.

She tore his shirt open, mindless of the buttons that popped and bounced across the room. When his chest was bare, her lips descended. His taste, his scent, stoked her already raging hunger. Without thought, she unbuttoned his pants, sighing as her hands pushed the fabric down. She cupped his ass, raking her nails along his skin.

He shivered, gripping her arms and tugging her close.

She kissed him, opening her mouth for him. His tongue was magic, fierce and demanding, greedy—the way she wanted him. His fingers fumbled with the closure of her bra before he cupped her exposed breast in his large hands. She leaned into him, embracing the frenzy of want between them.

She pushed him toward the bench at the end of the bed, smiling as he sat. "Lie back," she said, her voice husky. He did, his gaze blazing into hers. He lay there, gripping the legs of the bench while she straddled him—still wearing her boots and garter belt.

He closed his eyes as she arched forward, feeling every inch of him push deep inside. She moaned, rocking forward. Her knees hung off the side of the bench, her heels buried in the carpet. She had all the leverage, all the power. And she used it to her advantage.

His reaction fueled her overwhelming craving to control. He quivered beneath her, clenched with each thrust, hissing and cussing and groaning. The throb of him, the heated friction, the brush of skin on skin. His body was a work of art, all rough angles and smooth contours.

He sat up, lightly biting her shoulder, licking her neck. His lips latched on to her nipple, his tongue flicking the sensitized flesh and making her cry out.

She ground against him, wanting control. It wasn't fair that he could invade her body and steal her senses. She wanted to make him fall apart. She rested her hands on his knees, setting a frenetic pace. The muscle of his thighs tightened, his fingers biting into her sides, as he moved beneath her. His arms wound around her, supporting her as he drove into her.

His strangled moan, the pulse of him convulsing inside her, split her apart.

He held her in place as she rode out her climax.

How he managed to stand, she didn't know. One minute they were upright, the next, she was lying on his chest, the feel of cool sheets covering them.

She felt the rapid beat of his heart echoing her own. She knew this heart and loved the sound of it. Whatever she and Brent had had, it had never compared to what she'd felt for Spencer. She'd loved him down to the cellular level. His hands came up, smoothing her hair down her back in long strokes. She closed her eyes, reveling in the feel of him. The scent of him.

"You okay?" he asked breathlessly.

She nodded. She was good. So good she didn't want to move.

She felt him press a kiss to the top of her head. She looked up at him then, resting her chin in the middle of his chest. She covered his chest with her hand, staying connected to him. This connection had been her strength and her downfall. Now...she didn't know what it meant. She'd wanted this to be about sex, about freedom, but she knew it was more.

His fingers slid through her hair as his eyes bored into hers. He swallowed.

"I thought..." She sucked in a deep breath, the words coming without thought. "When I moved to California, there were days I didn't know how to...to live. Or function."

His heart seemed to stop. Then start up again, faster than ever.

"I thought there was something wrong with me—"

He shook his head. "No."

She placed a finger over his lips. "And there was. I poured all of my love, everything I had, into you. So when we were done, I had to accept I was wrong...to learn what love was. To remember that I couldn't let myself feel like that ever again."

He closed his eyes.

"That's why ending my marriage didn't destroy me. So thank you for that."

He looked at her then, his face so rigid and remote. He tried to sit up, but she shook her head, her hand firmly pressed to his heart. He covered her hand with his.

"That's why you and I can't have more than this. I know I wouldn't survive this time." But explaining why she could never love him didn't change the fact that she already did.

10

SPENCER HELD HER against him. He'd scarred her. Left her broken. "I'm sorry, Tatum. I'm so damn sorry."

She stared up at him.

"I did what I thought I had to do," he said.

She frowned then, confusion marring her features. "What are you talking about?"

"I hurt you when I should have fought for you," he confessed.

She tried to move, but he held her in place.

He knew he was entering dangerous territory but he wanted her to know the truth. "I knew you wouldn't leave unless I made you." His words turned gruff and hard.

She froze. "What?"

"Your mother—"

She held up her hand. "Don't. She has nothing to do with this."

"She has everything to do with this. I know it bothers you to talk about her. But it bothered me to know she was hurting you. I saw the bruises, Tatum," he argued. "And I couldn't live with it."

"Let me go, Spencer," she said softly.

He did.

She slipped from the bed, dragging the quilt with her. "I don't understand." She sat on the bench, her boots peeking out between the folds of the blanket. He waited. He should have kept his mouth shut, apologized without spilling his guts.

How many times had he woken up, dripping sweat and hating himself? If he could go back in time, he would handle it differently. He was a stupid kid who was trying to save the girl he loved. Breaking up with her hadn't been the worst part of it. Having her come back, day after day, asking him to give them another chance. *Whatever I've done, I can fix it.* Her words had shredded him. She wouldn't give up on him, on them.

"But you said... You said..." She looked so lost.

"I lied. I lied to get you out of here and away from your mother."

"She was depressed, sick— She couldn't control her moods. She didn't know what she was doing, Spencer—"

"It didn't matter." He shook his head, sliding from the bed to stand before her. "She hurt *you*, mentally and physically. Don't you remember how it was with us, Tatum? How much I loved you? I would have done anything, *anything*, to protect you."

She stared at him, swallowing. "You used *her* words to drive me away? You told me there was something wrong with me." She choked on the words.

There's something wrong with you, Tatum. Fix it, or no one will ever love you, not really. He'd heard Tatum's mom say them and felt the pain of those words. It wasn't the woman's fault that she was bipolar. But Tatum was the one that suffered when Jane Buchanan forgot to take her meds. Tatum was the one who cleaned up after her mother when she had a temper fit. Tatum was the one who took the abuse.

"I was all she had," Tatum said. "If I'd stayed—"

"No, you staying wouldn't have kept her alive." Spencer shook his head. "It would have destroyed you."

"You did a pretty good job," she whispered. "Because of you... Spencer, I believed you. *You* had never lied to me. You had promised...promised me..." She shook her head. "I could deal with my mom. I understood why my dad couldn't deal. But you? You were my safe haven. And hearing you say that to me...that was the first time I ever felt alone."

Her words wrapped around his heart, a vise of barbed wire.

She stood, finding her clothes and increasing his panic.

He stopped her, blocking her path. "I have no excuse. Only regrets. Every damn day for eight years I've thought about you, knowing I'd lost the best thing to ever happen to me. What I did was wrong but I can't undo it—no matter how much I wish I could." He paused, watching the play of emotions on her face. "Your dad wanted you in California, remember? You said no. Because of me. I was responsible. I was the reason you were being hurt over and over. Losing you was like cutting out my heart. But... I had to. I had to—"

She shook her head. "No, you didn't. Not like that. You were deliberately cruel. You knew my weakness and you used that against me." She sucked in a deep breath.

"If I'd asked you to go, would you?" he asked.

She opened her mouth, her brow creasing. "How can I know that? What difference does it make? You didn't just take away my choices. You made me doubt myself—my worth."

"I was a seventeen-year-old idiot who loved you—" He broke off.

"And I was the idiot who valued your opinion more than anyone else's."

It was hard to breathe. "I'm asking for your forgiveness. Maybe, in time, some understanding." If he told her he loved her, would it make a difference? "You deserve all the love, all the happiness a man can give you. You are amazing. Thoughtful, kind, beautiful. I'm sorry that my actions caused you to doubt that."

She stared at him. "I need you to leave. Now." She closed herself in the bathroom.

He dressed quickly, sighing at the sight of his shirt. Once he was dressed, he stared at the bathroom door. She was mad, and she had every right to be mad. She needed time and space. He'd give it to her.

He slipped from the room and headed to the coatroom, sliding into his blazer and buttoning it up before getting a beer and heading back to the party. If he was smart he'd leave. But he couldn't, not yet.

He ignored the questioning looks of Lucy and Patton, pretending his cousins' debate on V-6 versus V-8 engines held his attention. Thirty minutes and another beer later, Tatum arrived. Not only did she avoid making eye contact, she seemed determined to stay at least ten feet away from him at all times.

"What the hell did you do?" Patton asked.

"Don't ask." He glanced her way, willing her to look at him.

But she didn't look his way.

She spent the next few minutes helping his mother

pack up the presents for Cady and Patton. And another few minutes talking to the same older gentleman she'd been talking to before. He was saying his goodbyes when he saw Dean making his way to her.

She smiled at him, listening as his cousin undoubtedly tried to charm her. He looked at the floor at his feet, the wave of anger surprising him.

Patton said, "Tried to talk to her?"

He nodded.

"Did you talk to Lucy first?" Patton asked.

He glared at his brother. "What for?"

"She's a shrink. And a woman. Might have prevented the arctic treatment."

Spencer sighed, wishing he could take back the last hour. "Too late now."

"I can see that." Patton's pale eyes were fixed at the doorway.

Spencer glanced over in time to see Dean point up at the mistletoe he'd led her under. He should look away. He should ignore it and let it go. He'd won the bet, so of course he was going to try to rub Spencer's face in it. She'd turn and give him her cheek... Except she didn't. She was kissing him. Her arms were loose around his neck, her lips lingering on Dean's...

"Breathe," Patton reminded him.

"I'm breathing," he snapped.

But he couldn't look away. Tatum's smile. Dean's startled, but very pleased, expression.

"Go," Patton said. "Mom'll kick your ass if you started a fight."

He nodded, moving across the room as unobtrusively as possible. So why did it feel like everyone was staring at him?

He threw his truck into gear and drove into town, heading straight for Zeke's gym. It was late and the weather was bad, but there were plenty of guys willing to spar with him. After a quick warm-up he climbed into the ring and cut loose.

They had to take turns, giving him just enough time to catch his breath, stop whatever was bleeding and go again. When the gym closed at midnight, he drove to his mother's and the beat-up sleeper sofa in the near-arctic garage. Hell, at this point, it didn't matter where he slept as long as he could sleep. No matter what, he'd feel like total shit in the morning.

He hadn't been expecting to find his brothers waiting for him on the front porch.

He put the truck in Park and climbed the steps.

"Need a place to sleep?" Patton asked.

"Nah." He shook his head. "Garage."

"It's freaking cold," Zach said. "Let's go."

Spencer nodded, leading them into the garage and flipping on the lights. Folding chairs were located, a space heater was plugged in and Zach produced a large bottle of whiskey.

"Go to Zeke's?" Patton asked, pulling cups from their camping gear.

He nodded. "Is it bad?"

Zach and Patton exchanged looks.

"Make for some interesting wedding pictures," Zach said, laughing.

Spencer sighed. "Dammit."

Patton shrugged. "Fine by me." He poured out drinks.

There was a comfortable silence as they all knocked back their alcohol.

"Dean wanted to come," Zach offered, earning a hard glance from Patton.

"Not his fault," Spencer said, emptying the glass. "It's me."

Patton sipped his drink, flopping into one of the chairs and scooting closer to the heater. "Bad?"

He nodded.

"She hasn't really been here long enough for you to screw it up *that* bad." Zach sat in one of the other chairs.

He paced, the whiskey and the cold keeping him moving. "I screwed up. The sort of long-term, psychological shit that takes years to get over. And even if she gets over it, chances are she's never going to love me."

"And that's what we want?" Zach clarified.

"Yes, Zach." Patton sighed. "Do you listen to a thing I say?"

"No, not really." Zach smiled.

Spencer chuckled. "Remember our breakup?" he asked.

"The one where you were basically catatonic for a year?" Zach asked. "Yeah, good times."

Spencer flipped him off.

"That was a hell of a long time ago." Patton crossed his arms over his chest.

"I know we were kids, but I loved her. I mean, she was everything. Losing her was a nightmare. I believed we were forever. It felt like it would be. But if you love someone like that, you have to put them first, right?" He barely looked at them. "Her mom used to abuse her. Mostly mentally, but she got hit too. Tatum would make excuses, forgive her, but it ate at her—tore her down. And no matter how much I told her Dad could help, or the school could help, she felt responsible for her mom. Her mom used the guilt card a lot. Her dad kept asking her to come live with him, but she wouldn't go. Because of me."

Patton ran a hand over his face.

Zach set his empty glass on the floor. "So you dumped her."

Spencer nodded, sitting on the edge of the lumpy couch. "I made Dad call her father in California when she wouldn't leave. She wasn't safe here and I couldn't let it go on."

"I know you guys were pretty serious," Zach said, leaning forward. "So I'm assuming you pulled out the big guns for this breakup?"

"Cheating rumors." Patton glanced his way.

"Ouch," Zach said.

"Worse." He dropped his head in his hands. "Her mom…her mom used to say there was something wrong with her. That she needed to fix it or no one would ever love her. I said it to drive her away."

"Aw, shit, Spence," Zach groaned. "That's just mean. And teenage girls… I mean. You're king of the assholes."

"Why say anything now?" Patton asked.

"She said I was right." He shook his head. "She said that our relationship taught her never to love that much again. I had to tell her what I'd done. I had to."

Zach groaned.

Patton sighed.

He didn't bother lifting his head.

"So you begged for forgiveness?" Patton asked.

"On your knees?" Zach added.

"You saw how well that went," Spencer murmured. "I probably wouldn't forgive me, either."

"We need more whiskey," Zach said, reaching for the bottle. "It's gonna be a long night."

TATUM HAD NEVER had a hangover before. Everything ached. Her head, her eyes, her eyelids.

"Drink this," Celeste said, putting a glass of something green on the table in front of her.

"What is it?" she asked, her tongue thick and heavy.

"You drank all of these?" Lucy asked, scraping the army of miniature alcohol bottles into the trash. "Vodka. And tequila. Did you throw up?"

"Not yet." Tatum pressed a hand to her stomach. "Not to be rude, but why are you all here?"

"We'd talked about looking at the tearoom books, remember?" Celeste patted her hand.

"And you'd volunteered to make dessert tonight and, after last night, we thought we could help." Lucy sighed.

Accounting? She almost groaned. Baking? Dessert. For dinner. Tonight. At the Ryans' house. She groaned. Before they went caroling. Because she'd promised Mrs. Ryan at the auxiliary auction. "Oh, God."

"It's okay," Lucy said. "We've got plenty of time. It's only eleven."

Tatum covered her face with her hands. "So you're checking up on me?" she asked.

"Yes," Celeste admitted.

"I'm fine." She slid the glass across the table, sipping from the top. "That's awful."

"It is," Celeste agreed. "But it will settle your stomach."

She sipped again. "This is awkward."

"Why?" Lucy asked. "We've all been there. Men can be…morons."

"The question is, what can we do?" Celeste asked. "I'm a doer."

Tatum shook her head. "I was going to bake a black forest cake..." She covered her mouth.

"You have everything?" Celeste asked, hopping up and opening the refrigerator.

She nodded, pointing.

"Recipe?" Lucy asked.

She shook her head and tapped her forehead. "Secret."

They froze.

"Seriously?" Lucy asked.

Tatum shook her head, laughing weakly. "Red cookbook." She pointed.

"You're a hoot," Lucy said, squeezing her shoulder gently.

Celeste turned off the overhead lights. "Better?"

Tatum nodded. "Can you see?" she asked, peering through bloodshot eyes.

"Yep," Celeste said, already pulling out bowls.

"This sounds yummy," Lucy said as she read the recipe.

She sat, sipping her green concoction, strangely soothed by Lucy and Celeste's presence. At some point, she took a pain reliever. She felt almost civilized after the cake was in the oven and they made her take a shower.

But she emerged to find them standing, staring curiously at all the pictures, newspaper clippings, trinkets and one almost shredded pom-pom scattered around her room. In fact, her room looked like a bomb had exploded. She didn't remember much. She'd come home so angry, so confused. Apparently she'd taken it out on her room.

Stubbing her foot on the shoe box full of travel liquor at the bottom of the hall closet had seemed like an answer to her anger. Worse than anger was pain.

"You were a cute cheerleader," Celeste said, holding up a newspaper clipping.

Tatum sat on her bed. "I don't remember doing this."

"You drank a lot," Lucy offered, stooping to pick up the bits of paper and photos scattered all over the room.

"I had been planning on cleaning out the room," she muttered.

"I'll get a box," Lucy said. "No point in putting this stuff back up." She returned with the empty shoe box.

"I didn't drink all of it?" she gasped.

"No. You'd be dead." Celeste's smile was concerned. "I put it in the kitchen cabinet."

"We can throw it away?" Lucy offered.

"Don't worry," Tatum assured her. "I've so learned my lesson."

"Is this Spencer?" Celeste asked, offering the photo to Tatum.

She took it. "Yes." She stared at the image, her eyes burning with hot tears. She didn't need to look at it to know what it was. It was a picture she'd had pegged up above her bed. It was old and they were young. She was sitting on a chair and he was sitting on the floor between her legs. Her hand was at an awkward angle, because he was holding it. But what made it so special was the naturalness of Spencer pressing a kiss, almost absentmindedly, to her hand. Second nature. Like breathing.

He'd felt the same way, she'd known it—never doubted it. Until he'd...he'd crushed her heart. But now she knew the truth. He hadn't been some thoughtless hormonal teenage boy. No, he had to have the noblest of motivations. He was trying to save her. To protect her. Because he'd loved her.

Losing you was like cutting out my heart...

And just like that she was sobbing.

"Oh, Tatum." Lucy sounded heartbroken.

"Don't make yourself sick." Celeste ran from the room, reappearing with a cool, wet cloth. "Here."

Tatum pressed the cloth to her face, mortified.

"You can talk about it," Lucy prompted. "We won't say anything."

"I don't know if I—I can talk about it," she forced out.

"Then we don't have to," Lucy said.

Tatum nodded, her brain swimming. It took her a while to ask, "Could you forgive a person for lying to you about something?"

"Depends on what it was," Celeste said. "Some things are unforgivable."

Tatum nodded.

"I'd disagree," Lucy said. "If we're talking about a person you love, almost anything is forgivable."

Tatum glanced at the picture. "What if the person you loved most, the person who knew all of your secrets, used your weakness to drive you away?"

"Can you, maybe, give us a little more to go on?" Celeste asked.

Tatum did. From him telling her he didn't love her anymore to that horrible scene in the cafeteria when he said those words—the words that echoed in her ears for months after she'd moved to California. "There's something wrong with you, Tatum…" He'd kept going, saying her mother's words while his arm draped along some other girl's shoulders. "You need to let go. Move on. I don't love you anymore." She'd stood there, staring at him, wanting to scream.

"Why?" Lucy asked, her cheeks red. "Why was he so determined to make you leave?"

That was the part she had a hard time confessing. She knew her mother hadn't treated her well, that Spencer was right. But she'd spent so many years fooling herself. Her mother was ill, alone. She had to stay—to love her. No one else would. It was only after Spencer had broken her heart, after her father had shown up determined to take her with him and her mother into a treatment facility, that she relented. Leaving had been a relief.

"My mom…" She drew in a deep breath. "Spencer was trying to get me away from my mom."

They waited.

"Because she was mean to me."

"Mean to you?" Celeste repeated, her eyes going round.

"Oh, Tatum." Lucy hugged her. "People talked but I never thought… Why didn't you say anything?"

She shook her head.

"So he was a complete ass," Celeste murmured, "because he loved you."

"And when he found out he'd left scars, he wanted to make it better." Lucy was on the verge of tears. "Because he still loves you. Why else would he feel the need to tell you the truth now?"

Tatum froze, going numb. No. He didn't love her. He couldn't love her. He wanted her. "Maybe he just needed to clear his conscience?" But she wasn't sure she believed that. If Spencer wasn't the heartless bastard she'd thought, who was he? Too many years had gone by for him to be her Spencer. No, *not* her Spencer.

Her head throbbed. It didn't matter. She had a hangover—that was why she was emotional. Spencer, the past, none of it mattered. It couldn't. With him, she was… vulnerable. Vulnerable and needy. She didn't want to be either.

"What are you going to do?" Celeste asked.

She shrugged.

"What do you want?" Lucy asked. "That's where you need to start. If he does love you, it makes more sense for you to know what you want first."

She nodded, sniffing the air. "Chocolate."

"Always a good place to start," Lucy agreed, laughing.

"The cake." Celeste hopped up, running into the kitchen.

She looked at Lucy.

"Where was I?" Lucy asked. "Why wasn't I there?" She shook her head. "I should have been there to back you up, to scream at him when you wouldn't."

"Different lunch periods." She shrugged. "I called my dad as soon as I got home."

"That was the weekend you left." Lucy looked at her. "That horrible weekend. Spencer fell apart."

"I'm not going to feel sorry for him right now, okay? Not yet." Tatum flopped back on her bed. "Why do we make things more complicated than they need to be?"

Lucy flopped back with her. "Human nature, I think." She looked at her. "Are you going to come tonight? To dinner and caroling?"

Tatum closed her eyes. "I don't think so. I need time to pull it together. Right now, the only thing I know is my heart hurts."

11

SHE SKIPPED DINNER and caroling, claiming a headache. But when they stopped by, she wrapped herself in a blanket and stood on the porch to listen. She hadn't seen Spencer, but she'd felt his absence.

The next day Lucy came over and helped her start weeding through things. It wasn't as bad as she thought it would be. Brent had hired a professional organizer after her mother's death. They'd done an exceptional job of clearing out every piece of clothing, shoes, toiletries... Almost all signs of her mother. There were three large boxes she and Lucy tackled together. But there wasn't much. Mostly pictures and keepsakes gathered from before her father had left them. Nothing from Tatum's high school years, none of the letters Tatum had written when she and Brent had settled in his hometown.

When she'd pulled all the things she wanted, they'd hauled the boxes onto the front porch.

"I can call Dean?" Lucy offered. "He has a truck."

Tatum shook her head. "No, please don't. I feel terrible for what I did. I can't keep leading him on."

"You kissed him under the mistletoe." Lucy nudged her. "I didn't see tongue, or groping."

Tatum laughed. "Because there wasn't any."

"Then you're fine."

They sat on her front porch swing, enjoying the crisp air. Even though her yard was coated in a layer of white snow, the sun was shining down.

"It's a beautiful day," she said.

"It is," Lucy agreed. "But I'm starving. I think I'll order a pizza."

A faint thud from across the street drew her attention. Spencer was carrying a duffel bag, headed toward his truck. She watched him open the large toolbox in his truck bed, rifling through it before closing it again. He grabbed the bag, opened the truck door and tossed it inside.

He slammed the door and looked across the street.

She froze, panic sinking in. She wasn't ready to deal with him, not yet.

He lifted his hand in a wave.

Lucy waved back.

After a moment's hesitation, he headed across the street. And every step he took stirred up some new, conflicting emotion. It was easier when she just wanted him. Now...she shook her head. That *was* all. She wanted him. Nothing else. *Want* might be an understatement. Her body craved him like her lungs craved air.

He was red-nosed when he climbed the steps to her porch. But all she could see was the huge bruise along his right cheek, the taped cut on his eyelid and the gash across the bridge of his nose. She was up, reaching for his face before she realized what she was doing. "What happened?"

He stared down at her, closing his eyes as her fingers touched the bruise. "It's nothing," he said gruffly.

She blinked, pulling her hand back. He had a dangerous job. This probably wasn't all that unusual. "Tell me this has nothing to do with Dean." Had she caused a rift between him and his cousin?

He snorted. "Dean didn't do this. He wouldn't have gotten in this many punches."

Relief washed over her. Not that she preferred him getting beaten up on the job.

He saw the boxes on the porch and frowned, his whole demeanor changing. His jaw locked, his hand—resting on the porch railing—tightened around the wood. "Going somewhere?" His voice broke—she heard it.

And when his blue eyes locked with hers it was impossible to breathe.

He had no right to look…like that. Like he cared. Like she'd hurt him. He had no right to make her hurt for him. Words failed her, so she stared at him, confused and frustrated. And angry.

She was vaguely aware of Lucy saying, "I think I need to go pick up the pizza," before she left.

Spencer's gaze bounced from her to the boxes and back again. He seemed braced, waiting for something.

She opened her mouth, then closed it. She didn't know what to say. Or how to read him. After last night, everything seemed upside-down. Only one thing was certain—she wasn't up for any more life-altering revelations.

So why did she want to reach out for him? Maybe it was the wariness on his face or the hint of sadness in his eyes… Whatever it was, she wanted to comfort him. *Dammit.* She hugged herself.

His voice was rough. "Tatum—"

"On your way to work?" she asked, cutting him off before more things were said.

He sighed, his eyes narrowing. "Not until tonight." What was he looking for?

"Oh, well..." She stepped back, putting space between them. "Good time to get your Christmas shopping done... or something." Since she couldn't seem to be near him without touching him, she needed to remove herself. Her fingers were already longing to trace his stubble-covered jaw, to press a kiss to the corner of his mouth, to hold him close until his posture eased. All of which were very bad ideas. "See you later," she said, stepping around him and going inside.

But once she was inside, she froze. She didn't want to think or get emotional, but she didn't want him to leave. *Don't go.* She swallowed down the knot of fear and sucked in a deep breath. "Shit... Spencer—" she called out.

He was through the door in an instant, closing the distance between them as he pressed her against the entryway wall. She wrapped her arms around his neck, pressing her mouth to his. She wanted his kiss, his tongue, his touch—she craved him beyond reason.

His arms were steel around her, lifting her. She wrapped her legs around his waist and held on.

"I couldn't sleep last night, couldn't think." He cupped her face between his hands, pinning her with the raw hunger of his gaze. "I need you so bad it hurts."

She tugged his hair, ignoring all the possible ways she could interpret his words. It was easier to pull his head back to hers. He devoured her mouth, stealing her breath, making her light-headed. He carried them to her room, kissing her as though his life depended on it. She wanted him like this, fierce and hungry for her. Once she was pinned between him and her bedroom door, she reached down between them, unbuttoning his pants. His gaze bored into hers as her fingers freed him from his boxers. Her fingers wrapped around him, slowly. He was hot to the touch, smooth.

He let go of her long enough to tug her pants off. And then he was there, lifting her, his hands bracing her hips, parting her so he could fill her in one thrust. They groaned together, the sweet friction pulling her under. She smiled, her head falling back against the wall, savoring each stroke against her inflamed flesh.

"Don't stop." She pressed her ankles into his buttocks.

"I won't," he said, nipping her earlobe.

He didn't. His face was hard, driven, as he set a deep and frantic rhythm. His barely restrained hunger made her tremble. Her nails dug into his hips, mindless in her need. When he caught her lower lip with his teeth, she came apart. Hard. Fast. Out of control. It was oh so good. "Spencer," she gasped, shuddering at the aftershocks that rippled through her.

She wrapped her arms around his neck, pressing her forehead to his. She relished the rough groan that tore from his throat as he stiffened.

Seconds later she was lying on her bed, gasping, with Spencer at her side. Her mind was spinning, returning to her preorgasmic state of equal parts panic, frustration… and love. She closed her eyes, draping her arm across her forehead.

She understood why he'd done what he did. Their connection wasn't just physical. He had known her better than anyone else, had known she was hurting, and did what he had to, to stop it. She would have done the same.

She loved him. So much it scared her.

If she was smart, she'd keep her mouth shut. She didn't want to be hurt anymore. Heartfelt confessions and desire-fueled promises were all fine and good now, when they were still wrapped in discovery and lust. But there was no way this was real. That this could last. It was too…big.

No matter what Lucy believed, he'd never said he loved her, not in so many words. And while she was willing to accept what he'd done was because he'd once loved her—that didn't mean he still did. No, better to keep things as they were. It would hurt less this way.

She glanced at him and smiled.

He was sound asleep, snoring ever so softly. And he was gorgeous. This man was the boy she'd loved completely. He'd been lean and awkward then, but he'd loved her with a confidence that told her it was right. And she'd been too young to know better. With him, she'd never doubted herself or felt alone.

Until she did.

She studied his profile, the line of his brow, the angle of his jaw, thick brows and full lips. She ran a finger along his forehead, smoothing his hair back. He sighed, turning into her in his sleep.

Dammit.

If Lucy wasn't due back soon, she'd have no problem staying as she was. But Lucy *was* coming back, so pants were required. She felt Spencer's hand twitch and looked down. His hand held hers.

HE WOKE TO Christmas carols, laughter and singing.

It took a minute to orient himself. He was in Tatum's bed, alone, covered in blankets.

A shout of laughter made him grin. Tatum and Lucy, from the sounds of it.

He kicked back the blankets, ran a hand through his hair and glanced at the clock. It was almost 6:00 p.m. He had an hour before he needed to be at the station. He turned on the bedside lamp and stretched. It had been a long time since he'd slept a solid five hours without waking. It made sense that he'd done it in Tatum's bed. It was the one place he could truly relax.

He glanced around the room, taking in the changes. The pom-pom and trophies were gone. The walls were bare. Even the curtains had been pulled down. He remembered the boxes on the front porch, the tightness in his chest making it hard to breathe. Was she really packing up? She hadn't answered him. And it gnawed at his gut. He rubbed his hands over his face and rolled his neck. What would he do if she left?

More important, how did he convince her to stay?

He caught sight of the romance novel on her bedside table and picked it up. He shook his head at the cover and flipped it over to read the back. Something slipped from the pages and fell to the floor. He stooped to pick it up. A picture.

He stared at the picture, his heart thumping. A picture of them. They were on a field trip somewhere. One of the journalist students had snapped the picture and given a copy to each of them.

In a room intentionally stripped of all sentimentality, why was this picture out? This was something she'd held on to. Hope crashed into him. And happiness. He tucked the picture beneath the book and stood, heading into the kitchen.

Lucy and Tatum were in pajamas, sliding around the kitchen floor in fuzzy socks. Tatum's kitten-covered pink thermal pajamas and pigtails had him shaking his head.

She looked gorgeous, swinging a large wooden spoon around as she belted out Mariah Carey Christmas carols at the top of her lungs.

Lucy joined in, adding sprinkles to some of the stacks and stacks of cookies that covered the kitchen countertops. Among the tubes of icing and bottles of sprinkles, a gigantic gingerbread house was being built.

He leaned against the door, smiling. When they finished their performance, he clapped.

They both jumped.

Lucy burst out laughing. "Good to see you're alive and well. I was beginning to worry Tatum might have killed you."

Tatum glanced at him, cocking an eyebrow but not saying a word. Instead, the tip of her tongue licked a dollop of pink frosting from her spoon.

"She tried," he said, as he cleared his throat. Apparently they weren't keeping things a secret from Lucy.

Tatum frowned at him, dropping the spoon in the sink. "We made cookies."

"I see that." His brows rose. "I can eat a lot but—"

"They're for you to take to work," Tatum said. "It's Christmas."

As if that explained everything. She'd made cookies for him to take to work because it was Christmas. His smile grew.

"Her idea," Lucy said. "I just wanted to eat some cookie dough."

"They'll be appreciated." He winked at Lucy, content to watch Tatum fill a large storage container with festively decorated cookies.

"We're having a sleepover," Tatum said.

"Aren't you two a little old for sleepovers?" he asked, smiling.

"You're never too old for a sleepover," Lucy said, smiling sweetly at him.

"What's your schedule?" Lucy asked. "I know Juan's trying to get as many people to cover as possible—since the baby came early."

He nodded. "Not sure." But he hoped like hell he could avoid more overtime. His and Tatum's time was running out, and he wanted to make every second count. "It's been pretty slow."

"Spencer is sort of a hero right now. Did he tell you that?" Lucy asked Tatum. "Not that he brags on himself."

Tatum's eyes met his. "What did you do?"

He glared at Lucy. "Really?"

"Come on, Spencer, it's sweet." Lucy perched on the kitchen counter. "He was at the high school, doing some sort of don't-do-drugs thing when these boys got into a fight. He got in the middle of it, broke it up and saved one of the kids from choking to death."

Tatum looked horrified. "The other kid was trying to kill him?"

"No." Spencer sighed. "The dumb kid was sucking on a piece of candy. The fight broke out. He got punched. I guess he inhaled it when he got the wind knocked out of him."

Tatum smiled. "So you broke up a fight and did the Heimlich maneuver? I bet you made quite an impression."

"He made the front page of the paper. Aunt Imogene is framing it," Lucy said.

"What happened to the kids?" Tatum asked.

"I guess seeing his buddy turn blue made the other guy cool off real fast. They were all hugging and saying

'I'm sorry, man.'" Spencer laughed. "You couldn't pay me to be a teenage boy again. Too volatile."

Tatum giggled, staring pointedly at his injuries. "Hey, what's that on your face?"

He frowned.

"Y'all are fun." Lucy laughed.

"Pizza?" Tatum pulled a plate from the oven. "Sit, if you have time? It's veggie."

He shook his head. "I'll eat it in the truck. I should be heading out."

She wrapped the pizza in foil and set it on the container full of cookies. "Well…be careful."

He crossed the room, taking the container from her. "I will." He set the container on the counter, cupped her face in his hands and kissed her. He liked the startled look on her face, the perfect O her mouth made right before his lips met hers. She was so soft, so sweet. He broke away with a sigh. He pulled her close, sliding his hands up and down her back. "I promise," he whispered in her ear.

He grabbed his cookies and left, knowing a smart man would call in sick and crash their sleepover. He could decorate cookies with the best of them. Since his mother had no daughters, her boys all had basic cooking, cleaning and dancing skills. She considered all three of equal importance when it came to being a good spouse. As it was, he knew he was needed on the job—and hoped she'd let him make up for lost time later.

He drove to the station with the windshield wipers on high. After a sun-filled day, the sudden dip in the temperature and steady rain promised slick roadway conditions.

"Looks like tonight's going to be fun," he murmured, munching his pizza on the way to the station. Veggie or not, it was good.

He carried the cookies, nodding at his team as he headed toward his desk. After hanging his coat on the hook by his workstation, he shifted a stack of papers and put the container on the edge of his desk.

"I know you didn't make them," Patton said, pulling a cookie out.

"Nope." Spencer smiled. "Tatum did."

Patton grinned.

"Aren't you supposed to be off?" Spencer asked.

Patton shrugged, biting into the cookie. "Wrapping up a few loose ends."

"Patton, you could spend a month on loose ends." He pulled out the file he'd been working on. "Anything you need to catch me up on?"

"Where do I start?" Patton shook his head, sitting in the chair by Spencer's desk.

Spencer listened as Patton listed off what had rolled in since he'd left. There was a missing child linked to a known drug transporter—top priority. A neighborhood had over a dozen cars vandalized the night before, leaving a path of empty aerosol cans they were fingerprinting.

"Kids huffing?" Spencer asked. "Guess I'll check hospitals later, see if anyone turns up."

Patton nodded. "A twenty-four-year-old woman was found in the parking lot next to The Grind. Her blood work tested positive for Rohypnol, so they're doing a rape kit."

Spencer ran a hand over his face.

"And, last but not least, we have a van-load of teens in custody. They were coming back from a Dallas concert, smoke pouring out of their windows. Nothing like a moving hotbox to grab Highway Patrol's interest."

Spencer laughed. "People never fail to amaze me. They're damn lucky no one got killed."

"I don't remember what we were doing at that age, but I'd like to think we weren't that careless with other people's lives."

Spencer nodded. "We weren't. I can remember Zach trying to ski off the roof the year of the big blizzard. And I believe you—"

"Stopped you from breaking your neck more than once."

Spencer nodded, smiling. "Great. So I can expect a bunch of pissed-off parents who *know* it's not their kids' pot anytime?" Spencer asked, scanning over his notes. "The roofie thing, that's the third one this month."

Patton nodded, frowning.

"Any MO?" Spencer asked. "Same victim profile?"

Patton shook his head. "Doesn't appear so. Here." He handed him the file. "Feel free."

"What about the kid?" Spencer asked, looking at the whiteboard the clerk kept up as new information rolled in.

"It's a 1984 blue Dodge minivan with a gray bumper. We've had a few calls. Seems to be heading in our general direction." Patton sighed, staring at the abducted four-year-old girl's picture. "Sure would love to get her home safe."

Spencer nodded. "Custody thing?"

Patton nodded. "Dad lost rights because of his dealing. No one knows if he's using or not. And no violent record, just drugs. I'm hoping he's just a desperate dad doing a very stupid thing."

Spencer didn't say anything. Abduction cases were nasty, no matter what.

"Let me know if you hear something?" Patton asked.

Spencer nodded. "No news on Taggart?"

Patton shook his head, taking another cookie. "These are good."

"Are they?" He reached for one, popping it in his mouth. They were good. Not that he was surprised. Tatum had always liked to bake. Thinking of Tatum in her pink cat pajamas, pigtails bouncing, had him grinning from ear to ear.

"I take it she forgave you?" Patton asked, gathering his things up.

Spencer shook his head. "Not yet. But I'm working on it."

The intercom on his desk buzzed. "Got a call for backup. Immediate assistance requested to Cliffs Point and Jones Avenue."

"We're shorthanded, Spencer," Captain Ramirez yelled out.

"On it," Spencer answered, jumping up and tugging on his coat. "Go home to your fiancée, Patton. Take her a cookie." He winked as he sprinted out into the darkness.

12

"Hello?" Lucy answered the phone while Tatum hunted for the remote control. "What's wrong, Aunt Imogene?"

A chill settled in Tatum's stomach. She flipped off the television and stood, suddenly too antsy to sit still.

"Which hospital? Glenn Oaks? Okay." Lucy's gaze met Tatum's. There was a long pause. "I'll come get you…Yes, she's here…What?…I'll tell her." She hung up her phone.

"Spencer?" she asked, already knowing the answer.

Lucy took her hands. "He's okay."

"What happened?" she asked, her voice trembling.

"Don't freak out, okay? He was stabbed—"

"Don't freak out?" she repeated. He'd been stabbed.

"It could be nothing, Tatum, really. He's in stable condition." Lucy stood, hurrying to the door.

"Nothing?" she asked. "You said he was *stabbed*."

"I'll let you know…" She paused. "He…he said for you not to come."

Tatum frowned. "Oh."

"I need to take Aunt Imogene. She can't drive on the

ice, too jumpy," she said, hugging her. "I'll let you know as soon as I know more."

Tatum nodded, feeling numb. "Okay."

Tatum stared out the front window, watching as Lucy and Mrs. Ryan piled into her car and drove off.

He was hurt. In a hospital. But he was in stable condition. Stable enough to tell her not to come. She hugged herself, hating how cold she felt.

If he didn't want her there she shouldn't go. He had a good reason.

She started cleaning up the mess she and Lucy had made in the kitchen. But once the kitchen was sparkling, there was still no word on Spencer. She texted Lucy, asking for an update, but she didn't get an answer.

Lucy would call her if it was bad. She'd call, period, wouldn't she? She'd know Tatum was worried.

But since Lucy wasn't texting her, she did a load of laundry and straightened the living room.

An hour and a half ticked by before she couldn't take it anymore. She put on her thick black coat, tugged on mittens and a hat, and climbed into the SUV. She plugged Glenn Oaks Hospital into her navigation system and drove, slipping along the icy roads. The closer she got, the more she shook. Which didn't help with driving on the icy roads.

When she rounded a corner, her tires locked and her SUV slid. But she relaxed, stayed calm and kept control. She recovered and came to a stop at the red light. As she rested her head on her steering wheel, terrified of what could have happened, she heard the screeching of brakes and looked up.

A truck slid across the intersection and plowed into her passenger side.

She barely had time to register what was happening as her SUV was forced across the road and slammed into a lamppost. Her head smacked the driver side window, cracking the glass and making her see stars. A horn was honking, but she didn't know if it was hers or the truck's. All she knew was it wouldn't stop.

She sat there, stunned, a warm stickiness running down the side of her face.

Her phone vibrated then, but she was too dazed to reach for it.

Someone knocked on the window. "You okay?"

"Yes," she said. "Just...hit my head."

"We called 9-1-1," the person said, trying to open her door. "Door's smashed in."

"I'm okay," she said again. She tried the door handle, but the door wouldn't move. "I'll climb over." But then she realized her passenger side was crumpled in on itself, the hood of the truck firmly embedded.

A young man tried to open her door. "You might want to stay put. In case you hurt your neck."

"I really think I'm okay," she said, trying to unbuckle her seat belt. She pressed the button but nothing happened. "My belt's stuck."

"Must be connected to the car's computer," the man said.

There were sirens.

"Just sit tight."

"I don't think I have a choice," she said, laughing softly. She reached up, feeling along her hairline. She winced, pulling back blood-covered fingers.

What an idiot. Spencer had told her not to come—probably for this very reason. Lucy had told her he was stable. But *no*, she just had to see for herself. And now this. She rested her head against the seat back.

Her phone vibrated again and this time she reached for it. Lucy.

Spencer's fine. Stitched at the scene and back at work. See, no worries. Want to finish the movie?

She laughed then, which made her head hurt.

"You okay?" the man asked.

"I'm fine," she assured him, though she doubted he could hear her over the blare of the sirens.

What was she doing? She'd dropped everything to get to Spencer—after he'd told her not to come. She was doing exactly what she didn't want to do. Getting too involved, too attached. And now she was bleeding and trapped in a car because of it. *I'm an idiot.* An idiot whose head was throbbing.

The paramedics managed to pry open the back door to reach her. One assessed her injuries, strapping a large foam brace around her neck before they helped her out of the passenger side. The firefighters had to cut through her seat belt and force her seat back to get her out. By then, her head was definitely hurting.

"How do you feel?" the paramedic asked.

Embarrassed. I sort of hate myself right now. Pathetic. "My head hurts."

He nodded. "You knocked your head pretty good," he said. "Might need a few stitches."

Stitches? She closed her eyes.

"I need you to stay awake for me," he said. "Just in case you have a concussion."

And a concussion? "Okay," she said.

"Can we call anyone?" he asked. "Next of kin?"

She swallowed. "Nope."

He blinked. "You sure?"

She tried not to glare at the man. "Believe me. I'm sure," she said. She had no one.

The ride in the ambulance was short—she'd almost been there when she'd had her accident. When they arrived in the emergency room, she answered the same questions over and over, had ten different people shine penlights in her eyes, made her touch her nose, walk a straight line and had her head x-rayed.

She had a concussion. And needed eight stitches behind her ear, which was swollen and sore.

"I'm going to have an elf ear for Christmas," she said to the ER nurse. "How festive."

"You'd look pretty no matter what," the woman said, smiling. "I'm Aileen. If you need anything, just holler. I'm your nurse. Okay?" She handed her the remote control. "You'll be staying with us for a while so might as well find something to entertain you." Aileen pulled the curtain back. "So I can keep an eye on you. No sleeping, okay?"

"Okay," Tatum said. She flipped channels. She couldn't feel her incision; it was numb. But the rest of her wasn't. Now that she wasn't trapped in a vehicle, in immediate peril, her brain decided to replay all the times she'd been hurt. Not stitches or concussion hurt, but brokenhearted and defeated hurt. Her father's desertion, her mother, Spencer, Brent… How many times did she have to fall flat to learn to stay on her guard?

Her divorce should have liberated her.

Sleeping with Spencer should have empowered her.

She was in control now. And somehow she'd forgotten that.

No matter what truths had come to light about Spencer and their past, she was still antirelationships. She didn't have the strongest evidence that loving someone was a good thing. The crisscross cuts and angry coloring of her right arm was example enough.

No more pretending things hadn't gotten way out of hand with Spencer. She only hoped she was strong enough to end it.

She aimlessly flipped the channels, unease and nausea setting her stomach on edge. News. Sports. Travel shows. *It's a Wonderful Life.* She stopped, knowing George Bailey's tale would cheer her up. With any luck, she'd be able to go home by the time the movie was over. If she was really lucky, she'd look into getting an earlier flight to California.

"SPENCER," HE ANSWERED his phone, eating another of Tatum's cookies. He'd been back at work for an hour, closing out two files, and four cookies. And every time he took a bite, his mind drifted to Tatum. Her smile. Her laugh. Her tongue licking icing off the spoon. It was a good damn thing he was at his desk tonight, because he'd be shit in the field.

"It's Jared." It was hard to hear his cousin over the background noise. "I just heard. Is she okay?"

"At work?" Spencer asked. "I can barely hear you."

"Is Tatum okay?" Jared repeated, enunciating.

Spencer sat forward, a knot forming in his throat. "As far as I know. Unless you know something I don't know?"

"Aw, shit," Jared sighed. "You don't know?"

"Know what?" Spencer asked. "What the hell do I not know?" He stood, staring around the station, his panic building.

"Tatum was taken to the emergency room—"

"Why?"

"Car accident."

Jared's words ripped the air from his lungs—more effective than a gut punch. The roads were ice slicks. Even with his four-wheel drive, he struggled. Tatum hadn't driven in these conditions in years—that was the reason he'd told her not to come see him. That, and there was no point. He was fine.

His heart twisted and his throat dried up. "When?"

"A couple of hours ago. Sorry, Spence, thought you'd know—"

Spencer hung up the phone, grabbed his coat and ran from the police department. He pulled out of the parking lot, heading straight to Glenn Oaks Hospital.

The cop in him conjured up a variety of worst-case scenarios. Scenarios he didn't want to see or worry about.

Keep it together, Ryan. He drew in a deep breath, reining in his emotions to analyze only the facts. And he didn't have many. All the way to the hospital, no matter how much his truck slid on the roads, his thoughts were all Tatum. Was she okay? Was she hurt? Scared?

Dammit.

The truck slipped all over the road, so he kicked it into four-wheel drive and gunned it. By the time he reached the hospital, his fingers ached from his death grip on the steering wheel. He parked his truck and ran into the emergency room, flashing his badge.

"I'm looking for Tatum Buchanan."

The nurse flipped through the list. "I'll take you." She stepped around the desk and led him past a row of curtained partitions. "She should be able to go home shortly. We just wanted to make sure her concussion isn't too severe."

That was good news. Not good enough to make him relax, but it was a start. "What happened?"

"Ice." The nurse smiled at him. "We've had half a dozen accidents tonight and all of them were cars sliding on the ice. She was lucky, could have been a lot worse. The guy who hit her is in surgery."

Spencer's gut clenched. She was okay. She was okay. It would all be okay when he saw her. When he knew she was safe. It was hard to breathe.

"Aileen," the nurse said. "The detective is here to see your patient, Tatum Buchanan."

"Spencer?" He heard Tatum's voice and turned. "What are you doing here?"

He stood frozen. She had a wide strip of gauze wound around her temple, her long blond curls pulled over her left shoulder. She looked fragile, small, in the bed. "Hey." He moved to her without thought, pressing a hand along her cheek. "Where else would I be?" he asked, sitting on the side of her bed. "I would have been here earlier if I'd known."

"I'm...I'm fine," she said.

"That bandage around your head says otherwise." His voice was garbled. She was okay. He reached for her, taking her hand in his. Feeling her, warm and soft, made it better. "Why were you on the roads?" he asked, willing himself to calm.

She swallowed, staring at their joined hands. "I...I needed something from the store."

He frowned. "In the middle of an ice storm?"

"I didn't know it was that bad." Her voice was brittle. "Lesson learned."

"I'm just glad you're okay." He drew in a deep breath, focused on being calm. She didn't know he'd been scared shitless. That the thought of something happening to her was... He swallowed, twining his fingers through hers. "You're okay."

She nodded, then winced.

He winced too, squeezing her hand in his.

"You didn't need to come," she murmured, softly. "How did you even know I was here?"

He needed to come. He had to come. He had no choice. And there was no way he was leaving. "Cop, remember. I've got connections."

"Well, I'm fine. And you're supposed to be working." She tried to pull her hand from his, but he held tight. "Not babysitting."

He held on to her hand, biting back all the words he wanted to say. But now wasn't the time. She was in a hospital bed, for crying out loud. Not the best time to lay his heart on the line. It might be wrong to ask her to love him, but he had no choice. He loved her. He knew he always would.

"Miss Buchanan, once we get the doctor to sign off on your paperwork, you're cleared to go." The nurse smiled. "You shouldn't be driving—"

"I'm pretty sure my car's totaled," Tatum teased, laughing softly.

He closed his eyes. He'd seen too many accidents and fatalities on nights like this. She was safe. And he'd be damned if he didn't make sure she stayed that way. Seeing her here, wide-eyed and fragile, kicked his protective side into overdrive and his heart pumping. He cleared his throat and stood. "I'll take her home."

"Spencer—"

"I'm taking you home." He couldn't look at her, afraid she'd see just how close he was to breaking down. Whether it was his right or not, he needed to be with her.

13

TATUM STRETCHED, FEELING all sorts of aches and pains. She rolled onto her side, wincing at the jolt of pain that ran along her right side. She lifted the blankets high enough to assess her body. It wasn't pretty. Her thigh was covered in angry bruises, so was her hip, shoulder and upper arm. She groaned, going limp against the sheets.

Everything ached.

"That's gotta hurt," Spencer said, standing in the doorway.

"It does." She nodded, dropping the blankets back into place.

"I brought you something." He sat on the edge of the bed, offering her some pain pills and a glass of water.

"Best present ever." She sat up and took the pills, aware that his eyes were fixed on her bruises. "I know it looks bad."

He winced, shaking his head. "Can't help thinking you had a guardian angel last night. I saw your car."

She wanted to reach for him. She loved the concern that creased his face. And hated herself for it.

She'd lied to him last night. And she would keep lying

to him. He didn't need to know she was coming to him. Or that she loved him. Or that the way she felt, how overwhelming it was, scared her. She didn't want to be scared. She didn't want to hurt. Seeing his face in the hospital room—tender, almost…loving—cut her deep.

She couldn't get lost in him, not again. She closed her eyes. Neither of them needed to get hurt again.

He took her hand. "Hungry?"

She shook her head, pulling her hand from his.

He sat there, but she didn't look at him. She couldn't. She tucked her hands under the blanket.

"You need to eat something. Those meds are strong." He paused. "People have been bringing food and drinks by all morning."

People he'd been there to greet.

"At least let me make you some toast?" His voice was low, gruff.

She nodded, wincing at the tug of her stitches and bruising.

"Easy." He reached for her, but let his hand drop.

She lay back, staring at the ceiling overhead. Her heart hurt. She hurt.

It was almost Christmas Eve. Their deal was over. Done. She could fly to California without making a big deal out of it. That was what she wanted, what she needed, to stay in control. For this to be over. No complications, expectations or declarations had been made. No permanent damage had been done. Now was the best time to let him go.

"Lucy was here at the crack of dawn. She went to get your antibiotics," he called out. "Mom made some tea." He reappeared, balancing a plate on a brightly wrapped Christmas present. "You got me a Christmas present?"

She sat up, remembering the sexy lingerie she'd bought

for a final fling. She'd imagined seducing him slowly, under the Christmas tree, a fire roaring in the background. But now the thought of sex on the floor in front of the fire made her body protest. And her chest ache.

He sat on the edge of the bed, handing her toast with a smile. "I thought we'd already decided our twelve days was gift enough."

"I can take it back," she offered, eager to return the lingerie and scarves in the box.

"You can't take it back," he said, excitement edging his voice. "Not if it's what I think it is."

"You know what it is?" Disappointment gripped her. Okay, so sexy lingerie wasn't the most original idea, but she'd felt empowered buying it.

He ran his fingers through her hair, tilting her head back so she had no choice but to look at him. "I think so. And, no, I don't think you'll be up for that, either."

She met his gaze then, surprised. "You really think naughty lingerie is going to spice things up that much?"

He was quiet, his brows rising.

"Spencer?"

"Lingerie?" he asked.

"What did you think it was?" she asked, looking up at him. Did she really want to know?

He shook his head, a huge grin on his face.

Yes, she did. "Come on," she encouraged.

"I was *way* off base."

She sat up, wincing at the pull and throb of her bruises.

He frowned. "You need to take it easy."

She scowled at him. "You need to tell me what you thought I'd bought you for Christmas."

He shook his head. "No. I don't."

"It can't be that bad," she argued, frustration and curiosity warring.

"It's *not* bad." He ran a hand over his face.

She was beyond curious. "Can you give me a hint?"

"It required batteries," he said, watching her expression.

She shook her head. "Batteries?"

He ran a hand over his face again. "That first night, we talked about spicing things up."

She stared at him. Spicing things up? If things were any spicier, she might explode. But then understanding dawned on her. "A vibrator? You thought I bought us a vibrator?" If anything, he'd demonstrated that a vibrator wasn't an essential tool for sexual satisfaction. And yet the flare of desire that rolled over her told her it might be a hell of a lot of fun.

"I told you, whatever you want, Tatum." He stared at her, the corner of his mouth lifting into a grin.

Whatever she wanted… Sex with Spencer. Sex with Spencer and a vibrator.

Spencer.

Her eyes stung again. *Dammit*. No. That was over. He just didn't know it yet.

"All you have to do is tell me." The rasp of his voice made her toes curl. "I…I'd pretty much do anything for you, you know."

Her throat was tight and dry, her lungs empty. It was hard to breathe. Harder to say, "It's almost Christmas Eve."

His grin faded as he reached up. His fingers traced her hairline, captured a long curl and wrapped it around his fingers. "Let's renegotiate the terms."

Was he only referring to sex? Or something more?

She didn't want to know. She'd come to terms with the past, almost. But, if he did want something more... She couldn't. No matter how tempted she might be.

This was Spencer. No one else came close. No one else had this sort of power over her. Which was the very reason this needed to end. Whether or not this connection was normal, it was dangerously powerful.

"I don't think so." She nibbled her toast.

"Why?" He let go of her curl.

She forced a smile. "Because it was good. No, great. Exactly what I needed. No strings. No complications. Just sensation. Thank you for showing me how good intimacy can be."

His face was rigid, the tightening of his jaw making the beat of her heart falter.

She hadn't expected him to reach up, to stroke his fingers along her cheek, to run his thumb along her lower lip. "Tatum, maybe I want strings—"

"No, Spencer. I can't." She turned her head, severing the contact. "I'm flattered but... Thank you for the toast."

"She up?" Lucy's voice echoed. "Just tell me you're not banging an injured woman?"

He stood, tucking the Christmas present under his arm. She stared at the toast, focused on chewing.

"I'll go, since Lucy's here." He walked out, leaving her door cracked open, preventing her from falling completely apart.

"Merry Christmas." Cady was all smiles as she and Patton hung their coats in his mother's hall closet.

"You too," Spencer said, returning her hug and shaking his brother's hand.

"Patton showed me pictures of Tatum's car. Holy crap, she was lucky." Cady squeezed his arm. "She here?"

"She's in the kitchen with Mom." Spencer nodded, still numb from Tatum's casual brush-off. It was taking everything he had to be civil. When all he wanted to do was yell or punch something. Considering his bruises might be gone in time for wedding pictures, adding new ones wouldn't go over well.

Patton waited until Cady left before asking, "What happened?"

"Besides her wreck?" Spencer growled. He still hadn't recovered from that. And now... "Shook me up—I'm not gonna lie to you."

"And?" Patton asked, leveling him with his I-know-something's-going-on look. "Don't try to bullshit me."

He swallowed, his gaze bouncing around the room as he murmured, "She ended it." Saying it out loud made it worse.

Patton's hand rested on his shoulder. "I'm sorry, Spence."

"Can't blame her." He hesitated, knowing he was exposing more to his brother than he wanted. "Guess some things are too hard to recover from."

Patton looked at him, not saying a word. His expression was hard, unreadable. "You're not gonna give up?" Patton asked.

"I can't make her love me."

Patton sighed. "She's the one. She's always been the one."

"Not disagreeing with you." Spencer drew in a deep breath, trying to ease the tension as he added, "But thanks for the pep talk."

"That's what big brothers are for." Patton winked and headed toward the kitchen.

But Spencer didn't follow. He glanced at the clock. Eight o'clock. Christmas Eve. He should have four more hours to touch her whenever he wanted to. And, dammit, now that he knew she was saying goodbye, he wanted those four hours now more than ever.

Dinner was over, he'd made his way around the room and offered suitably affectionate holiday sentiments. And Tatum was in the kitchen, spending time with his family, instead of in his bed. As far as she was concerned, their time was up. While he couldn't keep his eyes off the damn clock.

He should leave. Not that he was looking forward to a night on the lumpy couch in the garage, but staying here was too much like torture. He finished off the beer in his hand and—fool that he was—headed into the kitchen.

Tatum sat at the table, patched and bruised, and poring over a family album. He loved the smile on her face, the easy laughter that filled the room when Cady turned the album page. That was all he wanted, right there. For her to be happy. Even better if he was the one who made her happy.

Maybe Patton was right. Maybe he had to fight harder—show her how much he loved her. How good they would be, outside of the bedroom and in. She had to give him a chance. The thought of losing her altogether made him hurt.

"Spencer, you were an adorable baby." Lucy grinned his way.

Tatum's gaze met his. Even with the bruising on her temple, she was the most beautiful thing he'd ever seen.

"Look at all those rolls," Cady added, tapping the picture.

"He's fat," Patton said, laughing. "Not chubby, but *fat* fat."

"Oh, hush," their mother said. "I'll find your baby book next and we'll see who wins pudgiest baby."

"Please," Cady agreed.

"Is this some sort of new holiday tradition I didn't know about?" Spencer asked. "Public humiliation?"

"There's no shame in you being an adorable baby, Spencer." His mother sighed. "You're so tense. I think you've gotten worse than Patton these days."

Everyone in the kitchen looked at him then. His brothers, his sisters-in-law and Tatum. She looked sad.

"He just needs some Christmas cheer." Lucy shoved a cup of eggnog into his hand. "Eat, drink, be merry," she said.

Conversation drifted back to him and his brother's childhood. Lucy patted a chair at the table, conveniently located beside Tatum, and he sat. He leaned her way, his hand itching to take hers. Instead, he studied her profile, the ease of her smile and the curve of her cheek.

She caught him looking. "What's wrong?" she asked him, softly.

He shook his head.

She frowned. "What is it?"

"It's almost midnight," he said, staring at her.

She swallowed, realization widening her green green eyes. "Oh..."

He could kiss her. He could tell her he loved her. But all he managed was "I...I want my time. Even if I have to take a rain check."

"A rain check?" she repeated, her cheeks turning a rosy hue.

He stopped breathing. More time with her. "A deal is a deal."

It was then that he realized the kitchen was silent.

"A rain check for what?" Cady asked.

"Did you two have plans tonight?" his mother asked, clearly delighted.

The silence stretched until it grew painful.

"We were going to watch *Elf*," Tatum said.

"I love that movie," Lucy gushed.

"Me too," Cady said, glancing back and forth between him and Tatum.

"Is this an exclusive viewing?" Patton asked, amused.

Spencer wanted to say yes. He wanted to tell his brother to go screw himself and the rest of his family to mind their own business.

"Of course not," Tatum said. "You're all welcome."

Spencer's heart sank. No matter how his hands ached to touch her, her answer was still no.

14

Tatum finished cleaning up the cups of cocoa, empty bowls of popcorn, half-eaten cookies and candy-cane wrappers. Lucy busied herself straightening the pillows and putting the television cabinet back to rights. And Spencer was asleep in the recliner in front of the fire. He'd dosed off halfway through the movie and had been snoring softly ever since. Every time she brushed past him, she hesitated.

"You ready for tomorrow?" Lucy asked.

Tomorrow. California. Leaving. She hoped, with time and distance, she could finally let go of Spencer. She couldn't exactly start over if she was holding on to the past. "Not quite."

"What time is your flight?" Lucy asked.

"Seven thirty," Tatum answered.

"On Christmas Day?" Lucy frowned. "You could have waited."

"I didn't know how depressing this year would be," Tatum admitted, sitting at the kitchen table.

"Not as bad as you thought it would be?" Lucy asked.

Tatum shook her head, smiling. Until now, it'd been great.

"Do you need a ride to the airport?" Lucy asked.

"No," Spencer said from the kitchen doorway, bleary-eyed and yawning. "I'm taking her."

"Well, hello, sleeping beauty," Lucy said. "Did we wake you with all of our cleaning?"

He smiled. "It's done. Looks like I woke up just in time."

Tatum couldn't hold back her answering smile. She didn't want tonight to be awkward. It was Christmas Eve, after all.

"Where's everyone else?" he asked.

"The movie ended about an hour ago," Tatum offered. "Zach and Patton were breaking down the extra tables and chairs at your mom's place."

"You slept through all that work too," Lucy said.

"My evil plan worked," Spencer said, turning the full force of his blue eyes on Tatum.

Tatum's heart thudded.

"Guess I'll be heading out," Lucy said, hugging Tatum. "Merry Christmas. I'll see you in Colorado for the wedding?"

Tatum nodded. "Can't wait. Thank you," she said, hugging Lucy.

She closed the door and turned to find Spencer leaning against the door frame.

"You don't have to stay up," she said. "I know how tired you are. Go to bed."

His eyes widened. "I will." He pushed off the wall. "How are you holding up?"

"I'm fine." She was tired and achy but she still needed to pack.

"Can I help?" he asked, following her as she flipped off all the lights.

She shook her head. "No. I just want to sit for a minute." She sat on the couch, staring into the fire.

He sat on the couch arm, not saying anything.

"I've got a taxi coming in the morning, Spencer."

"I'll take you." His voice rolled over her, warm and sure.

"No. Thank you." She scowled at him, laying her head back on the couch cushions.

He sat beside her, his proximity having an immediate effect on her. So did the concern in his voice as he asked, "Your head hurting?"

"You don't need to take care of me," she said. She felt good. Good enough to want him. Now. Badly.

"Why is me taking care of you a bad thing?" He frowned.

She frowned back. "Because...because I'm not your responsibility."

He frowned at her, then said, "Friends take care of each other."

She stared at him. *Friends?* That was all she was to him. Which was exactly what she'd wanted. So why the hell did it upset her to hear him say it out loud? *What is wrong with me?*

"If it was Lucy, would there be a problem?" he asked.

"No," she said. "But I'm not sleeping with Lucy."

"And you're not sleeping with me anymore." He smiled at her, but there was something off about that smile. He glanced at the mantel, his smile fading.

Her gaze followed. Almost midnight. Heat coiled in the pit of her stomach, setting an unexpected shiver along her spine.

He saw it. The clenching of his jaw, the slight flare of his nostrils... He moved from the end of the couch to kneel on the floor at her feet. But when he reached for her, she couldn't take it. She wanted his touch, craved the comfort and pleasure he'd give her. "Don't, please." Her voice wavered.

His jaw locked, clenched so rigidly she feared he'd crack a tooth.

She pressed a hand to her head, the dull ache turning into a more pronounced throb.

His expression shifted again, remote and distant. "You should rest."

"You should stop telling me what to do," she snapped, pushing off the couch to stand.

He frowned, rising to stand inches from her. "Why are you so pissed off? I'm playing by your rules. Rules you won't let me forget. Rules I would break if you'd let me."

"Spencer—" If he didn't leave soon, she was going to fall apart. "This was a mistake. I don't know what I was thinking... You and I—" She saw his eyes close, saw his hands fist at his sides. "I'm sorry." *I'm sorry I'm too scared to love you.* "I...I don't know where we go from here. If we *can* be friends. I'm pretty sure life would be easier for both of us if we weren't."

"I can't lose you again," he said, his tone flat, hard.

"You can't lose something you never had, Spencer. I can't do this again. Not with you. Let it go, please," she said, walking to her bedroom door.

"Dammit, Tatum, don't be like this—"

"Be like what?" she asked. "You're the one who keeps pushing this. I don't need your help. I don't want it." The lie rolled off her tongue, leaving a bitter taste of self-loathing. But she hesitated, unable to resist looking at him. "I'm sorry." *For so much.* He stood there, beautiful and tense, staring at her with searching eyes. "Good night, Spencer." She closed her bedroom door and her control broke.

His whispered "Merry Christmas, Tatum" was full of such anguish she almost opened the door. Almost. Instead, she slid down the wall, wrapped her arms around her knees and sobbed until the pain in her head rivaled the crushing pain in her heart.

SPENCER STOOD IN his black suit, wishing this day was over. The last five days had been hell. Attending the graveside service of Clint Taggart was the last straw.

Spencer watched Taggart's wife, the tears rolling down her cheeks as she clasped the hand of her young daughter. Taggart's other children were clustered around their mom, each looking lost and heartbroken. He was thankful his mother had lived a long life with his father before he passed. And that he'd grown up with a man in the house—as unyielding as he'd been.

"Not the way I want to go out," Patton said as they left the services for the airport. "But I'm sure it's a relief to know his death was an accident."

Clint's car had been found in a ditch four hundred miles north of Greyson, off some county road. After losing his job, he'd headed to a buddy's house to regroup. When he'd decided to come home, the weather intervened and sent him sliding off a bridge and into a ravine. He'd been dead for days.

"Doesn't make it any easier on his wife and kids."

"You don't think so?" Patton argued. "I think it'd be a hell of a lot easier. Clint may not have been the best cop on the force, but he wasn't doing something illegal. He wasn't hunted down by the bad guy. He had an accident. A tragic accident—but an accident."

Spencer didn't say anything.

Patton's phone rang, so he put it on speaker. "Yep."

"Patton, is Spencer there?" It was their mother.

"I'm here," Spencer answered.

"I'm trying to confirm rooms. Is Tatum still coming to the wedding?" she asked.

"I have no idea," Spencer answered honestly. He'd tried to think of Tatum as little as possible over the last few days. He ached for her, missed her. He'd picked up the phone a dozen times but never hit Send.

"You talked to her?" his mother asked.

"No," he snapped.

There was a long silence.

"Spencer Lee Ryan." His mother didn't tolerate disrespect. "You don't need to use that tone with me, young man. If you and Tatum are having trouble, that's your business. But I need to know—"

"Mom, can you give Lucy a call?" Patton intervened. "She'll know."

"Yes, yes, I'll do that. You two have a safe flight. We'll see you soon." And the line went dead.

"Promise me that whatever is going on between the two of you won't affect the wedding," Patton said.

His brother might be a sullen son of a bitch, but Spencer was happy for him. He'd be on his best behavior for the wedding. Spencer smiled. "Yes, sir."

It wouldn't be easy. Seeing Tatum would hurt. But not seeing her was worse. His heart felt like it was squeezed by a vise every second of every day for the last five days. It helped to know he would eventually recover, even if it felt like his world was coming apart.

Patton wasn't big on small talk, so Spencer didn't bother filling the silence. He stared at the same magazine pages for ten minutes, indulging in various reunion scenarios with Tatum. Reality would likely be cool civility, and that would be a stretch for him. It was too much to hope for more than that.

He dozed for the length of the flight and woke up with a crick in his neck. His mood continued to nose-dive when his luggage was nowhere to be found. And the rental car they'd requested wasn't ready. He paced the airport while Patton stayed busy—talking to Cady on the phone.

When they finally reached the hotel, he wanted a drink and, possibly, a nap.

His mother greeted him with a "Stop frowning" and a quick hug.

"Good to see you two," Zach said. "A little too much estrogen around here. Please tell me my big brothers have something big lined up for tonight?"

"You mean the bachelor-party thing?" Spencer asked, perking up.

Zach nodded.

Patton shook his head. "No. We're having rehearsal in an hour and dinner after that."

Zach and Spencer exchanged frowns.

"Buzz kill," Zach said, laughing.

Spencer's phone rang. It was the airline. They'd found his bag but wouldn't be able to deliver until the next afternoon.

"Spencer?" his mother asked.

"Airline found my bag," he said.

"Good. Can you pick up Tatum? Lucy said she's having a hard time getting a car." His mother waited, her blue eyes steady upon him.

Maybe picking up Tatum, alone, would give them a chance to deal with anything lingering—so nothing sullied the mood for Patton and Cady's big day.

He nodded. But after he'd hung up the phone and was driving toward the airport, he knew he had to be strong. He'd missed her, yes. He wanted her. He loved her. But Tatum had made it clear they were done and his heart was too shredded for more rejection.

15

Tatum smoothed her hands over her hair and straightened the tie on her sweater. Her skintight black pencil skirt, clinging cream wrap-sweater and tall black boots hadn't been the most practical traveling attire, but it had definitely drawn a lot of attention her way. Hopefully it would have the same effect on Spencer. He'd been right—they needed to talk. And even though she'd shut him down, she hoped he'd give her another chance. Being vulnerable was something she avoided at all costs. And she was nervous as hell.

The last five days had been good for her.

Gretchen had been a truly generous host, showing her the sights of San Diego, the coastal beauty and the friendly people. There'd been a lot of laughing, a lot of drinking, and too many late nights talking about what they wanted out of life.

Tatum hadn't wanted to bring up Spencer. But Gretchen had asked.

"Come on, I've been dying to know. This is the guy you compared everyone to? Your true love." She'd been teasing, but her words had struck a chord.

Spencer had always been her measuring stick. Even when he wasn't part of her life, he'd been there.

He *was* the only man she'd loved with all of her. Poor Brent never stood a chance. Even after the wedding, her defenses had stayed up.

With Spencer, her defenses crumbled. It was terrifying. And wonderful.

And the more she thought about him, the more she missed him, the more she realized she was a complete idiot. She knew why he'd told her the truth about their past. He loved her. He still loved her. Her whole I'm-in-control stance was a joke. She wasn't in control. Her fear was.

And being afraid of Spencer, of loving him, was the last thing she wanted.

Now she stood, eager and terrified, to see him. It had only been five days. But in those five days she'd gone from holding him at arm's length to holding him in her heart. She paced, bought a bottle of water at one of the news shops and was opening it when he walked in.

Keep it together.

His blue eyes found her immediately, the pull between them instantaneous. But she stood her ground and made him come to her. She didn't miss his head-to-toe inspection, or the fact that his jaw clenched so tight his teeth were in danger.

"Hi," he said, his voice raspy and low.

"Hi."

"You look..." He swallowed. "You look good. How's the head?"

She moved closer, using the electricity between them. She knew he wanted her. It seemed like the right place to start. She turned her head, leaning closer and lifting her hair to show him the scar. "Stitches are out. I'm still a little tender, though." Their proximity wasn't just affecting *him*. He smelled so good, too good. "And I have a patchwork of rainbow-colored bruises along my side." She lifted the front wrap of her sweater, exposing the plane of her stomach, her belly button and the remains of her yellow-green bruise.

His eyes lingered on her stomach. He swallowed, closing his eyes and drawing in a deep breath. He shoved his hands into his pockets and muttered, "I need to get my luggage. Then we can go."

"You look tired," she said. It was true. Not just tired. Worn-out. There were bags under his eyes. And his eyes looked…haunted. "Long week?"

His gaze searched hers. "Yes."

She held his gaze, unflinching. But when his attention wandered to her mouth she had to turn away. She wanted him to kiss her, oh so badly. But not yet. "Let's go get your bag."

She reached for the handle of her suitcase at the same time he did. Their fingers brushed, the stroke of skin on skin making her stomach tighten and her lungs empty. She'd missed him. This time, she leaned into him to draw his scent deep into her lungs. And when his hand wrapped around hers, tugging her into his arms, she melted. She could turn into him, press her lips to his neck… Instead, she pulled out of his hold and stepped back.

He stood there, staring down at her, his hand gripping her suitcase handle.

"Ready?" she asked, hoping she sounded unaffected. Because inside, she was on fire.

He nodded and set off toward the airline customer service desk.

While he spoke to the agent, she knocked her bag over,

spilling the contents onto the floor. So much for smooth. But as she bent to collect them she remembered he was fond of her ass. She straightened slowly, appreciating his sudden hiss of breath.

"Got it," he bit out.

She straightened, knowing she was teasing him but unable to stop. He couldn't seem to move. The plum lacy strap of her bra peeking from the deep V of her sweater had him mesmerized.

"Spencer?" she asked, laying one hand on his chest.

He glanced at her hand. But before he could cover it with his own she was moving toward the doors.

"Where are you parked?" she asked, glancing back over her shoulder.

He was staring at her rear—good. He frowned, tore his gaze away and pulled both suitcases behind him. The walk to the car was tricky. Her heels were tall and there was ice on the ground. Not to mention it was cold. But a padded coat wouldn't help with the whole remind-him-what-he's-getting part of her plan.

She climbed into the truck, the hem of her skirt riding up just enough to reveal she was wearing stockings and a garter belt. A garter belt that matched the bra she was wearing. Yes, she was playing dirty. And it was way outside her comfort zone but she could only hope it would work.

He started the truck, but they didn't move. From the corner of her eye, she saw the way he was looking at her thigh. And her stomach clenched, willing him to reach for her. She ran her hands over her skirt, smoothing the fabric over the slight glimpse of plum silk, and buckled her seat belt.

Awareness coursed through her. This wasn't how it was supposed to happen. He was the one who needed to be overcome with desire, not her. Instead, she was throbbing, wanting his hands on her, his lips... She cleared her throat. Cool, calm, collected.

Five minutes later, the car still wasn't moving. He was staring straight ahead, every muscle taut. Maybe she wasn't the only one fighting this crazy hunger.

"Is everything okay?" she asked.

He nodded, not looking at her, and put the truck in gear. They set off, navigating their way out of the airport and onto the highway. The silence grew unbearable.

"How are the wedding preparations going?" she asked.

He shrugged.

"When did you fly out?" she tried again.

"This morning," he answered. "With Patton. We had a funeral to go to."

She looked at him, surprised. "I'm so sorry, Spencer. Was it someone you were close to?"

"We worked together." His answer was curt.

"Was it on the job?"

He shook his head. "No. Car accident."

"I'm sorry for your loss." She wanted to touch him then, to offer some sort of comfort.

He looked at her, eyes blazing. "How was California?"

She swallowed. "It was wonderful."

His jaw ticked. "Have a good time?"

"A great time." She had. When she wasn't missing him. "I met some nice people. Gretchen has a brother who's a fireman, so he and some friends took us out one night. They were pretty hilarious." All of which was true. Gretchen's brother was a happily married father of two, but Spencer didn't need to know that.

"A fireman?" he repeated.

She nodded, wondering what he was thinking. "I tried a few new things too."

"Like?" he barked.

"Oh… Have you ever had Thai food?" she asked.

He shook his head.

"It's hot," she said, laughing. "My eyes were watering and my tongue felt paralyzed. Even the next morning."

"What else?" he asked.

"Tequila shots," she said. "They're yummy. But they make me a little crazy."

He looked at her then. "Crazy?"

"Zip lining." She waved her hand at him. "I had fun."

"Good." But his tone implied he wasn't pleased.

"Are there any plans for tonight? I'd love a nap. Maybe even a soak in a hot tub," she added, enjoying his reactions far more than she'd expected.

"Rehearsal, rehearsal dinner, that's it," he ground out.

"No bachelor party?" She paused. "Or bachelorette party?"

He shook his head as they pulled into the hotel driveway. She waited for the valet to open the door and climbed out, offering a smile. Spencer was immediately at her side, his hand big and warm on her back, steering her inside before she'd had a chance to inspect her surroundings. Not that she cared. Right now the only thing she was aware of was Spencer. And if she didn't put some space between them soon, she'd be throwing herself at him in no time.

Not yet.

"Key," he said, offering her the card key.

"Thank you." She took it. "Guess I'll go make myself presentable."

His eyes swept over her again.

She left him standing there and headed for the elevators. But when she climbed onto the elevator, he followed, pulling his suitcase behind him.

TATUM WAS IN serious danger. If the old man left them alone in the elevator, Spencer could not be held accountable for his actions. He'd never been this close to losing control. But seeing her in her skintight getup, knowing what she had on underneath, had his dick at attention and his brain malfunctioning.

When they arrived on floor seven, he brushed past her, eager to get to his room and take a cold shower. But she followed him down the hall until he reached his room. She went around him, to the door next to his.

"Looks like we're neighbors," she said, smiling his way.

He nodded stiffly, trying not to think about the fact that she'd be so close. His hands fumbled with his card key, dropping it.

She disappeared into her room.

"Dammit," he growled, picking up his key and resting his forehead on the hotel room door. She'd gone off to California and hung out with firemen? She'd tried new things? And come home wearing what she was wearing. He adjusted himself, his erection pressing against his already fitted pants.

He tried his key. It didn't work. He tried again. Still nothing. He punched the wall. "Dammit," he bit out.

He stared at her door.

He could go downstairs and have them fix it. Or he could call from her room...

He knocked on her door.

"Who is it?" she asked through the door.

"Spencer," he answered. He took a deep breath. *Stop*

being an asshole. Stop snapping and growling at everyone.

She opened the door. "What's up?"

"My key doesn't work." She was so beautiful, so soft. His hand itched to touch her, to stroke her cheek and slide through the length of her silky hair. "Can I call the front desk?"

"Sure," she said, stepping back.

He heard the sound of running water. A passing glance saw bubbles piling up in her bath. "Sorry," he murmured.

"About what?" she asked.

"Interrupting." His mind was assaulted with images of her naked. Her body flushed and wet... He swallowed, running a hand over his face.

She twisted her hair up, clipping it in place on the back of her head. "Are you sure you're okay?" she asked, her hands fiddling with the tie of her sweater. "You seem so...tense."

"I'm fine." He didn't sound fine. He sounded like he was going to explode. Probably because he *was* going to explode.

"You want to talk about it?" she asked. "It's what friends do. Talk."

His heart twisted. "So we can be friends?"

She shrugged. "I'd like to try. I've never seen you like this and I want to be here for you if I can. If you want me?"

He closed his eyes. "If I want you?" he muttered. "That's the problem, Tatum. That's the whole damn problem." He sounded harsh to his own ears.

"What?" she asked, startled.

"I want you." He moved forward. "I can't stop." His hands clasped her shoulders, pulling her against him. "So, no, I don't want to talk about it."

"Then what do you want?" she whispered.

"You." He bent, nuzzling her neck. "Dammit." She smelled like heaven. "Now."

She drew in an unsteady breath as his lips latched on to her neck. His hands slid through her hair, tugging her head back so he could taste her. His tongue slid between her lips, tearing a moan from her and racking him with a shudder.

He deepened the kiss, cradling the back of her head to explore the recesses of her mouth and leave them both reeling.

Her hands twined in his hair, shattering whatever remained of his self-control. He gripped her hips, lifting her up as he drove her back against the wall. He dropped to his knees, sliding the tie of her sweater free and pulling it down to her wrists—pinning them at her sides. With mounting impatience, he tugged her skirt until it was around her hips. He paused long enough to take in the view.

"You're so damn beautiful," he ground out, running his fingers across the plane of her stomach. She was gasping, her eyes pressed closed, her hands tightly fisted at her sides. He ran one finger along the garter, pressed a kiss at the edge of her filmy panties and gripped her ankle. He worked his way up her silk-clad calf, nuzzling the soft skin behind her knee until she was shuddering. He pressed her back, keeping her in place, while forcing her legs apart. His lips skimmed her heated flesh as his hand slid up the back of her leg. He lifted her leg, staring up at the raw need on her face. She needed release… and he would give it to her. When his hand cupped the curve of her ass, he nipped the velvet soft skin of her inner thigh.

"Spencer." Her voice broke, urgent.

He hooked her thigh over his shoulder. One hand gripped the soft curve of her ass, the other braced himself—holding her wrist against the wall.

Her panties were barely there, the frothy G-string hiding nothing. He nudged it aside with his nose and bent to his work. Her scent, the taste of her, overwhelmed his senses. She was ready, her skin contracting at the first stroke of his tongue. He kneaded the swell of her buttock, parting her for the slide of his fingers. He was relentless, his fingers deep, his lips and tongue working the tight nub at her core. On and on, he pushed her until she cried out, her hands slamming against the wall and her hips arched forward.

She slumped against the wall, spent and gasping.

He pushed off the wall, his breath powering from his lungs and blood on fire. His need for her was almost painful. But there was more. He knew he had no right to ask her to love him. But, right now, he had no choice. He loved her, he'd always loved her. It wasn't about wanting her body—it was about wanting her. He sucked in a deep breath, his heart pounding in his ears. "Tatum," he groaned. "I'm sorry. I… Damn, I…I hadn't planned on this happening."

The ragged sound of her breathing stopped. In that instant she went from soft and spent to wary. "No, don't apologize. You didn't do anything I didn't want."

He stared down at her, cupping her cheek. She still wanted him. That was something. "I missed you, Tatum."

She drew in a deep breath. "I had a lot of time to think while I was gone." She frowned. "You're right—we need to talk, I have a lot I want to say, but maybe now's not the right time." She shrugged away from him, her cheeks red.

"Why?" he argued, reaching for her. He needed to

touch her, to feel her, to know she was there. "Maybe there's no such thing as the right time. But there is right now." Panic pressed in on him. He knew what she was going to say. She was going to San Diego, she was going to leave him. Better to rip the damn Band-Aid off now. "Just say it."

"You have a hard-on. My skirt is around my waist." She sounded defeated as she pushed the clinging fabric back into place. "If we are going to talk, I need to know your words aren't coming from here." She grabbed his erection, making him jolt. "I'd like to know that your words are coming from here." She pressed her hand to his heart, then his head.

"Tatum, say it," he all but growled.

She looked so...nervous that his heart stopped. "I love you," she whispered. "I love you, Spencer."

Her phone was ringing. When it had started, he didn't know. And, at the moment, he didn't care. But the ringing sent Tatum into a tailspin, smoothing her tangled hair into place and holding her sweater closed.

He frowned, reaching for her, trying to process what he'd heard. She loved him? She loved him, and he was staring at her like an idiot.

She answered her phone. "Hey, Lucy."

He wasn't prepared for the anxious look in her eyes. Or the uncertainty on her face. "He's here," she said. "His key doesn't work." She paused. "I'll send him down."

Did she seriously doubt how he felt? Because he'd be happy to fix that—now.

He waited as she hung up the phone.

"Your mother needs you now," she said, brushing past him into her bathroom. "Don't forget to have your key fixed."

"Tatum—"

"Tonight is about Patton and Cady," she murmured.

"You can't seriously expect me to leave now?" he asked, putting his hand on the bathroom door. And ignoring the persistent ring of his phone.

She grinned. "I'd like to stay on your family's good side. And my bath is getting cold."

She shut the bathroom door in his face. He stood there, staring at the door. He pressed a hand against the door. "I can wash your back," he offered.

"Go, Spencer," she called back, laughing. "We can talk after. When I'm dressed and you're thinking straight."

He was reeling. She loved him. The ache that filled his chest didn't compare with the ache of his body. He wanted Tatum, there was no denying that—to the point of addiction. But he loved her beyond that.

He knew his life was risky. But life was risky. He'd rather face any adversity with her at his side than without her.

And he wanted her to know that—wanted everyone to know that.

His phone rang, making him cuss under his breath. He glanced at the screen before tucking it into his pocket. Once the wedding was over, he'd make sure Tatum knew exactly how he felt. And how damn good their future was going to be—together.

16

Tatum watched Cady and Patton move around the dance floor. It had been a gorgeous wedding. And, considering how firmly Patton insisted he wasn't a fan of weddings, he seemed to be enjoying himself. Or maybe he was just happy to be married.

"You look gorgeous," Lucy said, sitting beside her.

"So do you." It was true. The Ryans were a good-looking family.

"Dean's been checking you out," Celeste added.

"Dean's checking all the single ladies out," Tatum argued.

"Anyway, Spencer wins. He's almost walked into a wall twice. I'd say you two might finally be making progress?" Lucy asked.

Finally. He loved her—even if he hadn't said as much yet. She glanced at the dance floor. Spencer was dancing with his mother. He was laughing, his head thrown back—looking so gorgeous her heart hurt. They made their way to the front of the room, to join Cady and Patton.

"Looks like speech time," Celeste said, reaching for her champagne.

Cady went first. She was sassy and funny, making everyone laugh. But when she hugged her new husband, the tenderness on her face said it all.

"Cady showed me what it meant to live. Now all I want is to live every day with her." Patton's speech was short, but—from him—was truly touching.

Then Spencer took the microphone. "If my father were here, he'd say this toast. But, as he's not, I will. May you live as long as you want, and never want as long as you live. May the blessings of each day be the blessings you need most. May you have warm words on a cold evening, a full moon on a dark night. And the road downhill all the way to your door." Spencer paused. "My brothers are amazing men. Good sons, good husbands. They work hard, keep their word, are unwaveringly loyal, and when they fall in love—it's forever." He paused, his gaze finding and holding hers. He waited until everyone in the room knew he was looking at her before he continued, "I'd like to think I've learned from the best. Patton, Cady, congratulations."

Tatum stared at him, stunned. Her heart was tripping over itself.

When they fall in love—it's forever.

"Want to dance?" Dean asked, holding his hand out to her.

She was still processing Spencer's words as he led her onto the dance floor. He spun her into him, winking at her. She laughed, squealing when he dipped her.

"Is it a prerequisite for the Ryans to dance?" she asked, breathless when he spun her around.

"Yes. Aunt Imogene had a friend that owned a dance academy. She made us all take lessons, out of solidarity." Dean shook his head. "You look gorgeous."

"You don't look too bad yourself," she said, trying to keep up with him. While covertly searching for Spencer.

"He's behind you," Dean said.

Her heart stopped. "He is?"

"He's headed this way," Dean said, nodding. "Looks pretty pissed off to me."

"He does?"

"Not that he deserves you," Dean continued.

She smiled at him, pressing a kiss to his cheek. "You're a good guy, Dean."

He looked down at her. "Let's keep that our secret."

"Cutting in," Spencer said sharply.

She stared at him. "Is that a request?"

Spencer sighed, closing his eyes and taking a deep breath. "Yes. It is. May I cut in?"

"Watch it," Dean said. "She's all handsy."

She giggled, a mix of nerves—and hope.

Dean left, leaving them alone on the dance floor.

"Did you hear my speech?" he asked.

She nodded.

"What did you think?"

She brushed the hair from his forehead. "You love me?"

"Yes."

"I admit that makes me happy. Happier than I've ever been." She swallowed.

"I love you." He stopped dancing, cradling her face in his hands. "Always."

She sucked in a deep breath, feeling light and oh so blissful. She couldn't stop smiling.

He rested his forehead against hers. "Are you going to California? If you are, I need to get my résumé in order."

She laughed. "You'd go?"

He nodded, his expression stern. "I go where you go. I want what you want."

"You do?" Her fingers brushed through the hair at the nape of his neck. "And if all I want is you? And for you to love me."

"Done."

"No moving. Cady's already convinced half of Greyson I should handle their books."

"This is what you want?" His voice was low.

"As long as we have each other." She paused, the emotions she'd been fighting for so long clogging her throat. "I have exactly what I want."

He pulled her closer, swaying to the music. "I didn't know how much I'd missed you until you waved that poker at me on the front porch."

"I didn't wave it at you," she argued, laughing.

"Nothing has ever scared me like thinking I'd lost you again."

She stared up at him. "I'm sorry, Spencer. I promise, I'm not going anywhere."

"I'll hold you to it." He kissed her lips. "And you love me?"

"I love you," she said between kisses.

"Now, let's talk about that rain check." He ran his thumb along her lower lip.

"No more talking," she said, pulling his mouth to hers.

* * * * *

COMING SOON!

We really hope you enjoyed reading this book. If you're looking for more romance be sure to head to the shops when new books are available on

Thursday 20th November

To see which titles are coming soon, please visit
millsandboon.co.uk/nextmonth

MILLS & BOON

A STYLISH NEW LOOK FOR
MILLS & BOON TRUE LOVE!

Introducing

Love Always

Swoon-worthy romances, where love takes centre stage. Same heartwarming stories, stylish new look!

Look out for our brand new look
OUT NOW
MILLS & BOON

FOUR BRAND NEW BOOKS FROM MILLS & BOON MODERN

Indulge in desire, drama, and breathtaking romance – where passion knows no bounds!

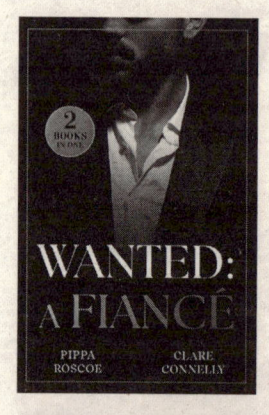

WANTED: A FIANCÉ
PIPPA ROSCOE / CLARE CONNELLY

Business Meets Pleasure...
Louise Fuller / Millie Adams

Christmas Baby Bombshell
Sharon Kendrick / Caitlin Crews

Bound to a Bride
NATALIE ANDERSON / ANNIE WEST

OUT NOW

Eight Modern stories published every month, find them all at:

millsandboon.co.uk

OUT NOW!

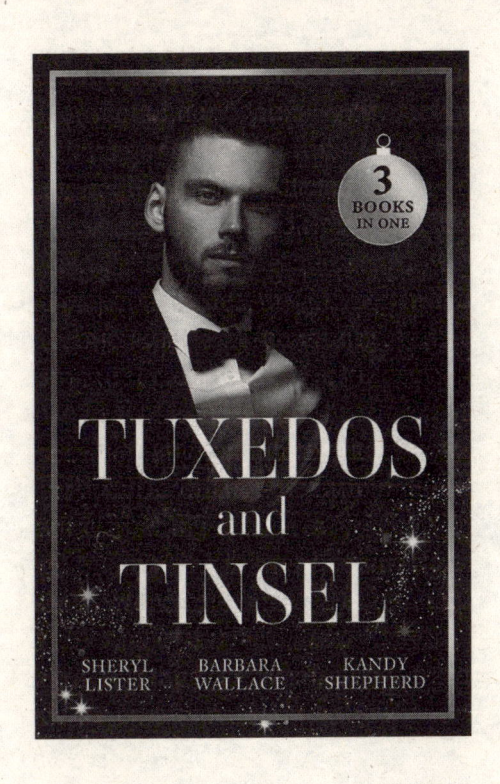

TUXEDOS and TINSEL

3 BOOKS IN ONE

SHERYL LISTER
BARBARA WALLACE
KANDY SHEPHERD

Available at
millsandboon.co.uk

MILLS & BOON

OUT NOW!

THE ITALIAN'S BILLION-DOLLAR Christmas

SHARON KENDRICK — **CAITLIN CREWS** — **SARAH MORGAN**

3 BOOKS IN ONE

Available at
millsandboon.co.uk

MILLS & BOON

OUT NOW!

3 BOOKS IN ONE

SECRETS UNDER THE Mistletoe

Sharon Kendrick Judy Duarte Brenda Harlen

Available at
millsandboon.co.uk

MILLS & BOON

OUT NOW!

Christmas in the Highlands

ANN McINTOSH · SUSAN CARLISLE · ALISON ROBERTS

3 BOOKS IN ONE

Available at
millsandboon.co.uk

MILLS & BOON

OUT NOW!

SNOWBOUND Christmas Nights

3 BOOKS IN ONE

SHARON KENDRICK
CAROLINE ANDERSON
SUSAN STEPHENS

Available at
millsandboon.co.uk

MILLS & BOON

LET'S TALK
Romance

For exclusive extracts, competitions and special offers, find us online:

- **f** MillsandBoon
- **X** @MillsandBoon
- **◉** @MillsandBoonUK
- **♪** @MillsandBoonUK

Get in touch on 01413 063 232

For all the latest titles coming soon, visit
millsandboon.co.uk/nextmonth